The Girl with the Suitcase

By the same author

FICTION

Georgia
Tara
Charity
Ellie
Camellia
Rosie
Charlie
Never Look Back
Trust Me
Father Unknown
Till We Meet Again
Remember Me
Secrets
A Lesser Evil
Hope
Faith
Gypsy

Stolen
Belle
The Promise
Forgive Me
Survivor
Without a Trace
Dead to Me
The Woman in the Wood
The House Across the Street
You'll Never See Me Again
Liar
Suspects
Deception
Betrayal

NON-FICTION

The Long and Winding Road

The Girl with the Suitcase

LESLEY PEARSE

MICHAEL JOSEPH

PENGUIN MICHAEL JOSEPH

UK | USA | Canada | Ireland | Australia
India | New Zealand | South Africa

Penguin Michael Joseph, Penguin Random House UK,
One Embassy Gardens, 8 Viaduct Gardens, London SW11 7BW

penguin.co.uk
global.penguinrandomhouse.com

Penguin Random House UK

First published 2025

001

Copyright © Lesley Pearse, 2025

The moral right of the author has been asserted

Penguin Random House values and supports copyright.
Copyright fuels creativity, encourages diverse voices, promotes freedom
of expression and supports a vibrant culture. Thank you for purchasing
an authorized edition of this book and for respecting intellectual property
laws by not reproducing, scanning or distributing any part of it by any
means without permission. You are supporting authors and enabling
Penguin Random House to continue to publish books for everyone.
No part of this book may be used or reproduced in any manner for the
purpose of training artificial intelligence technologies or systems. In accordance
with Article 4(3) of the DSM Directive 2019/790, Penguin Random House
expressly reserves this work from the text and data mining exception

Set in 13.5/16pt Garamond MT
Typeset by Falcon Oast Graphic Art Ltd
Printed in Great Britain by Clays Ltd, Elcograf S.p.A.

The authorized representative in the EEA is Penguin Random House Ireland,
Morrison Chambers, 32 Nassau Street, Dublin D02 YH68

A CIP catalogue record for this book is available from the British Library

HARDBACK ISBN: 978–0–241–67811–4
TRADE PAPERBACK ISBN: 978–0–241–67812–1

Penguin Random House is committed to a sustainable future
for our business, our readers and our planet. This book is made from
Forest Stewardship Council® certified paper

To my Irish family, the Keanes and the Glynns, both in Ireland and California.

It has given me so much joy getting to know you. I didn't expect such a warm and welcoming bunch of interesting relatives. I hope there will be lots of get-togethers in the future, and please keep on feeding me family stories.

I hasten to add that although Ireland is an important part of *The Girl with a Suitcase*, it *is* pure fiction, and no Irish people were hurt in the writing of it!

Perhaps I should have based it on truth and called it *The Girl in the Straw Boater*? The opening paragraph could've been when my seventeen-year-old self stepped down from the train at Roscommon to see Auntie Anne, Auntie Bridget and a host of other relatives, all complete strangers to me, coming along the railway tracks to meet me. I still cringe at that hat I wore. What was I thinking? Did I think I was in *The Railway Children*? J. J. Keane, my cousin, who was just six at the time, remembers it well.

Love you all and God Bless.

I

London, 12 September 1940

Elizabeth Manning had long since finished her pot of tea in the Lyons Corner House, but she was reluctant to go back to her hotel because it was good, free entertainment watching people coming in. She liked to assess outfits for style and quality, guessing which ones were hand-me-downs, or expensive. As she'd been managing a dress shop in Richmond for several years, it was her area of expertise.

Yet people's relationships fascinated her too, especially the younger women coming in on the arms of servicemen. She saw the way they kept glancing at their partners. Had they met just last night at a dance? Or were they sweethearts about to be parted as he went off to fight? She saw older couples too with tense faces, perhaps worried there might be another daylight bombing raid. Or maybe they were afraid for a son who was over in France. They could be anxious for a daughter who had moved away from home for war work. Or even planning to catch a train to see their grandchildren who had been evacuated the previous September.

A dark-haired woman, possibly in her twenties, had come in the door, but she faltered just inside, looking round nervously like a mouse who'd just come out of a hole in the skirting board.

Elizabeth was never afraid of going into restaurants alone, and she knew this was the young woman's problem. But then her own mother used to say she was born bold.

The Corner House was packed, and the Nippies, the name given to the waitresses, were nipping around faster than usual to seat customers. Elizabeth didn't want to be asked to vacate her table, and neither did she want to share it with someone old. But as she thought the hesitant woman was around the same age as herself, she beckoned for her to share her table.

Elizabeth liked the woman's somewhat shy smile and clear relief at getting a seat.

'This is so kind of you,' she said as she reached Elizabeth and pulled out a chair. 'I'm so hungry and I hadn't got a clue about where to go instead. Are you sure I'm not imposing?'

'Not at all,' Elizabeth said with a warm smile. The other woman had a faint Cockney accent, but her voice was soft and appealing. 'To be truthful I'm glad of some company. I'm Elizabeth Manning. Do sit down and we'll see if we can get a Nippy to take your order.'

'I'm Mary Price.'

It occurred to Elizabeth they were so similar they could be sisters. Both had dark-brown hair tucked up under their respective hats, pale complexions, and blue eyes. She thought they were a similar height and size too, though it was difficult to tell now they were both sitting. But Mary clearly wasn't as fortunate as her. Her hands were red and rough from hard work, and her navy-blue dress was dowdy, only lifted by a somewhat old-fashioned white lace collar.

Mary said she worked as a maid in Hampstead. It was her day off but she knew her mistress wouldn't have left anything out for her to eat when she got back. 'Mrs Bradley is really mean,' she said indignantly. 'Cook left soon after war was declared to go to the safety of her family home up north. Now I'm expected to do everything: cooking, laundry, cleaning and waiting on madam and her husband, with no more money. I went for an interview for a new job today down in Kent. I thought I was never going to get back, the train kept stopping.'

Elizabeth guessed that this deluge of information to a total stranger was probably because she rarely had conversations with anyone. Her off-white straw boater wasn't quite appropriate, too frivolous for such a sombre dress, but she admired her for trying to look confident. Elizabeth was intrigued by her and wanted to know more.

'So did you get the job?' she asked.

'I don't know, I was interviewed by the housekeeper, Mrs Wyles. She said she would speak to her mistress about me and then I'll be asked back to meet her in person. It's a very big house near Canterbury and they've lost a lot of their staff, to munitions, factories and to farming. So it might turn out to be even harder work than I'm doing now.'

A smiling Nippy arrived and Mary chose to have Welsh rarebit. Elizabeth ordered another pot of tea, this time for two, and a poached egg on toast for herself.

'Please forgive me for rattling on,' Mary said. 'How about you? Do you live and work in London?'

Elizabeth sensed someone other than a parent had had a hand in teaching Mary to modify her accent, and in her communications skills. Maybe it was a teacher, or even her employer.

'I did work in Richmond, but I've given up my flat there as I'm going to Ireland tomorrow and staying in the Charing Cross Hotel tonight.'

'How lovely.' Mary's dark eyes shone. 'I'm envious, I believe Ireland is beautiful. And you'll escape the bombs.'

'That isn't my reason for leaving. Until recently I was running a dress shop. But my boss decided to close the shop down. He said once clothes rationing comes in no one will buy new things, and he and his wife have moved to the safety of West Wales.'

'But the bombing won't last for long, surely?' Mary said.

Elizabeth smiled at her companion's naivety. She wasn't alone in underestimating the German determination to flatten London. The first daylight bombing had been in July, but it had become more serious five days ago, and since then it had continued daily and at night. So far, the bombs had been mostly dropped in East London, where whole streets were rumoured to be flattened, with scores of people killed. The newspapers and wireless were trying to minimize panic, yet even so they were calling it 'The Blitz', which suggested they were aware London could be razed to the ground.

But despite the media's efforts to calm things, everyone could see the night sky lit up by fire, hear the drone of countless bombers coming in to drop their deadly loads, and the thuds, bangs and crumps of explosions. Even well away from the East End, the air held a smell of brick dust, wet concrete, gas, fire and a strange cloying aroma no one seemed to be able to identify.

Elizabeth had been seeing Bernard, who was in the RAF. But he'd broken it off with her back in the spring, saying he needed to be free as he couldn't bear the thought of her worrying about him. He had been stationed at Biggin Hill at the time, not a pilot, but ground crew, and shortly after they parted, he was moved to another airbase further north.

She was upset at first, but he'd never been the most reliable of men, and she'd spent many an evening waiting for him somewhere, only to be let down. As it turned out it was good she was free to do what she wanted now.

There was evidence that most people in England had no idea of the hell that was yet to come. While brave pilots flew fearlessly into German planes in the Battle of Britain, and the German losses may have been instrumental in changing Hitler's mind about invading England, she and many like-minded people felt he still intended to destroy it.

'So, what do Mr and Mrs Bradley and you do when the air-raid siren goes off?' Elizabeth asked.

'We go down to the cellar under the house,' Mary said, wrinkling her nose. 'It's horrible, damp and gloomy, and Mrs Bradley keeps ordering me to go upstairs to make another cup of tea or to refill her hot water bottle. They don't talk to me and it's far too dark to be able to read. The camp beds are very uncomfortable too and imagine how cold it will get once autumn sets in. I can't cope with it for much longer.'

Elizabeth nodded agreement at the awfulness of Mary's predicament. As the two women ate their food and drank their tea, they discovered they had a good deal in common, both twenty-six, and without family. They had lost their respective fathers in the last war, and Elizabeth's mother had died of a heart attack just a year ago.

Mary commiserated but lied, saying her mother was dead too. The truth was that she'd disappeared several years ago with Ronnie, a very unpleasant bully who Mary had good reason to be frightened of. According to an old neighbour that Mary ran into in Oxford Street a while back, they were living in Essex. Sometimes Mary wished she could see her mother, even though she could never forgive her for turning a blind eye to what Ronald did to her. It was easier to claim her mother was dead than to have to admit that she had thought more of her fancy man than her own child.

'So will you be staying with family in Ireland?' Mary asked. She was already impressed by Elizabeth's poise and elegance. She spoke well and had lovely bright blue eyes and a creamy complexion. She was wearing a plum-coloured beret, which toned perfectly with the heather tones of her tweed coat. When Mary looked in the mirror, she saw a plain, pale girl with lacklustre hair, and knew, although she'd escaped the East End and tried to educate herself a bit more, she'd never shake off the stigma of her childhood.

'No family there at all,' Elizabeth replied. 'I've inherited a cottage from my godmother. Heaven only knows what it's like. It might have no running water and a privy at the bottom of the garden.' She laughed cheerfully. 'But it will be an adventure, and better than staying here wondering when and where the next bomb is going to fall.'

Mary looked at her new friend and wondered how anyone could be so blasé about going off to the unknown.

'You've got no friends there either?' she asked.

Elizabeth laughed. 'No, don't know a soul, I've never been to Ireland before either. But what is there here for me? A poky bedsitter in Richmond, and the choice of joining the Land Army, nursing or a factory making bombs as work. We've got food rationing already. Who can say what other horrors the government has in store for us?'

Mary could identify with that; she'd often sat in her room up in the attic in Hampstead and wondered if happiness was ever going to come her way. In the last few days of bombing, she'd even considered catching the first bus that came along out of London, and staying on it until the end of the route. She thought of it as a kind of Russian roulette. She could end up somewhere lovely, find a new job she liked, and perhaps even love. Or it might be an awful place, and she'd be forced to take the next bus back to Hampstead.

'Just lately I had been imagining running away,' Mary giggled, because that sounded so silly. Not even a proper plan. 'I don't think I can cope with Mr and Mrs Bradley much longer. They moan about everything;

anyone would think war had been declared just to spoil their comfortable life.'

'Come with me?' Elizabeth said impulsively. 'An adventure is always more fun if it's shared.'

Mary stared at her companion in disbelief. 'You can't be serious! I've only just met you!'

That was of course true, but though Elizabeth didn't want to admit it, she was terrified of going into the unknown alone. But with Mary at her side, stranger or not, she knew she'd be brave and confident. So she gave Mary a beaming smile. 'So what! I like you, we've got a lot in common. I think you need a bit of excitement and fun as much as I do. You haven't had much, have you? And what have we got to look forward to here? Bombing nightly, whole streets destroyed, opening the newspaper daily to read of still more tragedy.'

She knew it was reckless to ask someone she knew virtually nothing about to come and share her new life. But she needed a friend right now and she was pretty certain Mary did too.

Mary looked down at her now empty plate, playing for time. Elizabeth was right about her, but she didn't want to admit to someone she'd only just met how bad her life had been. 'There hasn't been much fun,' she admitted. 'But if I came with you, what if it didn't work out?'

'I can't be doing with considering "What ifs". Life's

too short for that,' Elizabeth said airily. 'But if it didn't work out you could always find another job like the one you have now.' She pulled a face as if she thought that was the worst possible outcome. 'They do say the rich are getting in a panic as their menservants have all been called up, and now the women are leaving for work in factories and on the land. Heaven forbid they might have to lift a duster or wash up a few dishes themselves.'

Mary giggled. 'I think I'd rather work in a factory or on the land, at least I wouldn't have a boss like Mrs Bradley on my back all the time. But seriously, Elizabeth, I am touched that you're impulsive enough to ask me – ninety per cent of me wants to throw caution to the wind and agree to go. But the other ten per cent is asking if it's sensible to do something so rash with a total stranger.'

Elizabeth looked at her with one eyebrow raised questioningly. 'What's the worst that could happen?' she asked. 'The cottage might be awful, and miles from anywhere, plus we fall out. But it may not be like that. The cottage might be lovely, we make lots of new friends, and have a great time. Come with me and try it. If you hate it, I'll give you your fare back to England.'

'I wouldn't expect you to do that,' Mary said with some indignation. 'But I haven't got my clothes and if I go to Hampstead to get them Mrs Bradley will get shirty with me about leaving without giving notice.' But she smiled as she said it because she suddenly realized she didn't give a damn about the Bradleys.

'I've got lots of clothes. I'll share them with you, we're about the same size. As for the sainted Mrs Bradley, write her a letter and say you went to see your aunt and she was so poorly you felt you must stay with her.'

The air-raid siren went off suddenly, instantly preventing further conversation. 'Blast it,' Elizabeth said, and jumped up. 'We'd better get to the shelter.'

The Nippy had brought the bill and taken the cash some time ago, but it was only now that they noticed the restaurant was half empty. Had everyone been expecting a raid? Or had they gone because it was now dusk?

They grabbed their gas masks and made for the door. 'There's a shelter in Trafalgar Square, I noticed it on the way here,' Elizabeth said, taking Mary's arm and leading her towards the road. 'Now, do you want to do this night after night, or be on the train to Rosslare tomorrow?'

Mary didn't know where Rosslare was, but she wasn't going to admit that. Or that going into an underground shelter with a lot of strangers was equally frightening.

Elizabeth paused on the kerb, looking across at the brick-built surface shelter in Trafalgar Square. 'People are saying those places aren't safe. We could go to St Martin's crypt, but I don't fancy that,' she said, then grabbing Mary's arm, she led her towards the steps down to the Underground. 'This will be safer. Nice and deep.'

Mary hadn't been in any shelter other than her employers' cellar, but she felt the Underground was the best place to be – it had lighting, and probably toilets somewhere, too.

As they went down the steps to the booking hall, there was a smell of bodily odours and more than a whiff of urine. Mary reminded herself that the Tube had never smelled nice, and people must have been using it as a shelter since the bombing started in earnest a few days earlier. She also remembered hearing something on the wireless that the government weren't too keen on people using the Tube as shelters in case they never wanted to come up outside again.

They went through the booking hall, following everyone else, and down an escalator which had been turned off.

'Let's stay as near to the exit as possible,' Elizabeth whispered in her ear as they went onto the nearest platform. 'That way we can be first out when the all-clear sounds. This will do,' she said, and plonked herself down on the ground, leaning back against an advertisement for Capstan Full Strength cigarettes on the wall.

Mary sat down beside her, looking around. It was a strange sight, the hordes of people equipped with pillows and eiderdowns who must live locally and have come down earlier to bag a good space, and hundreds more pouring in, businessmen in smart suits, manual workers in dirty work clothes, and whole families, some of the mothers with babies either in their arms or a pushchair. Then there were young people, all dressed up, perhaps come to the West End for the evening.

Mary had only ever seen Tube platforms full of standing people poised to push their way onto the next train. The scene before her was strange and bewildering. She was really glad she was with Elizabeth, who was so calm and knowledgeable.

'Give me your bag.' Elizabeth grabbed Mary's small brown handbag and stuffed it down between their hips. She then did the same with her own, which was much larger. 'I'm told a lot of thieves come in the shelters looking for rich pickings. I've got money, my train and ferry tickets, plus important documents in mine. If it was taken, I'd be stranded.'

Elizabeth's words sent a shudder down Mary's spine. She only had a one pound note and some loose change and it was all she had in the world. 'What do we do if we want a drink or to spend a penny?' she asked.

'I've heard people use the tunnel as toilets,' Elizabeth winced. 'I'm not going down there, that's for sure. As for drinks, I haven't a clue. But some of the people down here seem to have all the comforts of home.' She inclined her head to their right, where two middle-aged women sat on folding chairs, both knitting. In front of their feet was a wicker basket with a Thermos flask and what looked like packets of sandwiches and a box of cakes. They each had a blanket and a small cushion.

'How likely is it that bombs will drop around here?' Mary asked nervously. Last night she and the Bradleys had gone back into the house to their beds at midnight because there had been no bombs dropping nearby. But she had been told they were supposed to stay in their shelters until the all-clear sounded.

Elizabeth shrugged. 'I've no idea, I've been living in a basement flat, so I just stayed in there. To be honest I didn't hear much overnight, only distant rumblings. Last night I went out into the street about one in the morning and the sky was very red in the east, so I knew it was bad there, but it was quiet in Richmond. The West End hasn't copped any bombs yet, so we'll be fine. So let's try to enjoy our first time in a public shelter. I'm hoping before the night is out you will tell me you've decided to come with me tomorrow.'

Mary was impressed by her new friend's positive attitude – she ought to try and be more like her.

It wasn't pleasant to be sitting on a cold concrete floor, and the subway was stuffy, too hot and smelly.

And as for the noise! But that was to be expected with hundreds of people packed into a limited space. Yet Mary was glad she wasn't alone, indeed it didn't seem possible they'd only met a few hours earlier. As they pointed out amusing things going on around them to one another, or overheard snippets of conversations and arguments, Mary laughingly said it was like watching a comedy in a theatre.

'You're right,' Elizabeth agreed. 'Here we all are, a cross-section of human life, hiding from something that might kill us, and yet no one is distraught.'

'It's making me feel brave enough to say I will come with you tomorrow,' Mary said impulsively.

'Oh goody goody,' Elizabeth clapped her hands. 'That's just made the evening.'

Suddenly there was a loud thump from above them. Everyone on the crowded platform looked up and the thump was quickly followed by a loud explosion, and a whistling noise that seemed to be coming right through the roof of the Tube, burrowing its way down to them on the platform. People screamed and Elizabeth clasped her arms around Mary as most of the lights flickered and went out. Something was raining down on them. Not water, heavier, damp and rough.

'It's earth!' a male voice yelled close by. 'The bomb has come right through the road. We're going to be buried alive.'

Elizabeth pulled up their handbags, slung Mary's

round her neck and put her own big bag over Mary's face before tightening her arms around her. 'We'll be OK,' she said in a voice that didn't sound like hers. 'The bag is to protect our faces, so don't try to move it. But they will rescue us. I'm so glad I'm with you.'

All at once soil and rubble came down on them, thick and heavy. Elizabeth gave a shout of pain, and at the same time Mary felt a blow to her head. Then it all went dark.

'Elizabeth Manning?'

Mary heard the female voice as if it was at the end of a long tunnel. She tried to speak but it seemed something was in her mouth.

'Let me clean your eyes and mouth,' the voice said, this time much closer, and she felt something soft and wet against her eyes. 'You've had an awful time but it's over now.'

Finally Mary was able to open her eyes to see a nurse in her starched cap and apron, but she still couldn't speak because the nurse was delving inside her mouth and extracting debris. 'You were lucky to survive,' she went on. 'You have a nasty blow on your head, but as I understand it you were protected by your friend. The explosion drove down from the road into the ticket office and weakened the concrete and steel casing of the Tube. It really is a miracle that the rescue workers were able to dig most of you out alive.'

As the nurse picked debris out of her mouth Mary gagged, then, when she lifted her up a little so she could spit out the remainder of the soil, she winced.

'Well, Elizabeth. You've had quite a few stitches in your head,' the nurse said as an explanation. 'Now let me get you some water so you can wash the remainder of the dirt out of your mouth. I'll only be gone for a moment or two.'

Mary was not only sore all over, she was also totally confused to find herself in a hospital bed, without knowing how she got there. And why did the nurse think she was Elizabeth?

Lifting her head gingerly, she saw she was in a ward with about ten other women, but the lights were so dim she couldn't see if Elizabeth was among them. She supposed she must be in Charing Cross Hospital, and she was wearing a hospital gown. She wished she could remember what had happened.

The nurse reappeared with a glass of water and a kidney dish. 'Swill your mouth round, dear, it must be horrible. Seemed your handbag saved you, we were told it was shielding your face. We've got that in a safe place for you. Your dress was ruined, but we can find you something else to wear when you leave. We found a card in your bag that said you were staying at the Charing Cross Hotel. Someone rang there to tell them you were safe, and to hold on to your things until you can get them. We also saw the train ticket to Ireland. I'm sure they'll change it for you when you are ready.'

Mary rinsed her mouth out as she'd been told, then slumped back on the pillow. 'Was my friend brought in with me?' she managed to get out with some difficulty because her throat was terribly sore. As the nurse thought she was Elizabeth she thought for now it was best to ask about Mary.

'I will get one of the wardens to come and talk to you. We have many injured here, though some were given first aid on a train, before being brought up on stretchers. The rescue workers were very brave, they were advised to stop digging people out as the roof was unsafe, but they carried on regardless of the heat and danger. They say they got the last ones out by midnight. Surprisingly, the death count is very low. But you go back to sleep now, it's two in the morning.'

'If someone knows about Mary will they come and wake me to let me know?'

'I'll do my best, but you rest now.'

Mary felt they must have given her some strong medicine, for she did feel very sleepy. She touched the dressing on the back of her head and wondered how bad it was and if they'd had to shave her hair away. But even as these thoughts came to her, she felt guilty at not putting the nurse right about her name. What if Elizabeth was dead?

*

She woke to see weak light coming in through the criss-cross taping on the windows, and a sister with a pleated starched cap coming down the ward, looking at the names on the end of the beds.

'Are you looking for me?' Mary whispered to the sister. 'Have you found my friend?'

She came right up to the side of the bed. 'Yes, Miss Manning, but it's bad news, I'm afraid. Mary Price died in the Tube. You owe your life to her, I'm told. She had lain on top of you and took the full force of the rubble. The warden found her little shoulder bag with her identity card. She had it around her neck for safety. Do you know her next of kin so we can contact them?'

'She hasn't got any.' Tears poured down her face as she said it.

'We found a telephone number for the people she worked for,' the sister said. 'I'm going to ring them a little later. It's too early yet. I'm sorry I had to bring you such bad news. Can I get you a cup of tea?'

After the sister had gone, Mary had to close her eyes to shut out the gravity of what she had done, or perhaps not done. She wasn't sure which it was. She was to be Elizabeth Manning now. Sad, unloved Mary was gone; now, with a new identity, she could take on what Elizabeth had intended to do.

Could she really do that? Was she brave enough?

2

Eighteen years earlier, Whitechapel, East London

Hearing what sounded like a child crying in the back yard, Ruth Carstairs opened her first-floor kitchen window and leaned out.

It was a very cold January day, already dark though only four in the afternoon. Ruth could barely see the child's pale face in the darkness, but knew it was Mary, who lived downstairs.

'What the matter, Mary?' she called out.

'Mum ain't in and I'm freezing,' came the reply.

The two flats at 4 Crimp Street did not share a front door. The landlord had fixed up a flimsy partition in the hall to make them self-contained. Ruth upstairs had the street door. The Prices had the back door, accessed by the back alley.

Ruth Carstairs did not approve of Emily Price, or Ronnie Birch, but she certainly wasn't going to let an eight-year-old suffer because of her mother and the company she kept.

'You'd better come up with me, then,' Ruth suggested. 'Come round and I'll open the door.'

Ruth was sure Emily was in. She'd seen her from her kitchen window about an hour earlier coming in with a man. She'd heard his voice not long before Mary began hammering on the back door, and he certainly hadn't left, as she would've seen him. But then Emily Price was as careless with her child's wellbeing as she was with her virtue.

Crimp Street in Whitechapel was a short row of small terraced houses opposite the high wall of a laundry. Boys often climbed up on the wall to see the horse the laundry owners used for pulling their collection and delivery cart. And they also played noisy ball games against the wall.

Ruth was already at the front door when Mary got round there. 'Come on in, and sit by the fire,' she said.

The child's raincoat was not suitable for January weather and was soaked right through. Ruth told Mary to slip off her shoes and saw one of them had a hole in the sole where water had got in and made her sock wet, so suggested she take off the socks so she could dry them by the fire, and carried the raincoat up to dry it too.

Ruth wanted to laugh as Mary's mouth fell open in surprise at her flat. To her it was quite ordinary, but the view of her sitting room, with a roaring fire, book-lined shelves and the pretty chintz-covered sofa and armchair, was clearly nothing like Mary's home.

She took the child into her kitchen at the back of the

house. Again, Mary looked astounded at the red-and-white checked cloth on the table, and the matching curtain round the big sink to hide the clutter beneath. She looked too at the dresser holding all the matching plates and dishes.

'It ain't 'alf posh 'ere, do you use 'em all?' she asked.

'Of course, my dear. I bought pretty matching china because I wanted it on display. I'm sure your mother does the same?'

Judging by Mary's bewildered expression this wasn't so.

The child was very thin and pale, like so many of the children who lived in the East End. Her dark-brown hair was in dire need of a wash; Ruth felt it had been cut with garden shears as on one side it was just below her right ear, and an inch longer on the other. But she did have lovely eyes, very blue, although they looked sad.

'Sit down, dear,' Ruth said, pulling out a chair with a red cushion on it. 'Would you like tea, or cocoa?'

'Tea if it ain't too much trouble.' Her response was very faint.

Ruth cut her a slice of chocolate cake and put it in front of the child. She looked like she couldn't believe her eyes. 'Did you make this?' she asked.

'Yes, I did. I've had a few days off from my work and I find baking very soothing.'

'What's "soothing"?' Mary asked.

Ruth laughed softly. 'It's when something makes you feel relaxed and happy. Reading is like that for me too. Can you read yet?'

'A bit, but my teacher says I'm slow. But I really like it when she reads us a story.'

'If you'd like to come and see me again, I could help you with your reading?'

'Really?'

'Yes really, I am a teacher.'

Ruth looked at her and smiled. Mary thought she had a lovely face for someone old. Soft brown eyes that twinkled, pink cheeks and nice white teeth. She wasn't wearing any make-up, and her brown hair was cut short, but it had a bit of a wave in it and was very shiny. Her clothes were very plain, but somehow just right. A lavender-coloured twin set, and a checked skirt of a similar colour. She was wearing brown slippers, but Mary guessed she didn't ever wear high heels like her mother, but stout lace-up shoes.

'Normally I'm still at work at this time of day, as I have another job after school. But you could come on a Saturday, or around seven in the evening if your mother agrees.'

Mary had no intention of asking; she knew what the response would be. But as her mother always went out between half past six and seven to the pub where she worked, she need never know.

'Which school do you teach at, Miss Carstairs?'

she asked. Her teacher, Miss Stone, had talked about good manners and polite conversation just recently. She had said it was important to take an interest in other people, so asking what they worked at was a good way to start. She had pointed out it was very rude to ask how much money they earned, but if they did a job you didn't understand, you could ask about that.

'Bankcroft Road, but I also work at the council offices, helping people with their problems. I expect you know that when the Great War ended, many women were widowed and many of the soldiers who did come back were too sick to work.'

'My dad was a soldier and was killed in France,' Mary volunteered.

'Oh dear, I'm so sorry, Mary.' Ruth blushed and covered her mouth with her hand. 'I didn't know that.'

'It's OK, I never met 'im, 'e died afore I was born. We've got a photo of 'im on the mantelpiece, and sometimes I talk to 'im.'

'What do you talk to him about?'

'I ask 'im when Ronnie will go away. 'E's a nasty man. Mum just does what 'e says or 'e whacks 'er.'

Ruth Carstairs was used to such bald statements from children, but she still found it very upsetting that such bad examples were being set to them by adults. She had overheard this Ronnie character laying into Mary's mother many times and it was common knowledge in the area that he had pushed her into prostitution.

'Does he hurt you too?' Ruth tried to make the question as gentle and tactful as possible.

'I try to keep out of 'is way,' Mary replied. She probably imagined that meant she wasn't telling tales. But the way she avoided looking directly at Ruth told the true story.

That was how they left it that January day.

Teaching had been Ruth's goal for as far back as she could remember. She had even taught her younger brother to read when she was seven. She lost him in the Great War, not from battle wounds but typhus, and that cemented the idea in her head that education was the most important thing in life. Not just being able to read and write, but to educate those who hadn't had the advantages of a good home, as she had, in all aspects of hygiene, cooking nutritional food, and other household skills. Her parents did not understand why the daughter they'd brought up to share their middle-class values should turn her back on marriage and children of her own and go to live and work in a slum area.

But for each child she taught to read, to write a good letter, and each adult she helped through a bereavement, a crippling illness or other problems, she found happiness and satisfaction.

She saw in little Mary Price an ideal pupil. To give

her the confidence to feel able to break away from a careless mother and the strong, bad influences this area held. Also, reading, writing and other useful knowledge would enable Mary to make a better, happier life for herself.

Ruth had no doubt people would say she was a lonely spinster, trying to hold on to a girl who could become her family. But that wasn't her aim. She'd heard enough from downstairs over the last two years to know Mary was at risk. Ronnie, the man who controlled her mother, was a vicious piece of work, and Emily was too stupid to see that he had not only taken over her home and forced her into degrading work, but he almost certainly had plans for Mary too.

Sometimes when Ruth heard violence breaking out downstairs she was tempted to go and intervene, but she knew from experience with bullies that he would attack her too, and possibly he would make her life so miserable she would have to leave her little flat. Going to the police was a waste of time, they would do nothing. The best way she could help the little girl was to teach her useful skills, so one day she could get away completely to a decent job.

3

Dressed in a pretty blue floral dress, a white petticoat beneath and a beige cardigan courtesy of the hospital, Mary looked into the mirror in the bathroom and winced. Her swollen and badly bruised face and the dressing on her head gave a sad image of walking wounded. She still ached in so many different places, and was worried sick. But the dress she'd been given pleased her, it was far nicer than her old one.

She had been in hospital for two days, but now she had to go. The staff nurse on the ward was concerned that she hardly spoke, but then Mary was afraid she might blurt out something which would give the game away. The only excuse she could think of was that she was shy.

Now the terrifying prospect of retrieving Elizabeth's luggage was imminent. She was afraid the hotel staff would know she wasn't the rightful owner and call the police.

She was the same height, size and colouring as the real Elizabeth, and as she put on the hat the sister had given her, a pale blue felt with a brim, she hoped it hid her face enough. Elizabeth had said she'd left her suitcase at the hotel reception as her room wasn't ready when she checked in. Mary offered up a silent prayer that there would be different staff on duty now.

Taking a deep breath to steady herself, she opened the bathroom door. She had only to collect the handbag which had saved her, and she could go.

The sister who had given her the shocking news about her friend had gone off duty, which was a relief in as much as she wouldn't have to look her in the eye and take a dead woman's handbag from her.

Ten minutes later, reminding herself that she must now eat, sleep and everything else as Elizabeth, she walked out of the hospital. She had been given some aspirin for the pain and told she must see a doctor in a week's time to have the stitches taken out of her head. The big brown leather handbag had been wiped clean of soil and other debris by some kindly soul. As she picked it up she had a sudden mental picture of the real Elizabeth saying, 'Go on, you can do this! Have the adventure for both of us.'

Using it as a shoulder bag, she held it tightly, reminding herself again that her friend had used it to shield her, and therefore it still had that power. The Charing Cross Hotel was close by, part of the station. She walked onto the cobbled forecourt to the large doors, but paused before going in.

She turned to look across the Strand towards Trafalgar Square. There wasn't much evidence of the bombing, just a small crater cordoned off. She'd been told by a nurse that the emergency services had sent a stretcher-party car on the evening of the twelfth and the small hole they saw didn't appear to match the report, so they went off elsewhere to what seemed a more serious incident. But a 500-pound bomb had penetrated the ground and detonated in the ticket hall below.

This same nurse had informed her there were forty casualties in all that night, but only seven fatalities. Two of those had been Norwegians. She also said that the rescue team deserved medals for their courage.

The doorman at the hotel opened it wide for her and beamed a welcome. Mary smiled back at him then walked purposefully to the reception desk to ask about her luggage, trying to keep her head down to hide her face. The male receptionist clearly didn't know her, and returned almost staggering under the weight of a large brown suitcase and a smaller one. He must have been informed she was a bomb casualty as he asked how she was feeling now.

'Much better now, just a bit battered,' she replied. 'Now I need to pay for the room.'

Even as she said that she panicked a little as she wasn't sure there was money in the handbag. But fortunately he waved his hands. 'No charge, that's the least we can do,' he said, then beckoned a porter to take the cases and get her a taxi.

Before one came, she nervously opened the handbag and looked in. She saw a leather purse which held two one-pound notes, a ten shilling note and some change. She breathed a sigh of relief as the taxi pulled in.

'Where to, Miss?' the bespectacled driver asked.

'I'm not sure,' she said, nervously hopping from one foot to the other. She'd never been in a taxi before, but she'd been told London cab drivers were good men and knew everything. 'I was supposed to be going to Ireland, but I got caught up in a bombing raid, and I've got stitches in my head. So I think I ought to go to a guest house for a few days until I can get the stitches taken out. I didn't want to stay in Charing Cross because of the bombing. Do you know somewhere nice, but not too expensive?'

'I know just the place for you,' he said, his kindly face wreathed in a warm smile. 'It's in Blandford Street, just off Baker Street. Cosy rooms, safe and clean. The landlady is a relative, it's just called Number Eighteen.'

As they made their way there, she was itching to see what else the bag held, but now wasn't the time, so she sat back enjoying the ride. She felt rather grand, and hoped she could fool the driver into thinking she got in cabs all the time.

'You stay here, duck,' the driver said as they arrived. 'I'll just pop in to ask Marge if she's got a room. Won't be a moment.'

A stout, middle-aged woman wearing a brown dress and a crisp white apron opened the door. She looked pleased to see the taxi driver and kissed his cheek, and he pointed back to his cab and his passenger.

No. 18 was in a terrace of smart London townhouses. It looked well cared for, with shiny brassware on the navy-blue door and dazzling white net curtains at the windows. The railings in front of the houses in this street were still in place, although elsewhere many had been removed and taken away to help the war effort.

The driver came back grinning. 'Margery's got a room for you,' he said. 'As you've been injured, you can have it for one and sixpence a day. Is that OK?'

Again, she felt relief. She had enough to stay a few days and it sounded like it would be a good place. So she smiled and thanked him. He took the cases and together they went back to the house and he introduced her to Margery Blythe.

'You poor dear,' Margery said. 'Elizabeth, what a pretty name, may I call you that or should it be Miss Manning?'

'Just call me Beth,' she said impulsively. She had no idea why, it just popped out. But the moment she said it she realized it would be easier for her to cope with an abbreviation. 'That's what everyone calls me.'

'Fair enough,' Margery said. 'I must say Beth suits you too.'

Mary paid the driver. He wished her better and said he hoped she'd be happy in Ireland.

Margery was a warm, chatty lady. She commiserated on Mary's injuries and said the price she'd quoted was to include breakfast and an evening meal, and if she needed anything she was only to ask. 'My cooking isn't fancy,' she said, 'but most people don't want that. Of course I'll need your ration book while you're here.'

For a second Mary was thrown. But then realized Elizabeth's ration book was probably in the handbag or one of the suitcases.

The room Margery took her to was at the back on the first floor. 'It's not very big,' she said apologetically, 'but it's the only one I've got left.'

Mary was delighted. It was twice the size of her attic room at the Bradleys, with its own washbasin, and a double bed that looked very comfy and cosy, with a pink satin eiderdown.

'It's perfect,' she said, taking in the pretty rosebud wallpaper, thick curtains and the inevitable blackout blind. She liked the kidney-shaped dressing table with a frill round it, and there was a small desk by the window which overlooked surprisingly pretty gardens. She thought she could be happy here for ever.

After Margery had gone back downstairs, saying that supper would be ready at half past six, Mary sat on the bed and tipped out the contents of the big handbag.

There was a large brown envelope which had photographs, letters and the required ration book. She put it to one side. There was the usual handbag clutter: a powder compact, lipstick, nail file, nail scissors, a tiny diary and a couple of hair slides.

Elizabeth's identity card, birth certificate, her mother's death certificate, even her parents' wedding lines, were all there, including the telegram reporting that her father had been killed in action in France in 1917. Mary found the train ticket to Fishguard, but she couldn't find a ticket for the boat to Ireland. Then there were a great many letters, photographs, and a diary.

She went through the letters, sorting the handwritten ones from those that were typed. She arranged these in date order, and started with them first. There were several from a Mr Boyle, a solicitor in Waterford, Ireland. These bore out that the cottage had been left to her by her godmother. He said that the ferries had been withdrawn because of 'the Emergency' – she gathered by that he meant the war – but he had given her a telephone number for a cargo ship which would accept her as a passenger, though she might have to stay in a guest house in Fishguard until the boat was ready to sail.

That brought on panic. She had imagined she'd step down from the train onto a ferry, and considering she had no idea where Fishguard was, catching a train there was bad enough, but waiting in a guest house until she could get on a ship filled her with dread.

It was very tempting to go to the police right now and tell them that the bang she got to her head had made her forget who she was, but now she had remembered her real identity she wanted to put the record straight.

'Sleep on it,' she murmured to herself. 'You don't have to make a decision right now.'

That thought calmed her enough to continue looking through the letters. One from the solicitor was referring to a response from Elizabeth saying she would be coming over to take possession of the cottage. That again jolted Mary. Not only had that date passed, but Mr Boyle would be bound to want her signature before he handed over keys.

But then she found a slim folder containing typed carbon copies of all Elizabeth's replies to the solicitor, and they even included her signature. So it occurred to her she would only have to practise copying that signature perfectly, as there appeared to be no handwritten letters to trip her up.

Again she calmed herself and realized she didn't have to ring Mr Boyle immediately and tell him why she'd been delayed. There was plenty of time to make up her mind about what to do. Meanwhile she'd have a good rest in this lovely guest house.

Also in the brown envelope was a letter dated back

in July from Mr and Mrs B. Donaldson, the owners of the dress shop in Richmond, informing her that they were giving up the lease of the shop. They went on to thank Elizabeth for being the perfect manageress, and to hope she would find a new position quickly. Attached was a 'To Whom It May Concern' glowing reference which stated she'd been an honest and reliable employee, an excellent saleswoman with a real flair for fashion, and that all their customers thought highly of her.

There were a couple of letters from her old landlord too, the first saying he was sorry she was leaving as she'd been a very good tenant, and the second enclosing a cheque for the deposit she'd paid. He said he was pleased not to have to make any deductions from it as she had kept it in such good order.

The rest of the letters were mainly offering condolence on the death of her mother. Whether they were from relatives, or friends and acquaintances was unclear. They wrote the usual platitudes yet not one of them had offered help, or an invitation to visit. She thought they were quite blunt, as if written out of duty not affection, and she felt surprised her friend had kept them.

But at least it reassured her that no one would be worrying about Elizabeth Manning if they didn't hear from her.

She moved on then to look through the photographs.

Many were family ones, of her parents on their wedding day, her father in uniform, Elizabeth as a baby and then on through childhood. One lovely one was taken professionally when she must have been around sixteen. Many of them had dates and places written on the back. There was one of an attractive but small Georgian villa, with 'Home, 10 Marsham Road, Tunbridge Wells'.

Mary placed everything back in the envelope, intending to study all the photographs and letters again closely in the next few days. It was time to open the large suitcase.

Perfume wafted out as she opened it. She recognized it as Joy by Jean Patou – Mrs Bradley wore it on special occasions. Her first thought was how neat Elizabeth had been. The case was packed perfectly. Underwear in a monogrammed linen bag, shoes in cloth bags too and tissue paper protecting dresses, blouses, skirts and jackets. But it was a white cloth bag secured with an elastic band and which rustled as she picked it up that intrigued her. When she took the band off and shook out the contents, her mouth dropped open in shock.

It was full of bank notes, in bundles with rubber bands round them. Mostly £20 notes, and a quick count of just those made £700. The tens and fives made another £200, and twelve one-pound notes came to £912 in all.

She was stunned. She'd never had more than three pounds in her entire life. This was a fortune. Who had that much money just in a suitcase? A sudden and frightening thought came to her. She didn't know anything much about the real Elizabeth. Suppose she'd stolen this money and was going on the run! She'd said she ran a dress shop, but was that true? Since when did a mere shop assistant get to save this much money? If she had come by it honestly, surely she would've kept it in a bank account?

But Elizabeth *had* run a dress shop, there was a reference from her employers. Her landlord clearly thought a lot of her too.

Mary didn't feel she could keep this money, it was far too much. Yet it was so very tempting. It would give her the chance to change her life for a better one, and if she turned it in to the police she'd have to go back to the Bradleys.

She put the money back in the bag, telling herself that maybe Elizabeth's mother had given it to her on her recent death, or she'd sold some jewellery or some other valuable item.

She took the garments out one by one, astounded by the quality of them. She slipped a lilac-coloured short jacket over her dress. It fitted like it was made for her. She had very few clothes and all of them cheap things from markets. But remembering how Elizabeth had said she had enough clothes to share with her, she didn't feel guilty at revelling in the chance to wear such finery. There was only one special dress – she supposed it would be called a cocktail dress – mid-calf length, rose-pink satin and lace. It was beautiful, a dream of a dress. Apart from that her friend appeared to have picked stuff that was still glamorous, but suitable for every day. There were even two pairs of slacks, and several very soft jumpers, plus exquisite silk underwear.

In the smaller suitcase was a classic camel coat, a raincoat and a far smaller light-brown handbag, which looked more useful for now than the big one. Plus three pairs of shoes, size five, that fitted her perfectly too.

As thrilling as the clothes were, there were also a couple of desk diaries. A quick glance through them promised a wealth of information about the real Elizabeth. She told herself she would read every word of them, starting this evening after supper.

Completely overcome by this treasure, she lay back on the bed to gather her thoughts. She really wanted to be Elizabeth now. To wear nice clothes, to ride in taxis and stay in hotels. It was like a wonderful dream, but she was very much aware that taking another person's identity for gain was illegal.

'You are an imposter,' she whispered to herself.

Wishing you were someone else wasn't living a lie like an imposter. But for a good part of her life Mary had wished she was Ruth Carstairs' daughter. If it wasn't for that kind woman, she would probably have ended up like her mother.

She could recall the first time she met Miss Carstairs as clearly as if it was yesterday. It was raining, bitterly cold, and her mother was out. Miss Carstairs invited her in, and there began a warm and loving relationship which lasted until she was twelve. Absolutely everything good she knew came from Auntie Ruth, as she called her – reading, writing, sewing, cooking. Hours spent reading aloud to her, or learning to do joined-up writing, and to spell correctly. She sewed a blouse and a skirt for herself there, had cookery lessons, and learned her times tables and arithmetic.

Sitting by the warm fire in winter, in Auntie Ruth's snug and pretty living room, for a couple of hours each day, she managed to forget how different her real life downstairs was.

Home was dirty, everything shabby and ugly. It smelled of mould and damp, and Ronnie's sweat and cigarettes. The kitchen cupboards were always bare, a good meal was rare, and always the atmosphere was of something unpleasant looming. But then Ronnie and her mother went out every night, and if Mary hadn't got her dinner at school for free, and tea most days with Auntie Ruth, she'd have starved.

It was to Auntie Ruth that she finally sobbed out what Uncle Ronnie was doing to her. He'd come into her life when she was four, and had seemed nice. He'd wallpapered the tiny box room especially for her and bought her a proper bed. Up till then she'd shared with her mother. But gradually Ronnie stopped being nice. One wrong word from her or her mother and he'd hit them. Mary realized by the time she was nine that he made her mother do something at nights that she didn't like. She told Mary she worked in a bar, but that didn't seem like the truth.

She found out the truth when she was nearly ten. A boy at school said her mother was a streetwalker and went with men for money. Around the same time, Ronnie came back in the evening when her mother was working and raped her. It all fell into place. Ronnie took the money her mother made, and wanted to use her daughter for sex whenever he felt like it.

Nothing had ever hurt as much as what he did to her. Years later she could still smell his foul breath, his sweat, and remember the callous way he forced himself into her. But even the pain wasn't as bad as the humiliation. She felt dirty all the time, she was afraid to get close to anyone in case she smelled. And always the dread of wondering when the next time would be. She knew her mother couldn't or wouldn't help her, not just because she was afraid of Ronnie but because she took something in a brown bottle that made her dopey.

*

The sound of a gong from downstairs alerted Mary that she'd fallen asleep, and it was half past six and time for supper. She hadn't eaten anything since breakfast and that was only porridge. Now she came to think about it, she was very hungry.

4

The following morning Mary woke refreshed from a very good night's sleep, and decided she was definitely now Beth. In a dream she had seen Elizabeth smiling and clapping her hands. She interpreted that as her friend encouraging her to be brave and daring.

After telephoning Mr Boyle in Ireland, his response, showing more concern for her welfare than any irritation that she hadn't arrived on time, was further validation for her to be Beth.

He explained a little more about the cargo ship. 'Patrick comes back and forward twice a week with various goods,' he said. 'German ships do come into the Irish Sea, and of course a cargo ship could be fired on, so you must understand there is a risk. But Patrick is a good man and knows the waters very well. Now, if you let me know when you are getting the train, I'll telephone Mrs Griffiths at the guest house in Fishguard to let her know you are coming. Her husband will meet you from the train, and you'll have a room there until Patrick is ready to sail back here.'

Discovering she would be met and have somewhere to stay eased her anxiety. Not completely, but enough.

Had it not been such lovely weather, Beth might have been tempted to stay in all day and read Elizabeth's diaries. She knew it was vital to become Elizabeth, to learn little phrases that were particular to her, and to know who and what were important to her. In her diaries she might discover if there were any friends or distant relatives who might turn up.

But with the sun shining, the bruising on her face fading, and wanting some exercise, going out was appealing. She couldn't wait to have the stitches removed as they itched, but that was a few days off, so with her hat hiding the bald patch of shaved hair, she reminded herself Elizabeth had been a confident and sophisticated businesswoman, and she had to learn to be the same.

For a Londoner, she was woefully ignorant about the city. She needed to learn more about it, the major shops, hotels and landmarks. But that was exciting. The diaries were saved for the evening, and during the day, air raids permitting, she intended to educate herself.

With a map in hand, she found her way to Buckingham Palace, walked along the Embankment to Chelsea, and wandered around Hyde Park. She was shocked to see so much of the park dug up for trenches for people to shelter in. An elderly woman she got talking to said they were useless as shelters as they filled with water when it rained. So now the new plan was to turn them into allotments so people could grow vegetables.

Everywhere she looked there were sandbags piled up outside every shop and office. Likewise the black tape across windows to stop glass shattering! How many million miles of that had been used? Yet she hadn't seen much evidence of bombing so far. But then Margery had said the East End was taking the brunt of it.

As she was walking down Park Lane on her second day, intending to go and look at Eros all boarded up at Piccadilly, the air-raid siren went off and everyone rushed to the nearest shelter.

To Beth's surprise, this shelter, in a large basement under a motor-car showroom, was a good one. It didn't smell, there were lots of seats, and the clientele were jolly, talkative and laughed a lot. Many of them worked in nearby hotels, so it was a break from work they enjoyed. The all-clear went all too quickly that day, and she felt a bit guilty as she walked back to Blandford Street that she'd enjoyed herself when elsewhere in London people were being killed.

On the previous evening when the air-raid siren blasted out just after it got dark, she took the most recent diary down to the guest-house cellar with her. Margery had made her cellar quite pleasant for her guests' safety. She'd put some old easy chairs in there, the lighting was good, and as the boiler for the house was down there too it was not only dry, but warm. The only guests there that night were a middle-aged couple. Margery said all the other guests had gone out, and her husband was on duty as a fireman.

Beth took a seat by a table lamp and continued to read. It was mainly recording the days in the dress shop at Richmond, what she'd sold, a bit of local gossip, and the weather. Every now and then there was a reference to someone called Patty, who frequently dropped into the shop. Beth got the distinct impression that her friend wished Patty wouldn't drop in so often. At one point she'd written, 'She should volunteer for some war work or find a hobby that occupies her. It would take her mind off whether her husband is in danger in France. If she asks me one more time how she will manage if she's widowed, I just might snap at her and tell her we single women don't have the luxury of a man keeping us.'

She mentioned a man called Freddy quite often too. He had taken her to a dance and to the pictures, but he was just a good friend. 'I know he'd like me to be his sweetheart, but I can't,' she wrote. 'I thought it was true love with Bernard, but it wasn't. I'm not going to get involved with a man like him again.'

From these two little insights into her friend's thoughts, Beth realized that her namesake was at heart a traditionalist, not quite the happy-go-lucky, outspoken and freedom-loving girl she'd portrayed herself as. That was quite encouraging; if she had been able to play that part convincingly, then maybe Beth could too.

Elizabeth could also be very funny, with a wonderful turn of phrase when she described the bizarre things that had happened in her shop, strange customers, and those who annoyed her.

However the very last entry she wrote was insightful and threw a light on the chilliness of some of the letters, and why she'd asked Mary to go to Ireland with her.

I'm closing the door on my life here in Richmond. I've enjoyed working and living here, I've learned a great deal from observing people, and I've met many interesting, fun people, but lately I am feeling that most of them are false. Maybe this is just because I've been at a low ebb since Mother died and Bernard left me. I've certainly felt as if I was merely treading water, and that I could sink at the next setback. I was saddened to notice that people I considered good friends stopped coming to see me, or inviting me out. Do they really think I'd wail and gnash my teeth because it's over with him? Surely they know me better than that?

Being left the cottage in Ireland seems a bit like a thrown lifebelt. I'll cling on to it until I can come ashore, and find a new path. Maybe it will be fashion again, or perhaps something brand new. But meanwhile I can't wait to go on long walks, to explore Ireland and to make new friends. A year from now who knows what I'll be doing?

Beth mopped up tears from her cheeks. It was tragic that Elizabeth was the first woman she'd ever met that she felt at one with and she'd been snatched away so quickly. Yet as sad as it was that she had to embark on this adventure alone, she was determined to grab the lifebelt that had been passed on to her, and make a good life for herself in Ireland. She didn't want to fail her friend.

It occurred to her then that she ought to make notes of major points in these diaries and then get rid of them. Should anyone find them and compare her writing she'd be in serious trouble. She had been practising the signature, and become so good at it, she doubted she could use her old one anymore.

Yet all this made her consider Mary Price. Would anyone be sad to hear that she had died in an air raid? Presumably a list of casualties was kept somewhere. In the unlikely event her mother consulted such lists, or the police managed to contact her, she was likely to pretend to be heartbroken and drink herself into a stupor because that's what she always did. But it would be just an act to gain sympathy.

Mr and Mrs Bradley would have been informed,

and they would of course remark to anyone who remembered their maid that it was sad such a young woman should be taken. But in reality, they would be far more concerned about who was going to cook and clean for them now.

She was never going to miss the self-centred Bradleys or concern herself with how her mother was. She had no other relatives as far as she knew, and childhood friends had all faded away, but that was even more reason for succeeding in making a happy life for herself in Ireland.

As she trawled back in the diaries, Beth began to see that while her friend – or maybe she should call her 'her benefactor' – had had a pretty good life, with lots of parties, outings to the coast and a holiday in France with a group of friends, she had had more than her share of sadness too. Losing her mother in 1939 was a bleak time for her, and circumstances meant she had to clear out her rented childhood home in Tunbridge Wells. While reading how Elizabeth packed up her old dolls, toys, books and other things into boxes for a jumble sale, Beth sensed how hard it was for her to say goodbye to all the memories, particularly those of her mother.

Then just a few months later the man she thought loved her, dropped her. She wrote at the time, 'I don't know how I can go on without Bernard or my mother to turn to. I feel so terribly alone.'

Beth was sure, even though it wasn't stated, that the cash she'd found in the suitcase was left after winding up her mother's affairs, and selling various items. Elizabeth did mention around the same time that she opened a bank account in Richmond. As there was no bank book in the handbag, Beth had to assume she'd drawn out the money when she bought the ticket to Ireland. That was just as well, as Beth had never had a bank account and wouldn't have the least idea of how they worked.

One of the oddest passages in last year's diary was about her godmother, Miss Miranda Falcon. The only mention of her was when she died, in late 1938, a year before her mother's death.

> I got used to always getting a card and a postal order on my birthday, and then at Christmas, which just said 'love always from Auntie Miranda'. Nothing more. Mother insisted I wrote a thank you letter each time, and lectured me on the art of letter-writing, not just about whatever had been sent to me. If it was money you must never specify the amount, only something like 'I shall put it towards the book I want', or whatever is appropriate. I should also ask after Auntie Miranda's health, say a little about current news, and a bit about my own life. As Mother said, thank you letters should be at least two sheets of quality unlined paper, interesting to the reader,

asking about their interests and hobbies, and any places she may had visited.

Beth was glad of this advice. She'd never had any reason to send a thank you letter, and now if the circumstances arose, she could write one without making a blunder. 'Mother was very upset when she heard her friend was dead,' Elizabeth continued. 'She hadn't seen her for donkey's years but they'd been at school together. Miranda had become a governess, working for families in France, Italy and other places. She attended my parents' wedding and my christening. Mother said she wished she'd made more of an effort to keep in close contact. I don't recall ever meeting her.'

Elizabeth went on to say that although she always wrote to thank Aunt Miranda for the postal orders, Miranda never wrote back to her. Then her mother died and she couldn't ask her any further questions about this intriguing godmother.

'When I got the news from the solicitors in Waterford that I'd been left her cottage, I was astounded. It felt like a second chance in life, something to take my mind off the loss of Mother and Bernard. But I regret not trying to get to know her or visiting her while she was still alive.'

Elizabeth had followed that entry a couple of days later with a little nervous musing.

'Do I really want to go to Ireland? I'm told it's very beautiful but will I like living there? There is so much poverty, I believe, and I won't know anyone, I'll have no job. It seems ridiculous to throw caution to the wind, it could be the biggest mistake I've ever made. But on the other hand it would be very ungracious to turn it down.'

That night after the all-clear sounded, Beth dug out the bundle of old photographs and went through them painstakingly. The sort of people she'd known back in Whitechapel didn't have a camera to take photographs. However, weddings, christenings or husbands going off to war often prompted them to have a professional one taken. There were quite a few professional ones in Elizabeth's bundle, many still in cardboard folders, and as she flicked through them, she saw Elizabeth's parents on their wedding day, then one much older picture which, judging by the Victorian clothes, was of her grandparents' wedding, and one of Elizabeth's father in army uniform, dated 1914. Then finally her mother holding her new baby in her arms, presumably taken to send to her husband, as it was dated April 1914.

Beth pounced on a picture dated October 1914. It was a classic christening one, with a tree and the churchyard behind them. Baby was in her mother's arms dressed in a long lace-trimmed number and matching bonnet. Her mother was flanked by a dark-haired man in a suit and winged collar and an elegant lady in a gauzy picture hat. That had to be Miranda, the godmother, and maybe the man was a godfather.

In the file of letters and other documents was the telegram saying that Corporal Alfred Manning was killed in action on 2 February 1915, so presumably he hadn't been granted leave for his daughter's christening. There was nothing to say who the dark-haired man in civilian clothes was. Maybe he was a friend of Miranda's.

Studying the christening photo carefully, she noted Miranda's dress and matching jacket were beautifully cut, with embroidery down the front of the edge-to-edge jacket which suggested the outfit had been very expensive and very stylish. She just wished she knew what colour the outfit was, as even her shoes appeared to match. In contrast, Elizabeth's mother looked dowdy, her dress dark and too tight and the hem uneven. But maybe she'd spent all her money on her baby's christening robe. How sad it was that not long after she'd hear that her husband was killed in action, and he would never see his baby.

Beth lay back on the bed, surrounded by photographs and letters, and felt a little ashamed to be trawling through another's family photographs, yet she had to scrutinize them and note facial expressions to get some idea of what they were like, how they lived, who they were.

One thing that surprised her, revealed by both the letters and the photos, was that her friend hadn't had the rather privileged childhood she'd imagined. So that confident, classy air she had, she'd learned.

Thinking on that reminded Beth of Auntie Ruth again. Without that stalwart, intelligent and kind woman, little Mary might never have survived.

Theirs was a secret relationship. It had to be. If Ronnie had found out Ruth was befriending and coaching Mary, he'd have stopped it. So two or three times a week Mary would tell her mother she was having her tea at her friend Flo's home and instead went to Ruth.

For Mary those precious hours each week meant warmth, comfort and, indeed, love, which went on undetected for five years. It was Ruth who taught her to stop dropping her H's, and using the word 'ain't'. Under her guidance Mary soon began to read fluently and to do arithmetic. But there was so much more to the time they spent together. Ruth told her about other countries, and English history. She taught her basic cooking, sewing and knitting, and lectured her on hygiene. She said many times that as soon as Mary was old enough she should get a job as a nursemaid or housemaid, and leave home.

Ruth never said Emily Price was a prostitute, but she did say Ronnie had pushed her mother into bad things and he would do the same to Mary.

*

After just a few days Beth found she didn't really want to leave Blandford Street. She liked motherly Margery and her comfortable home, and even during the nightly bombings she felt safe in the cellar. She kept getting the jitters about going to Ireland. What if someone turned up who knew she wasn't the real Elizabeth Manning? But then she could hardly stay in England now for the same reason.

Beth knew her main failing was being indecisive. Perhaps that was because she'd been told what to do all her life. First by her mother, who ordered her about like she was her personal slave. Then at fourteen the Bradleys took over. Indecision had to stop.

Daily she was learning that the bombs, which sounded so close, were not, and were targeting the docks. She felt more comfortable, and her guilt at what she was doing abated. But after listening to Margery saying it was only a matter of time before the German pilots began to use the Thames, glittering in moonlight, as a pathway into the centre of London, she did want to run to Ireland and safety.

Beth decided that being here safely in London for six days was enough, and tomorrow after she had her stitches out, she would go straight to Paddington Station and exchange her rail ticket.

Once she'd done that and tucked the ticket into her purse she would know it was real. No turning back!

*

Two days later, Margery hugged Beth before she got into the taxi taking her to Paddington Station. 'Goodbye and God bless,' she said. 'If it doesn't work out there for you, come straight back. I'll always find room for you.'

Such warmth from the kindly guest-house owner was very touching. It was also a way out if she didn't like Ireland. But her confidence had been boosted by wearing Elizabeth's grey striped two-piece, with a pink blouse beneath it. She'd completed the outfit with a pink beret she'd bought from Selfridges. She could hardly believe that the sophisticated and fashionable girl looking back at her in the mirror was once drab, meek Mary Price who no one ever noticed.

As she got into the taxi Margery pressed a small bag into her hands.

'Just some things for the journey,' she said. 'The book is one of my favourites. I hope you'll like it as much as I did. It should make the train journey shorter, and there's some sandwiches, cake and fruit.'

Beth had to bite back tears at the older woman's kindness. She wasn't used to people caring about her.

Even with a good book to read, the train journey to Fishguard seemed interminable. The train was quite full, mostly women and children leaving London to escape the Blitz. Presumably they had relatives or friends in Wales. She didn't want to get into conversation with anyone, so she closed her eyes, and relived her last night in London.

She had wanted to experience what the Blitz was really like. She knew that most people would say she had already experienced it, being in the Tube when a bomb came firing down into it, and there, by luck, she survived. But she wanted to witness the spectacle of an air raid, what people did while it was happening. Was there panic? Fatalism, anger? So instead of going back to the guest house, she stayed out, knowing Margery would be horrified if she went out again later, and insist she went down to the cellar with her.

There had been three brief daylight raids during the day, two in the east, but one bomber broke away from the group and flew towards North London, where presumably he dropped his stick of bombs. There was something compelling about watching the planes flying in formation. It reminded her of a flock of geese flying off to a warmer place.

Down on the ground the ack-ack guns fired at the German planes, but she didn't see any of the planes shot down, and the barrage balloons hanging all over London didn't seem to be much of a deterrent.

It was about eight in the evening when she walked leisurely up Oxford Street towards Hyde Park. It was surprisingly crowded and there was an air of jollity which she hadn't expected. British soldiers, airmen and sailors, and then Free French and Polish airmen jostled with civilians window shopping or making their way home. Some of the men whistled at girls, Beth included, which made her blush and walk with her head down. But it was exciting to be part of the jollity even if she was surrounded by strangers.

As dusk began to fall, she picked up speed, anxious to reach the park before it became really dark. Until tonight she had never gone out after dark as she felt afraid in the blackout. With no streetlamps, car headlights showing only a glimmer of low light, and with not a chink of light coming from homes or offices, it was intimidating.

But Beth didn't feel afraid now, she had a torch to get home with and this time tomorrow she'd be in Ireland beginning a new life. She was just going to cross Park Lane to the park when the air-raid siren went off.

While all had been calm ten minutes earlier, suddenly people began to rush in all different directions, reminding Beth of how as a child she'd poured water on an ants' nest to see them all run. She hesitated, torn between running to the shelter she'd been in before, and sticking to her plan to stay out and watch.

She chose to run across the road to the park.

'Hey, Miss, you're going the wrong way for the shelter,' a male voice called out.

Turning, she saw a soldier. 'I know,' she said.

'You've got a death wish then, have you?' he replied, but his tone was light, as if amused.

'No, but it's my last night in London and I'd like to watch an air raid. I doubt they'll bomb the park.'

'There's other dangers in the park,' he said, coming right up to her and taking her hand. 'So I'm appointing myself your guardian.'

She didn't protest. It would be good to have a guardian, and he was slender, handsome, had a nice voice, and tawny eyes that reminded her of a cat they'd had when she was a child. Better to live dangerously than die of boredom.

He introduced himself as Jack Ramsey, then got her to run with him into the park.

They took up a position close to the trenches dug as shelters.

'At least we can jump in if worse comes to worst,' he joked.

Beth peered into the one closest, though it was almost too dark to see the bottom. 'It looks quite dry,' she said and laughed. She'd been told that even when they were being dug, before war was declared, people said they wouldn't go in them. They didn't trust the surface shelters either.

Jack shuddered and grimaced. 'They make me think of the tales my dad used to tell me about trench life in France in the Great War. The rats and stuff. It sounded horrible.'

Beth told him she'd lost her father in the last war, and added perhaps they should talk about something more cheerful.

At that point the bombing raid started, but like almost all nights since the Blitz began it seemed the East End was on the receiving end again as the planes were over that way. Searchlights scanned the dark sky, now and then illuminating a bomber. Their ears were assaulted by the crump, crump of bombs, flashes of vivid flames, and the staccato sound of gunfire coming from anti-aircraft guns mounted on roofs and from the ground. In this deafening barrage of noise, they could also hear ambulance bells and fire engines racing into that wall of sound, and suddenly the horizon was orange and red from buildings on fire.

Tears sprang into Beth's eyes, imagining those trapped in buildings or seeing their homes destroyed.

'Those poor people in the East End,' Jack said in her ear, his voice breaking slightly as if feeling the same as she did. 'I've been working there searching for survivors and clearing rubble. I couldn't believe what I've seen, whole streets gone. Beds hanging out of an upper floor where the side wall has gone. Curtains flapping where once were windows. I've seen women crying as they retrieved toys, kitchen utensils and other stuff from the ruins of their homes. I almost cried myself.'

There was enough light in the sky to see his eyes were glistening with tears, and she took his hand and squeezed it. It was too noisy to talk, and anyway there were no words necessary.

He put his arm around her, and kissed her cheek, and they stayed that way, silently watching the terrible yet magnificent show above them for some time. Beth's experience with both boys and men was extremely limited and none of it good, and she found it strange that she wanted to keep his arm protectively round her.

'Have you seen enough now?' Jack said in her ear. 'We could go to a pub and then we could talk?'

She nodded. The bombing seemed to have decreased, and the planes were concealed by smoke, only illuminated briefly as one was shot down.

Taking her hand, he led her towards Marble Arch, across to Edgware Road, and then to a small public house just off the main road.

After the noise outside it was quiet. No more than twenty people, mostly men who had chosen to ignore the air raid and have a beer instead before going home.

'What'll you have?' Jack asked.

'Just lemonade, please,' she said, feeling a bit foolish because she had no idea what women drank in pubs. She'd only been in three or four in her life. Her mother had been a gin drinker and the remembered smell of that on her breath turned her stomach.

They took a table in a corner.

'I'm going to Ireland tomorrow,' she blurted out. 'But thank you for being with me tonight, I think I would've been very scared on my own.'

'Do you have family there?'

'No family. But I've been left a cottage near Waterford by my godmother.'

She smiled at the way he raised his eyebrows in surprise. His tawny cat-like eyes were the first thing she'd noticed about him. Now she saw his sharp cheekbones and a wide, smiley mouth. It was a good face, a man who had been well brought up, and loved by his parents. She guessed him to be a bit older than her, perhaps twenty-eight.

'I don't think it will be anything more than a little croft,' she said. 'I might want to turn tail and run back here to the guest house I'm staying in.'

She explained that she had been in Trafalgar Square Tube station when it was bombed. 'My friend who was going with me was killed, but I was lucky getting away with just a small head wound. I only got the stitches taken out of my head yesterday,' she added.

'But where are you stationed?'

'Woolwich. Most of my company have been sent to France, but some of us were kept here to help with rescue and clearing work when the Blitz began.'

'So shouldn't you be with them now?'

'I got twenty-four hours' leave. I was with a few of

the lads earlier, but they wanted to go to Soho, so I was just wandering around exploring when I saw you.'

'So where are you from then?' She assumed by what he'd said he wasn't a Londoner.

'I'm Cornish,' he said. 'Me and some of the other lads have mining experience, which is useful in rescue work. I'd never been to London before.'

'And?' she said with a smile.

'I'd sooner be in Cornwall,' he grinned. 'I miss the sea, the big skies, and the tranquillity. But then I know rescuing people is worthwhile work, so I'm not complaining.'

'It's far better too than being shot at in France,' she said.

'They'll soon whisk me over there when the Blitz ends. But for now I'm glad to be here, to kind of see what we are fighting for. And I'm glad I was at Marble Arch tonight or I wouldn't have met you. But I'm sorry you are off to Ireland. Just my luck.'

'Mine too.' Beth blushed but forced herself to look into his eyes to respond. 'I'm glad I met you too and hope you stay safe.'

She couldn't believe she was forward enough to say that.

'So have you got a boyfriend in the Forces?' he asked.

She shook her head. 'Have you got a girl back in Cornwall?'

'No, I haven't, or here either. It's a shame you are going away. I would've liked to take you out. Will you write to me?'

'If you'd like that,' she said in a small voice. She liked him, but she was wary because she didn't know what was expected of her, or even if she was behaving normally.

'I'd like it very much,' he said, and got a small notepad and pencil out of his breast pocket. 'So the address?'

'I haven't actually been told that. But as soon as I know the correct one, I'll write to you.'

'You'd better,' he said with a smile, then wrote down both his army details and his home address in Falmouth and handed them to her. 'Who knows, you might come back to London, and I might get leave at the same time. A man can dream!'

He walked her back to the guest house a little later and kissed her goodbye at the door. It was without doubt the best kiss she'd ever experienced. All the others had been boys who grabbed at her, like she was for sale. She had thought she never wanted to be kissed ever again, but she didn't want this one to end, she felt something fizzing inside her, and suddenly she wished she wasn't leaving London.

'That kiss will make it hard to forget you,' he said, and cupping her face in both hands he kissed her nose, eyes and forehead before a second one on the mouth. 'Just my luck that I'd meet the girl who might very well be "the One" in an air raid, and she's off to another country,' he said, nuzzling into her neck.

Was he speaking the truth, or was this a practised line? She didn't know.

'If I am the One, we won't forget,' she said and laughed lightly. 'Ireland is only across the water. You just make sure you don't get injured.'

One last kiss and she had to hurry in because she was afraid she'd cry. Nothing had ever touched her like that before.

5

Beth shivered and wrapped her raincoat round her more tightly as she came out of the station at Fishguard Harbour. The coat had a warm lining, but not warm enough to keep out this strong wind.

Beth had never seen the sea before and had always wanted to. But she couldn't see much in the dark and what she could see looked spooky. The crescent moon gave off only enough light to show dark shapes of sheds, and between them glimpses of the sea, with mist hovering above it. There were a couple of boats moored, with a dim light on each, and she could hear the slap, slap of waves on the dock.

'Beth Manning?' a male voice boomed out. 'Dai Griffiths, come to take you to our guest house.'

Beth's relief at being taken to the guest house was quickly banished by being ushered into a gloomy, brown-walled, damp-smelling hall, and being met by the formidable Mrs Griffiths, a bony, hatchet-faced woman with iron-grey hair scraped back from her face. Her thin, colourless lips were pursed as if already in disapproval of Beth's appearance.

Until then Beth had imagined most guest-house owners would be warm, happy women as Margery had been. She'd also expected a light, welcoming place, but this house reminded her of the police station in Whitechapel, a place her mother once took her to scare her into being obedient.

Two days later, Beth was overjoyed to be finally leaving the Griffiths'. Her stay in their guest house had seemed interminable. Heavy rain made it impossible to go out exploring. But far worse was Mrs Griffiths. Beth had been told the Welsh accent was lovely, but Mrs Griffiths' grated. Questions came endlessly, not asked in the spirit of friendship or interest, but suspicion and disapproval. The guest house was as unattractive as her, completely lacking warmth or cosiness. After her first breakfast Beth retired to her bedroom to escape the questions. Not that the bedroom offered any cheer; it was spartan, with a single metal bed, a dining-style chair and a rag rug on the plain wood floor. The only picture was one of the Resurrection of Christ, so faded it was hard to work out what was going on. The bed linen was coarse and the single pillow like a brick, but at least there were three blankets and a worn but clean quilted bedspread. Mrs Griffiths had made her bed while Beth was eating breakfast, and she had a feeling if the woman caught her lying or sitting on the bed she'd be thrown out into the rain. Even the small mirror was fixed to the wall in the darkest place as if to stop any ungodly preening. One of the first things she'd said to Beth was 'I run my guest house as if the Lord is watching me. I expect my guests to be equally aware of his all-seeing eyes.' She had also listed things she disapproved of: alcohol, vanity, dyed hair, taking the Lord's name in vain, immodest behaviour and card games.

There didn't appear to be any other guests. Beth ate alone in the gloomy dining room. Breakfast was porridge followed by a boiled egg and toast. Lunch a brown soup, its ingredients undiscernible. Dinner, soup again, followed by fried fish and mashed potato. But there was a quite pleasant pudding of apple crumble and custard.

Beth found herself constantly hoping she'd get news of Patrick and his boat's arrival soon. She'd finished reading her book, and there was nothing else but a Bible. It was no wonder Mr Griffiths hadn't appeared again. Beth wondered how any man could stand to live with such a woman.

Finally, twenty-four long hours later, Mrs Griffiths informed Beth that the cargo ship would be moored on the wharf that evening. She added that her husband would take her to it, the curtness of her report implying that she expected no questions and Beth was to stand by in readiness for him.

Beth felt a surge of relief when Dai appeared, put her suitcases on a trolley and beckoned her to follow. Supper that evening, served at six, was macaroni cheese, with very little cheese in it. Beside the cutlery was the bill for ten shillings. Considering the warm welcome, comfort and good food at Blandford Street, it was exorbitant. Yet she wasn't brave enough to comment, much less to complain. She made a mental note should she come back this way again to find somewhere more amiable to stay.

However, Patrick welcomed her aboard with warmth, and apologized for the tiny cabin. He said she was welcome in the mess, where she'd have the company of any crew members in between their jobs, and to come up to the bridge if she wanted to.

He poured her a glass of brandy, and asked if she'd been on a boat before. When she said she hadn't, he said in that case she was lucky the sea was calm and recommended if she felt queasy to go out on deck. 'The worst thing you can do is stay below decks,' he said, and patted her shoulder in a caring way. 'Drink that brandy down, that helps too.'

The brandy burned her throat but it made her feel warm inside, and sort of comforted.

The boat wasn't loaded until after ten that night, but Beth was so relieved to be away from Mrs Griffiths' malevolence that she was enjoying being aboard, talking to the crew and looking at the sea. She'd been told they would arrive in Rosslare sometime between five and six a.m. Mr Boyle had told her to catch the train from there to Waterford, get herself some breakfast, and telephone him after nine, when he would come to take her to the cottage.

Beth stayed most of the voyage in the mess reading a dog-eared detective book. Now and then she did go on deck, but it was too cold to stand it for more than a few minutes. But she wasn't seasick, in fact she hadn't even felt queasy.

'You are a natural sailor then,' Patrick said when she visited him on the bridge at first light. 'Or maybe the macaroni cheese Mrs Griffiths made you has magic powers,' he suggested with a wry smirk.

He admitted he found the woman one of the worst harridans he'd ever met. 'I'm surprised Dai didn't strangle her soon after they got married,' he said with a loud guffaw. 'She must be about as comforting to come home to as a crocodile.'

She liked that he made her laugh, showed her what all the instruments on the bridge were for, but didn't cross-examine her. She liked too that he didn't seem to be fearful about German submarines. 'I spotted one last week,' he admitted, 'but I think they are more likely to be cruising around on the west coast of Ireland. Firing a torpedo at a small vessel like this is hardly worth the effort.'

The ferry crossing had been long enough, but the train to Waterford seemed endless, though in fact it was only a couple of hours. This was made far worse by the niggling fear that she was about to be revealed as an imposter by Mr Boyle. He might know far more about the real Elizabeth than she was expecting. Her godmother might have even given him a photograph of her at the time she made her will.

Surely such a serious crime as stealing an identity to gain an inheritance would be punished with a long prison sentence. Why hadn't she considered that before leaving England?

Yet it was too late to back away now, and stiff with sitting for so long, so tired she felt she could drop to the ground, she staggered with her heavy suitcases across the station forecourt to a small café.

It was tempting to put her head down on the café table to sleep, but she resisted and managed to order bacon, eggs and toast, along with a pot of tea.

The huge and delicious breakfast perked her up – she'd never in her life had such wonderful bacon. She was also charmed by the rosy-cheeked, friendly café owner, who quizzed her on whether she was on holiday, visiting family, or waiting for someone. Beth explained her godmother had left her a cottage, and she was waiting for a solicitor to arrive to take her there.

'Well, fancy that, to be sure it's grand she thought of you,' the woman beamed. 'And what would her name be?'

Back in England people didn't ask such direct

questions and it was a little alarming. But Beth saw nothing wrong with offering a name.

'Miranda Falcon,' she said.

The woman clapped her hands with delight. 'Miss Falcon, such a grand lady, but I liked her. Strong opinions, smart as a whip, but liked to stop for tea and craic. I was so sad to hear she'd passed. But aren't you the lucky girl, her house is a good one.'

Beth couldn't be sure whether 'good' meant it just wasn't tumbledown. She'd seen so many pretty but ramshackle houses from the train, some lacking windows and even doors. She'd seen women and children outside these houses, looking like the ragged poor back in Victorian times. She had already braced herself for no electricity and plumbing, as a woman on the train told her that few homes outside of the cities had such luxuries. It was worrying, but she reminded herself if it was truly awful, she could easily catch a boat back to England – after all, she had enough money to stay in a nice guest house for months, or even rent a couple of rooms.

But she decided she must be more optimistic. And to remember it was an adventure.

At nine o'clock Beth walked back across the station forecourt to telephone Mr Boyle. He said he would be with her directly, though she wasn't sure what that meant. But it was warm in the sun, and she placed her suitcases at the end of a bench and sat down to wait.

The main thing that struck her was the lack of cars. In the whole time she'd been in the café she'd only seen one. But then that would be the petrol rationing. Many people in England were putting their cars under wraps in garages. But here there were donkeys pulling carts, and the occasional pony and trap, a carriage or two, and many bicycles.

She knew as soon as she saw the green Austin pulling onto the station forecourt that it would be Mr Boyle. He wore a brown trilby, and he drove straight towards her.

'Good morning, Miss Manning,' he called out as he got out of the car. He was short and stocky, with dark-rimmed glasses, a rather hairy tweed jacket, and she put his age at around fifty-five. 'I trust you had a smooth crossing; the Irish Sea can be very rough.'

He shook her hand. His Irish accent was only a faint lilt, and he had a warm smile. He put her suitcases in the boot and opened the passenger door for her.

'It was fine, it seems I'm a good sailor,' she said as she got in. 'Just a very long night, what with train and ferry.'

'Well, you'll soon be in Clancy's Cottage – it's not far. Kathleen, a local woman who used to do for Miss Falcon, has taken care of it since she died. As I told you some time ago, I've been letting it out for holidays during the summer months, as there's nothing so bad for a house as to be allowed to get cold, unaired and damp. Kathleen gave it a thorough clean yesterday, lit a good fire, and got you a few groceries.'

As he started up the car, she felt a bit nervous because summer lets suggested he'd had a great deal more correspondence with her friend than she'd realized. What if they'd spoken on the phone? Would he realize her voice was different? And as he hadn't said where the house was, that suggested Elizabeth had known this.

'You'll excuse me if I seem a bit odd,' she said, feeling she must cover herself. 'But since the bombing I find when tired things slip my mind – my mother always accused me of being vacant. I can't even remember the name of the village where the house is.'

He chuckled. 'My wife is often vacant. I think I bore her. It's Dunmore East. Why they added East I don't know, there is no Dunmore West. But if you have any problems or forget something, you can always telephone me. I used to call on Miss Falcon when she was concerned about something. She was a very forceful lady, but even so, workmen often tried to take advantage of her. They never got away with it though, she used to say, "Robert, I might be an old woman but my mind is still sharp. I can sniff out a rogue at fifty paces."'

Beth laughed nervously. 'I wish I'd met her,' she said. 'She sounds fascinating. I don't know why she and

Mother didn't visit one another. She always remembered my birthday and Christmas, but it would've been lovely if she'd come to England to stay.'

'My dear, she was in a wheelchair for the last ten years,' he said. 'I dare say she was too proud to admit to that. She had a fall and damaged her spine. Not that it cramped her style much, she still had bridge evenings. And she liked to paint watercolours.'

'Why didn't she marry? Mother didn't say.'

'I believe she came from a rather grand but impoverished family,' he said thoughtfully. 'She was perhaps too bold for some men, and certainly not cut out for the little woman role.'

'What made her come to Ireland? Mother never told me that either.'

'She once told me she'd come because of a man from Waterford. But she fell in love with Ireland instead. Dunmore has often attracted artists and writers. But it is my opinion that she made it up about the man. I couldn't imagine a lady like her chasing a man across the Irish Sea. She liked to tease.'

He looked round at her in the passenger seat. 'What are you going to do here? Or will you sell the place?'

'I really don't know,' she said truthfully. 'I need time alone to think on that one. My brush with death in the bombing raid has kind of knocked the stuffing out of me.'

'Yes, it would do that,' he said, his voice soft with

concern. 'You could offer bed and breakfast. That way you'd have a bit of company. I wouldn't like to think of you being lonely.'

'That's very kind of you, Mr Boyle, but for a few weeks at least I think I need to be alone. London being so frantic, the Blitz, blackout and rationing, it was all a bit much.'

They lapsed into companionable silence. Beth looked out of the window and was soothed by the lush green fields all around and the trees beginning to take on autumnal colours.

'Well, here we have Dunmore,' Mr Boyle said as they approached a few cottages. 'Fishing is the main occupation, but some people work in business in Waterford.' Tis only a small village, but it's famous for being friendly.'

Despite being so tired, Beth leaned forward in her seat and felt a burst of wild excitement to see the sea in front of her. Book and magazine illustrations had put an image like this in her head. But the reality was better, white caps on the waves, a picturesque lighthouse at the entrance of the harbour, swooping seagulls, fishing boats, and the smell, so bracing and exhilarating.

Mr Boyle turned to the left, up past a thatched cottage, then right again along a narrow lane, where all the houses faced the sea. At the end he stopped.

'Here we are, Clancy's Cottage,' he said, waving his hand to the last house surrounded by a picket fence which needed painting. 'Miss Falcon liked the meaning of the name, which is Red Warrior. She saw it as an omen she'd be safe here.'

Beth looked at the cottage as he spoke, and noted Michaelmas daisies and chrysanthemums, so someone had been caring for it. But her eyes were drawn back to the beauty of the sea. Turquoise water stretching to infinity. She could hardly believe she was to have this view from the windows of the cottage. Whatever unpleasant surprises might await her inside, she was already in love.

Mr Boyle seemed to understand what the view was doing to her. He came round and opened the car door and held out a hand to her.

'It is a grand view,' he said. 'Miss Falcon once said to me, "I hope I can be looking out at it when the time comes to meet my Maker," and do you know, Miss Manning, she *was* looking out at it, she had her heart attack while sitting in her chair at the bedroom window. Kathleen found her soon after, and she said there was a smile on her face.'

'So the Red Warrior took care of her right to the end?' Beth said. She felt he needed to know she had been listening to him and he smiled in acknowledgement.

The cottage was small, with a window either side of a trellised wooden porch around the front door, covered in a pretty climbing plant. It had a tiled roof, and under the eaves were two more smaller windows.

'It's all so lovely,' she managed to add.

'Nature has been kind to you today, so it has.' Boyle smiled as he lifted her suitcases out of the boot. 'September can be very windy and wet, but she's shown you her best today, and I think that may mean you'll be happy here.'

The heat from the fire hit her as he unlocked the front door and led her into the living room. 'Kathleen's been in again this morning to bank up the fire, it seems. I won't stay with you now unless you ask me to,' he said. 'I know you must be very tired and will want to explore on your own. But first I'll carry these cases up for you, then show you where the account book is. Kathleen has kept these meticulously since Miss Falcon died. Anything she had to spend, soap, coal for the fire, the electricity and other bills, and her wages too. At first I paid the bills and gave her wages and any expenses, but once we started letting the cottage out, it came out of the rent. The balance is in the cash-box, for you.'

He opened a writing bureau and pointed to a cash-box and a ledger. 'I won't bother you with this now, but in a day or two when you've had time to check the figures and count the money, we can talk this over and anything else you need to know about.' He closed the bureau, then turned back to her. 'Kathleen said she'll pop round tomorrow to welcome you. But understand, Miss Manning, you don't have any obligation to keep her on, she knows you are young and will have your own ideas as to running the place. But she's a good woman and it might be nice for you to have someone to turn to until you are settled.'

'You are very kind, Mr Boyle,' she said. 'I really appreciate it. I'll be glad to meet Kathleen.'

Finally he reached inside his jacket and drew out an envelope. 'I was Miss Falcon's executor and handled the probate too. This is my final account and a cheque for the balance of your inheritance. I wish you much happiness here, and I will always be available to you, not just for legal advice, but as a friend.'

He left then, saying he had to call on another client, and she had his telephone number if she had any problems.

As kind and helpful as the man had been, she was glad to be alone again. The living room was cosy. She loved the round Victorian-style mahogany supper table in the window, the carved-back dining chairs which, although worn, were beautiful. Watercolours on the walls were of scenes and views she assumed were local and painted by Miranda Falcon. A thick, traditional Axminster rug covered the entire floor, very similar to one she remembered in Auntie Ruth's flat. She felt like flopping down on the chintzy sofa in front of the fire but knew she was likely to fall asleep, and she needed to look round first.

Behind the living room was the kitchen, with a

central, scrubbed table, and to her surprise and delight a gas cooker. There was a dresser crammed with dainty china and some curiosities, like a blue porcelain begging dog and a disgruntled-looking black and white cat. Flicking the light switch, she was thrilled to find it actually worked. And the big white sink had running water.

From the kitchen window she could see a garden that sloped up to a bank of evergreen trees and shrubs, and she felt there were rocks like a cliff behind them.

Across the tiny hall another door opened into a parlour. That ran from front to back, a window at both ends. This had clearly not been used for years, and seemed like a showroom for Victorian furniture, everything placed just so. There was a piano and needlepoint cushions which looked as if no one had ever rested on them, photographs in silver frames, and a big glass dome containing stuffed birds resting on branches of a tree.

She opened the envelope from Mr Boyle half-heartedly, only to stare at the contents in disbelief. The cheque was for £302 5s. 10d.

His invoice showed all his workings, but she would need to look at that properly later. She couldn't believe there was money on top of getting the cottage, plus the cash that Elizabeth had had in her possession.

Not even in her wildest dreams had she ever imagined having so much money. She would be forced to open a bank account now and that worried her. Did they do checks on people? What would catch her out?

But maybe a local bank would know Mr Boyle, a cheque from a solicitor must carry a lot of weight. And if all went well, she'd need to start to think seriously about what she would do with such a windfall.

She made for upstairs then. To the right at the top of the stairs was a bedroom the same size as the parlour below. Mr Boyle had put her suitcases in it. It had windows both back and front, and faded pink and white wallpaper. She prodded the brass bed covered in a patchwork quilt, and it appeared to have a feather mattress. She slid her hand in under the covers and found it warm from a hot water bottle. She was growing to appreciate Kathleen more by the minute. The button-back pink velvet chair by the front window was no doubt the one Miranda died sitting on.

On the other side of the landing was a guest room the same size as the living room downstairs, and behind it, to the back of the house, was a bathroom. That astounded her. She had been so certain there wouldn't be one. Now she had one of her very own, a pretty room with shells and fish on the wallpaper. Even the tiles around the bath were fancy, with turquoise sea creatures on them. It was all a bit too much and she began to cry.

She had purposely kept her expectations at a very low level as Margery had told her that Ireland was around fifty years behind England. It might be quaintly old-fashioned, but it felt like a real home, something she'd never had. She could never look back on the two squalid rooms in Whitechapel where she'd lived with her mother as a home. It had been more like a place of torture once Ronnie moved in.

She wiped her tears away angrily, and reminded herself that Ronnie couldn't hurt her again, and that she shouldn't even let her mind go back to thinking about what he and her mother had put her through.

A cockerel crowing woke her, and for a moment she didn't know where she was, as she hadn't heard that sound since her childhood. It seemed to be dusk, not really dark, and not light either, but the sound of the sea reminded her where she was.

She thought it was evening and she'd slept all day. But then she'd never heard of a cockerel crowing in the evening. Was it possible she'd slept all day and through the night too?

Running a hand down her body she found she was wearing a nightdress, yet she had no memory of undressing. Glancing across the room to the stool by the dressing table, she saw her clothes neatly folded on it. So she obviously did.

But it didn't matter whether it was night or day, she liked the bed, and stretched out like a cat under the covers, luxuriating in the warmth and comfort of it.

Her bed at the Bradleys' was a thin horsehair mattress, never comfortable, and in winter never warm either.

Bright sunshine hitting the back window woke her later and lit up the entire room. It was simply furnished, the wardrobe and dressing table painted cream, but someone, perhaps Miranda, had picked out the fancy carving on both pieces in gold. The pink button-back armchair looked like a family heirloom. Likewise the big Chinese rug with cream fringes. The Bradleys had one just like it in their bedroom; Madam was fond of saying that Chinese rugs were very valuable. Beth had always liked it, so thick and soft. Theirs had been just pale blue and white; this one was blue, pink and green.

There was a bookcase packed tightly with books close to the pink chair, and she guessed Miranda must have often sat there gazing out to sea before picking up a book. Beth wanted to do that too. She'd seldom had time to read whilst at the Bradleys'.

Someone knocking on the front door made Beth go to the window and look out. She instinctively knew the middle-aged woman was Kathleen, so she called out to say she'd only just woken up but would be down in two minutes. She slipped her dressing gown over her nightdress and went downstairs.

'Welcome, Miss Manning, to your new home. I'm sorry I called so early,' the woman said after confirming that she was Kathleen. 'But I thought you might have questions, or need something I hadn't left for you.'

'Please call me Beth, everyone does,' she replied. 'I seem to have slept right round the clock. But I'm very pleased to see you. I was so tired I just flopped into bed, and thank you so much for that hot water bottle. I thought it was the evening when I woke.'

'You must've needed it,' Kathleen said and laughed lightly. 'I'll put the kettle on, shall I?'

It made Beth smile to see how Kathleen didn't wait for approval, but went straight into the kitchen, filled the kettle and lit the gas under it. She had black wavy hair and very pale skin, her eyes were green, and although she was now possibly forty, she was still a beautiful woman.

'How kind you are,' Beth said, as Kathleen put two cups and saucers on the table. She then went to the back door and brought in a pint of milk she'd left out there to keep cool, and put some of it in a jug she took from the dresser.

'Since the Emergency began the sugar is on ration, so I hope you don't take it?' Kathleen said.

'The Emergency?' Beth questioned.

'It's what we call the war.'

'Oh!' Beth exclaimed. 'No, I don't take sugar. I've got my ration book though. Will I need it changed to an Irish one?'

'I'm sure you will – ask Mr Boyle, he'll know. We

have to be careful not to use much electricity now, and if you have a gas cooker, they come round to check you aren't using it. In Dublin they call him the Glimmer Man.'

'Glimmer?' Beth questioned.

'Oh, that's the little flame that fires up the gas. Some people put the kettle over the flame to keep it warm. They say they even put a pot of soup or stew on it. And it's not allowed. So the Glimmer Man comes round, and woe betide you if he finds it still hot. They can turn off your gas for weeks. But no one here has had a Glimmer Man call, so maybe it's just a story. But I'd advise you to be frugal with both the gas and electric, just in case they do send someone round or look at your bills.'

To Beth, the Glimmer Man sounded like a scary children's-book character.

'You'd be as well to get a few chickens as eggs are on ration too,' Kathleen said. 'Butter, cheese and just about everything else. The flour to make our bread is horrible. But at least there's no rationing on meat.'

Kathleen stayed for about an hour. She showed Beth the coal bunker in the garden, and where to turn on the immersion heater for the hot water. 'Miss Falcon put it on at night, so she could have a bath in the morning. She said the water in the tank kept very hot because she'd bought a special jacket for it.

Now, do you want me to come and clean for you?' she asked. 'Just a couple of hours a week, or a fortnight?'

'I'd like that,' Beth said. 'But maybe start next week as it's spotless everywhere now.'

'I haven't touched anything in the cupboards and drawers,' Kathleen said. 'But you might want to go through them and put Miranda's letters and other rubbish in the dustbin, or burn them – there's an old dustbin out the back for that. But anything else you don't want, put to one side and I'll find homes for them. There are some very poor people near here who will be glad of clothes, shoes, pots and pans and even furniture.'

'If I do decide to keep chickens—' Beth liked the sound of that '—can you tell me how to do it?'

'Of course, my dear,' Kathleen smiled. 'And I know a bit about growing vegetables too. There isn't much in the shops now, but you'll find Sean the milkman is very helpful about rationing and he brings other things like vegetables and eggs with him. He said he'd call to see you tomorrow morning. By the way, Mr Boyle has contacted the electricity company and other such people about you owning the property now.'

Beth was sure she must have dozens more things to ask, but she couldn't think of one.

Once Kathleen had gone, Beth rushed upstairs to get washed and dressed, in case anyone else came calling.

People called all day. Most brought something with them, a pot of jam, a bunch of flowers from their garden, a few potatoes and cake. But Beth knew that their real reason for calling was to find out what this god-daughter of Miranda Falcon was like.

It became clear to Beth that some of these new neighbours hadn't liked Miranda. They used words like 'educated, eloquent and clever', which most would see as praise, but as they used the words Beth sensed a hint of sarcasm, and undercurrents of jealousy, fear, and perhaps bewilderment too.

Particularly unpleasant was Bridie Collins, a woman of about fifty and clearly a leader in the community, who swept in with three other women. She kept picking up items, examining them and putting them down, as if assessing the value of everything, including the new and young stranger to the village. She had small, sharp eyes and an equally sharp nose. Small of stature, but with a formidable presence.

'So, you'll be staying then? Taking in guests? I heard it said you had a dress shop in England,' she rapped out.

'I used to manage a dress shop,' Beth said, trying hard not to be intimidated. 'I'll certainly be staying, it's a beautiful place and I'd like to see more of Ireland. As for taking in guests, I don't know yet.'

'And no husband?'

'No, and I don't want one,' Beth said, more firmly than she felt. She was sure that would be Miranda's response. 'But why don't you tell me about each of you and your families?'

The four women sat down then. Aisling, Caitlin and Nora looked a little uncomfortable with the way Bridie was behaving. But Beth made yet another pot of tea, and put out a cake one of her earlier visitors had given her. Aisling said she had five children, but the three eldest ones were at school, and she'd left the two youngest with her mammy. 'Miss Falcon liked children when they got bigger, but she couldn't abide babies,' Aisling said with a little chuckle. 'I made the mistake of bringing my Orla here when she was just two months, and she screamed the place down. You should've seen Miss Falcon's face! I didn't pop in to see her again for over a year, and never brought the wee ones with me again.'

'I like babies,' Beth said. 'But I've no real experience with them. But if you come again don't be afraid to bring yours.' All the women exchanged glances at that, almost as if that might be a reason to like her.

'Miss Falcon never told me she had a god-daughter,' Bridie said a few moments later. 'First we heard of it was when she died.'

'She was my mother's friend,' Beth said, 'since they were young girls, but their lives were so different. I believe Miranda was a governess living abroad most of the time, whereas my mother was just at home with me. It's hard to stay good friends when you find yourself with little in common, and too far apart to meet up. I don't think I met her, apart from at my christening, and I was too young to know her then. It was quite a shock to be told she'd left me this place.'

The women wanted to know about the bombs in London, and were shocked when she related being caught up in a raid, and showed them the bald patch on her head. They complained about the food rationing, and there was a note of bitterness about it. They couldn't understand why they had it like England, when Ireland was neutral.

'I was surprised at that too,' Beth said. 'But maybe they had to do that or people from England would be coming over here to buy up food.' She felt like sniping at Bridie by saying there was a whisper going round in England that Ireland was hand-in-glove with the Germans. In Beth's opinion she wouldn't blame Ireland if the whisper was true. England had treated them badly for centuries, and even now the Irish were looked down on. But she kept that opinion to herself.

Bridie did not warm up. It was clear she had her own agenda with both Miss Falcon and therefore her god-daughter. But the other three were very pleasant, offering help if needed and the best places to shop if she went into Waterford or Cork. Beth really liked Aisling, they were close in age, and she liked her bubbly personality. She thought they could become good friends.

Aisling was the last to leave, and took Beth's hand at the door. 'Don't mind Bridie,' she whispered. 'She's nasty, bigoted and poisonous, but everyone thinks that. None of us take any notice of her. But I'd like us to be friends, if you can stand someone with so many wee ones.'

'I'd like that,' Beth said, squeezing Aisling's hand. 'Pop by any time. But not with the witch.'

6

For three days after Beth's arrival in Dunmore it rained incessantly. Unable to go out to explore, inspect the village shop, or just walk around, Beth turned out the cupboards and drawers. She found enough old letters to fill a small dustbin, which she put to one side to go through later, plus some notebooks which Miranda had used like a diary but with many of the entries far apart. It seemed she only jotted things down when the mood took her.

There were just as many boxes and albums of photographs too. A quick flick through them suggested they were unlikely to be of any use in shedding further light on Miranda, as few had dates or labels to say who the people were.

Clothes were simpler to deal with. The oldest dress was a beautiful, intricately beaded pink evening gown, perhaps Miranda's mother's. There was another evening dress which was more 1920s, this one cream lace and slightly bigger. Beth couldn't bring herself to dispose of either, for the same reason Miranda must have kept them. They meant something and she hoped she might find out what in her notebooks.

A couple of neat jackets fitted Beth as if made for her, and she put those back in the wardrobe. The rest of the clothes were mainly sober, good-quality items, suitable for a middle-aged woman. These and the underwear and corsets went into an old suitcase she found on top of the wardrobe. She would give that to Kathleen to dispose of as she thought fit.

With that job done and room to put her own belongings away, she lit the fire, made herself some beans on toast, and settled on the sofa to read the notebooks.

Fortunately, Miranda's handwriting was not just beautiful, but easy to read. The oldest entry was dated 1900, when she was eleven and in Tunbridge Wells. There were mentions of Honor, her friend at school. Beth guessed this was the real Elizabeth's mother. They went to a dancing class together, and often stayed for tea at each other's homes. 'Honor hasn't got much imagination,' Miranda wrote at one point. 'She just wants to get married and have babies.'

Beth smiled at that, it seemed a perfectly good plan to her, but would Miranda reveal what her own plan was?

Sometimes weeks or months could go past without an entry. Then there might be something she'd been to, a show, concert or party. She often wrote rather waspish remarks about her companions, what they wore, how they looked, and her opinion on how they could improve themselves. Again and again

Beth found herself wincing at the young woman's scornful attitude to others.

As the years moved on, and Miranda was working as a governess, she excelled at brief, insightful observations about people, which also revealed quite a lot about herself. She was intelligent, opinionated, perhaps bigoted, generous to those she cared about, scathing about those she saw as fools.

The men who wafted in and out of her life got short shrift: 'Too dull. Lazy. Can't dance. No sense of humour. His breath smells. I hate the way he looks at me, it's like he wants to devour me. No ambition.'

She thought Mr Boyle had been right about Miranda coming from a grand but impoverished background. Her lovely handwriting, references to famous works of art, ballet, theatre and going to concerts were all pointers to a genteel upbringing. She even made a little aside about being like Jane Eyre, forced to get out into the world and work for a living.

Beth thought most women in that position would be happy to marry and let their husband support them. But maybe Miranda was too forward in her thinking for most men of that era. If she had any other family members, she never mentioned them.

She also read a great deal, and there were endless lists of books, often with her opinion of them. Beth had read very few of these, but of those she had, she agreed with Miranda – they were either terribly dull or brilliant. She liked painting, jigsaws, and now and then embroidery. Walking, gardening, swimming and playing tennis all got a thumbs up from her. But Beth liked best Miranda's views on her role of governess. She clearly resented having to be subservient to her mistress, a crashing snob who called the wife of her gardener 'vulgar' purely because her legs were tanned through not wearing stockings. Miranda wrote beneath this: 'If I'm to believe Mrs W's opinion, then I must be truly vulgar, I daydream of lying completely naked in the sun. Mrs W would have heart failure if she caught me doing that.'

However dismissive she was of adults, she seemed to like and understand children, which was at odds with what Aisling had said. She took pride in not just their reading and writing, but paintings they did or other handicrafts. Beth was indebted to Auntie Ruth for teaching her so much, yet Miranda was clearly an even better teacher, such a stimulating, intelligent woman.

She made references to letters from Honor quite often. She was disappointed her old friend was always writing about her baby, how beautiful she was, never cried, smiled constantly. But Beth was surprised by Miranda's waspish reaction to Honor writing to say her husband Corporal Alfred Manning had died in action. She copied out her friend's words on the subject: *I'm trying to be proud he died a hero fighting for his country, yet I can't help but be dismayed that I have to bring our daughter up alone*. Miranda felt her old friend sounded so very distant and cold, considering she was writing to the godmother of the child left fatherless. 'She could write reams of sappy, emotional prose on a cat being run over, or the old lady down the road never getting a visitor,' Miranda wrote, 'but not show grief and horror at her husband's death. I find that very odd.'

Beth wiped a tear away as she thought of all those women who lost their men in the Great War. She thought perhaps Honor was trying to be stoic and brave. But in the end she was with Miranda on this, for surely it was more normal to wail and cry to your oldest friend than to take all the grief inwards?

Yet however sarcastic and dismissive Miranda was of Honor, there was a tangible taste of the close friendship they'd had as young girls, even if they hadn't managed to hold on to it in later life, probably because Miranda moved in different circles and was often in other countries. Yet they carried on writing to each other for what had once been between them.

By the time Beth had read all the notebooks, or at least skim-read them, it occurred to her it wasn't Miranda she really needed to know; after all, the last time she saw her god-daughter was at her christening. With that in mind she went through all Miranda's letters, and picked out the ones from Elizabeth.

She seemed to be on a charm offensive with her godmother, considering she hadn't met her. But then she had been schooled in the value of a well written letter. Beth had never been trained like that, she never had relatives that wrote or sent presents, but Mrs Bradley used to go on and on about such things, often showing Beth examples of bad letter writing.

Elizabeth had written some amusing bits about plays and concerts in London. Perhaps she felt being entertaining was the best way to her godmother's heart. In one letter she had humorously described a customer trying to squeeze herself into a skirt a size too small. 'Mother often told me you believe in keeping yourself in trim and are always perfectly dressed. She said too that you used to call fat women hippos. I love that image.'

Reading another person's mail soon lost its appeal. Beth had hoped for men pledging undying love, or even admiration. A bit of scandal, or secrets. But most of the letters were very dull, from women who listed people they'd seen and places they had visited.

All of these she put on the bonfire heap, keeping only the ones from Elizabeth to read again later.

Even though she didn't really need to know about Miranda, she was still curious about her. How did a young woman from Tunbridge Wells who left home to be a governess come to live here in Ireland? Strange that she didn't ever refer to that move in her notebooks, when she had named all three places where she was a governess. Surely if someone had died and left her the cottage, or she'd bought it herself, it would be worth noting down? Perhaps it was as Mr Boyle claimed, a man from Waterford.

She went to a church school in Tunbridge Wells with Honor, and presumably had a quite average upbringing, but she only mentioned her parents in passing twice, and never after she'd become a governess. Her parents must have died. But odd that that wasn't noted!

In books, writers often referred to women with many of Miranda's traits as 'gentlefolk'. Was this learned behaviour from her years of being a governess? Beth was well aware she'd picked up a lot during her time with Auntie Ruth, and then the Bradleys. Not just things like how to lay a table, or the correct way to iron a shirt, but to drop her Cockney accent, and to use correct grammar.

About six months earlier, Mrs Bradley had remarked on that. 'I wouldn't have even allowed you to greet people at the front door when you first came here,' she said in that superior manner she had. 'But I must hand it to you, Mary, you speak excellent English now, no one would suspect you came from the gutter.'

Saying she came from the gutter really rankled, and she had wanted to retort that a real lady would not be so rude or insensitive. But of course she nodded and said nothing. Hoping that one day the woman would get her comeuppance.

Turning back to Elizabeth's diaries, it struck Beth that when Miranda died, Honor would've talked about her to her daughter. That would be natural behaviour, recounting things they got up to together when they were young, their hopes and dreams, tales about family members. Yet nothing was jotted down by Elizabeth. Not even that she was to inherit the house. It seemed as if she was only interested in the present, not the past, nor the people who had influenced her, or been good to her.

As Beth sat staring into the fire, the notebook slipped off her lap onto the floor and she didn't bother to retrieve it. She felt she was done with trying to unravel other people's pasts. Maybe she should stick with her present. Jack Ramsey sprang into her mind, and as she relived his kiss, she had a little tremor in her belly which she suspected was what people called desire.

'Write to him,' she said aloud. 'You've got to stop thinking all men are like Ronnie.'

Sadly all her childhood memories were tainted by Ronnie. It wasn't as if her mother would tell her romantic little stories about her father, possibly because their courtship and subsequent hurried wedding meant she didn't know him that well.

Beth was worldly enough now to appreciate that a young widow with a small child, struggling to make ends meet, must have felt Ronnie was a godsend.

But he wasn't, not once he'd got his feet well under the table. He not only slapped her so hard when her mother was out that she was left with marks on her face, but then progressed to beating her with a cane by the time she was seven. He didn't bother to only do it when her mother was out or drunk either, he did it in front of her, and if her mother tried to intervene, she got it too.

The evening in May when Mary was ten was still as shocking and painful as it had been then. Ronnie grabbed hold of her and dragged her into the bedroom. She screamed and he slapped her hard across the face. 'Time you learned what your mother does when she goes out,' he snarled at her.

Ronnie wasn't a big man but he was muscular and very strong as he'd been a trapeze artist in his father's fairground before the Great War. Mary had seen a photograph of him once in the glittery costume he wore on the trapeze.

But he was no longer that slender, lithe man with jet black hair and a wide smile. He was flabby, smelled of sweat, and his teeth were stained and rotten. He caught hold of her around her chest, pinning her arms to her sides, and hauled her into her bedroom. It was a tiny, dark room which smelled of damp. It held nothing more than the single bed he had bought for her when he first moved in with them, some shelves holding a few worn books, and a pink teddy bear her mother had bought her the first time she realized Ronnie was beating her.

Throwing her down on the bed, he stuck his hand up her dress and pulled off her knickers in one swift movement. Then he opened his flies and, kneeling either side of her hips, pulled out his cock. 'This what your mum does when she goes out,' he said, grabbing her hand and making her close her fingers around it. 'She gets it hard so the man can stick it in her. That's her job.'

Mary was astounded and terrified when his cock became twice the size in her hand. But then he pulled her legs apart and did just what he'd said.

Stuck it in her!

But it didn't go in easily; it hurt like she was being split in two, and when she screamed he grabbed the pillow and put it over her face. On and on the pain continued as he grunted like a hungry dog having its first meal in days, and she was struggling to breathe as his face was holding the pillow in place over hers.

Finally it was over, and he got off her, slamming the door behind him. She was so sore she couldn't even sit up at first, and just lay there crying. Later she heard him go out, and then she got up to go and wash herself in the kitchen. They didn't have a bathroom, they went to the public baths once a week. Emily was always talking about wanting a flat with a garden and a bathroom, and now Mary understood what Ronnie meant when he said, 'Do a few more a night and perhaps you'll get it one day.'

There was blood all down her legs and she was afraid he'd cut her somehow, but it was mixed with sticky stuff that made her shudder.

That was the day she left her childhood behind. She did her best to avoid ever being alone with Ronnie again, though she failed often. She soon learned that her mother was never going to take her and run away from Ronnie.

A year or so later she began to see her mother drank to blot out what she had become. She couldn't leave Ronnie because she was both dependent and afraid of him. Once, when she was very drunk, Mary had overheard her telling a neighbour that he'd hunt her down like an animal if she left him, and then kill her.

It was tempting to tell a teacher at school, in the hopes she'd be taken away from her home. But she didn't have the words to explain what Ronnie did, and even if she managed to tell it all, and was believed, wouldn't her mother be blamed?

Auntie Ruth's flat upstairs became her sanctuary, where she could feel clean and safe for a couple of hours. She sensed Ruth had some idea of what was happening by her kindness, the way she said Mary should look forward to when she could leave school and get a job with a home.

That was how it was for eight years in all, and though

Ronnie disappeared from time to time, sometimes gone for months, giving Mary the hope he'd gone for good, eventually he'd turn up again, sweet-talking her mother if he'd been building roads or doing demolition and had money. But even without money he got to stay, and he always managed to inflict another rape or beating on Mary.

But in a way it was worse to watch her mother slowly becoming older, battered and scared. All the remembered sparks of the lively, fun-loving mother Mary remembered from when she was very young fizzled out. Emily was thirty-four when Mary finally left for good, drink and degradation making her look a decade older. Mary knew that if she hadn't left then, Ronnie would have forced her into prostitution too.

Beth walked up to the bedroom overcome by those awful memories she tried so hard to forget.

She sank down on the chair in the window and looked out at the sea, with tears cascading down her cheeks.

Thanks to Auntie Ruth's help and affection, she'd worked hard at school, learned to cook, sew and do laundry well, because she knew domestic service was the only career open to her. When she felt sad and hurt, she would slip into a fantasy of living and working in a nice part of London far away from the East End, where her employers would be as kind as Auntie Ruth.

The Bradleys were not exactly kind, but they weren't cruel, and their Hampstead house was lovely, close to the heath. Mary watched her employers, their guests and their cook, and read newspapers and books, to learn as much about life beyond being maid-of-all-work, so that one day she could rise to a better position. She hoped by that time she would've forgotten her mother and Ronnie.

Ironically it was just a few days before the bomb and after she'd already applied for a new position in Kent, that Mrs Bradley, in an uncharacteristic moment of generosity and kindness, finally praised her. 'Mary, you are a gem,' she said, reaching out and taking Mary's hand. 'I've never had any maid before so capable or showing such initiative.'

That still brought a smile to her lips, and she hoped that after Mrs Bradley got the news that Mary Price was killed, she finally came to see she was unlikely to get a 'gem' again.

Beth mopped up her tears with a handkerchief. 'You must forget Mary,' she said aloud. 'Grieve for her now, then forget her and be glad you got lucky when you became Beth.'

Beth got up then and went to the desk where she'd seen notepaper and envelopes. Maybe Jack had forgotten her already, but she'd remind him.

7

Spring 1941

'Raining again,' Beth muttered grimly as she pulled back the bedroom curtains and saw the grey outlook.

Kathleen called such weather 'a soft day', as if she meant it was good for walking in. Back in England it would've been called drizzle, so, thinking that if the Irish braved drizzle so should she, Beth put on walking shoes and raincoat and ventured out. But down at the harbour she soon found the wind made the rain more like sleet, stinging her face, hands and legs. There was no pleasure walking in it, so she went home to finish sewing the kitchen curtains. Sometime ago she'd found a length of yellow gingham along with a Singer sewing machine in the cupboard in the spare room. There was enough of it to make a curtain to go round the big sink, and hide the pipework and buckets there, along with curtains to replace the washed-out and frayed ones that hung at the two small windows. Today she would finish making them.

She had been in Dunmore now for almost seven months. Back in November she'd got brave and walked through the rain to Waterford to open a bank account and to pay all that money and the cheque from Mr Boyle in. She was given a warm welcome by the bank, and no one said anything worrying about her signature, which was a huge relief.

Waterford wasn't very exciting, and it struck her as oddly ironic that for the first time in her life she had lots of money, but precious little to spend it on. If it wasn't for the Blitz raging in England she might very well have been tempted to go back right then, as she was lonely and very bored.

Christmas and New Year had passed uneventfully. She kept hoping someone would knock on her door, but no one came. She guessed that not one of the women she knew here and chatted to would attempt to invite her to their homes because they imagined she'd look down on them.

She could almost laugh at that idea. She was fairly certain their homes would look like a palace compared to her old home in Crimp Street. She passed the time reading, three books in two days her record so far, and felt grateful that Miranda had kept such a well-stocked library. It seemed to have rained constantly ever since.

She had worked every day since she was fourteen, and being idle seemed so unnatural. War work in a factory had taken on a rosy image of camaraderie and fun. She was even imagining renting a flat back in England, somewhere green and pleasant because there was only so much cleaning and rearranging she could do at Clancy's Cottage, and time passed so slowly.

Aisling had come to see her a couple of times, but she was nervous and rather uncommunicative, as if thinking Beth was a cut above her, and she had no right to imagine they could be friends.

Beth had been like Aisling once. So she tried to bring Aisling out of her shell by asking about her children and her husband, Donal. He was a fisherman and it was obvious by Aisling's threadbare and much-mended clothes and shoes that they were very poor. But she was proud, and as much as Beth wanted to help, she didn't wish to offend her.

The miserable weather wasn't helping. Spring seemed very slow to arrive, and she felt if she could just take some long walks to break up the day she would be happier and less lonely.

Yesterday she had asked Kathleen what Miranda had done with herself all day. Kathleen looked puzzled by the question. 'She was a lady, they don't do anything. To be sure, she'd paint or read. That's all.'

When Beth thought back, Mrs Bradley did nothing much either. At one time she'd had Mary, a cook and a housekeeper, plus a woman who came in to do the rough work, scrubbing floors and the like, and a gardener. When Cook and Mrs Hamilton, the housekeeper, left, Beth took on their work too. So often Beth had gone into the drawing room during the afternoon and found her mistress staring mindlessly out of the window. At that time she'd wished that just for once she could sit in a comfortable chair and do nothing. But now she had that endless time, day in, day out, she hated it.

Lying in bed at night, Beth often heard bombers overhead, and sometimes during the day she saw flashes in the sky which she thought were planes being shot down. But it was nothing like the terrifying sounds she'd heard back in England. From her bedroom window she could see ships through the murky weather, but she had no idea if they were German or British warships, or maybe cargo ships taking goods to Liverpool or Bristol. She had been told Ireland was still supplying butter, cheese and meat to England, as it had for donkey's years. But there was talk of German submarines around the coast.

She would switch on the wireless sometimes, but it was very crackly and the news was always vague. The only worthwhile thing she remembered hearing was that land was being offered to Irish people as allotments, with free seed and manure. She wondered if anyone round here had one and would appreciate an offer of help with it.

The next day it finally stopped raining in the early afternoon, and the sun came out, making Beth seize the moment to go for a walk. After being cooped up for so long it felt marvellous. She could see tiny leaf buds on the trees and hedges and the thought that spring was finally on its way made her heart leap with joy. She went down to the harbour. In the past months she'd spent hours at her bedroom window gazing at the sea, never tiring of its vastness, and the size of the waves breaking on the harbour wall when the wind got up. Today the sunlight glinting on the white wave caps was beautiful.

She began to think of all the things that had happened in the last years. In April, Denmark and Norway had fallen to the Germans. Prime Minister Chamberlain was replaced by Winston Churchill after Holland and Belgium were invaded. There was the Battle of Britain, and at the end of May the evacuation of Dunkirk had begun. Soon after that, in June, Paris was captured too.

All that had happened even before the Blitz began in early September, and of course the events which led her to Ireland. Huge dramas which affected so many nations and people, yet her own life remained so dull. Now, as she stood looking out to sea, she thought how vast it was, not just reaching the coast of England, but all those countries now taken by the Germans. Heaven only knew what the people there were going through. She thought that maybe she should be grateful her life was dull – at least it was safe and comfortable.

The sea had been ferocious sometimes during winter. She would shiver just to look at it, and planned when it got warmer this year to go down to the beach and paddle. She wished she could swim, and wondered if you could teach yourself. While with the Bradleys she'd often walked to the swimming ponds on the heath and watched the people in the mixed pond. It looked like a wonderful, exhilarating thing to do on a hot day. 'But that's for another day, later in the year,' she murmured out loud. 'Today you'll walk as far as that road that leads to Cork.' She hadn't been to Cork yet. Aisling told her there was a bus, but not the times and where to catch it.

Once she'd reached the road to Cork, she just kept on walking, looking at the little cottages. Some were very neglected; one very bad one had two pigs wallowing in mud in the front garden, and the smell was awful. But some of the cottages were whitewashed and pretty, their neat front gardens with a few early daffodils out. She knew from Kathleen and Aisling most people living here had big families and few had modern amenities like bathrooms.

She was hoping to meet someone she could get into conversation with to ask about allotments, and who might like some help. But the few people on this road flew past on bicycles, small horse-drawn gigs, and a couple of donkey carts. She guessed she would have to telephone Mr Boyle to ask about the allotments; he seemed to know everything that went on in this part of Ireland. He'd given her a list of people who were handy to have onside, whether that was for wood or peat for the fire, painting and decorating, electrical work or driving her somewhere.

Beth did not like the smell of burning peat, it clung to the curtains and her clothes, but fortunately, as well as the stack of peat bricks, there was a large supply of dry logs in the shed, along with a few sacks of coal. Miranda, it seemed, had been a stockpiler. There was enough sugar and flour in the pantry to last a couple of years, plus a great many tins of peaches, apricots and pineapple. Kathleen said she'd started buying in extra things when it was first mentioned there might be a war, and this was apparently four years ago.

Kathleen shook her head as she related this to Beth. 'Ach, she could be a strange woman at times. She counted the pennies, yet sometimes was a spendthrift. She was often mean, then just when you least expected it, she was generous. In all the years I worked for her I could never be sure how she'd react about anything. Most contrary.'

It said a great deal about Kathleen's honesty that she hadn't taken any of the hoarded items. Beth was impressed by that, so she gave some of the flour and sugar to her. She'd given some to Aisling too, plus a couple of tins of peaches.

Although the road to Cork was pretty, flanked as

it was by emerald-green fields and many orchards with cows or pigs grazing beneath the trees, it was disappointing that there were no further shops. In Hampstead there would always be a post office or grocer's, often a baker too, well away from the main shopping areas. As a child in the East End, there was a shop on nearly every street corner. But Kathleen had told her most people lived on a very basic diet of potatoes, cabbage and bacon, and if they could get some other meat they'd cut it up fine with any vegetables they could get to make a big pot of soup or stew that would last all week.

As Beth walked on, she felt she didn't belong in Ireland at all, a country where the poor far outnumbered the affluent and were ruled with a rod of iron by the Church and the mainly English landowners.

Yet in England there was the possibility of rising through hard work, at least for those prepared to be subservient to the Mrs Bradleys of this world. For Irishmen going to England to try and better their families back here, it wasn't so simple. Back-breaking work on the roads and railways, living in slum-like conditions in places like Camden Town, was all they could look forward to as they sent money home to their families. And they were stigmatized, called Paddies, navvies, and worse.

She felt very uncomfortable with what she knew, especially as she'd gained her own comfortable life by deceit. She felt she must think of something she could do while she was here to help people.

She heard horses' hoofs and the rattle of a gig behind her, but she couldn't move over any further as the ditch beside the road was full of water. The horse came so close to her she could smell it and feel the warmth of its breath, and suddenly she felt a blow to her shoulder and back which knocked her off her feet into the water-filled ditch.

It was coming to in cold water which made her aware she must've been knocked unconscious, if only for a short while. The water was deep, so it was a miracle she wasn't drowned, but when she tried to get to her feet and out of the ditch the pain in her shoulder prevented her. The mud was sucking at her feet, and as she tried to turn to use her good arm, she couldn't move her feet. She put her elbow on the bank of the ditch and tried to lever herself up, but the pain was so intense she nearly blacked out. Worse still, her feet appeared to be sinking further and further into the mud, and she was chilled to the bone by the cold water, which had soaked right through to her skin.

There was no point in yelling for help, she hadn't seen anyone else walking on the road, and there had been few carts, gigs or bicycles passing her. The driver of the gig who hit her must have felt something – why didn't he stop to check?

She removed the sodden red scarf from around her

neck, and held it tightly to wave when the next person came along. She waited and waited, growing colder and more frightened by the minute, and still no one passed. Her wrist-watch had stopped when she fell in the ditch, but she guessed by now it was after five as it was fast growing dark, but surely someone returning from work would come past soon.

She waited and waited, but no further carts, bicycles or gigs came by. The sun went down and suddenly it was dark. She was so cold her teeth were chattering. Again and again she tried to get out, but her feet were now imbedded in the mud. Each time she put her arm on the bank to try and lever herself out, the pain was so excruciating she was afraid she'd black out, fall into the water and drown.

Dr Finn McMara was driving his gig home from seeing a couple of elderly patients in Dunmore, when he spotted something ahead at the side of the road. He thought at first it was a parcel perhaps fallen from a cart or other vehicle. But as he got closer he saw it was a person who, all but for their head and shoulders, was submerged in the ditch. Closer still he realized by her long dark hair it was a woman, but she was face down on the ground, presumably unconscious.

Pulling up his horse, and ordering it to stay, he climbed down from the gig, taking a torch with him. 'Jesus, Mary and Joseph!' he exclaimed on seeing a rip on the shoulder of her coat, and blood flowing from it. He knew immediately she'd been knocked off the road by some sort of vehicle, and almost certainly a gig very like his own.

He took off his coat, got a blanket from the gig and laid it down, lifted the woman's head onto it, then knelt down to examine her. He was surprised that she was young, he guessed under thirty. Her pulse was weak but she was still alive, though icy cold.

'Let's get you out of there,' he said. Her eyes flickered as he put one hand under each of her arms and began to pull her up. He felt resistance and knew her feet were stuck in the mud. 'I'll have you out in a few minutes. I am a doctor,' he assured her, knowing that the pain of pulling at her was likely to distress her further.

There was a low moan from her, and a squelching sound of her feet coming out of the mud. But she'd been deeply stuck, and it took all his strength to get her up, haul her onto the blanket and wrap her up in it. He saw the mud was right up to her knees, and he needed to get her into the warm quickly.

'Can you tell me your name or where you've come from?' he asked, rubbing her face with a corner of the blanket to bring her round.

'Dunmore,' she said weakly.

He guessed immediately this was the much-talked-about god-daughter of Miranda Falcon who had inherited Clancy's Cottage. Nothing happened in these parts without everyone knowing, and he'd been Miss Falcon's doctor for the last five years of her life. News had reached him almost as soon as her heir set foot in Dunmore. There had already been bets laid by the more travelled people that she'd soon leave because no young unmarried woman from London would be able to adjust to living in such a quiet place.

'Let's get you home,' he said, and he lifted her into his arms and onto the gig seat. She squealed with pain as he did so, but he told her he would soon get her warm, and her wound dressed. Supporting her with one arm, he managed to turn the gig around to go back towards Dunmore.

When Finn McMara arrived in Waterford, he was thirty-five, married with two boys, John Joe aged seven, and Michael aged five. He had been in general practice in Dublin until his widowed father retired six years earlier, and he'd come home to take over the practice in Waterford and keep an eye on his father, who was not in the best of health.

His wife Lily hadn't wanted to leave Dublin, and certainly not to live in the large, draughty family house, with the surgery downstairs. Neither was she thrilled, when she found she was pregnant again, to have a third child so far away from her family and friends.

But Finn had promised her that it was a mere temporary measure. He would find another doctor to take over the practice as soon as possible. He meant, but couldn't bring himself to say, that that would be when his father died. But his father had died eighteen months ago, and with all the talk of war coming, he had not made any attempt yet to sell the house and practice. Their boys were thirteen and eleven now, their daughter, Ilsa, five, and they were happy and safe here. The boys certainly didn't want to go back to Dublin.

Lily felt this part of Ireland was too backward, she had no friends or family here, and though she and Finn were often invited to the houses of the local landowners, a barrister, the chief of police and a couple of teachers, Lily found them all terribly provincial, and their wives eye-wateringly dull – but of course they hadn't lived and worked in London as she had.

Lily had in fact been a model for a fashion house before she married Finn, and had graced the pages of many women's magazines. In Dublin people found that fascinating and were bowled over too by her long flame-red curly hair, emerald green eyes, beautiful oval face and haughty manner. Down in Waterford and Dunmore, a former model was practically a fallen woman – and she was a Protestant too.

Finn drove the gig at a gentle pace so as not to jar his patient's shoulder. He glanced sideways at her pale, almost luminous complexion and her dark-brown, lustrous hair, and wondered about her.

He had found Miranda Falcon to be mean-spirited. She had the wherewithal to help others even if it was only a few new books for the school, some food parcels for those in need, to knit a warm jumper or two for children or give some money to local charities. But she had never done this, and therefore he found it suspicious that she'd left her entire estate to a young woman she'd only met at her christening. She once spoke to him disparagingly of Honor. 'We grew up together but she was unimaginative, dull and quite stupid. She married the first man who asked her, a timid little man who only joined up for the Great War because it was expected. Then, when he died soon after the child was born, she put him on a pedestal, and went on and on about him until she died. I can't imagine the child has any spirit coming from such parents. She writes the occasional letter to me, I think just to get on my good side. But I will make her my heir, there is no one else. I just wish I could remain a fly on the wall and witness what a disaster she makes of it. She works in a dress shop – that won't help her here.'

Finn couldn't imagine why anyone would be so nasty to a child they had sworn to protect in the sight of God. Couldn't Miranda have helped earlier, suggesting college or some kind of training to give her a good start in life?

But it wasn't any of his business after all. His job was to get the girl warm, set that shoulder if necessary, and let her know that somebody cared about her, for he was pretty certain Miranda's attitude to her neighbours meant that no one in Dunmore would make much of an effort to befriend her heir.

8

Beth was hardly aware of the person who rescued her from the ditch. She knew it was a man, and a gentle one too, and she sensed he knew what he was doing.

She also knew he took her home in some sort of cart. She could smell the horse, hear the wheels on rough ground, and each bump in the road sent a sharp stab of pain to her shoulder. Yet that was all she knew. It wasn't until he fumbled for the door key in her soaked raincoat, helped her into the warm, and sat her on a towel on one of the kitchen chairs in front of the fire that she came out of the grey fog in her head.

She watched him stir up the fire with the poker and put another log on. It was then that it dawned on her he knew who she was, and was familiar with the cottage.

Beth couldn't stop shivering. She felt the cold had gone right to her core and she'd never be warm again. He told her his name and that he was a doctor, and had been Miss Falcon's too, but he needed to cut away her sodden jumper as she'd never get it over her head, and he needed to wash and dress the wound on her shoulder immediately. Thankfully she had a vest on beneath the jumper, but just exposing a bare shoulder to a man she didn't know, even if he was a doctor, made her blush furiously.

But he was quick and gentle, then wrapped her up in the shawl left on the sofa.

'May I have permission to go upstairs to get a bath towel, your nightdress, dressing gown and slippers?' he asked.

'Yes of course,' she said, hoping she hadn't left anything embarrassing about.

When he came back down he first washed all the mud off her feet and legs, then went into the kitchen while she undressed and put the dry things on. He said he was making her tea to warm her up.

He waited till she was ready before coming back into the living room. She had moved to the armchair and was crying more from relief than anything else. She'd managed to get her nightdress on as it buttoned down the front, but she could only get her good arm in the sleeve of her dressing gown. The rest of the garment was draped around her.

'I'm sorry,' she sobbed out. 'I had begun to think I'd die in that ditch.'

'For a moment I was afraid you *were* dead,' he said, crouching down on his haunches beside her chair and touching her shoulder gently. 'But you weren't, thank heavens, and your shoulder is just dislocated. I can fix that, but it will hurt just while I do it. Afterwards it will be sore, but bearable. I'll put your arm in a sling, give you something for the pain, and put a hot water bottle in your bed, which is where I think you ought to go.'

'Thank you, Doctor,' she said in a small voice. 'I'm so glad it was you who found me. I was so frightened. Why didn't the person who hit me stop?'

'I think it was a tinker,' he said with a shrug. 'He was probably drunk and unaware he'd hit anyone.' He rolled her wet clothes in the towel and took them to the kitchen along with her soaking, mud-covered shoes. He got her to sit back on the kitchen chair, and, standing behind her, held her left arm and shoulder, then jerked them suddenly. Beth screamed at the sharp pain, but almost immediately knew he'd put it back in line. She was even able to bend her arm again.

'Don't try to put your dressing gown on yet,' he said. 'I'll make some tea then strap it up for you.'

It was only then that she got a good look at her rescuer. He was tallish, perhaps five foot eleven, with a slim, athletic build, slightly too long hair, and thin, light-brown moustache. It was a good face, not exactly handsome, but the kind anyone would warm to, as his eyes were like milk chocolate and surrounded by laughter lines. She knew in her heart he was a man who liked to laugh, and that he'd been born kind. She liked to think that was how her father had been. He put Miranda's shawl around her shoulders and then went back into the kitchen.

'Shall I make you something to eat?' he called out. 'I see you've got soup in the pantry and there's some scones. Or I could make you a sandwich.'

She had made the scones that morning, so she asked for two of them buttered with jam. 'And have some yourself,' she called back.

It was only once he was back sitting on the sofa with his scones and tea that Beth remembered his horse. 'Will your horse be all right outside?' she asked.

'Are you suggesting I bring her in?' he said.

Beth laughed, and he joined in.

'That's better,' he said. 'I always like to leave my patients laughing.'

He filled up the hot water bottle and took it upstairs to her bed, then came down and took some pills from his bag. 'You can take two of these now and I'll leave you some to take first thing in the morning. But I shall be round to check on you after my morning surgery.'

'I'm sorry I messed up your evening,' she said. 'And it's pitch dark now.'

'I'm just glad I was coming home that way,' he said. 'Don't worry, I have lights on the gig, and my horse knows the way even blindfolded.'

He placed the fireguard in front of the fire for her. 'Will you be able to go upstairs alone?'

She smiled up at him. 'You are thoughtful. I'll be fine now. I don't want to waste more of your time.'

He left then, and Beth got up and walked to the window to see him getting his horse to turn the gig round and go off down the hill.

In bed later, the hot water bottle next to her sore shoulder, she thought how lucky she was that the doctor came along. She doubted many people went along that road after dark. If nothing else, it would give her something interesting to write to Jack about, should he ever write to her. She had written to him before Christmas, but to her disappointment she'd had no reply. She'd more or less given up hoping now, assuming he'd had another girl all along. But in idle moments she would daydream about him, and tell herself that if he had gone to North Africa, perhaps the mail was held up for months.

The next morning Beth found her whole body stiff and aching, not just her shoulder, and she had a job to get down the stairs to make a cup of tea. It was very cold down there too, as she hadn't thought to bank the fire up last night. She didn't think she had the energy to rake it out and relight it, so she made some tea and took it back to bed with her.

She dropped off to sleep again, but a banging on the front door woke her. The alarm clock had stopped as she hadn't wound it, so she had no idea what time it was. She opened the bedroom window and called down to her visitor.

The attractive but anxious face looking up at her wasn't the doctor, but Kathleen.

'I can let myself in if you like,' she called up. 'The doctor told me you had an accident, but I didn't like to just barge in with my key.'

Beth got back into bed. Kathleen came into the room a few seconds later.

'What a good thing I ran into the doctor this morning,' she said, coming closer and putting her hand on Beth's brow. 'An accident like that would be enough to give you pneumonia, to be sure. But you don't seem to have a fever. Just the same you'd better stay in bed.'

'I was going to get up but the fire had gone out and I hadn't got the energy to make it.'

'Don't you worry your head about that, I'll see to it,' Kathleen said. 'And I'll make you some breakfast. The doctor won't be here till after one. The good Lord must have been watching over you, to send him along last night.'

'You are very kind,' Beth said, 'but I mustn't keep you from something more important.'

When she'd arrived, Beth had had a job to get Kathleen to discuss her wages. In the little account book she'd kept after Miranda had died she'd only taken two shillings for jobs she did here without jotting down the time it took her. That included cleaning the cottage after paying guests had left. There was £9 5s. in the cash-box. She'd taken the money for the food she'd bought when Beth was expected, but not for cleaning the cottage from top to bottom, or for coming in the next morning to light the fire and put a hot water bottle in the bed.

Beth had to be quite forceful in the end, saying she admired Kathleen for having such a kind heart, but it wasn't right to work for nothing and made Beth feel awkward. So they finally agreed on an hourly rate, and Kathleen would continue to jot the hours down in a notebook and be paid monthly in cash.

'You need help today,' Kathleen said, smoothing Beth's cheek as if she were a child. 'You just stay in bed in the warm, I'll look after you.'

It was the first time she could remember anyone saying they'd look after her, and Beth's eyes filled with tears. She lay back on the pillow and turned her head away so the older woman couldn't see.

When Dr McMara arrived, Kathleen left after telling her there was some homemade soup on the stove for her supper, and promising to pop in the next morning.

'She's an angel,' Beth said to the doctor as he sat on the edge of her bed and checked her blood pressure.

'To be sure she is,' he said with a smile. 'Ever since Miranda hurt her spine, she did everything for her, bathing her, dressing her, the works. But there's so many people around here who have benefited from her help and kindness, so different from some of the begrudgers.'

'What are they?' she asked, thinking it was some kind of Irish expression.

His eyes twinkled. 'They are the ones who hate anyone to have good fortune. Miranda came across it a great deal, and you will too. So don't you get upset if anyone makes a sharp remark to you. I'm not convinced that coming here was actually good fortune for you. You are too young to be alone, and without work to fill the time you're going to become very bored.'

'I'm still thinking about what I want to do,' she said. 'I'd like a job. When my shoulder is better, I'll go into Waterford and see what's about.'

'It isn't like England,' he said, shaking his head. 'Unskilled jobs here tend to go to family members or else you need qualifications like nursing or secretarial. Why do you think so many young Irish people rush over to England?'

'Are you suggesting I should pack this place up and go back?'

'No, I'm not saying that. It must be hell in London right now with bombs dropping continually. And if the Germans do invade England—' He paused, as if the thought of that was too awful to talk about.

'Well then?' she asked.

He shrugged. 'I'm an example of someone who ought to have left. Ireland is in the grip of the Catholic Church, and maybe I was a coward giving in to my father's wishes to take over his practice. My wife claims I am.'

'I think it was a good and kind thing to do,' Beth said indignantly.

He chuckled. 'Did Miranda railroad you into coming here?'

'No, she didn't. I used to write to her sometimes, but there was nothing in her letters to suggest she'd leave this place to me.'

'Weren't your family worried about you coming?'

'I haven't got any now. My father was killed in France during the Great War. Mother died in 1939.'

'I'm sorry,' he said, and she was touched that he looked not just sorry but embarrassed.

'You weren't to know,' she said quickly. 'Why would you?'

'There was a great deal of speculation here about you when it got out that Miranda had made you her sole heir, mainly because she didn't tell anyone anything about you,' he said with a little chuckle. 'Some people are convinced you are her child, and that she'd abandoned you to an orphanage when you were a baby. I knew for a fact she'd never had a child, and I doubt she ever wanted one. But folk around here like a bit of scandal to brighten their lives.'

Beth laughed. 'I have to admit I couldn't really see why she chose me. She might have been my godmother, and a childhood friend of my mother, but she never visited, and letters were few and far between.'

'She was a lady who burned all her bridges, I think,' he said, leaning closer to Beth and tapping his nose as if this was secret information. 'She once told me that she was guilty of cutting people off when they got too close. I suppose by that she meant both sexes.'

Later, after Dr McMara had left, Beth lay in bed considering every last thing he'd said to her, and musing that she was a bit attracted to him. She was also sure it was reciprocated. They had chatted for far longer than anyone would consider normal for a home visit. The conversation had flowed effortlessly, they had laughed at the same things, though when she thought back it was all inconsequential stuff, nothing important. But when he untied the sling around her shoulder, and felt to make sure it had gone back into the right position, his fingers lingered, caressing her shoulder, while he looked right into her eyes. It felt almost like a mild electric shock, and she didn't want him to take his hand away.

'You have beautiful skin,' he said. 'It's like porcelain.'

She might never have had a good experience with a man before, but she certainly knew a doctor shouldn't be making personal remarks to a patient. But it was the way it made her feel which surprised her. She should've brushed his hand away, or said something sharp, but she had liked it and wanted it to continue.

Even now he was gone she had a bubbling feeling of excitement in her stomach. She closed her eyes and thought of his lovely brown eyes and the gentleness of his hands. As he left he reached out, lifted her hand and squeezed it. 'Stay in bed and keep warm,' he said. 'I'll pop in to see how you are tomorrow.'

9

Beth found herself unable to stop thinking about Dr McMara. He had come on three successive days to check her shoulder. She was certain the last two visits were not necessary. She could move her arm perfectly, and it just felt bruised, something that only time would cure. But she wanted to see him, and she was sure he felt the same.

Casually she asked Kathleen about him when she came in to do the laundry. 'He's a kind man,' Beth said. 'My doctor in London was so grumpy and disinterested. What's his wife like?'

'A beauty,' Kathleen replied, feeding some sheets into the mangle with one hand and turning the handle with the other. 'She was a fashion model. But with three wee ones, a big house and having to take messages from the doctor's patients and the like, she has such a busy life I doubt she ever thinks about what she used to do.'

That wasn't what Beth had hoped to hear. First she hoped he was unmarried. And if he had to be, an ugly shrew of a woman would've been ideal. 'How fascinating,' she said. 'I imagine with a past like that she'd find it hard to settle in the country. Is she still glamorous?'

'Oh yes, still a head-turner, but very capable. I helped her out a bit when wee Ilsa was born, but she recovered very quickly and didn't need me anymore. She's one of those who doesn't like people prying into her life.'

'It wouldn't occur to me that someone helping me would pry.' That wasn't true. Beth hid anything she thought would tell Kathleen something about her past. 'You'd need to have big secrets to worry about such things.'

Kathleen bent over to pick up the wicker laundry basket full of damp washing to take it upstairs. Beth moved to help. 'Let me take a handle, that's too heavy for you alone,' she said, catching hold of it. The washing was going to be hung in the guest bedroom as it was raining.

'You're a good person, Beth, but don't be too trusting thinking folk won't pry,' Kathleen said with a chuckle as they made their way up the stairs with the laundry. 'Just don't let Bridie Collins in here. She'd ferret out everything from a stain on your petticoat to sending coded messages to the Germans in a blink of an eye, so she would. And she'd pass it on as quick as look at you.'

Beth laughed. 'I'm not likely to invite her in again, I didn't like her.'

'No one does, but we put up with her,' Kathleen said as they went into the guest bedroom and put the basket down. 'She was crossed in love. Her very own sister snatched her sweetheart and they ran off to England together. She's never got over it. If her sister dared to come back here, she'd skin her alive.'

Beth grinned. She loved stories like that, especially when she didn't like the person they were about. She pulled the big wooden clothes horse from under the bed and stood it up in a Z shape.

'So tell me more about the doctor,' she asked as she put some underwear on the bottom rungs. 'He seems so charming. Is he really or is that window dressing?'

Kathleen gave her a sharp look as if suspecting her, and shook out a pillowcase.

'He's a good man, too good some would say, as he gets no life of his own. It will be a sad day for us all if he goes back to Dublin where he could make far more money.'

Beth sensed she'd gone as far as possible without alerting the older woman to her reasons for asking so much.

They had nearly finished hanging up the washing when she heard the whistle on the kettle downstairs.

'Time for elevenses,' she said, and, picking up the empty basket, went down, Kathleen following her. She made the tea and put the pot on the table. Kathleen got cups and saucers out of the cupboard, and fetched the milk from the pantry.

'So, tell me more about you,' Beth said as they sat

down. 'You always ask about how I am. I don't even know if you have children.'

Kathleen smiled. 'To be sure I do. Two girls and a boy. But they are over in England now. Both the girls are nurses, we breed them here.' She laughed as she said that, and Beth knew that was because every hospital in England had a quota of Irish nurses. 'My boy is an apprentice engineer in a shipyard in Newcastle. He's only got one more year, and I hope he'll come back home then. All the shipyards here and in Belfast need his skills, but I pray he doesn't get caught in a bombing raid. Shipyards are targets for the Germans. Luckily one of my girls is in Cheltenham, the other in Wrexham. I think they'll be safe. But I still worry.'

'I'm sure you do,' Beth said. 'And miss them too. Have you always lived in Dunmore?'

'I have,' Kathleen said, and poured Beth's tea for her; she always remembered Beth liked it weak. 'I had big plans of going to England as a girl, but I met Pat, and that was that. We got married when I was eighteen. We lived with his folk for a few years, they had a small farm by Waterford. Pat is a carpenter, but he also helped on the farm. But then my mammy died, and Daddy soon after, so we came back here. Pat's folk died a few years later too. Pat still keeps a few cows and pigs at the farm, and uses the sheds as his workshop.'

'No one living in the farmhouse?'

Kathleen sighed deeply. 'No, it's empty and getting very damp. It's something we argue a lot about. He thinks if he does it up, we could go and live there. But I like it here with a view of the sea, and I don't want to be trudging through mud and cowpats. I think he should do it up, but to rent it out in summer. He could fence off the little front garden so the animals don't get in there, and folk like being on a farm for a holiday, and it's easy to get to a beach or into Waterford or Cork.'

'That sounds sensible to me,' Beth said.

Kathleen gave a dry, humourless laugh. 'Irishmen don't do sensible! And it's nostalgia too, as it's the place he was born.'

They chatted for some time. Beth was very glad of some company. She had a feeling Kathleen's marriage was shaky. She never said anything to that end, but odd little cryptic remarks told a different story.

'You know, Beth, before you fall in love with an Irishman and marry him,' Kathleen said, returning to her favourite theme, 'Irishwomen having no rights, a man can beat his wife like a dog and he'll never get charged with assault. Between the police, government and the Church, they have everything sewn up to keep women subservient. Just last week, Eileen, a girl in the village, was found to be pregnant. The poor girl is only fifteen, but her parents called Father Fermagh and he packed her off to the nuns in Tuam, near Galway.'

'She'll be better looked after there,' Beth said.

'Not so! You can't imagine what those places are like, Beth. It's as bad as prison. The only time she'll see her baby is to breastfeed it. Then if the baby survives it will be off to an orphanage, and Eileen will be sent to an industrial school. They are hell come to earth – beatings, half-starved, not to mention being interfered with.'

Beth couldn't bring herself to ask who would interfere with the young girls – was it boys, the priests or even the nuns? 'Why shouldn't the baby survive?' she asked instead, thinking this was safer ground.

'Babies don't survive with no care or mothering. They say a third of those born die before six weeks. I tell you, Beth, those places are hell, and the nuns cruel devils. I was educated by them, so I know. But I really fear for poor Eileen, she's a bit slow, and needs her mammy. Some boy took advantage of her and he'll be bragging about what he did to her and no one will punish him. Last year a girl in Waterford came back from the nuns, baby gone, they didn't even let her see it for a moment. She was thin, weak and deeply troubled. The nuns claim to arrange adoptions, but many think they sell the babies to rich Americans.'

'Heavens!' Beth exclaimed. She was uncomfortable hearing all this and she couldn't believe it was true. She had no doubt that Kathleen believed it, but it was so awful it sounded like a story, being embellished further with everyone it was told to. 'That's truly awful,' she said.

Glancing out of the window she saw the rain had stopped. 'I think I must go out for a walk and clear my head.'

She put her walking shoes on and her coat.

'Mind you keep your ears pinned back for tinkers,' Kathleen called out as she opened the door. 'Don't want you being knocked into any more ditches.'

It was good to get out of the house, not just because of the distressing story of the unmarried mother, but because Kathleen had just put tea towels in a pan on the stove and the smell of it always reminded Beth of the Bradleys'. They'd had a gas copper to do the washing in, and every Monday morning the smell was the same as she had to grate carbolic soap into the hot water and whisk it with the copper stick. It was an awful job, hauling out boiling hot, heavy sheets and towels and getting them into the sink to rinse them. But the smell of the tea towels today almost made her blab out about the Bradleys. Fortunately, she stopped herself just in time.

Thinking of that copper and the hot water made her take her hands out of her pockets to admire them. While with the Bradleys they had been as bad as Kathleen's, red raw and ugly, her nails all broken. When she met Elizabeth she noticed she had beautifully manicured nails and smooth hands, and immediately felt ashamed of hers and tried to hide them. But while at the guest house in Blandford Street she'd got some special cream from a chemist which she applied nightly, before going to bed wearing cotton gloves. They improved very quickly. Since then she'd lavished care on them, and now they looked as if she'd never done washing in her life. Her nails were perfect ovals too.

Almost slipping up about her past this morning was worrying. She had been very careful with Kathleen at first, but she soon found there were danger points. Cooking was one. Kathleen had often remarked on how much Beth knew. She quickly said she'd learned at school and her mother used to make her cook their dinner quite often. In fact she took it a stage further and said she'd always done most of the cleaning too.

It wasn't natural to chat without occasionally speaking of old memories. She couldn't use Elizabeth's background, because she didn't know enough about it. She knew Kathleen must find it very odd she had no little anecdotes to share, tales of relatives, or even the places she'd been. At first, she got round this by seldom engaging Kathleen in chat, but the older woman must have thought her a cold fish, or a snob who didn't talk to staff. But in recent months she had asked Kathleen some questions about her life, if only to show she wasn't either of those things.

One night soon after she'd got here, she couldn't

sleep for imagining the police had traced Mary Price through her ration book, then gone to the Bradleys to get them to formally identify her body. In the cold light of day this seemed very unlikely, as during the Blitz dozens of people were killed nightly, and the police wouldn't have had time to do anything more than report a death to the address they'd found on the body. Mrs Bradley would've said that Mary had no relatives, and they certainly wouldn't have volunteered to pay for her burial.

Elizabeth must have been buried in a mass grave. And that troubled her.

The air was crisp and fresh, and the sun, though weak, felt warm on her face. As she walked, she thought once again on the wisdom of coming here. How different it would've been if Elizabeth was here with her, no need for pretence, sharing everything, cooking meals, cleaning, even doing the washing. Instead, she had more money than she'd ever dreamed of, more than a man here in Ireland could earn in his entire working life, but she was terribly lonely. She wished she had a friend with her now, someone to laugh and chat with.

Perhaps she ought to try and get a lodger, but why would a single woman want to come to Dunmore if she was working in Waterford or Cork?

Daydreaming about how good it would be to have

a companionable lodger, Beth had walked nearly two miles without noticing. Then suddenly up ahead she saw the doctor's gig with its distinctive two white bands on the back. It had been left by a farm gate, and his horse, Henny, was dejectedly grazing on some weeds.

Henny looked round at her as she approached, almost as if she'd recognized her, so Beth went over to her and stroked her nose, and reassured her that the doctor would be out soon.

She hadn't been with the horse for more than a couple of minutes when she heard the doctor saying goodbye to someone further along the road. She couldn't see him as there was a hedge and trees in the way.

Her heart quickened, and then she saw him walking towards her.

'Well, there's a surprise!' he exclaimed. 'Or are you after stealing my horse?'

Beth laughed. 'I thought she looked sad.'

'She puts that face on every time I make a home visit. Now, where are you off to?'

'Just walking. I thought I might go right to Waterford, and buy myself some knitting wool to knit a jumper.'

'Well, hop on up and I can take you almost the whole way as I've got a call to make in that direction.'

Delighted that he seemed as pleased to see her as she was to see him, Beth climbed up beside him.

Henny set off at a trot, and Beth found she liked being higher up, able to see over hedges, and feel the wind in her hair.

'Are you well now?' Dr McMara asked.

'Very well, but bored,' she admitted. 'I'm not used to doing nothing all day. I'd like a job. I don't suppose you know of anyone who would take me on?'

'Most people in these parts have difficulty in just feeding their families.'

'I meant in a business, not domestic work,' she said quickly. Yet even as she spoke she realized she had no skills other than cleaning, plain cooking and laundry.

'Mostly they struggle too,' he said. 'You could maybe volunteer at the hospital, they are always glad of an extra pair of hands.'

'That's a good idea,' she said. 'I found a bicycle in the garden shed. If I could get someone to oil it and pump up the tyres, I could ride it into Waterford.'

'Ask Kathleen, she'll know someone. Do you want me to teach you to ride it?'

Beth laughed. 'I used to ride my friend's bike when I was about ten,' she said. 'I just hope it's true you don't ever forget.'

'And there was me thinking I had the perfect excuse to see you,' he said.

Beth turned her head to look at him. That sounded like flirting, but he was smiling so maybe only joking. 'I think the good people of Dunmore would find it extremely suspicious if their doctor took to giving bike-riding lessons,' she said.

'Everyone around here is suspicious of everything. Catholics seem to see Sin in even the most insignificant word or deed,' he laughed. 'I do hope Kathleen recommends a man over sixty to see to your bike, or he'll have to be off to the confessional telling the priest he had impure thoughts imagining your bottom on the saddle.'

Beth giggled.

Just a few minutes later he drove the gig towards a gate into a field. 'I always stop here to visit auld Peggy because her cottage is on a bend and anyone coming along fast, like your tinker the other night, and poor Peggy might be hurt. It's only about half a mile into Waterford now.'

He jumped down and came round to her, taking her by the waist to help her down. But he didn't let go of her as she reached the ground. In fact he held her tighter.

Then he kissed her. A real kiss on the lips. As his lips touched hers, she knew full well she should back away, but she didn't. It wasn't a passionate kiss, but it also wasn't an entirely chaste one.

'No, Doctor,' she said a little too late, and pushed him away. 'You shouldn't do that.'

She could feel her face had gone red, but he was smiling down at her.

'Why not?' he said. 'You are lovely and I couldn't resist.'

'You are a married man,' she said. 'What if someone saw that?'

'There's a cow watching,' he joked, pointing to a black and white one looking right at them.

'Don't be silly,' she said, but she wanted to laugh, and more alarmingly she was hoping he'd kiss her again. 'Now, I must go. So behave yourself with old Peggy!'

'I'll not give up on you,' he called out as he tethered Henny.

Beth didn't dignify that by looking round. But it made her smile.

10

On the walk back from Waterford carrying a bag of cream knitting wool, needles and a pattern for a lacy jumper, Beth told herself that in future she would avoid any contact alone with the doctor. Furthermore she would stop daydreaming about him. He was, after all, a married man, with a beautiful wife and three children.

But she knew telling herself this wasn't a fail-safe solution. Firstly, she couldn't understand why she would feel this way about the doctor, when all previous experience with men – except for Jack – had proved them to be brutes only interested in sex. Secondly, and this was more worrying, she didn't feel as if she had complete control over her actions. If only there was someone she could talk to about this madness. Because that was how it felt, being mad, like she had no free will anymore.

That evening she settled down by the fire to start knitting her jumper.

She had learned to knit from Auntie Ruth, and just holding the needles in her hands made her remember sitting by the fire with her, the wireless on, the fire crackling, and the repetitive movements of knitting soothing. She'd only made squares then, all different colours, and Ruth would join them together to make blankets. When finished, she gave them to the old folk who lived in the nearby almshouses.

She owed that kind, caring woman so much, but the best thing was that she managed to give Mary hope for her future.

Back then all Mary daydreamed of was one day living somewhere like Ruth's. A clean, bright place with lots of books, vivid-coloured cushions on the armchairs and sofa, and one of those tall lamps which shone a nice soft light. In winter she'd always have a fire lit, and a fluffy red rug in front of it so she could lie on it to read a book.

She was fairly certain Ruth had some idea of how bad it was downstairs, because she was always saying Mary must prepare herself for leaving home. Not just to be able to speak well, attain a good standard of education along with domestic skills, but to feel confident in her own abilities. She suggested that once Mary was fourteen it would be best for her to go into service for a few years, to gain experience, have a decent home and to have the company of other staff.

Mary always wished she had been brave enough to tell Ruth the truth about her home, but she didn't dare. Ronnie said if she told anyone about him or what her mother did, she'd be packed off to an orphanage. He painted the very grimmest picture for her, that she'd be hungry and cold all the time and that they'd beat her and lock her in a dark cupboard if she complained. Even her mother would claim that all girls from orphanages ended up working like slaves for people and that they never had a good or happy life.

Mary was twelve when Ruth gave her the devastating, last-minute news that she was leaving her flat the next morning and moving out of London. 'I wish I could take you with me,' she said as Mary threw herself into her arms, crying. 'But I can't, sweetheart.'

Mary tried to persuade her to stay, but to no avail. Ruth couldn't even give her a good reason for why she was leaving.

As shocked and heartbroken as Mary was at losing her only friend, she was astute enough to guess that Ronnie had threatened Ruth. For some time, he'd been making snide remarks about her thinking she was better than anyone else in the street, and a nosy cow. More worrying was that he was well known for hurting anyone who crossed him.

'Mary, listen to me,' Ruth had said, wiping her own tears away with the back of her hand. 'I want you to promise me you will do as I suggested, to apply for a position in service when you are fourteen. Ask your teacher to help you with this, and she'll give you a reference too.'

'I don't want to go into service,' Mary insisted, still clinging to Ruth.

'I know, it wasn't what I wanted for you either. I dreamed of college, a good career and independence,' Ruth said, her voice cracking with emotion. 'But going into service doesn't have to be permanent. It will give you a good place to live, much better food, warmth, and the companionship of other girls. Yes, it might be tough at times, but far better for you than what will happen if you stay here and let Ronnie push you into bad things. In a couple of years you can apply to go to college, or find a better job. You are a clever girl, so learn all you can from the people you work for, remember the things I've taught you too, and I know you will do well.'

It was soon after Ruth left that Mary realized her mother was not only a drunk and a prostitute – something she'd known for well over a year – but she also took some medicine along with all the drink to numb herself. Sometimes she didn't seem to know her daughter, and she lay on her bed lifelessly all day until Ronnie reminded her she had a job to do.

Mary's life had always been bleak, but without her dear friend upstairs it became unbearable. She was often hungry and Ronnie continued to force himself upon her, and she lived in fear he might make her pregnant.

That she didn't get pregnant was the only luck she had at that time. She was always scared, not just of Ronnie and her mother, but bullies at school who loved to pick on her because her clothes were even shabbier than theirs, and because of what her mother did for a living. After school she would go to the library. There she was safe from Ronnie and she could escape into books. She tried praying but that didn't work. She thought of walking to the docks and jumping in, but each time she went there, the dockers were still around.

So she did what Ruth had said. When she was nearly fourteen she asked her teacher to help her find a live-in job with nice people. Perhaps Ruth had confided her fears for Mary, because the position with the Bradleys in Hampstead was what Miss Grahame found her. She even bought Mary a better dress and shoes for her to wear for the interview, and gave her a glowing reference.

After the dirt and poverty in Whitechapel, Hampstead was an Eden. The Bradleys lived in a tree-lined street, and everyone had pretty front gardens. She had a tiny room up on the top floor, but it was bright and clean. The bed wasn't too good, but at least there was no Ronnie to molest her.

She had walked out of her home in Crimp Street without even a glance back. Ronnie had been slumped in a chair, and her mother was still in bed. She didn't say goodbye. She'd packed and left a small bag hidden out in the yard to pick up as she left. It contained her nightdress, the teddy bear Auntie Ruth had given her when she first began going to her flat, and the small brown leather shoulder-bag she'd given her when she said she was leaving. It was that bag Elizabeth had round her neck for safety when she died. Apart from those two gifts, everything else in the cloth bag was shabby and unimportant.

She vowed that day that the only reason she would ever think of Crimp Street again was to remember Auntie Ruth. But she soon found that nasty memories had stuck more firmly in her head than good ones.

It was at the Bradleys she took up knitting again. Cook showed her how to follow a pattern and to do cable stitch and lacy patterns. The first garment she made was a pink baby's matinée jacket for Cook's new granddaughter. She was so proud of herself when it came out perfectly, she went on to make a navy blue cable-stitch sweater. She wondered what Mrs Bradley did with it once she'd heard Mary was dead, as she'd actually admired it, and complimented Mary on her knitting skills. But she probably packed up all her things and sent them to a jumble sale.

Mrs Bradley was very shrew-like – small, thin, and her movements so fast it was like she was a clockwork toy. Her beady little eyes picked out a smear on glass, a cobweb, or an item left undusted, and she never praised anyone. But to have good food, warmth and safety made up for that. As every year went by, Mary told herself that she would find a better position in a few months, but she was scared of the unknown, and that she might end up somewhere worse.

When war broke out and the other staff left, Mary did think it was the perfect opportunity to leave and apply for war work. But Mrs Bradley said point blank that she hoped Mary wasn't thinking of going too. She felt she had to stay then. But the following year she'd had enough, and in uncharacteristic boldness, she applied for the job in Kent.

After returning to London from her interview she had walked into that Lyons Corner House, and her future was decided by meeting Elizabeth Manning. For the first time in her life she felt fate was smiling on her, which was why when Elizabeth suggested she went to Ireland with her, she didn't refuse out of hand.

Had the bomb attack not happened, she might have backed out the next day, but finding herself in hospital, and knowing that Elizabeth had died protecting her, made her feel she must go.

Looking back at how shy and timid she'd always been, she could hardly believe what she'd managed to do by herself, things she'd once have thought far too difficult or scary to attempt. To stay in a guest house as if she was brought up to do such a thing, to exchange her rail ticket, and speak to a real solicitor on the telephone. Then to leave England alone, and to keep up the pretence of being Beth, and act like she was born to this new way of life, really was quite astounding.

Who would have thought she would find herself having a pretty little house and garden by the sea, and with a housekeeper too? The only thing that she wasn't comfortable with was the money. It was wicked enough to be an imposter but somehow worse to think she had taken money that didn't belong to her.

There was nothing she could do about it of course, not unless she went to the Garda and admitted she was not Elizabeth Manning. That would result in her going to prison, a terrifying prospect. So maybe she could deal with her guilt by using the money to help people in some way.

She woke the next morning to hear the postman putting something through the letterbox. Still in her nightdress, she ran down the stairs, curious, as she had only had two letters in her entire life, both here. The first had come from Mr Boyle just after she arrived, wishing her every happiness in her new home and saying if she needed his professional advice, he would be happy to act for her. The second had been from the bank in Waterford confirming that her account with them was now open, and enclosing a cheque book. But even at Christmas there wasn't one card from anyone, not from Margery at the London guest house, nor from Jack. Kathleen did give her a card and a little present of a knitted tea cosy that looked like a cottage, but these were left on the kitchen table.

Puzzled at who this letter was from, she studied the blurred, unreadable postmark. She couldn't make anything out, and the envelope was so grubby it looked like it had been walked over many times. As for the rather scratchy handwriting, she certainly didn't recognize that. Yet she assumed it must be from Margery as there was no one else likely to write. She ripped the envelope open and, gasping at the signature, flopped down on the sofa to read it.

It was from Jack Ramsey.

Six or seven months ago when she wrote to him, she'd been bitterly disappointed when he didn't reply. But she carried on hoping for a letter for some time, until eventually she felt he had forgotten her and that he was never going to write.

Yet her heart leapt to find this letter was from him, and judging by the state of the envelope, it had been halfway round the world before arriving here.

'Dear Beth,' she read. 'I'm in North Africa, where I was sent shortly after I met you. And I only got your letter sent on to me a short while ago. I expect this reply will also take ages to get to you too, and I wouldn't blame you if you tore it up!'

Beth began to cry then. It could of course be a lie, a pathetic excuse, but it sounded like the truth. She wiped her eyes and read on.

But even if your letter took for ever to get to me, I was thrilled to hear from you, because I hadn't forgotten anything about you. I kept telling myself you were too busy in your new home to think of a man you'd only spent a couple of hours with. I even hoped you'd found love, or at least some new friends in Ireland, as I didn't like to think of you being lonely.

I can't of course tell you where I am exactly or what I'm doing, but the old work of clearing up bomb damage and searching for bodies in the wreckage of homes sometimes feels far better than the real and present danger here. It's very hot, the flies torment us, sand gets in my uniform, in my boots and hair. I find myself dreaming of pouring glass after glass of water from the tap in Mum's kitchen, and running down to the beach for a swim.

You described the beautiful view of the harbour and sea from your cottage window, and I made myself happy by imagining one day looking at that view with you, or taking you to meet my mother and to show you what a lovely place Cornwall is.

I have so many questions, but until I hear that you've got this letter and that it made you happy to remember me, I don't think I should ask anything, and only tell you I am going to request some leave and, if I get it, hope you could meet me in London?

There's so much I want to know about you, Beth, but I'm sure when and if we do get together I'll be stuck for words. I was so happy to get your letter and I write in hope that you've thought about me as often as I have about you. If you do want to see me, I'll send you a telegram with the date of my leave. As I understand it, mail is getting through much quicker now. One of my mates got a letter yesterday from his mum that had only taken a week to get here. But I have to go now as I'm on duty in ten minutes.

Thinking of you.
Yours, Jack x

Beth ran upstairs after reading the letter, jumped into bed again and re-read it, a shiver of delight running down her spine.

She could go to London. It was such a long way, the ferry, then the train, but she had nothing better to do. She could ask if they had room for her at No. 18 and if they did she could call it a little holiday, and a chance to do some shopping.

Jack's letter was replied to that same morning. She said how pleased she was to get it and said she was willing to meet him in London, and reminded him of Margery's telephone number at No. 18, just in case he'd lost it. She also wrote to Margery to explain about Jack and that she needed a room for a little London holiday but couldn't say the date yet.

After posting the two letters, praying that the one to Jack would get there quickly this time, she went for a long, energetic walk.

That evening as she went upstairs to bed, she

realized that the day's events had stopped her from thinking about the doctor. She was very glad of that and thought how silly she'd been to daydream about him. Jack was a far more suitable candidate.

Margery's reply came five days later. She said whenever it was that Jack got to England, she'd find room for Beth, and she'd be very pleased to see her again. She said the constant fear of bombs was affecting many people now. Her husband was exhausted with the endless firefighting, and there had been several bombs dropped close to No. 18. Just a couple of days ago Ernest Bevin, the Minister of Labour, had called for women to fill vital jobs, so she was expecting she would soon be getting enquiries from single women coming to London for work and wanting somewhere to stay. She said too that both she and her husband were in need of a real rest, and she had thought of writing to ask if they could come to Ireland to stay with her, but she was afraid that was too much of a cheek.

Beth posted a letter back later the same day to say it wasn't a cheek to ask and she'd love them to come. Perhaps they could arrange it when she came to London?

Remarkably, Jack's reply came just three weeks after his first letter, so clearly the army were making more of an effort with mail for the soldiers. 'Dear Beth,' he wrote,

Your letter made me whoop with excitement and oddly enough my sergeant informed me even before I'd asked that I was due for some leave along with several of my pals here. He said he'd let me know the date when the ship which would be bringing fresh troops got here.

So with luck I could be back in England by June. I'll have to squeeze in visiting my family, but that depends on how I get back. I'm sure you realize I can't tell you that. Can't wait to see you! Mum tells me they've had bad bombing in Plymouth, and she's heard a lot of horror stories about troops in Africa. She sounded very anxious. But I suppose mothers are the same everywhere, convinced their child is in danger.

I'll write as I leave here, then send a telegram when I'm in England.

Love, Jack x

As thrilled and excited as she was to know Jack was so eager to see her, the bit about mothers being the same everywhere caught her off guard. Her mother had always known she had put her child in danger, and condoned it.

That was a reminder that she didn't have a safety net if things went wrong. But she poured herself a second cup of tea, and said aloud that she didn't need a safety net, and she wasn't going to let the past spoil the possibilities ahead of her.

Just that week, Aisling's husband, Donal, had given the bike a good clean, fitted two new tyres, and oiled it. Now Beth had a few short trial runs, and once she knew she could still ride and felt confident, she set off for Waterford to find out train times and check the ferry situation.

It began to rain as Beth cycled back from Waterford. By the time she got home she felt like a drowned rat, but she was happy; the bike was a joy to ride, despite the wet. Beth wheeled it round the side of the cottage to the open-fronted shelter for logs. Once again she felt grateful that Miranda appeared to have thought of everything.

The fire only needed a bit of a prod and a couple more logs to liven it up, and with the curtains drawn and the wireless on it soon felt warm and cosy. It would be good to see Margery in London, and she thought she would buy a warm coat too. She'd been very cold during the winter, and the camel one was a bit too smart to wear here. She would have to ask Mr Boyle if clothes rationing was definitely starting on 2 June as she'd heard, and whether that meant she had to apply for coupons even if she was only visiting England.

As she sat down by the fire with a cup of tea and toasted a crumpet, she smiled to herself about buying a coat in London. In all the time she worked for the

Bradleys, she was too timid to go into shops, much less try anything on. She'd bought a cheap skirt and blouse from a market stall, and once she picked up a cardigan at a jumble sale. Mrs Bradley had provided her uniform, a navy-blue serge dress, and two aprons. She occasionally spent her wages on a book from a second-hand shop, or knitting wool, and the rest went on stockings, underwear and face cream. She hadn't earned enough to go and buy a new dress.

Today in Waterford she'd bought some fancy face cream and a lipstick for Margery. Even before she left England such things were disappearing from the shops. She thought she'd take some meat with her too, as that wasn't rationed here.

It was just on nine o'clock, when she was thinking of going to bed to read, when she heard loud screaming. She opened the front door, but it was too dark to see anything, and the noise had stopped. She was just about to close the door when it began again, louder and more desperate sounding than before. She slipped on outside shoes and her raincoat, and, picking up her torch, made her way down towards the harbour, where the sound appeared to be coming from.

Another scream and she heard a woman begging for whoever it was hurting her to stop. The sound was coming from one of the three small cottages set up on the hill, and to Beth's horror she realized it was Caitlin's home.

Beth had only spoken to Caitlin a couple of times since she met her with the other women when she first arrived in Dunmore, and that was just to say hello. It was Kathleen who'd pointed out where she lived, and said the big man outside chopping wood was Mick, her husband. Beth remembered he was well over six foot, red-headed, with very broad shoulders, and hands like hams. She also noted he was unshaven and dirty. Now she was sure it was he who was beating Caitlin, she felt justified in her earlier disapproval of his appearance.

Maybe it was because of how Ronnie had treated both her and her mother that her timidity left her and, gripping her torch more firmly, she marched up the steps to the door and banged on it loudly.

The door was flung open, and there was Mick in front of her filling the whole doorway. Beth gulped. The sheer size of him and his angry face was daunting, but she could hear Caitlin crying as if from the back of the cottage.

'I was concerned at Caitlin screaming,' she said more bravely than she felt. 'May I see her to check she's all right?'

'Who the feck do you think you are?' he retorted, taking a step closer to her. His breath stank of whiskey. 'Bugger off or you'll get some too.'

'A man who hits a woman isn't a real man at all,' she threw back at him. 'He's just a bully.'

He lunged at her, fist raised to punch her. Beth lifted her foot to trip him and neatly sidestepped him as he crashed down the steps and landed on his face.

'Oops!' she said, and quickly got past him. She was buoyed up by feeling she'd got the better of him, but she wasn't going to hang around and risk him hitting her.

It was only later as she collapsed on the sofa, out of breath and her heart pounding, that she realized she'd done a very stupid thing. Brutes like that didn't like to be bested. He was bound to retaliate, and he might hurt Caitlin even more because of it.

Yet knowing she had stood up to him was a good feeling. She'd taken all the horror Ronnie had done to her silently, and she had no doubt that that had empowered the man even more.

The following afternoon Beth was just washing her hands after sweeping up fallen leaves in the garden when Kathleen called round.

'Come on in, I'll make a cup of tea,' Beth said.

'I came to say you were very brave to take on Mick Collins,' Kathleen said, reaching out to squeeze Beth's shoulder affectionately.

'You heard about it?' Beth said in surprise.

'Nothing happens here without the world and his wife knowing,' Kathleen said. 'To be sure, Mick is a nasty piece of work. Poor Caitlin rues the day she set eyes on him.'

'Why doesn't she leave him?' Beth asked as she got the cups and saucers out of the cupboard.

'Where would she go with three children and no money?' Kathleen shrugged her shoulders. 'Besides, the Church would say as his wife she has to stay and make the best of it.'

'Surely the Garda could do something?'

Kathleen's laugh was hollow. 'You can't hope they'll help. Most of them are as bad as Mick.'

Beth looked askance at the older woman. 'Surely not.'

'Welcome to Ireland, Beth. I once read somewhere "No one can love like an Irishman." It's my opinion whoever wrote that wasn't married to one. To be sure they are all full of the romantic blarney until that ring slips on the finger. Then it's gone.'

'Get away with you. You're an old cynic,' Beth said, giving Kathleen a playful tap on her arm.

The kettle whistled and Kathleen moved to make the tea. 'Just think hard before you agree to marry anyone,' she said with a smile. 'But you're a smart girl, and a brave one. So maybe you don't need a warning from me.'

11

July 1941

As the train sped towards London, the windows blacked out except for a tiny oblong to see station names, Beth pulled her camel coat round her tightly. It wasn't cold but she was bored, as the light was too dim to read. She silently prayed for sleep and no bombing raids to damage the train track, or anything else that might prolong the journey. She had been on tenterhooks since she got Jack's latest letter telling her his leave was approved, and he was coming. She understood he was not allowed to give any details of how he was getting home for fear of it falling into enemy hands, but he would phone or send a telegram when he could.

Beth couldn't wait, and just sent a letter to his mother's address to say she was leaving for London straight away. Margery had a room for her, and he could telephone there.

The crossing from Rosslare had been very rough. So many people were sick, and the smell of it was enough to turn Beth's stomach too. But she didn't succumb to sickness. She'd found a seat in a corner and immersed herself in a book, avoiding looking at or talking to anyone.

She was so glad to be away from Ireland. After the night that she tackled Mick Collins for beating his wife, she was scared he might come round to Clancy's Cottage to cause trouble.

Thankfully he didn't.

Kathleen claimed it was because he was afraid to retaliate, as he knew she had friends in high places. That idea made Beth laugh. It was true she knew Mr Boyle and Dr McMara, but were a doctor and solicitor enough to make Mick nervous?

Caitlin called round three days after her beating when her children had gone to school. She was wearing a brimmed felt hat to try and hide her injuries, but once she was in the cottage and took it off, Beth saw both her eyes were black, the side of her face was purple with bruising and she winced as she moved as if her ribs were broken.

'I just wanted to thank you for trying to stop Mick,' she said haltingly, and Beth noticed she'd also lost a front tooth. 'He got in a rage about his work. It is hard for him to provide for his family on ten shillings a week.'

Beth guessed it had taken a lot for Caitlin to come and see her because, in the Irishwoman's eyes, Beth was upper class and therefore would have no idea of what life was like for the poor. She wished she could admit to Caitlin that she'd once lived a life just like hers. But that was out of the question.

'I wish I could've done more,' she said instead. 'And I was frightened I might have made things worse for you.'

Caitlin sighed at that. 'I think he quite admired you. Very few people stand up to him. But he isn't always like that.'

Beth was certain most beaten wives claimed that of their brutish husbands. She remembered hearing her own mother insisting Ronnie couldn't help his behaviour, because it was due to his experiences in the First War. As if war experiences made a man rape a child!

'I wish I could at least offer some practical advice,' Beth said. 'But he shouldn't be doing this to you, Caitlin, it is so wrong.'

'I thought of running away to Dublin,' she said in almost a whisper, perhaps imagining Mick could hear her. 'I mean taking the wee ones and finding a room there, and a job. But would I be able to manage without a man?'

'If you can bring up three healthy children, which I'm sure you did mostly alone, then you could easily manage without a man. But it's a big step getting on that train! You would need to plan ahead, know what you are going to take with you, and to pick a time when Mick wouldn't be around to stop you. Then of course you'll need money for rent and food, enough to tide you over until you can get the kids in school and find a job. Have you got any money of your own?'

Caitlin shook her head. 'Sometimes when he comes home drunk I go through his pockets and take some of his money. But that's to feed the children. It could never be enough to escape.'

'If you really want to go, I'll help you with some money.' Beth knew that she shouldn't be offering that to a woman she knew nothing about, but Caitlin's position was awful, and it was likely to get worse.

'Oh no! I couldn't let you do such a thing,' Caitlin said, her eyes widening with surprise. 'It's grand of you, but I couldn't accept it.'

'Well, the offer is on the table if things get worse,' Beth said. 'I'd even come up to Dublin with you and help you find a place to stay.'

The clickety-clack of the train wheels was soothing but Beth still couldn't drop off to sleep. She tried to lose the image of Caitlin's battered face, and the helplessness in her voice, but to no avail. She had been serious in offering Caitlin help; she felt that it would go some way to making up for being an imposter. But perhaps that was crazy.

She knew the reason her own mother ended up with Ronnie was because it was so hard for a widow to bring up a child alone. Caitlin had no skills, and few employers would take on a married woman, especially one with three children. She supposed there were Catholic charities she could go to, but they wouldn't approve of her running out on her husband, and they might even take her children from her and put them in an orphanage.

It was no wonder women in Caitlin's position felt they had no choice. They either had to live with the beatings or run and live by prostitution!

Beth must have dropped off for a short while as she dreamt she was dancing in Jack's arms wearing the rose-pink dress.

She almost laughed aloud, because she couldn't dance – she'd had no opportunity to learn. But she *had* brought the dress with her. She had tried it on countless times, staggered by how well it fitted her, and that the colour made her look pretty – something she'd never experienced before. She just hoped Jack would take her somewhere suitable to wear it.

Beth got a very warm welcome from Margery at No. 18, and after giving her the presents of face cream, a lipstick and scented soap, along with a large rib of beef and some bacon, she'd gone upstairs to unpack. Margery had shed a few tears, and Sid, her husband, said the rib of beef was the best thing he'd seen in years.

Unpacking brought up worrying memories from ten months earlier. She remembered lifting out Elizabeth's clothes, overwhelmed because they were so stylish and expensive. She was wearing the lilac-coloured jacket now, with a sleeveless dress she'd made herself, just glazed cotton with splodges of lilac on a white background. Kathleen had been impressed she could sew so well. She'd almost blurted out about Ruth, because she'd taught her how to use a pattern and a sewing machine. But as always, she managed to stop herself.

It was strange that she wanted to tell people about Ruth, but never about her mother, or where and how they'd once lived. But perhaps that was just because all the memories of Ruth were good ones.

Jack was going to find it very odd if she didn't ever come out with a few anecdotes about her childhood. She might have come out of herself immeasurably in less than a year, doing things she'd once thought would terrify her, but she knew she wasn't capable of inventing fictional personal stories. It crossed her mind that maybe she could claim the bang on her head had made her suffer some loss of memory. Would Jack believe that?

After unpacking, Beth went into the dining room where Margery was doing some dusting. She smiled at Beth. 'So, when is he getting here?'

Beth explained about the military secrecy and added that he might be visiting his family in Cornwall before coming to London.

'I expect he'll stay at the servicemen's place up near

Baker Street,' Margery said. 'So how do you know him? Not that it's any business of mine, of course,' she chuckled. 'Why don't you sit down with me for a bit and have a cuppa, at least until there's an air-raid warning. I want to know all about Ireland too.'

It was good to chat to Margery. Kathleen was great in so many ways, but Beth felt she probed too much and she had to be on her guard when questions came round to the past. Margery, on the other hand, lived in the present. She wanted to know about Ireland, what the cottage was like, how far to a shop, and about the locals. And whether Beth was lonely.

'Yes I am a bit,' Beth admitted. 'To be truthful if it wasn't for the war I'd lock up the cottage and come back. The scenery is beautiful, the cottage lovely, but I think I'd rather be doing war work here.'

She went on to tell her about the evening when she was knocked into the ditch. 'I've never been so cold and frightened. I thought I'd be stuck in there for ever. Thank God the doctor came along and rescued me.'

'So what is he like?'

Beth smirked. 'Kind, attentive, and I'm ashamed to admit I got a bit of a crush on him. If Jack hadn't written and suggested I come here, I might have made a fool of myself.'

'A married man?' Margery raised an eyebrow.

'Yes, with three children, and by all accounts his wife is beautiful.'

Margery nodded as if she could see the whole picture. 'To be honest, Beth, I was worried about you when you left here. You'd had a bad scare in the bombing, lost your friend, and you've no family. I thought of you like an abandoned kitten, needing a home and some mothering. Girls in that position are very vulnerable to a silver-tongued man.'

Beth blushed. 'You are such a kind lady,' she said. 'But I'm tougher than I look. I've got options, I don't have to stay in Ireland, and I've got a bit of money stashed away.' She went on then to tell her about Caitlin. 'Now there's someone who really does need help! But I suspect she'll just put up with the beatings from her husband. I wish I could do something to help women like her.'

'You can't, my dear. All you can hope for is that her husband mellows with age. It's the same here. Thousands of women are trapped by poverty in bad marriages. To be fair to them, these men probably weren't born to be brutes, but gruelling jobs for little pay, substandard housing and disappointment makes them turn to drink, and that's a recipe for trouble.'

'I wonder if there is some way you can tell a man who is likely to become a brute,' Beth said thoughtfully. 'After all, these women must have been in love when they married.'

'I think there are little pointers,' Margery sighed. 'Jealousy, possessiveness . . . I think women get the idea these are good traits, suggesting he'll never desert her, and that she is very special. But it is a form of bullying and that's like a stranglehold on their marriage. Soon he's policing what she wears, how she does her hair, and if she disobeys violence often erupts. We had a couple as tenants here when we first bought this house. She had to do exactly what he said. He stopped her friendships, kept her from her family too. Then the hitting began.'

'Crumbs,' Beth exclaimed. 'Did you and your husband hear this?'

'Yes, we kept out of it at first – he was in the fire brigade like Sid. But one night he knocked her down the stairs, and Sid kicked him out. She was distraught, claimed he couldn't help himself and the pair of them found somewhere else to live. Six months later she was dead. Found by the police in a pool of blood at the bottom of some stone steps to their basement flat, and he'd run away.'

'Gosh, how awful!'

Margery pursed her lips, the memory being a disagreeable one. 'And I was just like you, Beth, wishing I could've saved her; let her stay here. But she'd have gone looking for him, she would never have stayed here and made a new life for herself. Some women you just can't save.'

Beth spent the days after her arrival shopping and exploring London. Margery had told her clothing coupons had begun, and gave her the address to get some, though she added she suspected some shops would just let her have goods without coupons if she said she lived in Ireland.

Margery was right about that, at least in the cheaper shops, but she did get a gorgeous three-quarter black and white winter coat from the Army and Navy Stores in Victoria Street. It was half price in the summer sale. That took all the coupons she'd got. But she was able to buy a couple of pretty summer dresses elsewhere without them.

But looking in shops began to pall. So she stayed in most days and helped Margery at the guest house. It felt good to be busy and appreciated. Margery said she'd never had such a good worker before, and that there would always be a job for her here if she got tired of Ireland.

When Jack finally telephoned to say he was with his parents in Falmouth, Beth felt not just joy to hear his voice but relief the ship hadn't been torpedoed, something she'd worried about. He told her he'd liked being on board, and slept most of the time as it was great to be out of the gruelling heat. 'I'll need to stay here for at least three days to keep Mum sweet, but maybe you could come back to Cornwall with me before I have to get the ship back to Cairo.'

Beth wasn't sure his mother would like that and said so.

Jack laughed. 'Not my mum, she'll want to meet you. As will Dawn and Andy, my brother and sister. Besides, we have to make the most of this leave, heaven only knows when I'll get another one.'

It was a few days later, just after nine in the morning, when Margery knocked on Beth's door to say Jack had arrived.

'He's a bit embarrassed to call so early but he came on the sleeper train,' she said. 'I must say, he's very handsome and he's got a nice way with him. I put him in the dining room, and you can join him for breakfast.'

Beth hurriedly put on some lipstick and brushed her hair. She left it loose as she was pleased that it looked shinier and longer than she ever remembered.

She had been worrying that she wouldn't recognize Jack, but as she walked into the dining room he looked far better than she remembered. That night he'd come straight from a bomb-site, his hair dull with dust, and he'd looked tired. But now he leapt up eagerly from the table, his uniform was crisp and smart, plus he was very suntanned and his teeth were dazzling white against it. Those tawny eyes which she thought she'd forgotten sparkled brighter than the image in her head. She longed to kiss his wide mouth and touch those sharp cheekbones. But she was struck dumb, even though her heart was singing.

'You are lovelier than ever,' he said in a small voice, and moved to embrace her.

Fortunately, the other guests had all left the dining room earlier, and as he kissed her, she held him tight, hoping that would convey what she couldn't say.

They sat down at the table as Margery came in. 'A pot of tea for you, and I'll bring some toast in a couple of minutes.'

Pouring the tea for Jack brought back Beth's voice, and she asked about his family, and what it was like to be back in Cornwall.

'Dawn – she's twenty-two – is seeing a fisherman. Mum says he smells of fish too. As for Andy, he's seventeen and he's applied to join the navy. They argue a lot – Dawn tends to boss Andy around. But it was good to be with them. We went to the beach, looked up two of my old friends still in Cornwall. The rest are in the services. It was really nice after the heat and dust in Africa. Mum's cooking was good too, though the rationing makes it hard for her, like everyone.'

This quick insight into his family brought Beth up sharply, as she imagined he'd expect her to do the same.

'I'm afraid you might find me a bit odd, not just because I've no family to tell you about,' she said, putting one hand over his, 'but that bang on the head I got in the bombing has made me forget some things. Not about you, luckily, but I'm struggling with stuff from before that day.'

Jack shrugged and grinned. 'We don't need to look back, only forward,' he said, then grinned as Margery came back in with two plates of bacon and eggs. 'Gosh, that looks wonderful. My mum was finding it hard to put anything on the table. If she hadn't been keeping chickens there would be no breakfast. She said she hadn't been able to get bacon for some weeks.'

'You've got Beth to thank for that,' Margery said. 'She brought the bacon with her. And a huge rib of beef too. I'm going to cook it for tonight's dinner, so make sure you're back for six-thirty.'

After Margery had gone, Jack said he had planned to take Beth to the Tower of London. 'But it's closed because of the Blitz,' he added. 'So shall we go on a boat to Greenwich? I've never been, have you?'

'No, never,' Beth said, smiling at the thought of him trying to find something fun to do. 'That would be lovely.'

It was a warm, sunny day and they decided to walk to the Embankment, only to find there were no passenger boats running because of daylight bombing raids.

'You'd have thought I would've known that,' Jack said, looking a bit crestfallen.

Beth tucked her hand through his arm. 'Never mind, I like walking around London, especially the very old parts, and the parks.'

When Jack took her up the Strand into the Savoy for

coffee and cake, she found it hard to not let her mouth drop with the palatial splendour of the famous hotel. Fortunately Jack was almost puppy-like in his glee, and didn't even bat an eye at the cost. 'It's a treat to come in here,' he said happily. 'I've wanted to experience how rich people live in London, but I needed to do this with someone who looks like they belong here.'

'But it's too much for you to pay,' she whispered. 'Let me help.'

He looked affronted at that suggestion. 'You're my girl, and nothing would make me take your money.'

They walked along to the Law Courts, and found their way to the ancient Inns of Court where all the solicitors and barristers had their offices. There they sat on a bench in the sunshine watching men in black gowns and wigs hurrying off, perhaps to court, clutching bundles of documents tied up with pink tape.

'There's a whole world in London that I really know nothing about,' Beth said thoughtfully. 'The law is just one bit of it.'

Jack put his arm around her and squeezed her closer to him. 'Imagine how it is for me, the boy from Cornwall more used to fishing boats and tin mines than men in wigs. Maybe we can learn about them and everything else together.'

He kissed her then, regardless of the wig-and-gowned men going past, and it felt like soaring up to the sky.

They walked around the City of London, looking at the old banks and other buildings. Jack talked a little about Cornwall, the pretty fishermen's cottages, the turquoise sea and the narrow cobbled streets. 'I so much want to show it to you. Once you've had Cornish fish and chips you'll never buy them again in London.'

The air-raid siren went off suddenly and they ran to the nearest shelter at Chancery Lane Tube. 'Just our luck,' Jack said, as they joined the mass of people trying to get into safety. 'But maybe in years to come we can tell people we spent our first date in a bomb shelter.'

Beth was apprehensive about going into another Tube station after what happened at Trafalgar Square, but she liked that he was talking long-term, and that took her mind off being scared. She knew of course that it was far too soon to hope they would fall in love and stay that way, regardless of the war and the distance between them. But there were good signs; he talked so easily about being a soldier, life down in Cornwall, his childhood and anything else she asked him about. She just wished she could be so open.

She had imagined when she read Elizabeth's diaries and letters that she had gleaned enough about her life to be her. She might look as well dressed as Elizabeth, but in fact she was like one of those cardboard dolls little girls fitted paper outfits onto. Inside she was still Mary Price, whose total experience of life was a miserable childhood, and being a lowly servant. How long would it be before Jack realized she was no more than a façade, with nothing behind it?

The raid appeared to be a fairly distant one, and the all-clear came only an hour after entering the Tube station. It was good to walk out into fresh air, and to see the Holborn area just as it was earlier.

'I came here on a shout just before I left England,' Jack said, pointing out two buildings undergoing extensive repairs. 'But that café,' he added, indicating a café called Mick's across the street, 'they had their windows blown out, and they'd put a sign outside saying "More Open Than Usual". That's the spirit of Londoners, Beth. Refusing to be cowed with fear. And he's got new windows fitted now.'

Beth laughed. 'I think it's wonderful people can find something to laugh about. Who would have thought it?'

'I know,' Jack said. 'I don't think I could.'

'I often wonder how people learn to cook for so many people,' Beth said thoughtfully. 'I know I couldn't do it.'

'Can you cook Beth? And do you like it?'

'Yes I can. I learned a lot from a neighbour I called Auntie Ruth. She taught me to knit and sew too.'

Beth found it odd that she felt compelled to talk

about Ruth. But then the time spent with her was the best part of her childhood. 'My first job was in service, and I learned still more from Cook when I was helping her.'

Jack looked a bit stunned. 'To be honest I never imagined you working at anything. Too well brought up and stuff.'

It was her chance to dispel a few myths and make a story for herself. She took a deep breath. 'People often think that about me, but with my mother widowed we certainly weren't rich. I had to help out financially. But I'm not sorry I went in for service rather than working in an office. I learned lots of useful skills. It was through meeting someone when I was with the Bradleys that I ended up running their dress shop in Richmond. I loved that, but when war broke out they decided to shut it down. About that time I inherited the cottage in Ireland.'

'So the shop is why you've got such lovely clothes?' he said.

'Yes, one of the perks of the job,' she said with a smile. She felt she'd told him just enough now, and she felt better in herself that she'd admitted being in service, so she'd never get tripped up by forgetting herself.

They decided to go to Hyde Park then, and caught a bus in that direction.

It was lovely in the park, so warm and sunny, they

bought ice creams from a kiosk and went down to the Serpentine to watch people in the small boats. Jack said there wasn't enough time to hire one, but perhaps they could do it tomorrow or the next day.

Jack bought a bunch of flowers for Margery at Green Park station, and they went up Bond Street then to make their way back to the guest house.

Then Jack asked Beth about her mother.

She gulped. She hadn't expected that question so soon and was unprepared. 'Sadly she died just before war was declared. A massive stroke!'

That was the worst thing. She might have no love for her mother; but to claim she was dead seemed like the ultimate betrayal.

'I'm so sorry, Beth,' he said, putting his arm around her. 'Gosh, I must stop interrogating you.'

'I don't see it as interrogation, only interest. I'm just glad she went quickly,' Beth replied, anxious to move on to an easier subject. 'After clearing out our old house, and having no one to stay for, it seemed a good idea to move to Ireland.'

'And now?' He raised his eyebrow questioningly. 'Is it what you expected? Have you made friends there?'

'Not really. There are women I talk to, but not real friends. I do get a bit lonely and bored, as I've got nothing much to do,' she admitted. 'I knit, read, go out on my bike. I need a job, really, my savings won't last for ever. I'm told it's a good place to have paying guests. I might do that next spring. Or I could let it out permanently too, and come back to England.'

'I keep thinking about what I'll do after the war,' Jack said thoughtfully. 'I'm a carpenter by trade, and I'd like to make bespoke furniture, but I'm not certain I'd get any business in Cornwall. One of my army pals comes from Kensington. He said that's the area I should focus on as there's plenty of wealthy people living there. Or Pimlico, Hampstead, Highgate, any of those would be good.'

It was tempting to tell him about the interesting small shops in Hampstead and that that was where she worked in service, but she was loath to encourage him in that direction for fear of revealing more.

'I think that's a wonderful idea, but you could start out somewhere like Bath or Cheltenham, which would be cheaper, and there's plenty of rich people there too. You'd need a workshop with it, wouldn't you? Perhaps with rooms above where you could live.'

He looked surprised. 'Good idea,' he said. 'You aren't just a pretty face. Would you like to marry me and live in the rooms above with me?'

She knew that wasn't a proposal, more of a joke. 'Ask that question again when the war is over,' she laughed and then went quiet.

'Penny for them?' he said. 'You've gone very quiet.'

'I was thinking what a lovely day this has been, but

then I wondered how long it will be before I can see you again.'

Jack drew her into his arms, backing her into a shop doorway, and kissed her. Like all his previous kisses it made her feel like being given one chocolate and wanting more. Cupping her face in his two hands and looking right into her eyes, he gave a deep sigh. 'I wish I could promise you that it will be in a few months' time, but the truth, Beth, is that the fighting is very fierce over there and it looks like it's going to get much worse.'

That sounded to her as if he thought he might be killed there. 'How can you be so brave?' she asked. 'If it were me I'd want to run away to safety.'

'That isn't an option,' he said, caressing her cheek. 'I joined up to fight for my country and I will go on doing that whatever the cost.'

'Just stay safe for me,' she said in a small, tremulous voice.

'Enough now, we need to get back and have that dinner Margery promised. Don't spoil the time we have together by worrying about stuff we can't alter or ignore.'

12

Beth found herself unable to drop off to sleep that night for thinking about Jack and his kisses. Just the thought of them made her feel hot and bubbly inside.

She had expected that anything more than the most chaste of kisses would bring back memories of Ronnie and all he did to her. She had met someone a couple of years ago and gone to the pictures with him. He kissed her in the cinema and it was horrible — a sloppy wet one and his tongue like an eel. He also shoved his hand up her skirt. She excused herself to go to the toilet, and left the cinema.

But Jack could kiss her for all eternity. She wanted him, and in truth had they been alone somewhere, she might have even got carried away.

Long ago, thanks to Ronnie, she had made up her mind she would never have sex until she was married, and even the thought of that made her flesh crawl. So why on earth was she beginning to think it might be not only acceptable with Jack, but wonderful?

It was possible she had grown out of her Ronnie phobia; after all, she had never tested the water with any other man. But she couldn't bank on that. She had already entered her relationship with Jack dishonestly.

She remembered that Auntie Ruth often said that one lie always leads to another, and everything she'd told Jack about herself was a lie. With such a huge volume of dishonesty, even criminality, how could she ever tell him the truth? He would assume she was a virgin and she wasn't even that.

As a child she'd escaped from reality with daydreams so many times, imagining herself as a ballerina, a high-wire act in a circus, a film star. The more far-removed the fantasy was from Whitechapel, Ronnie and her drunken mother, the better and the safer she felt.

From now on she could escape into a little daydream of living with Jack in a flat above a workshop and listening to the sound of him sawing wood downstairs. She would walk to the back window of the flat and look out into a sun-filled garden, washing flapping on the clothes line, and the woods beyond looking beautiful.

Plugging herself into that fantasy made her forget nastier thoughts and drop off to sleep. She awoke refreshed and excited at spending the day ahead with Jack.

At ten, Margery called out to Beth that he had arrived. As she came down the stairs, Margery was inviting him in, offering breakfast again. 'I've got some sausages and bacon, and as two of my guests left early without having breakfast, they are going begging. I bet the food at the army hostel is dire!'

'I didn't stop for it,' he laughed, 'but you are right, it is dire. I'd love some if Beth doesn't mind.'

'Of course not,' Beth spoke out, touched that Margery was so generous. 'And you can tell me what you'd planned for today so I can dress appropriately.'

She had put on one of the summer dresses she'd bought. It was pink and white gingham, with puffed sleeves and a flared skirt.

Margery carried a tray into the dining room and put Jack's breakfast in front of him.

'I made extra toast so you can join Jack,' she said to Beth. 'And a fresh pot of tea.'

'This is so kind of you,' Jack said, smiling up at the older woman. 'No wonder Beth likes staying here.'

'I'd keep her here if I could,' Margery admitted. 'It's a treat to have someone young and sweet-natured staying. Mostly we get older people, and some of them never stop grumbling. Our Beth has still got stars in her eyes, and I hope she can stay that way for ever.'

'Have I got stars in my eyes?' Beth whispered once Margery had gone.

'Yes, like you are expecting every day to be better than the one before.' He reached out and took her hand. 'I get the feeling you had a sad childhood, and maybe that's why.'

Beth's stomach churned. She hoped he wasn't going to follow that line any further.

'No worse than anyone else's,' she said defiantly.

'So maybe it's just a look that's special to you,' he said. 'But I hope you'll always look that way for me.'

Breakfast eaten and washed down by more tea, they sat for a while discussing what they could do. Beth suggested St James's Park so they could see Buckingham Palace from the Mall. Jack nodded. 'That would be good this morning, but I was told last night there is a tea dance at a hotel in the Strand in the afternoon. Do you like dancing?'

Beth giggled. 'I like the idea of it, but I've never learned to dance and never been to one either.'

Jack looked shocked. 'Really? Well, I can only do the waltz, but I thought all girls could dance.'

'That's a bit like saying all boys can play football or swim.'

'I can teach you to waltz,' he said. 'It's really easy. But have you brought a suitable dress with you?'

She nodded, her excitement at wearing the lovely dress outweighing her fear of looking foolish.

She went upstairs a little later to put the coral dress on, and put a cotton duster coat over it. Jack whistled. 'You look like a film star. I'll have other men cutting in to dance with you all afternoon.'

Beth looked alarmed. 'I hope they don't, I don't want anyone else to know I can't dance.'

'Then I'll hold you so tightly no one will be able to prise you from my arms.'

*

St James's Park was beautiful, the perfume from the rose beds incredible. The lake was full of swans, geese and many different varieties of ducks. They bought a little bag of special food for them, and some of the birds were so tame they might have eaten out of Beth's hand.

A man with a monkey on his shoulder dressed in a little red jacket was playing a piano accordion on the bandstand. After a few numbers the man walked around his audience, the monkey holding out a hat for tips. Jack was just moving forward to give some money when a couple of policemen arrived, and the accordionist took off across the bridge over the lake.

'As it's a royal park I don't suppose entertainers are allowed,' Jack said sorrowfully. 'Shame, it was nice.'

They had a cup of tea and a rock cake in the park café and Beth noticed Jack was frowning.

'What is it?' she asked.

'I was trying to decide the best time to tell you that I've got to go back to Plymouth tomorrow,' he said glumly. 'There was a message for me at the hostel last night.'

'Oh no,' she gasped. 'Why?'

'I don't know, but there'll be a good reason,' he said, his eyes welling up. 'Such a shame we can't have a few days in Cornwall together as I planned. I so much wanted you to meet my family.'

Beth felt like her heart had sunk into her shoes. This

wasn't fair, to have such a nice time together and then have it snatched away.

But she could see he was troubled, and she didn't want to make it any worse for him.

'We've still got today together,' she said, reaching out to caress his cheek. 'When the war is over we will have all the time in the world.'

They walked down the Mall and across Trafalgar Square, and paused to watch people feeding the pigeons. Then a photographer came up to them and asked if they'd like their picture taken. 'I can have it developed by Monday afternoon, and I'll have it over there by the National Gallery for you to see it,' he said. 'Just a shilling deposit now, and I'll take that off the full price of two shillings when you come to collect it.'

'I could collect it,' Beth said, realizing Jack wouldn't be able to.

Jack smiled. 'How much for two copies?' he asked, looking at Beth. 'You could send me the other one?'

Jack haggled a little and finally the photographer laughingly agreed he'd do two for two and sixpence, as they were clearly in love and about to be separated.

Beth blushed furiously as she removed her coat so her dress could be the star of the picture, but she noted that Jack wasn't embarrassed at all by haggling. That pleased her – back in the East End everyone haggled.

A little later they went off to find the tea dance in the Strand Palace Hotel. Although the dance had only started a few minutes before, there was quite a queue for tickets. Beth left Jack in the queue to go to the cloakroom and leave her coat. As she waited for him to join her with the tickets she gazed into the ballroom, astounded by the splendour of it. She had expected little more than a plain hall, but this had a shiny wood floor, gorgeous crystal lights, and a huge rotating ball covered in tiny mirrors which cast a snowflake effect over the few couples who were dancing. Even the gilt chairs around small tables had velvet seats. As for the band, she had only expected a quartet at most, but there were eight musicians wearing evening dress, black bow-ties and shiny patent-leather shoes. She had never imagined a dance hall to be like this. The scullery maid who'd worked at the Bradleys' about three years before war broke out used to tell her that she went to a dance in Camden Town most Saturday nights. She said there were lots of rough men, and quite often fights broke out. Beth had wondered why she went, as it sounded frightening.

'So, what do you think?' Jack asked, breaking her reverie.

'It's wonderful,' she smiled. 'Not a bit what I expected.'

'Well, let's hope there isn't an air raid, or we might get stuck in a damp, smelly cellar,' he said, then, putting his arm around her, led her through the door to the dance, handing in the tickets on the way.

'No other girl here looks as good as you,' he whispered, tightening his hand on her waist as he took her in his arms to dance. 'The waltz is just one, two, three,' he said. 'Just follow me and you'll get the hang of it immediately.'

Apart from a couple of times when she tripped against his feet, she did get the hang of it very quickly, and loved it. By the third dance she was confident enough to be able to take note of other dancers, without even thinking of the steps. Almost all the men were in uniform. The few civilian men were mostly past call-up age, with wives in dresses that looked like relics from the Twenties. And there were a few spivs wearing sharp suits, bow-ties or cravats. Jack whispered they were probably black marketeers or gangsters. Their women were glamorous, reminding Beth of Hollywood stars with their platinum-blonde hair and dresses that looked as if they'd been poured into them.

For the first time ever, Beth felt good about how she looked. Her dress was a great colour and she knew she looked classy, but sexy too, as the handkerchief points revealed glimpses of her knees and lower thighs as she moved. She saw other women looking at her admiringly, something she'd never encountered before, and, held firmly by Jack, she felt powerful.

The dance floor grew more and more crowded, and Beth was pleased to see there were lots of people who couldn't really dance, and just shuffled about in time to the music. When the band struck up a quick step, a tango or some other dance Beth had never heard of, the floor cleared a little, giving the dancers more room. Beth watched them entranced and vowed she would find someone to teach her when she returned to Ireland.

At the tables and chairs set back from the dance floor, a couple of waitresses darted about taking orders. Jack got them a table and ordered tea and cake for two.

'It's really romantic, isn't it,' Beth said. It wasn't just the lighting, or the music, it was an atmosphere of hope, love and tenderness. She could smell perfume and hair oil, sense the effort people had made with their appearance, and loved the way so many of the couples were looking at each other with love as they danced. She wanted to say she hoped all the soldiers, sailors and airmen here today would get through the war unscathed to hold their sweethearts in their arms again, but to say such a thing might become a jinx, and Jack might be one who wouldn't return.

There were more dances after their tea, and Beth wished she could stay safe in Jack's arms for ever, just floating around the dance floor in a world of dreamy music and twinkly lights where nothing bad ever happened.

The dance finished at six, but no one looked in a hurry to leave. 'This was the perfect place to bring me,' she whispered in Jack's ear as they shuffled their way out. 'I hope it won't be too long before we can do it again.'

He just smiled, helped her on with her coat, and took her hand to lead her outside.

'I'm afraid we have to be patient, as I think it will be a long time before I can see you again,' he said as they walked up a side street towards Covent Garden. 'You will write to me?' he asked.

'Of course I will, every day if you like. But I don't expect you to do it too. You'll be far too busy.'

He paused, took her face in both hands and looked into her eyes. 'I've fallen in love with you, Beth. I'll never be too busy to write to you, even if it's only a couple of words. I'll be thinking about you all the time.'

She knew by the intensity of his eyes that he meant it. 'I love you too, Jack. It's really too soon to say such things when we've only had these two days together, but I know you mean it, and so do I.'

Suddenly the air-raid siren blasted out, and people all around them began to run. 'The church crypt in Covent Garden is the closest shelter!' someone yelled out. Beth and Jack ran too, because they could hear planes coming closer.

It was a bad raid. The crypt of the church seemed safe enough, but they winced each time a bomb dropped as it sounded as if they were right above them, and dust trickled down between the ancient stones holding up the walls.

Beth stayed in the circle of Jack's arms on an old pew. There were perhaps sixty or seventy other people in the crypt with them, but it was quiet, no one was doing much talking, and while there wasn't much light, their faces looked anxious.

Finally, at half past nine, the all-clear sounded, and an air-raid warden, his uniform covered in dust, let them out. 'A bad one tonight,' he said wearily. 'A bank in the Strand flattened, a whole row of houses gone, we think many people killed too. Look where you're walking, there's a lot of glass and roof slates underfoot.'

Despite it still being light, the air was heavy with brick dust. As they made their way as quickly as possible across Leicester Square and on towards Regent Street, they saw many small fires in buildings and a tremendous amount of rubble and broken glass.

The joy Beth had felt all day was now replaced with dread. Any day now Jack could be killed.

Suddenly she saw what war really meant. Not the inconvenience of being on a train with just a tiny slit in the blacked-out window to tell where you were. It wasn't just banging into things with no street lighting or hearing sad stories of homesick evacuees. She had enjoyed chatting about the shortages of food stuffs in the shops, the rising costs, and laughing about bossy air-raid wardens who bristled with their newfound importance. But war wasn't that at all; it meant death for many. For some, terrible deprivation, grief and terror, and many men would come home with missing limbs, their personalities changed for ever.

Being in Regent Street and seeing boarded-up windows brought back a sudden and sharp memory of the last time Auntie Ruth brought her here one December. She was nearly twelve, and all the shop windows were decorated for Christmas and ablaze with light, so Mary had hardly noticed the dark or cold. It was the last Christmas before Ruth moved away. That evening she bought Mary a new pair of shoes, as the ones she was wearing had holes in the soles and rainwater came in. 'Leave them on,' she'd said once she knew Mary liked them and they fitted properly. 'We'll ask the assistant to throw your old ones away. You have my permission to tell your mother a white lie about them. Tell her your teacher gave you them, say they have a box of clothes and shoes that other children have grown out of.'

Mary didn't have to tell the lie. Her mother and Ronnie were out when she got home and neither of them ever noticed or cared what she had on her feet. They were worn out by the time she went for the interview with Mrs Bradley, so it was good her teacher gave her another pair.

Ruth gave her a knitting bag before she left. It was made of tapestry and had wooden handles. She'd packed it with odd balls of wool and several different sizes of knitting needles. 'I wish I could give you something more personal,' she said sadly. 'But I thought Ronnie was likely to take it from you.'

That knitting bag was the one thing Beth wished she still had, but of course that was still at the Bradleys', almost certainly thrown out by now.

'You're very quiet,' Jack said as they walked up Regent Street. 'What is it? Because I've got to go?'

'No, it's not that,' she said and tried to laugh. 'Up till now the war seemed . . .' She paused, not knowing how to explain.

'Far away! Affecting other people. A disease you can't catch?'

'Not quite as simple as that, but a distant threat. Now I know we could be killed just walking home to the guest house.'

Jack stopped and pulled her into his arms. 'We aren't going to be killed tonight, and please, Beth, don't start thinking like that. I love you and hopefully the war will be over soon and we can get married and live happily ever after.'

'Yes, that's a really lovely thought,' she said, and made herself smile. She shouldn't be dwelling on the past, or death and destruction, not when he'd spoken of getting married.

'So, is fish and chips a better thought? There's a shop just around the corner. I'm starving.'

It was painful saying goodbye, knowing it might be months or even years before they'd see each other again. Jack's kisses were even more tender and prolonged, and it made her think he did know what lay ahead for him in North Africa. And it wasn't going to be good.

Later as she lay in bed trying hard not to cry again, she reached for the little dog-eared card Jack had pressed into her hand as they parted. On the front was an illustration of two little dogs snuggled up in a basket. 'I'm sorry we didn't get the time we planned for,' he'd written. 'If things get bad for you in Ireland, you can always go to my folks. Please write to Mum so she can see you are just as lovely as I told her you were. Write to me and stay safe. I love you, Jack.'

Saying he'd told his mother about her was comforting, though she guessed any mother would be suspicious about her son being struck by a girl he'd only just met.

Looking back at the day, apart from being told it was the last one, it had been just perfect, rounded off by fish and chips straight out of the newspaper, which, despite Jack's scathing remarks about London fish, she loved. Not to mention the sweetness of his kisses before she said goodnight.

On Monday she'd go and collect the photographs, get a couple more up-to-date knitting patterns, and perhaps some nice fabric to make new cushion covers. The ones at Clancy's Cottage were very shabby.

She would try very hard not to think any more dark thoughts about the war.

13

1943

Beth pulled back the bedroom curtains to see it was raining heavily again, the third day of rain. Dejected, she sighed and got back into bed. It was now May. She'd hoped to do some gardening today as the tulip bulbs she'd planted back last autumn were over and the weeds had sprung up round them.

She picked up the framed photograph of Jack and her in Trafalgar Square from her bedside cabinet, and her eyes filled with tears. Missing Jack and worrying about him was awful, but on top of that she was lonely and felt imprisoned by the bad weather.

But the photograph always cheered her, a reminder of the best of days, Jack in his uniform and she in her gorgeous tea-dance dress. She wished it was possible to get colour photographs, but even in black and white it was a good picture. The famous fountain and the head of one of the big stone lions were a superb backdrop, and their faces shone with how they felt about one another.

With Jack off to Plymouth to join his ship, she had

spent the day after the tea dance crying, until Margery came upstairs and, seeing her tear-stained face, told her to pull herself together, pointing out that Jack couldn't help having to cut their time together short. 'He's a soldier, he must obey his orders. We all have to do our bit, Beth. My Sid has to fight fires, I have to support him and all the people who come and stay here, some of whom have lost loved ones. You have to support Jack if you love him.'

'How can I if he's hundreds of miles away?' Beth sobbed out.

'By writing to him, so he knows he's got you to come home to. Now, dry your eyes and come down and have a cup of tea.'

Beth stayed another couple of days at No. 18. She helped Margery tidy up the garden, whitewashed the walls in the cellar, and took down all the net curtains in the house and washed them. Just doing some practical jobs made her feel better.

'I think I ought to go back to Ireland tomorrow,' she said as she and Margery gave each of the bedrooms a spring clean, Margery pulling out the bed to clean beneath it, and turning the mattress before remaking it, while Beth wiped the window frames clean then slid the sparkling nets back onto their canes and rehung them. 'I can't leave Kathleen to look after the place any longer.'

'That's probably for the best,' Margery sighed. 'You

associate this place with Jack. But heaven knows I shall miss you terribly.'

Beth got down from the window and embraced the older woman. 'I wish my mother had been like you, I'd never have left home,' she said, nuzzling into Margery's neck.

'Perhaps one day you'll come back and tell me your whole story,' Margery said softly.

Beth just hugged her tighter. She knew that if she was ever to tell anyone about herself, it would be this kind, unjudgemental woman.

'I'd better take a walk to the station and find out if the ferries are running. If not I'll have to call Patrick,' she said as she broke away. 'I'm going to miss you too, so much.'

Beth arrived back in Dunmore with a head full of plans: decorate the cottage, tidy up the garden, look for a dance teacher, volunteer at the local hospital. But summer turned to autumn so quickly, with too much rain to do the garden, a shortage of paint preventing her decorating, and she couldn't find a dance teacher. As for volunteering at the hospital, the sharp-featured sister she spoke to said, 'We need a couple more nurses, but not a do-gooder that will get in our way.' That was enough to make Beth turn tail and run.

News reports from England were deliberately vague, presumably to keep people's spirits up. But on her weekly visit to the cinema in Waterford, she learned on Pathé News that the RAF had dropped 100,000 bombs in an hour on Düsseldorf in September and that the army had recaptured Tobruk. They learned the German siege of Leningrad was still going on, the RAF had bombed Berlin, but, closer to home, that 173 people were crushed to death trying to get into Bethnal Green Tube station. Beth couldn't help wondering if there were people she'd gone to school with.

Margery wrote most weeks, telling Beth about guests, going out of her way to amuse her with the funnier tales, but there was also mention of bombing quite close to Blandford Street. She'd had no bookings yet for Christmas but she supposed people were waiting until nearer the time.

When Beth wrote back she didn't say that there were times she felt she could go mad with boredom and loneliness — not when London people were in fear of their lives — so she stuck to telling Margery about what she was knitting, little bits of local news, and that she was always anxious about Jack.

Jack's letters were both amusing and loving. Without saying where he was or what he was doing, he managed to convey the heat there, the atmosphere of the crowded, rather squalid towns, and the camaraderie in his unit. But more recently his letters were slow arriving, sometimes three or four coming together, then nothing for a few weeks. She tried very hard not to think that his letters might stop altogether one day.

Christmas had been dismal. The only cards she got were from Margery, Mr Boyle and Kathleen. She saw people she knew walking past her cottage, yet none came to the door. A handmade card eventually came from Jack, arriving at New Year. He'd drawn a forest of Christmas trees in pencil, with various little animals and birds perched on the branches. She had no idea he could draw, especially so well, and she put it between two sheets of cardboard to be safe until she could get it framed.

Christmas had never been a good time for her. Her mother was always drunk and bad-tempered, Ronnie either creepy, trying to get her to sit on his lap, or violent if something set him off. As a child she had often wondered who had the happy Christmases she read about in books. Christmas with the Bradleys had just been hard work. They had cocktail parties before Christmas, then family and friends arrived on Christmas Eve and stayed for three days. On top of all her usual chores there were extra fires to be lit in bedrooms, dresses and shirts to be pressed, she had to help cook in the kitchen and wait at table too. Cook, who had in the past worked for titled people in country mansions, used to snort with derision at the Bradleys' attempts to appear monied and grand. 'They are merely middle-class nobodies, pretending to be upper class. No one with any class expects the maid to wait at a dinner table. Nor do they expect a cook of my standing to manage without an assistant and scullery maid.'

At least in the past, however much work was involved, Beth had the company of the other staff, there was friendly banter between them and laughter. But as Cook and Ruby, the maid, left in 1939 when war was declared, Beth had been expected to fill all the roles – cooking, lighting fires, cleaning, laying the table and everything else in between. The only thing the Bradleys did themselves was to answer their own front door. Her Christmas present from them was a new apron. It had been tempting to strangle Mrs Bradley with it.

'You must get up,' Beth finally said aloud, aware it was past ten and Auntie Ruth had always said staying in bed was a bad habit to get into. She thought maybe she should write to Margery and ask if she could visit her. The bombing in London wasn't so bad at the moment, and the Irish Sea would be calmer by now.

It struck Beth as she washed and dressed that once upon a time she would have thought her present way of life to be perfection. No worry about money, good food, no hard work or people bullying her. The cottage was lovely, and there was no doubt the view of the sea from the windows was breathtaking. During the winter she'd often sat on the chair in the bedroom watching the fury of the storms, waves crashing into the sea wall with such ferocity it was a miracle the wall didn't crumble.

'You should count your blessings,' she said aloud. 'Would you really like your old life back?'

By the afternoon it had finally stopped raining and the sun was trying to get out from behind the clouds. Beth put on a cardigan and went out into the garden. She hadn't been out there for over a week because of the heavy rain, and to her surprise it looked very pretty. The laburnum tree was heavy with its tassels of yellow blossom, there were forget-me-nots, and daisies she hadn't planted, plus clumps of green leaves thrusting out of the soil. She had no real idea what they were but they were healthy and strong.

Her spirits were suddenly lifted. It seemed like a message that the miserable times were over, and there were good things in store for her.

She went back into the cottage to get her raincoat, thinking she would go on a bike ride, something she hadn't done for weeks.

It was exhilarating to cycle fast and feel the wind in her hair. She stayed on the coast road, which in reality was more of a track. There were a great many puddles and many of them she rode through, lifting her feet the way children did and laughing at the joy it gave her.

All at once she noticed up ahead a man standing out in the middle of the lane. On seeing her he waved his arms to stop her. He was around thirty, with dark unkempt hair. He wore working men's clothes and a red bandana tied around his neck. Reason told her to ride on, but then a murderer or robber was hardly likely to lie in wait for his next victim on such an isolated road.

'Help me!' he called out as she got within hearing distance. His Irish accent was very strong. 'My father has had a fall, and I can't get him up on my own. I can't leave him either to call a doctor. He has no phone.'

She could understand why he couldn't summon help elsewhere, this was the first house she'd passed for at least two miles. 'I'm sorry to hear that. Should I ride on and get help?' she asked. 'I mean, if you can't lift him I doubt I'll be much help.'

'Maybe that's so. But he's outside, half in a puddle, he'll catch a death of cold if I leave him there. Will you just try?'

Despite the man's rough appearance he had a nice face, with speedwell-blue eyes and very white teeth.

'OK, I'll give it a go,' she said, getting off her bicycle. 'Lead on.'

It appeared to be a small farm, set back from the road, with a courtyard in front where chickens were pecking. She saw a couple of black and white cows beyond a hedge, and in the courtyard a donkey was looking out from a stable door.

The old man was lying on his back by an outhouse, in a deep puddle.

'How did you get here?' she asked the younger man, seeing no vehicle.

'I walked. It was grand with the rain stopped, an' all. I live about five miles that way.' He pointed towards Cork.

She thought it rude to ask more questions when the elderly man was possibly badly hurt.

'I'll take his shoulders, if you could get his feet,' he said. 'Sorry, it means you'll get yours wet.'

'That's OK. Wet feet are nothing to worry about,' she said, and let him grab his father under his arms, while she waited to be told when to grab the feet. 'Which way are we going, back or to the side?'

'To the side. Make sure you are steady on your feet before we try to lift him. I don't want you falling in too.'

The old man appeared to be unconscious, but as his son lifted him, he shrieked in pain. 'It's all right, Pop, I'll soon have you out,' he said comfortingly and signalled for Beth to take his ankles.

The old man was wearing boots and it was hard for her to get her hands around his ankles, but she grabbed him a bit further up his legs and lifted. He was a dead weight, and it was clear the water in the puddle or mud at the bottom was sucking him down. But on the count of three they lifted and took sideways steps.

'Nearly there, Pop,' the man called out over his father's desperate cries.

They laid him down on a dry part of the courtyard. His face was chalky white, and it made her remember the night the doctor had rescued her from the ditch.

'Shall I ride to call an ambulance, while you get some blankets to cover him? He's very cold, he must've been lying there for ages,' Beth said.

'I'll go, if I can borrow your bike,' he said. 'I know people across the field with a phone. You won't be able to find their place.'

He was on her bike and away before she'd even had time to agree, or to ask if it was OK to go into the cottage. She looked at him speeding up the road and in that second she felt he might not be the son, but a thief, and now he had the only means of transport to get away, leaving her with an injured old man.

That might well be the case, but for now she had to get the old chap warm.

'Can you hear me?' she asked, kneeling beside him. His eyes were open but staring vacantly. 'Your son has gone to call an ambulance, but can I go in your home and find some blankets?'

'Who are you?' he asked, his tone sharp and eyes wary.

'Beth Manning. I live in Dunmore. Your son flagged me down to help him. What's your name and where does it hurt?'

'I hit my head.'

She lifted his head a little, enough to see a great deal

of blood on his woolly hat. She wasn't going to take his hat off, she'd leave that for a professional. As she got up to go and get some blankets she looked over by the puddle he'd fallen into. There was some blood on the concrete but nothing like a sharp stone that might have caused such a bad wound if he tripped and fell on it. She scooted into his cottage, and immediately felt further panic to see the state of it. It was hard to tell if the living room was always an untidy mess, or if someone had ransacked it. On the couch was a blanket which looked like a dog's bed. She picked it up and then went up the stairs to look for more.

There were two bedrooms, the main one also looking as if someone had searched it. She took a blanket from the bed, and then it struck her that there was no dog. Had there been one it would've barked. That was odd. Farmers always had dogs, and the first blanket she'd picked up smelled of one. Her stomach churned, wondering where he was.

Once downstairs again she wrapped the old man up with the blankets. 'Sorry, this one is a dog blanket and a bit smelly,' she said as she tucked it round him. 'What breed is he?'

'Prince!' he exclaimed. 'Where is he?'

'He's probably asleep somewhere,' she said soothingly. 'Once the ambulance gets here I'll go and find him.'

'He wouldn't leave me here,' he said, and his voice cracked with emotion.

She felt she knew then what had happened. Someone, either the man she saw or another, had come to rob the old man and hit him when interrupted. Maybe the dog tried to defend him and the thief killed the dog.

If this was the work of the man she spoke to, she could identify him, but setting that aside, she needed to get help for the old man now. She knew she hadn't passed any houses or telephone boxes, so that only left going further up the road to see what was there.

She knelt down beside the old man. 'I need to get help for you,' she said. 'I can't leave you out here, it will be dark soon. So who is your nearest neighbour?'

He looked fearful now. She didn't know if this was because he was picking up on her anxiety, thinking about his dog, or asking himself who the young man was.

'Was that young man who helped me get you out of the puddle your son?' she asked.

'Both my sons went away,' he said, his faded blue eyes filling with tears. 'They don't write anymore.'

'I've got to get help for you,' she said. 'Can you hold on? I'll be as quick as possible.'

Beth sped off, running as fast as she could up the lane in the direction of Cork. She willed someone to drive this way to flag down, but people just weren't driving now due to petrol rationing. She hadn't run for a very long time, and she was soon out of breath and had a stitch. But she kept on; she had to find help for the old man.

Finally she saw a cottage, smoke coming out of the chimney, and she prayed silently that they had a phone. Or at least that they knew where the nearest phone box was.

She charged up to the front door and hammered on it.

'All right, all right, I'm coming,' a woman called out, and the bolts were drawn back.

'The old man,' Beth managed to get out, holding her side and pointing back down the track. 'He's hurt.'

'Get your breath,' the woman said, 'then tell me calmly.'

Her Irish accent was barely noticeable. She was possibly in her forties, with a plump pink face and well dressed in a twin set and tweed skirt. Just a glance at the polished wood floor in the hallway gave Beth hope for a telephone.

'Do you have a telephone? The old man has a bad wound on his head and he's lying on the ground. He needs medical help.'

The woman nodded. 'Are you talking about Able Connor? His farm is the next place down.'

'I don't know his name,' Beth blurted out, then told her about being flagged down, helping to get the old man out of the water, and the young man riding off on her bike.

'Oh my goodness,' the older woman gasped. 'I will telephone the police and ambulance now. Go into my kitchen and get a drink of water. You look like you need it.' She pointed down the hall.

Two gardai arrived within five minutes, and took Beth back to old Mr Connor's farm. On the way she told them about the young man. The ambulance turned up soon after and the men lifted Able on a stretcher into it, after first taking his pulse and listening to his heart. They drove away with him immediately.

'His dog,' Beth said to the two policemen. 'Do you think he killed it?'

'We'll look, Miss,' one said. 'And check his home. You sit in the car for now, we'll take you home then and you can make your statement there.'

It was when the younger of the two policemen came back into the farmyard after going round the back, and she saw his shocked expression, that Beth began to cry. She knew he'd found the dog dead, and that brought all the recent events to a head and shock set in.

'He's beaten old Prince over the head with a shovel,' the man reported to his companion. 'I think if this young lady hadn't turned up he might have killed old Able too.'

Beth wasn't so sure of that, or why did he stop her? Was it just to get her bicycle or did he really want her help to get Able out of the puddle? And how did he know she was coming down the road? He surely couldn't have heard her. Or was that just chance and he was looking to see if it was all clear?

'Don't cry,' the older garda said, reaching into the car to pat her shoulder. 'You've had a nasty shock. Stay in the car to keep warm, and we'll take you home when we've finished here.'

Two hours later, the gardai gone and the light gradually fading, Beth sank back on her sofa feeling completely drained. They would establish if Able had any relatives and contact them. Meanwhile a friend of his was going into the house tomorrow to check if anything had been taken. Beth knew the young man left empty-handed, but of course he could've filled a bag with stuff before she got there and hid it in a hedge to retrieve later.

The Garda claimed he was probably a tinker. He may even have had a horse tethered further up the road, so they would be keeping an eye on that lane, and looking for her bicycle in case he dumped it.

It was very unsettling, and unless she got the bicycle back she'd be trapped in Dunmore.

Perhaps it would be good to go somewhere else for a short break. Maybe on the train to Dublin?

14

Three days after the robbery and assault at Able's farm, the poor old man died. At eighty-two, left lying in a puddle in fear of his life, and then hearing that his attacker had killed his dog and ransacked his house, once in hospital Able just gave up. According to Kathleen, everyone was gossiping about it and she warned Beth she should expect people to waylay her to talk about her part in the tragedy.

The Garda were calling it manslaughter and had stepped up their efforts to find his assailant. They found Beth's bike some five miles from the crime scene, but they couldn't return it to her yet as it was evidence. They also found Able's medals from the Great War under a hedge close to the farm. They thought the case must have fallen out of a bag of stolen items hidden there.

Sean Connor, Able's eldest son, came over from England. Kathleen said he was 'mad with grief'. Beth privately wondered, if he thought so much of his father, why he hadn't come to see him more often. Apparently, the last time he came was in 1931 when his mother died. But she didn't air her opinion, and she bypassed all questions about her role in the crime and made no comments, hoping it would make her neighbours lose interest in her more quickly.

However, she felt she had to go to Able's funeral or risk offending the locals.

It was a very cold, wet day and the church stank of wet, slightly mouldy wool overcoats. The Mass seemed interminable. Afterwards, at the wake in the pub, she overheard several people asking Sean what he was going to do about the farm. He said airily that he had already sold the cows and donkey, but he was hoping someone would take the chickens, and when asked if he wouldn't like to run the farm, he treated that as a joke and said he had had enough of it as a young man.

Beth thought that Able's lifetime of hard work and caring for his family was what should be at least acknowledged, if not praised, yet his son appeared only concerned with money.

Rory, the younger brother, hadn't bothered to come, and as the local men were swigging back pints as if the pub was about to run out of beer, and their women were gossiping in loud voices, which to Beth seemed irreverent, she slunk away after only twenty minutes.

The following morning, Dr McMara called on Beth. She had occasionally seen him in his gig around Dunmore, usually from a distance. He'd stopped to pass the time of day with her several times, which was always a little embarrassing, a reminder of the silly crush she'd had on him.

'I just wanted to ask how you are,' he said, smiling broadly, his eyes twinkling as she remembered. 'Finding Able the way you did and meeting the man who did it must prey on your mind?'

She thought it was kind he could be bothered to call, and felt obliged to ask him in for a cup of tea. She just hoped he wouldn't take advantage again.

'I'm absolutely fine, Finn,' she said. 'It was distressing to find an old man in that situation, but I haven't been dwelling on it. I just hope they catch the man that did it. Do sit down, the kettle has just boiled.'

'He's probably miles away now,' the doctor said thoughtfully, following her into the kitchen and sitting down at the table. 'As you've probably heard, the Guards are not great detectives. Too complacent in their comfortable jobs to put themselves out.'

Beth thought that was a bit harsh but she wasn't going to argue. 'I just wish they'd give me my bicycle back. I feel marooned without it,' she said as she warmed the teapot and lit the gas under the kettle to bring it back to the boil.

McMara took a pad out of his pocket and wrote a name and address on it. 'Go into Waterford and see Steven Malley, he'll sell you one, and to be sure he'll buy the other one off you when you get it back. He's a good man, he has new ones and second-hand.'

'That's kind of you to help,' she said, putting the note on the table and getting out some teacups.

'So, Beth,' he said, after admiring the new curtains she'd made for the kitchen, 'a little bird told me you have a soldier boyfriend.'

Beth poured the tea. The little bird could only be Kathleen and it reminded her to be careful what she told her in future.

'He's in North Africa now,' she said warily, putting the milk and sugar on the table for him to help himself, and some biscuits she'd made. 'He's nice but I don't know him very well. We write, but that's no substitute for seeing him regularly.'

'I bet he's dreaming about you every night,' Finn laughed lightly.

'I hope so,' she said, and changed the subject to war damage, and wondering how people in England would fare with the cost of repairs.

'The poor devils in the East End of London,' he said. 'Whole streets gone, and all their belongings. But from what I hear they are all being very stoic about it and helping one another.'

Beth almost launched into her own experience of how grim some of those streets were, and maybe them being bombed was a good thing. But she stopped herself just in time and said how touched she was that people in the more affluent areas of England were donating clothes and household items.

They stayed on that theme for some minutes, then Beth got up. 'I'm sorry to chase you out, Finn, but I'm in the middle of writing to some friends back home. I must get on with it to catch the post. But it was good to have a chat.'

His eyes twinkled. 'There's me thinking you might invite me for lunch,' he joked. 'But now you've got a sweetheart you don't have eyes for this old man!'

She laughed. 'It was good to see you, and thank you for the address to get a new bicycle.' She held out the plate of biscuits she'd made. 'Take a couple to eat on your round.'

Unsettled a little by Finn's visit, Beth decided she would take the bull by the horns and walk into Waterford immediately to see Steven Malley. For once it wasn't raining and it felt warm in the sunshine.

She was nearly into Waterford when she noticed a few tinkers camped in a field. She paused by the gate to admire the five beautifully painted caravans, and smiled to see two little girls singing as they groomed a donkey, who appeared to love their attentions.

There was a group of four men further back in the field, who looked as if they were mending or erecting a fence, and a couple of women sitting by an open fire. Concerned that the adults would feel she was spying on them, she moved on.

Two hours later, Beth was joyfully riding her new bicycle home. It was dark green, had a far more comfortable saddle than the old one, and Steven Malley had adjusted the height for her perfectly. She had intended to buy a second-hand one, but all Steven had were men's bikes with a crossbar. He told her that his business was built on repair, and he normally only got a few new bikes in to order, mainly children's ones, but when war was threatened and he'd heard petrol would be hard to get, he'd taken a chance and ordered a couple.

He wanted six pounds for it. She had no idea if that was cheap or expensive. However, it was worth it to be able to get around, and as Steven had thrown in a bell, a padlock and a basket on the handle bars to put shopping in, she was delighted with her purchase.

As she approached her cottage, she heard horse's hoofs behind her. Looking back, she saw the rider was a man but he was already turning the horse as if realizing he'd come the wrong way.

Soon after she got in, the wind got up and the sky looked threatening, so she lit the fire in readiness for a storm. The rain came along with the dark: gentle at first, gradually getting heavier, until it was a deluge. The first flash of lightning was startling, then the clap of thunder made her almost jump out of her skin. Further lightning lit up a small fishing boat coming towards the harbour.

She went up to the bedroom to get a better look, and during the many lightning flashes the boat was clearly illuminated as it was buffeted by big waves. Finally to her relief she saw it had managed to navigate into the harbour, and saw a dark figure, presumably the harbour master or another fisherman, running along with a long boat hook to help secure the vessel.

Satisfied the boat was now safe, Beth went back downstairs, drew the curtains and put the radio on to drown out the noise of wind and rain while she cooked her supper.

The storm went on and on, and finally at half-past nine Beth decided to go to bed with a hot water bottle. She lay there listening to the storm, thinking about what she'd discussed with Finn. Knowing that most people in the East End lived a hand-to-mouth existence, she couldn't really imagine how they could pay for a roof being torn off or all their windows broken.

She woke with a start to find she was still hugging the now cold hot water bottle. Then she heard a creak which sounded like someone on the stairs. She strained her ears to listen, and another creak came, this time one she recognized as near the top.

A cold chill ran through her. She reached out for the bedside lamp, but it didn't work and she thought the power must have been cut off in the storm.

'Who's that?' she called out, throwing back the covers and leaping to grab a heavy brass giraffe on the chest of drawers. Kathleen had suggested she give it to the next jumble sale as it was a pain to clean, but Beth had joked it would make a good weapon as the neck fitted neatly into her hand. Waving it might frighten a burglar enough to flee.

As she lifted it in readiness, the bedroom door opened and, although it was dark, she could see a faint silhouette of a slim man, taller than her. He smelled of something vaguely familiar.

'What do you want?' she asked.

He didn't answer but stepped closer and the smell grew stronger.

She didn't see him raise his arm, or the weapon in his hand, not until he lifted it right above his head.

Beth ran at him, the giraffe firmly in her hand, and got the first blow to his chest before his cudgel came down on her. His blow missed her head but landed on her shoulder, making her reel back. It hurt, but the pain emboldened her.

'Right, you bastard!' she yelled at the top of her lungs. 'Get out now before I do you a permanent injury.' With that she leapt forward and hit him again and again with the giraffe, still screaming loudly in the hopes that a neighbour would hear and come.

'All right, I'm going,' he said, backing out of the door. 'You're mad, mad!'

He reached the top of the stairs and she ran at him again, arms outstretched to push him down the stairs. He fell backwards, his head thumping on each stair.

A banging on the front door alerted her that someone else was there. In a confused state she thought it was his partner-in-crime and screamed even louder.

With that she heard the front door being booted in.

'It's me, Miss Manning,' a voice called out and she recognized it as Mr Sayers from next door. He was a small, wiry man, who she'd heard had once been a fly-weight boxer. 'Are you hurt?'

'No . . . yes!' she shouted back, realizing the blow to her shoulder had broken the skin and she was bleeding. She made her way down the stairs and gingerly past the intruder. 'But I'm fine, really. Is he alive? I think there's been a power cut.'

'Mine is all right next door,' Sayers said and he peered at the fuse-board by the door. 'Ah,' he exclaimed. 'He turned it off.' Flicking a switch, light flooded the hallway and he saw the man at the foot of the stairs.

He made a low whistle. 'It's a tinker, to be sure, I saw him ride his horse up the lane this afternoon.'

'I saw that man too,' Beth admitted. 'Do you think he was checking out places to rob?'

Sayers went over to the injured man and felt his pulse. 'I think that's very likely. He's alive but unconscious. Could he be the man you saw at Able's farm?'

Beth went over to check. His face was dirty and with his eyes closed she couldn't be absolutely sure. But intuition suggested he'd been at the tinkers' camp where she stopped on the way to Waterford. Maybe he'd seen her ride back later and followed her to find out where she lived? Even if it wasn't the man who attacked Able, it could be a brother. As the only witness to the crime, perhaps he felt she should be frightened into silence.

A shiver ran down her spine. 'I don't know. Possibly. But we must get an ambulance for him and call the Garda.'

'I can't go and leave you alone with him,' Sayers said. 'He might come round.'

'Then I'll go,' she said. 'There's a phone box down at the harbour.'

'But you are hurt too! And in your nightclothes.'

Beth hadn't really thought about what she was wearing or her own injuries. But she glanced at her shoulder and saw the bloodstain, and was embarrassed to be in her nightdress, aware her shoulder really hurt, and that she was cold. She went over to a hook by the door, took down her raincoat and put it on. She picked up the brass giraffe again and brandished it. 'You go to the telephone. If he comes round I'll whack him with this.'

Sayers chuckled. 'You're a plucky one, Miss Manning, and no mistake. I'll be just two ticks, and be back to stay with you till help comes.'

Beth felt dizzy as soon as her neighbour had gone. She pulled a chair out from the kitchen to sit on, and put a towel on her shoulder under her raincoat to staunch the blood, but the effort of doing that made her feel quite faint.

Looking down at the tinker, she hoped he wouldn't wake up as she wasn't sure she had the strength to hit him again. Despite the dirt on his face he was a good-looking man, with shiny black curly hair, and a fine straight nose. Now, with good lighting, she could see the red patterned bandana round his neck, like the one Able's attacker wore. The day she met him she thought it gave him a rakish charm, as did his long coat and worn, muddy riding boots.

But more telling was the smell coming from him. It was peat from a fire, and the young man at the farm smelled of it too. It was a smell which often wafted out of cottages as she passed, and she didn't like it.

She reached out and touched his coat. It was soaked right through from the rain, and she wondered if he'd walked here, or whether a horse was tethered somewhere nearby. What was he intending to do to her? Rob her obviously, but maybe to terrify her into silence about Able, or even kill her?

His eyes flickered and she stiffened in fear, clutching the brass giraffe more firmly.

'Yes, it's me,' she snapped out firmly, 'and I'll whack you again if you move. My neighbour has gone for the Garda.'

His eyes opened fully and they were as brilliantly blue as she remembered.

'I didn't come to hurt you,' he said, his voice a little croaky. 'I saw you looking at the camp and just wanted to ask you not to tell the Garda where I was.'

'No one creeps into a house at night, turns off the electricity and comes upstairs in the dark unless he wants to hurt or rob. Do you think I'm a fool?' she spat out with anger. 'As it happens, I didn't even see you at the camp. I was admiring the lovely caravans. But now you are hurt and you're in even more trouble.'

'I've been an eejit, but you could say I wasn't the man at the farm? I just came in to rob you?'

Beth shook her head in disbelief that he imagined that was a good plan. But then he was so handsome he probably had women doing whatever he asked.

'The farmer died because of you,' she said.

'I didn't hit him, he fell and banged his head on a stone.'

'And did his dog die the same way?' she said angrily.

'I had to feckin' hit the dog. He was going to bite me.'

He was gradually raising himself to a sitting position, keeping his bright eyes directly on her, and Beth grew dizzy again and felt unable to cope.

'Let me go,' he said, his voice soft and melodious. 'Turning me in could be the worst thing for you.'

'Why?' she asked.

'Well, you must be running from something to come here.'

A shiver ran down her spine. Did he know something, or was it just a wild prod to gain her reaction?

'I inherited this cottage, I certainly wasn't running from something,' she said, more defiantly than she felt.

'Oh yes, I heard that, but a young woman coming here alone when there's a war going on in England? That's odd. And suspicious! The Garda will question you, even if only because they think you might be a spy.'

His words scared her, and he was looking at her as if he knew that.

'I've got three paistí under five and another on the way,' he went on. 'How will my wife manage without me if they lock me up?'

For some odd reason it was the use of the Irish word for children that affected her. She knew the struggle her own mother had been through with only one child. She couldn't reply for a minute or two.

'Let me go,' he pleaded, clearly realizing by her silence she was unsure. 'I can slip out the back and over the fields, and you can say I went when you fainted. I hurt your shoulder, didn't I?'

'But you'll have concussion,' she said weakly. 'You might collapse out in the fields.'

'Your concern is touching,' he said and got to his feet. 'Us tinkers don't often get that.' He reached down and pulled a knife from his boot and pointed it at her. 'Let me go without any fuss, or I'll have to use this.'

Part of her wanted to stand up to him and whack

him again so he couldn't get away. Yet she wavered, perhaps because gypsies, or tinkers as they were called here, were blamed for so much. She dropped the brass giraffe to the floor, knowing she hadn't the strength or the will to fight him. 'Go then, but bring your little ones up to be honest.'

He slid the knife back into his boot, and moved forward to drop a kiss on her forehead, and then he was gone quickly and quietly out through the kitchen, leaving just the faint aroma of peat and a small pool of blood on the hall floor.

Her head was swimming, she couldn't seem to focus her eyes, and the next thing she knew Sayers burst in, panting like he'd run for miles.

'Sorry I was so long,' he wheezed. Then, stopping short, he looked to the bottom of the stairs. 'Where is he?'

'I passed out I think,' she said in little more than a whisper. 'He must have gone.'

Sayers scratched his head. 'I couldn't raise the Garda or an ambulance, and went to the pub, told them what had happened. They said they'd ring from there, but they advised me to let him go. Tinkers are more trouble than they're worth. But you need your shoulder seeing to. Come into the kitchen where the light is better and I'll take a look. When I was boxing I often patched people up.'

*

An hour later Beth was back in bed in a clean nightdress and with a fresh hot water bottle. Mr Sayers had been as good as a doctor. He dropped the top of her nightdress down over her arm, cleaned the wound and dressed it. He said it was only superficial, but she would have a big bruise in a few hours. After securing the front door with the bolts inside, he went out by the back door and round the side to get to his own home. He said he'd be back in the morning to mend the front door, and would phone the Garda and report what had happened.

As Beth lay in bed listening to the rain outside, she thought back to what she'd done. Strangely she felt no real guilt – maybe it was his kiss on the forehead that banished it. He was right, she would've faced many questions if Able's case went to court and she was called as a witness, which would bring journalists. They might dig around in her past, and she didn't want to risk that. True, the man should've been punished, but what about his young family? She couldn't imagine anyone here helping them.

But one thing was absolutely certain, she must get out of here for a while.

15

August 1943

After the drama at the farm and then the break-in, Beth felt she needed to get away, but it was several more weeks before she decided where to go. Now, as she stepped down from the train in Bristol, she was very relieved that the long journey was over. It was two in the afternoon and a glorious sunny day, which was very welcome after the incessant rain in Ireland. She had considered Dublin or Galway, but decided that England was a better plan – after all, it would appear natural to people for her to go home. After studying the map, she picked Bristol because it had good train links both from the Irish ferry and to London, and also to Cornwall for when Jack returned. She had been told it was a lovely city, surrounded by open countryside and close to the sea. But to Beth the real attraction was that she was unlikely to run into anyone she knew.

Whilst she was aware the city had received more than its fair share of bombing in 1941, with many dead and a great many homes and ancient, beautiful buildings destroyed, from what she'd read it seemed the Luftwaffe were now focusing more on places with dockyards or shipbuilding, like Southampton, Cardiff and Newcastle. Margery had stayed with her husband in a small guest house in Bristol called Down House just before the war started. She said it was comparable to No. 18 for amenities, and in Clifton, the most desirable part of the city. Now all Beth was concerned with was getting to the guest house and resting after the long and tiring journey.

The break-in at Clancy's Cottage seemed a long while ago now, but according to Kathleen, who appeared to have a direct message service from God – or at least from the Garda – the tinker had not been found. The camp Beth had seen near Waterford vanished like smoke, and Kathleen said she doubted the Garda would make much effort to find them.

In fact, Sergeant Michael Flannery who had come to interview Beth after the break-in had all but dismissed the case. After all, nothing had been stolen, and apart from the cut on her shoulder, the only real damage was to the front door, and that was caused by her neighbour. Beth was relieved; she'd been expecting to be interrogated. But she found it very odd that they were not pursuing the attack on Able. His son had gone back to England, leaving the farm in the hands of an agent.

It was Mr Boyle who finally made her mind up to go

away. He came to see her just two weeks ago, saying he'd been contacted by an old friend who was looking for somewhere for himself and his young family to rent for three weeks in August. 'I told him that you were the only person I knew who had a home with the kind of comforts he'd expect,' Mr Boyle said hesitantly, as if expecting her to be offended he'd even asked such a thing. 'I ran it past Kathleen, and she said you had been speaking of going back to England for a holiday and to see friends.'

'I have been,' Beth agreed, and her spirits lifted at finally being encouraged to go.

'Kathleen would be happy to clean for them. Do the laundry and such like. They could pay you ten pounds a week, in advance. They would pay Kathleen directly too.'

Beth said she'd mull it over, just so she didn't look suspiciously eager. But the house would be safe with someone in it, and the money made it a sensible plan.

She had already written to Jack telling him about the attack and saying she wanted to go away somewhere. Just a few days ago she'd had a reply in which he sounded alarmed that someone had broken into her cottage. He said she should go to his mother's in Falmouth. But by the time his letter came, she'd already decided on Bristol, booked a room at the place Margery had recommended, and agreed to let the cottage. She wrote to him and said maybe while she was in Bristol she could go down to Falmouth to meet his mother. She suggested he wrote back care of Margery at No. 18 and she'd send him her new address as soon as she was settled.

She hadn't packed much, as most of her clothes were too warm for summer. She was looking forward to shopping for a couple of dresses and sandals. Right now she was sweltering with her raincoat over a wool dress. It would be so good to sit in a park and sunbathe.

Margery was right. Down House, in St Paul's Road, was as charming as her own guest house. The owner, Mrs Levy, a tall, slender brunette with olive skin who immediately suggested Beth call her Rachel, was very welcoming. She took her up to see a room at the back of the house on the first floor, and said she was happy to provide an evening meal, along with breakfast.

'We've been lucky so far in the bombing,' she said. 'Several bombs have landed near here but, touch wood, we haven't been affected. However, in the unlikely event of getting an air-raid warning, there is an Anderson shelter in the garden. I got someone to clean it out the other day. But make sure you take something warm to wear if the worst happens.'

Rachel asked her why she'd come to Bristol. Beth explained that she wanted a change of scene, and she'd rented her home out for a few weeks. 'I've got a boyfriend in the army, in North Africa. Ireland is too far to go when he's on leave, but Bristol is convenient whether he arrives back in London or one of the ports on the south coast.'

Rachel commiserated, but said she could probably find him a room for a couple of nights if he ever needed one. 'These are difficult times for everyone,' she said with a sigh. 'People losing their homes, loved ones overseas, rationing and the fear of bombs. We should all do our best to make things a little better for people.'

Beth settled into Down House very quickly. It was good to be in walking distance of shops, and the wide open spaces of the Downs. Just a day or two into her stay she found herself thinking she could live happily in the leafy city for ever. She had quickly sent a letter to Jack telling him where she was, and alerted Margery he might write to her or telephone there. But she knew how long mail took to get to and from England, so she tried not to get excited.

She bought a couple of summer dresses and some sandals, and as the weather was so nice, she spent most days on Brandon Hill, a lovely small park which overlooked the whole of Bristol, just a short distance from the guest house. Rachel had a good selection of books which she was happy to lend, and lying in the sun reading was Beth's idea of heaven.

Clifton, Beth learned, was built for the wealthy

merchants at the time that Bristol Docks were second only to London for trade in innumerable goods, from glass, sherry, cotton and sugar, to shot for guns, and of course shipping. But the merchants and other wealthy people involved with these companies didn't want to set up home down near the docks because of the foul smells, nor anywhere near the Horse Fair in the centre of town, where the worst slums were. So the greatest architects and builders of the day were hired to build a town on the hill looking down onto the River Avon. The elegant terraces rivalled those in neighbouring Bath, and the wealthy flocked to buy them.

Beth had learned all this from the museum, which had been bombed, but the valuable exhibits had been taken out of harm's way before the Blitz began, as they had in other big cities. Now part of the museum had reopened with many photographs and drawings of old Bristol, and she enjoyed reading about this splendid city which had so much fascinating history.

She did get the local paper to check on situations vacant, but there was nothing that inspired her, just domestic work either in private homes or hotels. But she was in no hurry, feeling that something would present itself in due course.

On Beth's fourth day, she was just coming out of the museum, when a slight, elderly lady in front of her tripped on the steps and fell. Beth rushed to help her.

'I'm not hurt, just winded,' the lady said, her voice

posh but soft. 'But if you'd be so good as to help me to my feet.'

'I think I should call an ambulance,' said Beth. 'Especially as you banged your head.'

'My dear, I appreciate your concern, but the last thing I want is a trip to the hospital, so please just help me up.'

The command in her voice was such that Beth felt she had no choice but to put her hands under the lady's arms and lift her to a standing position.

'That's the ticket,' she said with a chuckle as she leant into Beth. 'The only thing damaged is my pride. But bless you for coming to my aid.'

Beth thought the lady had the sweetest face, with pale blue eyes and rosy cheeks, but she also thought she might be a bit dazed. 'Well, I'm at least going to take you somewhere for a cup of tea,' she said firmly and pointed across the road. 'Over there in the Berkeley Tearooms.'

Beth had found this place the previous day and was told they held tea dances a couple of times a week which were popular with servicemen home on leave. She had liked the atmosphere, the marble floor and a rather splendid domed ceiling. She had already earmarked it to take Jack to when he got leave.

'I'm Beth Manning,' she said as she tucked the old lady's arm into hers to cross the road. 'And your name?'

'Rose Cullen,' she said and smiled up at Beth. 'Beth always makes me think of the book *Little Women*.'

'I'm not as virtuous as she was.'

'Well, anyone who takes me off for a cup of tea is virtuous in my eyes.'

Beth felt an odd flash of déjà vu; she knew she hadn't met Rose before, but the sweetness of her face and kindness in her eyes were a reminder of Auntie Ruth. She wanted to know all about this lady.

Once seated in the Berkeley, a pot of tea and tea cakes in front of them, Rose told Beth that she lived in a lane just off Pembroke Road, which Beth knew was close to Down House. Rose had been widowed for ten years, with one son, Myles, who lived in Canada. 'He begged me to join him there after Duncan died,' she said. 'But I love Clifton and my home, I have so many happy memories here, and I find Canadians rather dull. Oh, I know it's a vast, beautiful country and so many aspects of life there are better than ours, but really, do they have to be so smug about it?'

Beth giggled. She'd never met any Canadians so she couldn't judge if Rose's view was accurate, but she liked people who said what they thought.

'So what does Myles do for a living?'

'He's an orthopaedic surgeon. His wife, Shirley, is a theatre sister, but they don't have any children, too career minded. If they had I might have been keener to settle there.' She paused reflectively for a moment.

'I've been for a holiday with them three times, but I find their way of life exhausts me,' she said, and smiled as if reliving it. 'Off to dinners, parties and meetings for this and that all the time. I went along with them to many of these do's, all dressed up in my finest, but though people were kind and welcoming, it wasn't for me.'

'Do they come to visit you?'

'Well, they did come every year in the spring until war broke out. They'd whizz round to see all Myles's old friends, and a couple of Shirley's relatives, so I didn't have them under my feet all the time. But I always felt a sense of relief when they left. At my age you need peace, not gallivanting around. That sounds as if I don't love Myles, I do of course, but we've grown apart. His world is alien to me. I don't mean the medical side of it, his father was a doctor too, but the big cars and houses, the striving to achieve more and more. I always hoped he'd work here, where I could watch his progress with his patients, and though I'm very proud of him, it feels as if he isn't my boy any longer.'

Beth put her hand over Rose's. She sensed that this old lady felt it was her fault he moved away. 'You've been the best kind of mother,' she said. 'You've allowed him to follow his dream, never holding him back. I bet he loves you a great deal for that.'

Rose looked thoughtful. 'Yes, I believe he does, but

I think he'd like me better if I was to agree to live in Canada.'

Beth laughed at that. She found Rose so refreshing. She had to be in her seventies, yet she was still pretty and well-dressed, alert and articulate.

They continued to talk, and Beth explained how she came to be living in Ireland.

'I do like Ireland and the people,' she said. 'But I'm lonely. The days seem endless, mostly, and it's virtually impossible to find work. If the cottage was in Dublin it might be better, that's why when I was asked if I'd let the cottage out, I jumped at it. I picked Bristol rather than London to come to as I thought I was bound to be able to find a job here, and it's easy to get to other towns.'

She went on to tell Rose about Jack, pointing out that she hadn't spent long enough to be certain he was the One. 'I'm not so silly that I'd leap into anything with him or any other man just so I'm not lonely,' she added.

'So you want a job, then? No parents to go to or other relatives?'

'Yes, I do want to find a job, and my parents are dead.'

'I'm sorry about that, Beth. You are too young to be alone in the world.' She reached out and patted Beth's cheek affectionately. 'You'll have no trouble finding work here; you are very well-presented. That striped dress is a real classic and your dark hair is so shiny. Plus you have a lovely manner, not too bold but not a mouse either. What sort of experience have you had?'

Beth almost told her practised story about running a dress shop. But something stopped her. Whether that was because she felt Rose was worldly enough to sense a lie, or that Beth couldn't bear to lie to her, she didn't know.

'I've mainly done domestic work,' she said. 'In my last position I was running the house single-handedly for the last two years as the other staff all left for war work. When I heard my godmother had left me her cottage I thought I'd plunge in and see what Ireland had to offer.'

'What did you find?'

Beth smiled at the question. 'There's awful poverty for most, but the people are so warm and engaging. It's sad they've been kept under the iron grip of the Church and the government. Historically the English treated them appallingly, too. But it is a beautiful place. The view from my cottage of the harbour is such that I could sit and stare out of the window all day. If I had found a job, or even someone to share the cottage, I doubt I'd have even thought of coming back to England.'

'So will you be looking for domestic work?'

'If I could find the right position, more housekeeper than general dogsbody. Plus decent live-in accommodation, not a draughty garret.'

Rose chuckled. 'Why don't you walk home with me? I've been intending to get some help for several months, but I've done nothing about it as I live in fear of one of those domineering types turning up on my doorstep, and browbeating me into submission.'

Beth gave a peal of laughter. 'I can't imagine anyone browbeating you.'

'Well, they might bore me into an early death,' Rose said, her eyes twinkling. 'So would you like to come and see my home? No strings attached. If you don't like the house or the job, I won't browbeat you. We can still be friends.'

Forty minutes later, after a leisurely stroll with Rose, stopping to window-shop en-route, they arrived at Lamb Lane. It was a mews to the big Georgian houses in Pembroke Road, originally designed to keep rich people's carriages, with the servants living above. Some of the properties would've been workshops for artisans.

Rose's house was perhaps the latter, as it had big double doors to the right of the front door, and it seemed to be nearly twice as wide as other properties in the street. It was also very smart, both the double doors and the front door painted a glossy dark green with shiny brass letterbox and knocker.

'Duncan might have been a doctor, but his hobby was carpentry. When we bought this place it was in a terrible state, but he had the dream of making what was once a stable into a carpentry workshop,' Rose said as she unlocked the front door. 'I used to tease him and say he only wanted the workshop to escape me.'

Beth had not been in that many people's houses, so really all she knew was Mrs Bradley's style, lots of good-quality family furniture, and patterned, fringed rugs over polished floors. She expected Rose's to be the same.

She followed Rose along a wide corridor with a thick pale-green carpet beneath their feet, into a large sitting room with French doors leading onto a courtyard garden.

Beth gasped in surprise. It wasn't a bit like the Bradleys', but sleek and modern, in a style she thought was called art deco, and which she'd only ever seen in magazines.

Rose laughed. 'You thought it would be old fuddy-duddy?' she said teasingly.

'No, just more traditional,' Beth said, wide-eyed at the sight of two large cream sofas, and cabinets and side tables made of pale wood and glass. 'This is kind of Hollywood.'

'We did have quite a few passed-down antiques, but a couple of years after Duncan died, I shipped them over to Myles. He loved them, and wanted reminders of his grandparents. Duncan and I had more modern tastes; he wanted to make stylish furniture. He made that cabinet,' she said, pointing to the honey-coloured one Beth had already noticed with stained-glass triangular shapes fitted into the doors.

Beth gasped. 'How clever of him, it's so beautiful.'

'It was a shame he didn't get the long retirement he planned, doing what he loved. That cabinet was the last one he made. Once I'd sent the old furniture to Myles, I bought other pieces similar to those Duncan would've liked. It made me feel he was still with me.'

Beth saw Rose's eyes had filled with tears and she moved to embrace her. 'I'm so sorry you lost him.'

Rose stayed for a moment or two, her face resting on Beth's shoulder. Then she looked up and tweaked Beth's cheek.

'He was very sick come the end, and he was glad to go. I hope your Jack does turn out to be the One and you are as happy as Donald and I were.'

Rose took Beth then to see the rest of the house. A door in the sitting room led to the kitchen, again light and bright, with big windows onto the garden, and a solid-looking table and chairs.

'We always ate here unless we had guests,' Rose said. 'The dining table and chairs in the sitting room have never been used since I bought them at Waring and Gillow's down the road.'

She opened a door. 'And this,' she said with a flourish of her hand, 'is Duncan's workshop.'

It was huge, with daylight coming through the windows in the big doors. It had a workbench along the party wall, and the internal wall had what looked like a custom-made storage unit, with cupboards and drawers beneath. Above, countless pegs held tools in groups, hammers, chisels, screwdrivers, clamps and the like, arranged by size.

'Goodness me, that's impressive,' Beth said. 'And so clean. No dust and not a cobweb in sight.'

'I enjoy looking after it,' Rose said. 'I talk to him in here, I can feel his presence.'

Beth felt something too. She sensed it was love, Duncan's love of his carpentry and Rose's love for him.

Rose opened a low cupboard to show her a huge collection of boxes. 'All screws, nails and stuff,' she said. 'I spent all one day sorting them into sizes, then labelling the boxes. Duncan always intended to do it but never got around to it. I see it as my memorial to him.'

She walked back to the door, flicking off the light and smiling as if to tell Beth she was moving on from sad reminiscing. 'Now, let me show you upstairs and the garret I'm hoping you might like.'

'I wondered where the stairs were,' Beth remarked as Rose opened a door she hadn't even noticed as they came down the hall. Behind the door was a small area, and stairs went up from there. Light shone down from a skylight.

'It wasn't like this when we bought it,' Rose said when they got to the top. 'The staircase was a death trap, right in the middle of the workshop.'

Rose's bedroom was at the back, with a bathroom next to it. At the front were two bedrooms looking out onto the lane, the smaller one used as a study, the far wall holding shelves and thousands of books.

Rose went to the second bedroom and opened the door. 'This could be your garret,' she said with a smile. 'What do you think?'

Beth took in the rose-strewn chintz eiderdown on the pretty brass bed, a washbasin, a desk and chair, and a luxurious pink carpet, and felt she'd found her dream home.

'It's lovely, perfect even,' she said. 'But we need to talk about my duties and I need a day or so to think about it and to speak to my solicitor in Ireland about the cottage. Would that be all right?'

'You take as long as you need, Beth,' she said. 'But I really hope you'll come.'

16

It was inevitable that Beth would willingly take Rose up on her offer of a job and home. Nothing had ever felt more right. She really liked Rose, her house was lovely, and Rose had impressed on her that it was an open-ended arrangement, so if she decided to go back to Ireland, or anywhere else for that matter, she could leave with no hard feelings.

But perhaps the main reason Beth wanted to work for Rose was because she felt the same way about her as she had for Ruth. Some things she felt were meant to be, and this was one of them.

Rachel gave Beth a warm hug as she was about to leave Down House to work for Rose Cullen. 'I wish you every happiness,' she said, her voice cracking with emotion. 'I've loved having you here. But I hope you'll pop in from time to time to tell me how things are with Mrs Cullen and with your young man. And don't forget, I can find room for him if he needs it when he gets some leave.'

Beth was surprised that such a reserved woman could show such affection. 'I'm going to miss you too, Rachel, I've loved staying here, and you've been so very kind,' Beth said, struggling not to cry.

All her life she'd wanted someone to say they liked her, cared about her, and believed in her, and it took two guest-house landladies to make her see she did have something in her worth loving.

As she walked away with her suitcase, it occurred to Beth that maybe Bristol was where she belonged.

The day before she had telephoned Mr Boyle in Waterford to tell him her new address and that she'd be caring for an elderly lady. She didn't want to say it was a real job. Something told her the less personal information she gave people in Ireland the better. But she asked if everything was well at Clancy's Cottage, and if Kathleen was still happy to look after it.

'All just grand here,' he replied. 'The Mackillicks have only been there a couple of days, but they are loving it there. Some of their friends are after wanting to come straight after they leave. That's three weeks, and someone else I know, a couple from Liverpool, they'd like two weeks while their roof is mended. It got damaged in an air raid.'

Beth couldn't help but smile at the good news; it made her feel less guilty about leaving the cottage. 'And Kathleen?'

Mr Boyle assured her that Kathleen loved looking after it, but said she missed her chats with Beth.

'Tell her I miss her too. Now, I want you to put up the rent a bit,' she said. 'You can keep the extra. I can't expect you to do it for nothing.' Rose had said she was sure the solicitor had already added his fee, as she'd never known a solicitor do any work for nothing, but Beth thought it needed to be clarified.

'To be sure, that's not necessary,' he said, but there was a smile in his voice. 'But I appreciate the thought.'

'I shall have to come back in October or early November to get my warmer clothes, and we should meet up then for a chat. In reality I can't see me coming back permanently for some time, and I wanted to ask your advice about selling the cottage.'

'Well, dearie me,' he said, sounding shocked. 'After Miranda left it to you?'

'I know, I feel bad about that, but obviously it hasn't worked out as I hoped, and I can't expect you and Kathleen to look after it for ever. I'm not talking about selling right now, I need your advice about that. But if I do decide to do it, would you handle the sale for me?'

'To be sure,' he said. 'But best to wait till the Emergency is over. Families will want holidays when their men come home, and when your young man returns, he might want to marry you and settle here?'

'That's a lovely thought,' she said, keeping her tone light. 'But none of us know what this war has in store for us. Like you said, wait till the Emergency is over. If the Germans invade England I might be on the first boat back to my cottage.'

*

Beth felt satisfied she'd left the solicitor with a clear idea of what she wanted, and was delighted he had other guests lined up. That left her free to be a good and reliable housekeeper for Rose.

She suspected Rose only wanted a companion, not a housekeeper; at their last meeting she'd talked about cooking, and it was clear she liked to do that herself. So that left laundry, cleaning and gardening for Beth to do.

Rose had insisted on paying Beth £3 a month, which seemed far too much considering she was living in. Mrs Bradley had paid her just £2 a month and she'd done everything there. But Rose would not budge on this; she said she believed in paying people properly.

A new job and home were exciting enough to chase any dark thoughts away, but she was worried about Jack. His letters were few and far between, and although he tried to be cheerful and amusing in them, she could sense underlying exhaustion, anxiety and fear. The newspapers were not as upbeat as they had been at the start of the war. Although the British had successfully landed in Sicily, progress was slow going.

She couldn't help wondering how servicemen would adjust to civilian life when the war ended. It was difficult to imagine how any man who had killed, or seen his companions die in battle, could possibly settle down with a wife and children and go back to an ordinary job. She did have a memory from early childhood of strange men in Whitechapel who shouted and sometimes hid in alleys or behind market stalls, crying like children. She remembered being told they had shell shock. She got the idea they'd been frightened by something in a shell, but couldn't imagine any shell being big enough to scare anyone. It was Ruth who explained the true meaning, and that it was unfair nothing was done for these poor men who had often fought bravely in the Great War.

She hoped and prayed Jack wouldn't come back like that.

Just a week after moving into Lamb Lane, she and Rose were having breakfast with the doors onto the garden wide open as it was already very warm at eight in the morning.

'I am enjoying having you here so much,' Rose said suddenly as she poured them both another cup of tea. 'I used to feel the days were so long before you came, but now the time flies by.'

Beth smiled. 'I found that in Ireland, and wished I had work to go to. But this isn't like a real job, more like having a little holiday with a lovely aunt,' she said.

She was speaking from the heart. Each day revealed something new about this remarkable, lovable woman, whether that was a walk to admire the Clifton Suspension Bridge or taking Beth to Christmas Steps, the ancient shopping street that had been there from before the 1600s. Rose said she had lived in fear the bridge might be destroyed by bombers using the River Avon to reach the city, and even more afraid for Christmas Steps, as so much of the old city had been destroyed in raids.

But even when they didn't go out, just an afternoon sitting in the little courtyard garden reading, knitting or sewing, or indeed doing some baking together in the kitchen, was so relaxed and pleasant.

The only thing Beth was struggling with was rationing. In Ireland she'd been able to get eggs, meat and a great many other things which she now found were scarce in England. This morning she'd made them porridge, and they'd just the last couple of spoonfuls of honey on it. The sugar had run out yesterday.

'My real work must start today,' Beth said with a broad smile. 'I've got to use some ingenuity and find some food for us. I thought if I managed to get some yeast we could make our own bread. Any ideas about where I could get it?'

'Ask at the baker's in Princess Street. I doubt they'll part with any fresh yeast, but they might have the dried stuff. I'm told it's quite good. Don't be afraid to tell them it's for me. I've been a good customer of theirs for years. And the butcher round the corner from them in the Mall – introduce yourself as my housekeeper and ask what he's got. It might only be scrag-end or liver, but agree to that and he'll slip you a couple of rashers and maybe some chops. Just don't speak about it, or everyone in the queue will want the same. He'll just tap his nose and put it on my account.'

'I'll feel like I'm a spy,' Beth laughed. 'When do I have to give him the coupons?'

'I'll come with you at the end of the month to settle up with cash and coupons. Vegetables should be fine, hopefully there might be runner beans and even some strawberries in the shops.'

Later that same morning, Beth walked home from Clifton Village to Lamb Lane with a full shopping basket, feeling rather pleased with herself. She'd got yeast, the dried variety, and had been told how to use it. She'd managed to get a pound of sugar, gooseberries, some runner beans, and a pot of honey, plus whatever was in the parcel from the butcher. She really liked the village. The shops, though not very well stocked because of shortages, were at least interesting. Clifton was an affluent area, and hadn't been heavily bombed the way other parts of Bristol and its suburbs had been.

But the well-dressed people strolling past her in the sunshine, looking relaxed and untroubled, were not representative of Bristol as a whole. Beth knew that the poor people both here and in the East End of London, in Liverpool, Birmingham and other cities, were struggling to survive. Many of them had seen their homes and all their belongings destroyed in the almost nightly bombing during the Blitz. Rose said many people were living in the woods around Bristol, not in a real tent even, but a makeshift shelter. In other towns they huddled into derelict houses. So many hundreds killed, even more wounded, and unlike the well-to-do here in Clifton, they wouldn't have any savings, no cushion against disaster. She knew from her own experience what hunger was like, to wear second-hand clothes and shoes with holes in them, to make friends with another child in the park, only to have their mother drag their child away from her, as if poverty was catching.

She had money now and good clothes thanks to Elizabeth Manning. Those things opened doors which would otherwise be closed. Yet she still felt she was on the outside looking in, always an imposter. Daily she wondered if that would ever change.

As Beth got closer to Lamb Lane, she shook herself out of those negative thoughts. She had fallen on her feet. Cooking, cleaning and laundry were pleasant to her. To stop for elevenses and decide what to have for lunch and what else needed doing was something she'd never experienced at the Bradleys.

During the afternoons, whether they went out or sat in the garden, Rose would talk about her late husband or her son as a boy. Sometimes she reminisced about her childhood with her two older sisters, living in the New Forest.

'But enough about me,' Rose said one afternoon. 'I want to know about you as a child.'

Beth had been expecting a question like that ever since she arrived here. She couldn't bring herself to make things up, not to this kind, open-hearted woman.

'I don't remember much,' she said. 'After the whack on the head in the bombing raid, my memory seems to have failed. The things I can remember are all a bit grey, like old photos. I remember Mum washing clothes with a scrubbing board, and getting me to wind the handle on the wringer. But not a lot more. We were poor 'cos my father was killed in the First War, so we didn't go anywhere.'

'Did you go to church?'

'I think so. Maybe Sunday School. I do have a vague memory of being in a church hall. Do you think memories will come back?'

She was aware Rose was looking at her intently. 'I do believe we suppress bad memories,' she said at length. 'Maybe one day you'll be able to share them with me.'

That sounded to Beth as if Rose didn't believe the bang-on-the-head story, and hoped that one day she'd reveal whatever she was hiding.

The weeks flew by. Beth loved everything about being here with Rose: the lovely house, the close proximity to shops and other amenities, and a feeling of safety, something she'd never experienced before. Even in Ireland she always had a feeling her security could end suddenly.

Whether she and Rose turned on the wireless to laugh at Tommy Handley, their evenings were always jolly. They made rag rugs, cutting old clothes and leftover fabric into strips and then forcing them with a hook through the canvas. They tried to make their offerings attractive by choosing toning fabrics. Unpicking jumpers to reuse the wool was another thing. It could be knitted into hats, scarves or even new jumpers. Sometimes they played cards or draughts, and when there was dance music on the wireless, Rose coached her on the quick step.

'You really need a man to practise with,' Rose said. 'Shall I go out in the street and find one for you?'

Beth laughed at the thought of some passer-by being stopped by an old lady to come into her house and dance. It was a lovely image, but of course Rose was only joking. She often made ridiculous statements with a poker face. Another one of her lovable traits.

One day, as Beth was about to cross at the Pembroke Road junction and was checking there wasn't a cart or cyclist coming, she spotted a familiar-looking man coming up St Paul's Road.

Her heart almost stopped, as she thought it was Ronnie, and a cold sweat broke out all over her. 'It can't be him,' she said to herself, and went behind a thick tree trunk to get a better look. She had last seen him when she was fourteen, fifteen years ago. Back then he had looked fit, muscular and straight-backed, and kept himself very neat, clean-shaven and wearing good clothes. But this man was hunched over, almost bald, and his clothes were very shabby. Yet she was sure it was him – something about the rather graceful way he walked, a reminder he came from a circus background and had been a trapeze artist.

She watched, still hidden behind the big tree, until he had crossed the road and gone towards Clifton Village. Only then did she come out from behind the tree and run to Lamb Lane and safety.

17

'What on earth is wrong with you, Beth?' Rose asked.

It was four in the afternoon and Rose had sensed something was wrong when Beth came back from the shops. She'd done exceptionally well at the shopping, braving queues and not only getting sugar, but another pot of honey, more dried yeast, some strong flour for making bread, plus meat and vegetables.

Rose would've expected her to want to start on making bread immediately, but instead she had remained sitting, nursing a cup of tea, without saying a word. She looked pale and worried too.

'Did someone say something unpleasant to you?' Rose asked. Clifton was full of people who thought they were a superior being. Because she had been the doctor's wife she never experienced this herself, but she had heard women making cutting remarks to those they considered beneath them.

'No, everyone was nice,' Beth replied, but she didn't smile as she said it. 'Especially the butcher.'

'Well, he's got an eye for a pretty girl,' Rose said. 'So why the sad, worried face? You can tell me, whatever it is.'

'I saw someone I used to know.'

'Well, that's good isn't it? An old flame?'

'Never! But I can't imagine what he's doing in Bristol.'

The way she snapped out 'Never' told Rose a great deal. Beth loathed the man she'd seen.

Rose had been told a thousand times that she had a gift for sensing stuff about people. On her first meeting with Beth, she'd known this was a young woman holding a big secret. On the face of it Beth had everything. She was intelligent, capable, attractive and well-dressed.

But she was incredibly cautious and suspicious, not trusting anyone, yet craved affection.

Rose had tried to analyse what little Beth had told her about her past, mixed with observations she'd made. Beth was afraid of this man she'd seen, so what was he to her? Not her father, he'd died in the Great War, so it could be a stepfather or an uncle who scared her. Did he molest her? Or was he just cruel?

The other observation Rose had made was about Beth's speech. Most people would claim she had no discernible accent, but that would be because she was softly spoken. Yet Rose could hear hints of Cockney. It was almost ironed out, either by a teacher, or her mistress when she was in service, or indeed a conscious effort on her own part, but now and again when she was a bit excited it slipped out. She claimed she grew up in Tunbridge Wells, but there was no Kentish accent.

Then there was the mystery of the godmother who left her the cottage; wouldn't most people inheriting be likely to speak of their good fortune and also about the person who gave it? Beth never did. She said once she used to write to the woman as she was her mother's friend, but Beth had never met her, aside from at her own christening. She said she had a photograph taken at the christening and judging by Miranda's clothes she was a wealthy woman. That all sounded true, but so distant! Rose wondered if in fact Miranda was Beth's mother, and she had handed over her baby to her married friend.

Rose knew many young gentlewomen did that rather than face the disgrace. And the foster mother must have been very glad of the money paid to her when Miranda was notified that her husband had died.

That would make complete sense of Miranda leaving her cottage to Beth. A sort of apology.

Over the next few days, Beth tried to forget the man she'd seen and told herself that Ronnie had no connection with Bristol and that it was probably just someone who looked a bit like him. After all, it was fifteen years since she'd seen him, and people could change so much in that time. He'd be in his late forties now, perhaps even older. But she vowed whenever she was out, she'd keep watching for him.

A couple of letters arrived from Jack, warm, loving

letters, yet she sensed how weary he and his comrades were. He mentioned the heat and the flies a lot, and wanting to go out mackerel fishing when he got home.

But he wanted to know about her life, how she was getting on with Rose, what they did all day, and whether she kept thinking about him. When she wrote to him, Beth told him what she considered really boring stuff, like weeding the garden, or putting clean sheets on their beds. But he seemed to love such detail; he said it made him feel he was there with her, and one day when they were married he'd help her change the bed, turn the mattress and even hang washing on the line.

It was endearing to imagine a man sitting writing in a tent, in blazing heat, perhaps only just returned from some skirmish which had killed or wounded some of his friends, having a little fantasy about helping with laundry or making beds.

It was approaching October now, the streets strewn with fallen leaves, and each time a squall of wind came it was like walking through golden confetti. She and Rose often walked up to the Downs in the afternoon, and on one occasion a German bomber flew over so low they dropped face-down on the grass, expecting bombs to rain down on them. But it flew on to the Avon Gorge, following it down towards Portbury Docks. They heard that evening that it must have got separated from the rest of the squadron, and dropped its stick of bombs on the docks before wheeling off to fly back to Germany.

'I keep thinking the bombing is over now,' Beth said quietly as they walked home. 'Then that happened, and I realize we've just had a lull before the next onslaught.'

'If only the news made it clearer how things are going,' Rose sighed. 'There is so much going on in different fronts, in Italy, the Allies invading Sicily, the Japanese in Singapore and Malaysia, and then the uprising in Warsaw, when the Jews fought back against the Germans for a whole month. But we don't hear what happens to the ordinary people in these places. I had so much hope back in January when the 6th Army surrendered after the Russian victory in Stalingrad. Even more hope when the Americans got here in force. But we are still very much in the dark about what is happening. Are we winning? Or losing?'

'We have to believe we are winning because we are in the right,' Beth said. 'I keep wondering about the fate of the men taken prisoner, on both sides. We don't hear much about that, do we?'

'Perhaps we aren't reading the right newspapers,' Rose said, putting her hand on Beth's arm comfortingly. 'But I'm sure Jack is fine.'

Beth guessed that Rose was glad her son was in

Canada and in a reserved profession. She wouldn't, of course, voice that to Beth. She was too kind.

'Shall we put up the decorations today?' Beth asked on the first day of December. She had fished them out of a store cupboard a few days earlier, and they had discussed when they would get a Christmas tree. Too early and it would start shedding before the big day; too late and only skinny, threadbare ones would be left.

The compromise was to get one around the 15th and to keep it cool in the garden until the 20th.

Beth was so excited to open the boxes, as Rose had countless beautiful glass baubles collected over the years, and fantastic paper garlands bought at classy shops like Harrods back when Myles was a little boy. She even had electric fairy lights.

Beth had only ever had paper chains and a scrawny tree bought at Whitechapel Market at close of business. She used to put bits of cotton wool on the branches to pretend it was snow, then strings of silver bells she'd made by modelling milk bottle lids round a thimble. There was a shoe box with some glass baubles, some of which her mother had had as a child. But each year there were fewer and fewer because some had been broken. Neither Emily nor Ronnie wanted to waste money on new decorations, when that money would buy drink.

In November, Beth had gone back to Ireland for a week. It had been a stormy crossing, and had rained almost the whole time she was in Dunmore. Everything in the cottage was neat and tidy, and Kathleen was excited as Mr Boyle had booked a family of four to stay for two weeks over Christmas and New Year. She loved the green wool jacket Beth had brought her. It had belonged to Rose, but never worn because it was too big for her. It looked wonderful on Kathleen and fitted her perfectly.

It was bliss to Beth to do nothing much for the week she was there. Reading, a bit of weeding when it wasn't raining, visiting Aisling and Caitlin, both of whom were pleased to see her and seemed to be in good spirits. Caitlin said her husband was drinking less and being nicer to her, though she admitted she'd be on the next train to Dublin if it wasn't for her children.

Beth found it quite amusing that these two women and Kathleen appeared to hold her in such reverence, almost like a visiting celebrity.

Dr McMara came by, having heard she was home, and wanted to know if she had any intention of coming back permanently. She said she didn't know, but in her heart she knew it would only be a place for a holiday. She was wanted, needed and valued by Rose. And when the war was over and she and Jack married, she hoped they could stay near Bristol.

'So, is the young man well?' the doctor asked. 'Still in Africa? And does he still love you?'

'As far as I know,' she said, 'yes to all three. It takes such an age for letters to get through sometimes, he could be on his way back now.'

But a week of sitting around was enough for her. She packed her warmer clothes into the empty case she'd brought with her, bought some beef, pork and bacon to take back for Rose and Rachel, and after a goodbye hug for Kathleen, she left without a backward glance.

'So what's the verdict? Decorations up or leave them a couple of weeks?' Beth asked.

Rose smiled at her impatience. 'I bet as a child you used to hunt for presents before Christmas.'

Beth laughed at that. There would've been no point in hunting for presents, there were none. The most she ever got at Christmas was a few sweets, though Ruth always kept a few surprises upstairs for her. But she couldn't tell Rose about her childhood Christmases – she'd cry.

'Next week,' Rose said firmly. 'I know perfectly well you've already been through them. Mice may have got in the boxes and damaged some of them. Meanwhile we could go up on the Downs one day this week and see if we can find holly with berries.'

*

Rose and Beth came back the following Tuesday afternoon all rosy-cheeked from the cold wind as they'd walked to the Downs, and with a basket of the holly they'd found. As Rose opened the front door the telephone was ringing.

'I'll put the kettle on,' Beth said, and carried the basket to the back door to put outside in the cool, while Rose answered the phone.

'It's for you,' Rose said, holding out the receiver and looking worried. 'It's Jack's father.'

Beth's heart lurched. A call from his mother might be an invitation to come for Christmas, but his father did not bode well.

'Hello, Mr Ramsey,' she said. 'Is everything all right?'

'No, I'm sorry, it isn't,' he said. 'We've had a telegram from the War Office. Jack is reported missing.'

Beth's knees buckled under her and she reached for a chair to steady herself. 'No, no,' she gasped, tears instantly welling up in her eyes.

'It could mean he's been taken prisoner, or wounded, but his name was omitted from the list of men taken to hospital,' Mr Ramsey said, and his deep voice was cracking with emotion. 'We have to wait for clarification.'

Beth didn't know what to say. 'How has Mrs Ramsey taken it?' she asked eventually.

'As you'd expect, Beth, devastated,' he said. 'She

couldn't bring herself to break the news to you. Now, would you like me to read the telegram to you?'

'Yes please.' Beth could hardly get the two words out.

'"Regret to inform you that Private Jack Ramsey reported missing in action. Letters will follow shortly."'

Beth felt as if all the blood in her body had suddenly drained away. She thought she had prepared herself for bad news about Jack, but clearly she hadn't. She loved him and thought they'd be together for ever after the war. How could fate be so cruel?

Perhaps Mr Ramsey understood how she felt, indeed he was probably at the same stage as she was. 'He's just missing, not reported dead,' he assured her. 'If he's in a hospital, the army or Red Cross will find him. If he's been taken prisoner I believe he will be taken to Italy, and the Red Cross with contact us. We have to say our prayers for him, Beth, and hold on to the belief our boy will come back to us. He told us in his last letter he wants to marry you. So we understand how shocking this news must be for you.'

'Yes, I love him,' she whispered. 'So much.'

'Have faith, Beth, and rest assured we will contact you as soon as we get further news.'

After thanking Mr Ramsey and sending a message of condolences to his wife and the rest of the family, Beth slumped onto a chair and, holding her head in her hands, let out a wail of pain. Rose came over and enfolded her in her arms, rocking her gently till her tears subsided and Beth could tell her all that Jack's father had said.

'There is nothing I can say to make you stop imagining the worse,' Rose said eventually. 'It's true he could be wounded in a field hospital, or taken prisoner by the Germans, and neither scenario is comforting. But I can tell you that all bodies of men killed during action are identified if possible. That was very difficult during the Great War because of the thick mud, and the dangers to the stretcher-bearers who went out under fire to bring the wounded and fallen back. But the fighting in Sicily isn't the same as North Africa. I don't know what it's like there, but I imagine it's mountainous, and I believe they even have an amnesty time when they can bring bodies back behind the lines.'

'It seems to me this is punishment for things I've done,' Beth sobbed out.

'What can you have done that was bad enough to make Jack go missing?' Rose said.

A fresh burst of crying was Beth's response.

18

In the days that followed the terrible news, Beth found she was left with what felt like a big black stone inside her. No room for laughter, joy or even tears, she just went through the days like a clockwork toy. At night, lying sleepless in bed, she tried to cheer herself by imagining Jack in a prison camp, writing her a letter to tell her he loved her, which would arrive any day. But her mind kept flitting to imagining him in hospital, heavily bandaged, his limbs all broken and burned, and him crying out in pain. She thought that this was because it was true.

All thoughts of putting up Christmas decorations were gone. If Rose asked her to do something, she did it, but there was no chatter or smiles. She was so wrapped up in grief she couldn't even appreciate how hard it must be for Rose to be with her.

She couldn't go shopping; to stand in a queue was beyond her. She couldn't eat either, but cleaning was fine, as it was mindless.

Rose watched Beth one morning, nibbling the edge of a quarter of a slice of toast. Once she ate two full slices with jam or marmalade, plus anything else on offer. Weight was dropping off her, she looked gaunt, and it was less than ten days since the news came.

Finally, Rose knew she must intervene, even if she seemed cruel.

'Beth, this has to stop,' she said firmly, plonking the teapot down on the breakfast table. 'You'll be no good to Jack when he comes back if you go on like this. It's close to Christmas, we need to buy the tree, put up the holly and other decorations, and see what we can get to eat in the shops. If you care anything for me, pull yourself together and come back to me. We can wait for more news of Jack together.'

Beth turned to Rose, her eyes dead. 'I don't want to live without him,' she said. 'I deserve this misery.'

'There is no evidence he is dead,' Rose said sharply. 'He's merely missing. That could mean he wasn't put on a list of prisoners of war, or they were so busy at the hospital they could even have put the wrong name down. But the army is thorough, Beth. They will track him down. He'd be horrified if he knew you'd gone to pieces like this.'

'It's a punishment for something I did that was bad,' she whimpered.

'Who is punishing you? God?'

Beth continued to cry and hang her head.

'If that was the case, which I don't for one moment believe, why should Jack's family be punished? He isn't just the man you love, he is loved by his parents, brother, sister, aunts and uncles. Can you possibly imagine God is so vindictive he'd punish all of them for something you did?'

Still she cried and said nothing.

Rose thought for a moment how she should handle this. Had it been anyone else behaving this way she would have been tempted to tell them to go, as she didn't like living under a black cloud. But she had grown to love Beth and she sensed that would only send her spiralling down even further.

'There is only one thing to do, Beth, and that is to admit to me what you've done. I'll be the one to judge if it is a heinous crime.'

'How can I tell you? You'll hate me and make me leave.'

'Allow me to decide what I will do,' Rose almost snarled at the girl. 'But I warn you, Beth, fond though I am of you, I do not have infinite patience, and I believe that once you've confessed what you did, you'll feel better, and together we can decide what to do about it.'

Beth looked up at the older woman, her eyes full of pain. 'I'm ashamed, that's why I can't tell you,' she whispered.

At that Rose's eyes prickled with tears. She moved to Beth and clasped her in her arms tightly. 'Tell me, let it out, I can't bear to see you burdened this way.'

It crossed Rose's mind that if Beth had really done

something wicked like killing someone, she couldn't conceal that crime, but Beth was one of life's gentle people, she wasn't capable of physically hurting anyone.

'I'm not Elizabeth Manning!' Beth blurted out. 'She was killed in a bomb blast in 1940. I was with her and survived. My real name is Mary Price. I took her identity.'

Rose had not expected anything like that and she felt her legs turn to jelly with shock. She needed to sit down, but she continued to hold Beth in her arms while she thought about how she should react.

'I didn't intend to take her name,' Beth went on. 'I had a head wound, and when I came round in the hospital at Charing Cross they called me Elizabeth because she had used her handbag to shield me. She had my bag with my identity card.'

'All right, then.' Rose took a deep breath. 'Now, you have to tell me exactly what you did, and what you know about the real Elizabeth.' She moved Beth onto a sofa and sat opposite her in an armchair. 'From the beginning, how you met Elizabeth and your situation, the whole thing.'

Rose had always been good at picturing things she was told. And Beth told her story clearly, without trying to whitewash herself.

Bit by bit, the complete story unfolded.

As it did, Rose thought Beth had similar spirit and

determination to some of the French heroines in the Great War who put themselves in real danger to help thwart the Germans. There was no doubt in Rose's mind that Mary had had the bleakest of childhoods, and that it continued even during her time in service, without a soul to turn to for comfort. Yet Beth didn't attempt to absolve her actions by revealing any of that. She was not suffering from self-pity, just shame and fear of divine retribution.

To Rose it took courage to do what she had done. She'd stepped into another woman's shoes who had all the advantages she'd never had, she put on Elizabeth's clothes and became her, and once she'd gone that far, who could blame her for seeing Elizabeth's plan right through to the end? A ferry to Ireland and claiming the house.

She had said almost in passing that before the bomb blast Elizabeth had begged Mary to come with her to Ireland, saying they could share clothes and a happy life. So in reality she hadn't stolen anything, she'd just gone along with her friend's plan.

'I'll have to give this a lot of thought,' Rose said at length, knowing she couldn't possibly praise the girl for her actions. 'What you did is illegal, but I can't for the life of me see any benefit to anyone in reporting it. Elizabeth had no family and I suspect the law will do exactly the same as for someone who died without a will. They will take the cottage and any money.

Plus they are likely to put you in prison for fraud. That would be catastrophic. So now I want you to tell me about your childhood, mother and so on. So I can see the big picture.'

They paused for more tea and toast. Beth drank the tea but only nibbled at the toast. Her face was chalk-white and her hands were shaking. Rose had never felt so sorry for anyone as she did for Beth. But she knew she must do the right thing, and just maybe that wasn't informing the authorities.

The story about her childhood, her weak, drunken mother and Ronnie, who had continually abused little Mary, was hard to hear. Now Rose understood why Beth had seemed so scared when she thought she'd seen the man at the end of the road. She listened to how Ruth, their neighbour, had tried to help the child, and her heart went out to that good woman. But for her, little Mary Price would no doubt have been pushed into selling herself on the streets by the evil Ronnie. Mary did well to take her advice to go into service and to try to rise above her hideous background.

Rose knew, as Beth got to the end of the story, that she couldn't possibly hand her over to the police. A girl like her would never survive in prison.

Rose had always been of the opinion that a serious decision should only be taken after sleeping on it. But it wouldn't be fair to Beth to say she'd got to wait till tomorrow for the verdict, so, some shopping now, perhaps a glass of sherry to fortify them, and wait to see if that would show her the way forward.

Rose got up, poured two glasses of sherry and handed one to Beth. 'Drink that and then let's go out and buy a Christmas tree. You've been very brave and honest, but I need time to mull over where we go from here. It's a nice crisp afternoon out there and sometimes a walk can clear the head.'

Beth did perk up a little once they set out. Rose pointed out Christmas trees in windows, garlands on front doors, and said she thought they should go into Christ Church in the next day or two to see the Nativity scene, as that always made Christmas for her. She wasn't angry with Beth, but she wasn't going to be too soft. 'I always think that Christmas can be a healing time,' she said. 'It teaches us to appreciate family members, and to forgive and forget. When I was a girl the vicar in our church used to say at the midnight service on Christmas Eve, "Open your hearts and let the Christ Child in." He meant of course to stop family disputes, to embrace those you've fallen out with, to value what you have. But as a small girl I always imagined this fat little baby flying through the air to settle inside someone, like a real birth, only in reverse.'

Rose was pleased to hear a tight little giggle from Beth, and when she turned to look at her, she saw the earlier dead look in her eyes had gone. She reached out and patted Beth's cheek. 'That's better, you've got through the worst part of this by owning up. So let's put it aside for now, and enjoy the spirit of Christmas all about us.'

As Rose had expected, there were slim pickings left in the shops. They managed to get two oranges, some margarine, lard, and four sausages. Thankfully, mainly due to Beth, they had got some provisions weeks earlier, and made a Christmas cake. Rose liked Beth's suggestion that they could eke the sausages out by making sausage rolls. She was also very glad she'd ordered and paid for a chicken some months ago from a farmer. He would deliver on Christmas Eve and no coupons were needed.

The Salvation Army band was playing carols on the corner of Princess Victoria and Regent Street and they stayed for a while to listen. To Rose it was the essence of Christmas, and she could see by Beth's rapt expression she felt the same.

They had spotted a man selling Christmas trees in Boyce's Avenue, just across from where the band was playing, and on the way home they selected from him a medium-sized, nice bushy tree, and with Rose at the top end and Beth taking the heavier trunk, they began to carry it home.

As they walked across the green in Victoria Square, Rose noticed a man skulking in the bushes. Maybe it was only because of Beth talking about Ronnie, but this man fitted his description. Furthermore he was looking intently at Beth.

Beth was oblivious to anything but the prickly trunk she was holding and trying to tie a handkerchief around. Rose could see the man was dishevelled, dirty, all the hallmarks of a rough sleeper. Such men often came to Clifton because they were more likely to receive handouts, both from ordinary people and a couple of charities run by the churches, than they would down in the city centre. People were inclined to pay them for little outdoor jobs like sweeping paths, cutting grass, mucking out stables.

She didn't alert Beth – she'd had enough grief for one day – but Rose decided that in future she wouldn't allow her to go out alone.

As they went on down the road towards Lamb Lane, Rose glanced back several times, pretending she was checking on Beth, but there was no sign of the man. So maybe he wasn't Ronnie, just a man looking at a pretty girl?

Once home, Beth lit the fire, then filled a big flower pot with soil while Rose cooked the tea. Rose watched Beth from the kitchen, pleased to see she was moving speedily again, and acting on initiative, not asking what to do.

'We should maybe leave the tree outside for a couple more days,' Rose said, breaking off from mashing some potatoes to go outside and join Beth. She was pressing the tree trunk into the pot now. 'We don't want it bald on Christmas Day.'

'No, that would never do,' Beth said and smiled. 'Mrs Bradley, the woman I worked for, used to be a fiend about Christmas tree needles. Just one left on the floor was a hanging offence.'

Rose laughed, delighted that Beth appeared to be able to talk now about that part of her former life. 'Come on in now and tell me more about her and her household,' she suggested. 'It's got to be a whole lot more interesting than eating Spam and mashed potato.'

By nine that evening Rose knew a great deal more about Beth: about the interview she'd been to before the bomb struck Trafalgar Square Tube, about how she went into the Lyons Corner House nervously because she wasn't used to eating in restaurants, and how Elizabeth beckoned her over to share her table. Rose knew the Corner House well; she often met friends there when she was in London. So she could picture the busy scene. She could also picture how nervous Mary Price was to be sitting with a well-dressed, confident woman like Elizabeth. The same age, height, similar colouring, but a world apart in experience. But as they chatted, Elizabeth must have found the same thing in Mary as Rose had when they first met. Vulnerable, yet capable, sweet-natured, yet some steel in her spine. Maybe Elizabeth knew this could become a true friendship, and perhaps, too, she liked the idea of bringing the shy, unworldly girl out of the shadows. Yet she must also have realized that Mary was the kind to care for people, to want to cook and clean for them both, sew on her buttons, darn her gloves. And she'd never try to outshine Elizabeth.

Yet in the end it was Elizabeth who saved Mary's life. She held her tightly against her chest, her big bag protecting this new friend's head and face. A noble act of true affection.

So how could Rose turn her over to the police? She could almost hear the real Elizabeth Manning whispering that she was glad Mary had done what she did, and that she deserved good fortune.

Rose handed Beth a small glass of brandy. 'That's for making me happy and eating dinner, if you could call it that.'

'I quite like Spam,' Beth said cheerfully.

'Just as well, as it's the mainstay of the pantry,' Rose laughed, her blue eyes twinkling. 'I think tomorrow we will make sausage rolls and some mince pies.'

'Before you turn me in?'

Rose looked at the girl sharply, thinking it was a cheeky remark. But in fact Beth had turned pale again with fright.

'Oh no, my dear, I can't do that. I've weighed up everything and I can't see any benefit in it to anyone.

You didn't steal anything, you just reclaimed your friend's belongings and then made use of them. It wasn't right, of course, but you know that. I think in the next few weeks we must discuss what to do with the cottage in Ireland. If you do something with it which is good – say, for instance, giving it to a charity who will let sick people convalesce there – you can be left with a clear conscience.'

The expression on Beth's face was like the sun coming out from behind a cloud.

'So do I go back to being Mary Price?'

Rose shook her head. 'No. To do so might flag up things or people you don't want to come into your life. What's in a name anyway?'

'And the money?'

'That's up to you, my dear. You've got quite enough on your plate right now with Jack missing, and the war ongoing. I think it's best to shelve that and everything else for the time being.'

'Oh, Rose.' Beth began to cry. 'You are so kind, much kinder than I deserve.'

'Enough of that tosh now,' she said. 'Drink your brandy and we'll check if there's anything worth listening to on the wireless. We should put up the holly and the rest of the Christmas stuff tomorrow.'

Close to midnight, as Beth lay in bed hugging a hot water bottle, she heard planes overhead and braced herself for a bomb, but there was no bang. In fact it was so quiet she could've been in the heart of the country. She offered up a little prayer for Jack's safety and thanked God for sending her to Rose.

Ruth had taught her to say prayers, just as she told her stories from the Bible, and of Jesus. When she came to think about it, Ruth had been like a fairy godmother, and Rose was another. She hoped one day she could be a good influence on someone, as they had been to her.

19

Spring 1944

Despite many letters and phone calls to the Red Cross and the War Office from Beth, Rose, and Jack's parents, by the spring Jack had still not been traced to either a hospital or a prisoner-of-war camp.

Mr and Mrs Ramsey had received a few letters from his captain, always encouraging them to be optimistic, telling them it was possible that Jack's details had been entered wrongly, or omitted accidentally on registers, and that letters from POW camps were notoriously slow in getting back to England.

Yet he also said that none of the other soldiers in Jack's unit had seen him being injured or captured. He explained that they were under heavy fire that day, and therefore it wasn't possible to keep tabs on everyone.

Beth had kept in close contact with the Ramseys, and Jack's father was angered by a suggestion from some ignorant person that Jack had deserted. He said that was as improbable as Jack being wounded and and falling into a ravine, with no one noticing. Beth wished Mr Ramsey had never said that, as she began to imagine that was what had happened. Rose insisted that was ridiculous, but the little worm of the idea had burrowed into her head and wouldn't go away.

Christmas had passed very quietly, and on 31 December Rose and Beth had walked down to the Victoria Rooms, originally built as a concert and banqueting hall and meeting place to commemorate the start of Queen Victoria's reign. It had been given to Bristol University in the 1920s, to house the Student Union, and the rather splendid fountain at the front was quite likely to have coloured water from time to time, the ink tipped in by students. It was the usual gathering place for people to see in the New Year, and Rose remembered a particularly raucous occasion when one of the students who got in the fountain had nearly drowned.

One of the many reasons Beth adored and admired Rose was her interest in and enthusiasm for young people. Few ladies of seventy-two would venture out on a bitterly cold night just to join younger people and celebrate the New Year. She got a tin whistle out of her pocket at midnight and blew it loudly, kissed three young airmen on their cheeks after singing Auld Lang Syne, and joined in a conga line.

It was so cold this year the water in the fountain was beginning to freeze. The sight of so many men in uniform home on leave was yet another reminder of Jack being missing, so Beth was glad when Rose was ready to go home.

'I just hope those three boys come home safely,' Rose said as they walked back, Rose holding Beth's arm. 'I think this year will be when we really see what the RAF can do with the big planes, bombing German cities. It seems to me we are gearing up for a big finale.'

'Do you mean we are going to win?' Beth asked.

'Did you ever doubt that?' Rose asked incredulously.

It was another thing to love Rose for. She was such a positive person. She refused to grumble about her age, rationing, shortage of food and the complete disappearance of so many things in the shops. She not only made do and mended her own things, but often the neighbours' too. Beth had met many of them over Christmas, when Rose invited them in for a drink and mince pies. She'd made two beautifully dressed rag dolls for the little Jewish girls who'd arrived on the Kindertransport from Germany and were living with a couple in Pembroke Road. Beth had noticed that she was raiding the larder and giving away food to these and other people. There was no end to her generosity.

Towards the end of January the news broke that the Allied landings at Anzio in Italy had begun. At first Beth felt sure, if Jack was in a POW camp in Italy, that all prisoners would be liberated. But that hope died when it became clear that the Germans were fighting back tooth and nail. Besides, it was also possible the Germans had already moved all the prisoners back to Germany.

Following Rose's lead in helping others, Beth began knitting in earnest – hats, scarves and gloves. She found that many of the haberdashery shops had odd ounces of wool, leftover dye-lots they couldn't sell, so she bought them. It didn't matter to her what colour the wool was, she was knitting multi-coloured striped items. When the weather grew really raw in February she took a big pile of finished articles to the women who ran the clothes stall in Christ Church Hall to help people who had lost everything in bombings. It made Beth happy to see children in her hats, scarves and mittens. She also became respected by the rather starchy women who ran the stall, and felt less guilty of her crime now that she was helping people – plus knitting these things took her mind off Jack's plight.

She had long since stopped looking over her shoulder for Ronnie too. She believed she had been mistaken – after all, it made no sense that he would've come to Bristol.

Beth telephoned Mr Boyle in Waterford from time to time, but he didn't seem fazed by being left to manage her cottage, and had new dates booked to tell her about. He paid Kathleen and the utilities from the rental money, and asked if she wanted the balance sent to her. She asked him to hold on to it for the time being. Kathleen, it seemed, was still happy to take care of the cottage and was appreciating Beth's letters, but apologized for not always responding, as she wasn't a good letter-writer. Both Kathleen and Mr Boyle, however, were concerned that she still had no news of Jack. They both thought she should stay with Mrs Cullen, who sounded lovely, and they prayed for good news.

March came in with a hint of spring in the air, and green shoots of bulbs appeared in the garden, which cheered both her and Rose. Then, right at the end of the month when the garden was bright with daffodils, it turned really warm, and Rose thought it would be a good day for cleaning out the old workshop.

Leaves had blown in under the double doors back in November, and the whole place was dusty and untidy as they'd tended to just dump stuff in there when it was too cold to linger long enough to put things away properly.

Rose opened the doors wide onto the lane, and Beth swept the floor vigorously.

'That's creating even more dust on everything,' Rose wailed, running her fingers across the tools.

'I'll go and get the mop and bucket,' Beth said. 'Once the floor's washed, we'll only need to dust the tools with a damp duster.'

Rose was bending over trying to pull out a couple

of boxes because she saw leaves and sweet wrappers had blown in beside them, when she heard a man say, 'Where is she?'

Without moving or even looking round, she sensed it was the man Ronnie. He had a rough voice and his tone was threatening.

'Where is who?' she asked, straightening up and holding her broom tightly for security.

'Don't yer give me none of that, I've seen Mary with you. Get 'er!'

Rose offered up a silent prayer that Beth would stay in the house, and said, 'My good man, I have no idea what you are talking about. There is no Mary here, so kindly go away.'

'There's nuffing worse than a posh bitch,' he snarled, taking a threatening step forwards. 'Now call 'er!'

He was in an even worse state now than when she saw him three months earlier, with unkempt beard and hair, a long black coat covered in stains, boots tied on his feet with string, and the collar on his shirt black with filth. He smelled appalling too.

'Fuckin' get 'er!' he yelled and from his coat pocket pulled a brown cudgel shiny from constant handling. It was about two feet long and Rose remembered, as a girl, village boys making such things from tree branches, whittling them with a penknife so they had a fat ball shape at one end, becoming gradually narrower to fit their hand. They threatened boys from other villages with them, but she never heard of them hitting anyone.

But she guessed this foul-mouthed man wouldn't hesitate to hit her with it. Her broom was no deterrent.

'Come now,' she said in her loudest voice, hoping Beth would hear and telephone the police, 'there is no one here by that name, but I can see you are in need, let me go inside and I'll get you something to eat and some money for you.'

'Money? I don't want no fuckin' money from you, just that little bitch to come out and see me. I was like a dad to 'er and she owes me.'

Rose moved sideways just enough to be able to reach a chisel that had been left on the side instead of in its place on the wall.

'Look, I'm sorry you are distressed,' she said, 'but you've got the wrong place. There is no girl here. Just me, and I'm a widow.'

Her hand closed around the chisel handle, but at the same moment the door through to the house opened and Beth saw Ronnie. She dropped the bucket of water, slopping it all over the floor, and leapt to Rose's side to protect her.

'This man seems to think someone called Mary is here,' Rose said, looking intently at Beth in a silent message to follow her lead. 'This is Miss Manning, my housekeeper, and I doubt she's ever seen you before.'

'No, I haven't,' Beth spoke up. 'So clear off now or I'll call the police.'

'Hoity-toity!' he exclaimed. 'You learned to talk posh too. But I knows who you really are.'

He moved closer, reaching out to grab Beth's arm. Quick as a flash Rose stabbed his arm with the chisel. It was so sharp it went right through his coat and he yelped.

'You've had fair warning.' Rose's voice was loud and clear. 'Come one step closer and this will go through your heart.'

Beth snatched up a large shovel. 'Go and call the police,' she said to Rose. 'I'll deal with this man.'

She had the vivid memory of being too small and frightened to fight him off, but she was a strong woman now. She lifted the shovel above her head, hating him so much she wanted to split his head open with it. Rose had backed up through the door to the kitchen, and Beth heard the ping of the phone as she picked it up.

'Last chance,' Beth said, taking a step nearer him and standing feet well apart to keep her balance. 'Go now, or you get this. How dare you come here disturbing an old lady.'

Her blood was up, and as he lifted his cudgel and took another step towards her, she whacked him with every ounce of strength she had. He fell to the workroom floor like a sack of potatoes. As he lay there crumpled up, she lifted the shovel to hit him yet again and kill him.

'No, Beth!' Rose's voice from behind stopped her. 'Enough! The police are coming.'

Beth began to cry then with shock, and the memories the man on the floor had brought back. However much she wanted to kill him she knew Rose was right to stop her. Murder would mean prison.

The police arrived very quickly, followed five or ten minutes later by an ambulance, and Rose took charge. While Ronnie was examined she told them he was a stranger who had threatened her. They pronounced him alive but unconscious, and Rose stood by the ambulance men wringing her hands as if distressed. To the police she explained how the man had barged into the workroom, convinced she was harbouring someone he knew. She repeated how he had sworn at her and threatened her with his cudgel, how Beth came into the workshop then, spilling the bucket of water she'd brought with her, and had insisted on dealing with the man, but in reality getting Rose to telephone for help. Beth had picked up the shovel to hold the man at bay, and only hit him with it to stop him attacking her and possibly Rose too.

Faced with Beth's tear-stained face, and Rose's dignified, detailed account of events, the police were entirely sympathetic. Rose pointed out his cudgel, now on the ground.

'If he'd hit either of us with it, which he threatened, I don't think we'd have recovered. Beth was very brave to stop him.'

Ronnie was taken away on a stretcher, and the police said they would arrest him for threatening behaviour once he regained consciousness.

'I don't think we want to press charges. Just warn him not to do it to me or anyone else again,' Rose said. 'I think the bump on his head will probably act as a deterrent.'

When the ambulance and police had gone, they mopped up the water on the floor, washed it over properly and then closed and locked the double doors.

'We'll sort the rest in a day or two,' Rose said. 'Now, let's go and have a cup of tea and try to put what happened into perspective.'

Beth was still shaking with shock at what she'd done, very much aware, if Rose hadn't intervened, of what might have happened. 'You were very calm,' she said to Rose. 'Thank you for supporting me, and backing me up in claiming not to know that horrible man.'

'He had done you so much damage in the past, it was the least I could do,' Rose said with a nonchalant shrug. 'Let's hope the police make him leave Bristol and never return. It's been an unpleasant drama, but thankfully it's over now. That man was a really nasty piece of work.'

'I wonder if my mother is still alive,' Beth said in little more than a whisper.

Knowing there wasn't a good answer to that question, Rose just went to Beth where she sat at the dining table, and put her arms round her, resting her face on Beth's head. 'I like to think of you as the daughter I never had,' she said softly. 'If your real mum is alive, at least she got away from Ronnie. But I think it's more likely she's passed away and that's why he's sleeping rough.'

'When and if Jack comes back, do I need to tell him everything?' Beth whispered, as if afraid of being overheard.

'You know you do,' Rose replied. 'And I'll be around to help you. But let's light the fire and put the wireless on, and maybe we'll have a large sherry each for shock.'

20

A burly police sergeant called on Rose and Beth a few days after the attack. Rose invited him in for a cup of tea, and he told them that Ronald Birch was about to be discharged from hospital, but had been cautioned against attempting to go anywhere near Mrs Cullen's home and advised to leave Bristol immediately.

The sergeant looked across the room to Beth and chuckled. 'He's got a sore head, but was still adamant that you are Mary Price, his stepdaughter. Nothing like sticking to a lie for grim death! He said he'd left London two years ago after his wife, Mary's mother, died, and went to various cities to try and find you.'

Rose knew how hard it must be for Beth not to show interest in what Ronnie had claimed. To do so might expose her, or at least make the sergeant suspicious that she was Mary Price. Yet Rose felt as an elderly lady, and perhaps a busybody, she could ask some questions on Beth's behalf.

'What did his wife die of, then?' she asked casually.

'Birch said it was tuberculosis. He got all worked up and angry that Mary had gone into service, probably to a big house with all modern amenities, yet she didn't care that her mother was living in damp, insanitary conditions.'

'I dare say the poor girl left home to get away from such a nasty stepfather, and surely it's a man's job to look after his wife?' Rose said. 'Why wasn't he called up anyway? Even through all that dirt I didn't think he looked old enough to be exempt.'

'He claimed he was fifty-eight but had lost his identity card,' the sergeant said, pursing his lips, clearly not believing a word of that. 'I made an enquiry to find out more about him, but haven't heard anything back yet.'

'What part of London was he from?' Rose asked, looking the picture of innocence.

'The East End. He said he buried his wife in Whitechapel, where they were living when she died.'

The sergeant finished drinking his tea and got up. 'Now be careful, you two. Don't answer the door unless you are expecting a caller. I don't think for one moment he'll come back here now he knows how competent you can be with a shovel,' he grinned. 'But if you see him hanging about, or he should come to your door, telephone the police immediately.'

'We will,' Rose nodded.

'Well, that went quite well,' Rose said after Beth had shown the sergeant out. 'I half thought we both might be charged with assault. They can do that if they think the force used in self-defence was excessive. Good job we are frail little women!'

Beth laughed. 'Nothing frail about us two. Do you think Ronnie was telling the truth about my mum dying?'

Rose didn't answer for a moment. 'I don't know,' she said eventually, rather hesitantly. 'Do you think he even married her?'

'I think it probably *is* true about her dying, but I can't imagine Ronnie ever being sentimental enough to go through with marriage. I also doubt Mum would've ever been sober enough.'

Rose paused before answering. It struck her as odd that Beth used the word 'sober'. Most people, when asked about their mother, would've said 'well enough'. It was clear the scars from childhood were still raw.

'When the war is over, you could go to Whitechapel and check the burial records. Just so you know for certain.'

'I never want to go back there,' Beth said firmly. 'Dead or alive, I don't care.'

Rose was sitting in a chair in the garden. It was now May, and very pretty with the little cherry tree dripping with pink blossom and masses of small rockery plants billowing over onto the paths. She had been reading, but she'd stopped to study Beth. She was kneeling, planting out some pansies she'd grown from seed. The last few days of warm sunshine had given her face, arms and legs a golden tan. Her chestnut hair was loose on her shoulders, and very shiny. She looked quite lovely, though Rose was aware Beth saw herself as very plain.

She rarely mentioned Jack now, but Rose knew this wasn't because she'd stopped caring, more that she was trying to prepare herself for bad news.

Rose knew next to nothing about army procedures when a soldier was missing, but she thought – as probably did Beth – that poor Jack had been blown up, and it had been impossible to identify his body. The Red Cross were very thorough. If he'd been in a POW camp or hospital, they surely would've found him by now. Besides, even if Jack was unable to write a letter himself, he would've got someone else to do it for him, to put his parents' and Beth's minds at rest.

Every day when she and Beth went up to the shops in Clifton Village, they heard about someone's son, brother, father or nephew who had either been killed, taken prisoner, or was recovering from serious injury here in an English hospital. They also saw many men on crutches, with missing limbs, or head injuries. Not as many wounded as Rose remembered after the Great War, thank heavens. She recalled how busy Duncan was in his practice at that time, seeing men with both wounds that wouldn't heal and shell shock. Many of these men he made no charge for treating. As he said, 'They fought to keep us safe, the least I can do to show my appreciation is to try and make them whole again.'

'Why the tears?' Beth suddenly asked Rose, snapping her out of her reverie.

Rose wiped her eyes with a hanky. 'Just thinking about Duncan and something he said. I hadn't realized it had made me cry.'

Beth crouched down beside Rose and took her hand between hers. 'Tell me?'

Rose related the little story, and saw Beth's eyes well up too. 'He sounds like such a good man,' she said.

Rose smiled at Beth and patted her cheek affectionately. 'He was. He used to get very angry about the way servicemen were neglected when they came home. But he'd be very happy to know I've got you here for company. If we'd known you when you were a little girl we would gladly have adopted you.'

There was nothing Beth could say in answer to that, she was too choked up with emotion.

Two days later it was tipping down with rain, and Beth and Rose were making some pasties to eke out the tiny meat ration. The telephone rang and Rose went to answer it, leaving Beth to cut the pastry into small circles.

'It's Mr Ramsey for you,' Rose called, covering the receiver with her hand. 'He sounds distressed.'

Beth leapt to the phone. 'Hello, have they found him?'

Rose watched Beth's face drain of colour. 'No!' she shrieked. 'No, that can't be true.'

Beth slumped down on a dining chair to listen to Mr Ramsey. Clearly Jack wasn't dead, but something very serious was wrong. Rose could only stand by helplessly, her heart going out to both Jack's parents and Beth.

Finally, Beth put the receiver back, her eyes as dead as a fish's on the fishmonger's slab. 'His legs were blown off,' she said, then rested her arms on the table and dropped her head onto them, sobbing.

Rose felt faint. This was not a problem that could be solved easily. There were prosthetics, of course, but to a young man, losing his legs would be living death in his eyes.

She sat next to Beth and pulled her into her arms.

'Where has he been all this time?' she asked, knowing that platitudes were almost an insult to someone getting such awful news.

'The Red Cross manager who contacted the Ramseys thinks he was taken to a hospital in Sicily, then moved to Italy as a POW, where he was moved several times more, before ending up in a sick-bay of a German POW camp. It's all unclear because he was wrongly identified in the beginning and was, and still is, too sick to communicate properly.'

'What can I say? It's a nightmare, for both his parents and you,' Rose exclaimed. 'Is there anything we can do?'

'Only write to him. Mr Ramsey said he'd put the details in the post for me. But I can't stand the idea that he's lost his legs! That's too gruesome for words. How will he work? How will he be able to bear it?'

Rose thought that her last question was the major one. How would he? Getting married, having children, running down the beach in Cornwall, playing football, all things which must now seem out of reach to him. But she wasn't going to say that.

'Duncan used to tell me that it was amazing what people can teach themselves to do when they come to terms with serious injuries and disabilities.'

'Maybe, but if it were me, I'd want to end it all.'

'That is defeatist talk,' Rose said sharply. 'We will have no more of that.'

In the days that followed, Beth felt completely crushed. All her dreams and hopes for the future involved Jack. She had compiled a list of things she wanted to see and do with him when the war was over. She'd kept a diary of her feelings day by day. Put all his letters in a scrapbook, and even begun to knit him a jumper. Now all she saw in her head was the picture of him in a wheelchair.

She was absolutely certain she could still love him, despite the lack of limbs, but would he want that? She realized because she had spent so few hours with Jack, she knew only one small bit of him, the physically fit, bright, ambitious, kind and sunny-natured bit. She'd never seen him angry, challenged in any way. Was it even possible for any man to rebuild a life after being dealt such a huge blow?

It was a week later that a letter from Jack arrived for Beth. It wasn't written by him and it came via the Red Cross. It seemed as if her first letter to him hadn't yet arrived.

'Dearest Beth,' she read, her face alight with joy that after so long he was actually dictating a letter to her,

> *I hope the long silence hasn't worried you too much, but I'm OK, as well as can be expected so far from home and in a ward full of other sick and wounded men. The days seem very long and I try to escape from the boredom by imagining what you could be doing. I hope you are keeping busy with Mrs Cullen. My father will have told you how it is for me, and I will quite understand if you decide to abandon the plans we had.*
>
> *Sorry I couldn't write this myself, but my right hand was injured too. I dream of Cornwall a lot and of dancing with you wearing that beautiful dress. I'm hoping a letter will come from you soon.*
>
> *Love, Jack xxx*

Beth passed it to Rose, her joyful expression of just a few moments earlier now a look of extreme anxiety. 'It doesn't even sound like him.'

Rose read it and passed it back. 'It's very hard to dictate a letter, Beth. Whoever wrote it for him might be almost a stranger. He isn't going to pour his heart out to someone he doesn't know well.'

'I know that,' Beth said, nodding. 'But I couldn't hear his voice. He didn't tell me anything about the treatment he gets, or the other patients. And what does he mean when he says he'll understand if I abandon our plans?'

'You know what he means,' Rose said firmly. 'He's giving you a way out.'

'But I don't want a way out,' Beth said indignantly.

When Beth listened to the news on 4 June about how Allied troops had entered Rome and liberated the city, she felt nothing. Not excitement or joy, she just felt numb. Two days later, on 6 June, when troops landed on the Normandy beaches, she did feel something, but it was mainly concern for all the wives, mothers and sweethearts who would be crying for their dead or wounded men before the Germans were pushed back.

Rose insisted on them going to the pictures to see *Casablanca*, the film with Humphrey Bogart and Ingrid Bergman. The exciting and often poignant story did lift Beth's spirits a little. Yet it wasn't until Pathé News came on after the film that she realized Rose had hoped the scenes of courage and gallantry on the Normandy beaches would help to take her out of herself. Rose's plan worked. It would've been impossible not to see all those brave young men prepared to fight and possibly die for their country and not be moved. As tears flowed unchecked down her cheeks, the hard knot of sorrow inside her softened. She made a silent vow to herself that when Jack came back she would be whatever he wanted, be that nurse, companion or just friend.

Rose kept a close eye on Beth in the days that followed. On the face of it she seemed calm, resigned and indeed relieved that she finally knew where Jack was, even if his situation was tragic. But Rose was concerned that she was comforting herself by slipping into a kind of Joan of Arc fantasy, where her crusade would be to dedicate her life to making Jack happy and well looked after. In one respect that was both brave and big-hearted, but Rose feared she hadn't really faced up to the reality of what life would be like taking care of someone so severely disabled.

Rose did know a little of what that was like. She had been a member of a women's group attached to Christ Church after the Great War, and one of the things they did was to visit men who had been wounded. These men were not from wealthy Clifton families; often they and their wives and children were living in appalling conditions in a couple of damp, squalid rooms, or with aging parents. Rose remembered seeing photographs of weddings, of healthy, smiling faces alight with love and hope for their future. Now that once strong, handsome groom had to get around on crutches, or was confined to bed, angry and bitter that once he'd been called a hero, but now society had turned its back on him. Their children were listless, pale and thin, always hungry, and the mother like a wraith, worn out with the struggle to keep her family alive. Could she still love that man who belittled her, hit her, and ordered her out to get him the drink he craved?

Rose remembered Duncan telling her about the wife of one of his patients who mixed rat poison into her husband's porridge, killing him. She said at her trial she could no longer bear clearing up after the doubly incontinent man. She asked the judge if he could do that, day after day. Duncan doubted he could, but the poor woman was still hanged and her children sent to orphanages.

However sad Beth felt, she rallied herself by not just writing cheerful letters back to Jack, but by volunteering in Hambleden House, a convalescent home for wounded servicemen up on Bristol's Downs. Rose understood she wanted to learn how men like Jack were coping with missing limbs or burns, and to find out what she could do to aid their recovery.

Yet while Beth was rushing off two afternoons a week to help wounded men recover, there were more challenges in store for Britain. There had been great delight when the Allies liberated Paris in August, and people were beginning to think it was the beginning of the end. But first came the so-called doodlebugs or buzz bombs the Germans began firing on England. They were unmanned, and when their buzzing engine stopped, they would drop down to kill and destroy property. They didn't have a long range, though, so most fell in the south of England.

But then, much worse, in September came the V-2 rockets. These silent and deadly missiles gave no warning, and caused untold damage and death in London.

One afternoon, Beth was reading a newspaper article about wounded soldiers being brought back from France to Charing Cross Station, the picture showing volunteers plying the men with drinks and sandwiches.

She looked up thoughtfully from the newspaper and asked, 'Do our servicemen ever get sent home if they are taken prisoner yet are wounded?'

'No, never,' Rose said. 'Just imagine what the logistics of that would be.'

'So what do we do with the German sick or wounded here?'

'We take care of them. The Germans do too, by all accounts. I think it's in the Geneva Convention that we must. Anyway, nurses and doctors are much the same the world over, their care doesn't depend on nationality.'

Beth wasn't so sure about that. If Germans could send Jews to prison camps she doubted they tucked up sick and wounded POWs in comfy beds at night. But she said nothing – Rose thought well of everyone. She just hoped against hope that no one was neglecting or hurting Jack. She'd only had two letters so far, and neither of them gave any real idea of how he was.

21

October 1944

'Do you go out dancing, Beth?' Sergeant Harold Irwin asked whilst Beth was making his bed. He was called 'Sarge' by the other patients, but the nurses and assistants like Beth called him Harry.

He was sitting on a chair with his plastered leg up on a stool. He'd been brought in a couple of weeks earlier with an infected broken leg. It was said he'd made himself a makeshift splint and continued on the march from Normandy towards Belgium because he didn't want to leave his men. That heroic act had resulted in his leg breaking again in another place and becoming infected. He was very lucky he was treated before gangrene set in.

'I've only ever been dancing once,' Beth admitted as she smoothed out the bottom sheet and tucked it in with hospital corners as Sister insisted. 'My Jack took me to one in London. But I think his dancing days are over now. He's lost both legs and he's a POW in Germany.'

'What rotten luck,' Harry exclaimed. 'Especially

with a beautiful girl like you waiting at home for him.'

Beth blushed. Sergeant Irwin was thirty-eight and very handsome in a rakish kind of way, with dark chocolate eyes, too-long curly fair hair, and lips that curled up in the corners like a continual smile. All the women at the convalescent home had remarked on his looks – one of the older nurses thought he looked dangerous; a younger one said he was 'swoon-worthy'.

Beth just liked him. He was brave, interested in people, amusing, caring, and very intelligent, though, as she had waspishly told him, 'It wasn't intelligent to walk miles with a broken leg.' He'd responded: 'If I'd known a girl like you was due to come along, I would've sat by the road in France and waited for you.'

He came from Bristol, and said he was delighted he was brought to his hometown rather than being dumped in Folkestone or Dover. Beth saw him as a lucky man, well-liked by other men, and loved by his elderly parents, who she'd met when they visited him last Thursday.

Beth only volunteered here on Mondays and Thursdays. Rose had encouraged her to do another day, saying she could see it was helping Beth's anxiety about Jack. But Beth didn't think it was fair to leave Rose on her own so much.

'Tell me more about your Jack,' Harry said. 'Are you married? Engaged? You aren't wearing a ring.'

'No, we're not married or engaged. We met during a bombing raid in London and I only knew him for a short time because I had to go back to Ireland, and shortly afterwards he was sent to North Africa.'

'Poor devil. I've heard it was pretty hairy there.'

'I wouldn't really know about how bad it was – his letters from there were always cheery. But since I was told he was missing, nearly a year ago, there was no word from him until we got the news he was in the sick-bay in Germany. But you must've had a bad time too, in Normandy?'

His face clouded over. 'Yeah, it was awful, so many good men killed and wounded. But we've got the enemy on the run at last. I didn't break my leg there, though. It happened as we were chasing after the retreating Germans. I got up on a tank to get a better view, slipped off onto a rock and broke it. Not all injuries are caused by bullets!' He grinned sheepishly as he said it, and she felt he was embarrassed about it.

Beth plumped up his pillows, then put the top sheet on.

'Let's hope that teaches you to be more careful,' she said lightly.

'You said you were going back to Ireland. You don't sound Irish?'

'I'm not. I was lucky enough to be left a cottage there by my godmother. I was full of enthusiasm when I first went there, but there's no work and it's a bit lonely. I came to Bristol for a little break and met the lovely lady I now work for.'

'Are you going to be able to cope with Jack's missing legs when he comes home?'

If anyone else had asked that question she'd have snapped at them. But the gentle way Harry put the question suggested he understood the problems that wives, girlfriends and other family members had with amputees.

Beth shrugged. 'I really don't know, Harry. I want to claim I'll be fine. But he's been missing for months and is in such a bad way that someone else writes his letters to me. If I could just talk to him, find out how he feels. It's the not knowing which makes it so difficult.'

Harry nodded in sympathy. 'Most servicemen find it hard to talk about such things. But stick with it. As he gets used to his situation, he'll probably find it easier to communicate. Where are your family?'

'I haven't got any. Jack's family are in Cornwall.'
'Will they help?'
'I'm sure they will. I haven't met them though, only spoken to his father on the telephone.'

'So Jack's said nothing about how he sees the future?'
Beth nodded.
'What do you want to happen?'
'I wanted to get married, I still do, but—' She faltered.

'You can't see where you could live, or how,' he suggested. 'You don't know how long it will take to get him prosthetic legs, or for him to learn to walk with them.'

'Yes, that's about the size of it,' she said, and her eyes involuntarily filled with tears.

Harry reached out and took her hand, squeezing it in sympathy. 'There must be hundreds of girls in the same boat as you,' he said soothingly. 'And even more men in POW camps and hospitals worrying themselves sick that their girl back home has already met someone else or will reject him when she sees his injuries.'

'Have you got a girl here?' she asked.

'No, and I'm glad about that as there's no one to hurt or disappoint. I expect Jack is half hoping you'll give up on him, he wouldn't want to spoil your life.'

'That's quite an insulting view. If you love someone you want to take care of them,' she said, angrily wiping her tears away.

'It's also quite insulting to imagine a man should be happy to be taken care of,' he retorted.

Harry's eyes were twinkling. She knew he didn't mean to humiliate her, but his bed was made, and it was time to go and prepare the tea trolley. 'I'll deal with you later,' she said as a parting shot before walking out of the ward.

Her face was flushed as she arranged the cups and

saucers on the trolley. She wasn't sure what she'd meant by dealing with Harry later. Was it an attempt at flirting with him? If so she should be ashamed at herself.

As she walked home later, Beth found herself having guilty thoughts about Harry. He was very attractive, but surely she shouldn't be noticing that. She knew he was a regular soldier, not conscripted. She wished that instead of telling him about her anxiety over Jack, she had asked him something safe, like whether he would be staying in the army after his leg was healed and the war was over.

'You look perkier!' Rose said as Beth came in. 'Something nice happen today?'

Rose put a cup of tea and a slice of cake for Beth on the table. She had become adept at finding recipes that didn't require eggs or sugar. Some were good, others were, as she said herself, like eating wood shavings.

Beth sat down, tried the cake and smiled approval. It was a fairly good one. 'Nothing in particular,' she said. 'It was nice walking back across the Downs, though. The leaves on the trees are all changing colour now, maybe it's that.'

She found it extraordinary that Rose could pick up on her every mood. Yet she never gave her opinion unasked.

'And what have you been doing?' Beth asked her.

'Aside from this cake, I bottled some raspberries.

Miss Tomlinson gave me lots of them. Apparently, she's got a glut this year and she's sick of eating them.'

'How can you get sick of eating raspberries?' Beth giggled. In her opinion their neighbour bought friends by giving them things. She knew if she called round with something people would invite her in, and she was quite hard to get rid of. 'So what did you say to banish her today?'

'I didn't need to, she was on her way to someone for lunch.'

Beth went into the kitchen to put the kettle back on, and saw the six Kilner jars full of raspberries cooling on the table.

'You should've waited till I got home,' Beth reproved Rose. 'I don't like the thought of you handling boiling syrup.'

'I was making jam and bottling fruit before you were born,' she retorted. 'And I still have all my faculties.'

Beth laughed and went over to hug her. 'Yes you have, but to be on the safe side, wait for me next time.'

'Miss Tomlinson claimed you'd be off soon now you've heard from your young man. I tried to tell her he'd lost his legs and was still imprisoned in Germany, but she didn't seem to grasp the seriousness of that.'

'I think she's a bit senile now,' Beth said, but laughed because they'd both had conversations with the old lady, and she was always getting things wrong. She'd probably be looking for her raspberries tomorrow, having forgotten she gave them away.

The telephone rang suddenly, shrill in the quiet of the sitting room. Beth moved to answer it.

As soon as she heard Mr Ramsey's voice she sensed it was bad news.

He paused, as if gathering the strength to speak. 'I'm sorry, Beth, there is no easy way to tell you this, but Jack passed away a couple of days ago. We just got a telegram from the Red Cross. A letter will follow.'

To Beth it felt like a black pit had just opened up in front of her, and she was about to fall into it. She forced herself to be more rational.

'But why? I thought he was on the mend,' she said, tears coursing down her cheeks.

'We don't know,' Ramsey said. 'We will when we get the letter. But we think it was the infection. It's always that for the most severe wounds. We are trying to tell ourselves he is in a much better place now, but it doesn't help. Our beautiful boy gone.'

Beth had no words, her head was spinning so fast she had to drop to a chair. 'I'm so, so sorry,' she whispered. 'I can't believe it really. He's so much alive in my mind.'

'Ours too, Beth,' he said, his voice cracking. 'Stay strong, and we'll try too. I'll ring again as soon as we know more.'

He was gone. Beth sat there with the receiver in

her hands, unable to move, not even to wipe her tears away.

'He's gone?' she heard Rose say. 'Oh, darling, I'm so sorry.'

Rose enfolded Beth in her arms, rocking her. For some ten minutes Beth stayed there, not speaking. It was the end of every dream and happy thought she'd ever had about him. She felt she had nothing now, no future, hope, not even the will to go on.

'Thank goodness I've got you,' Beth said eventually, her face still pressed against the older lady's chest. 'We've become hardened to news of death, and now it's my turn and I can't believe how much it hurts.'

'It will for a while,' Rose said softly. 'When I lost Duncan I didn't want to go on alone. But day by day it does get easier. I was lucky I had my son, he pulled me through.'

'Everyone is going to say it was for the best because he wouldn't have wanted to spend his life in a wheelchair.' Beth sat up suddenly and her eyes blazed with anger. 'Why couldn't I have seen him just one more time, or even talked on the telephone. He shouldn't have had to survive in pain for all this time, should he.'

Rose tilted Beth's chin up to look at her, and dried her cheeks with her hanky. 'I agree, that was terribly cruel. But every aspect of war is cruel, my darling. Families forced apart, homes destroyed, hideous injuries, and dreams shattered. If women were in charge of countries there would be no war, anywhere, or so I believe.'

'If those women were all like you,' Beth said. 'But I can think of many women who'd make a pig's ear of it. My mother included.'

'I've always wondered what "making a pig's ear of it" actually means,' Rose said. 'I wouldn't have the first idea how to make one.'

If it wasn't for the seriousness of the moment Beth would've laughed. Rose often queried the sense in common phrases.

'Well, I've made a bit of a pig's ear of my life so far.'

Rose said nothing, just caressed Beth's cheeks in deep sympathy.

For over two weeks Beth carried on as normal, shopping, cleaning, gardening and going to the convalescent home. But she said nothing about Jack to anyone. She felt as long as it didn't become common knowledge, she could tell herself it wasn't true, or a mistake – after all, the Red Cross had to keep tabs on so many POWs. She didn't want people saying it was for the best, and she didn't want to cry in public anymore. It was bad enough at night, crying herself to sleep, waking the next day and having to face that there would be no reprieve from her misery.

Rose did her best to help. She didn't keep asking her how she felt, offering advice, or sympathy. In fact, an outsider would imagine she either didn't know Jack was dead, or didn't care.

But Beth knew better.

Then two weeks later on her Thursday stint at the home, she got there to find Harry dressed in civilian clothes and sitting on a chair just outside the ward, without the plaster on his leg.

'When did that come off?' she asked.

'Yesterday, and now I'm going home.'

'That's marvellous,' she said. 'How does your leg feel?'

'Stiff, a bit weird, I'll need a stick for a while. But last night it was bliss to sleep without the plaster. But come and sit with me for a minute or two. You've lost weight and your smile. Are you going to tell me what's up?'

No one else had guessed something was wrong, but she might have known observant Harry would pick up on it.

'Jack died,' she said simply, and sat down beside him. 'Please don't say it's for the best.'

'I won't,' he said and took her hand and squeezed it. 'But I'm very sorry, nonetheless. And for his folks. Was it the infection?'

'Yes, his father got further news just a few days ago. He's being buried there. So not even a funeral to pay our respects and offer a few prayers. But his parents are planning to have a memorial service in Falmouth. I'll go there for that. But tell me about you?'

He reached out and smoothed her hair back from her face. 'How like you to concern yourself with an old soldier like me,' he said quietly. 'I'll go back to my regiment in a couple of weeks, I expect, and they'll find me a few desk duties to keep me busy. It looks like it might all end soon. We've liberated Paris, and I'd like to be back in action to enjoy the last rites, and come back to England in triumph.' He looked every bit the conquering hero as he spoke, and it warmed her inside where there had been nothing but misery since Jack died.

'You just make sure you don't take any more risks. No climbing on tanks or hurtling over fences,' she said. 'I'm going to miss you on the ward.'

'Not as much as I'll miss you, Beth. There is something about you. I can't quite find the name for it, but you are strong yet gentle, caring and funny too. Not easy to forget.'

'Neither are you,' she laughed, and realized it was the first laugh since before the news of Jack. 'But I appreciate the compliment. And I wish you all the best for the future.'

He leaned forward and, cupping her face in his hands, he kissed her on the lips. Not just a peck, but long enough to be meaningful.

'I suppose I should apologize?' he said. 'But I won't because I couldn't leave here without doing it.'

Beth was shocked, but his dark eyes were twinkling,

and those rakish good looks delighted her. 'I'm glad you did,' she admitted. 'But now I've got beds to make, and dressings to change on wounded men.'

22

That evening, Mr Ramsey telephoned to tell Beth he had arranged the memorial service for Jack in Falmouth. It was to be the following week.

'It's a tall order, as you'll have to change at both Plymouth and Truro.'

'I don't mind that at all,' Beth said. 'I'll arrange to have time off work.'

'Bless you, Beth, it will mean so much to us to have you there. Let me know your arrival time and I'll meet you at the station the day before. We hope you'll be happy to stay with us.'

'That is very kind of you,' she said.

'I just wish we weren't meeting you for the first time for such a sad occasion,' he said sorrowfully. 'We know Jack wanted to marry you, and so we see you as part of our family.'

'That is a lovely thing to say, Mr Ramsey. I'll organize train tickets immediately. Meanwhile is there anything I can do to help you and Mrs Ramsey? Anything I can bring for the wake?'

'Just yourself, my dear,' he said. 'That will be more than enough for Jack.'

As Beth had walked home earlier across the Downs,

her head had been buzzing with the memory of Harry's kiss. It made her feel lighter, more optimistic about the future, and happier. But after the phone call from Mr Ramsey she felt guilty that she was even thinking about another man when Jack was barely cold in his grave.

Rose, ever perceptive to moods, brought it up later that evening.

'When you came in this evening, you had flushed cheeks and brighter eyes. Even your voice was bouncier. Then Mr Ramsey called and all that went. I understand that being asked to attend a memorial service in Cornwall for the man you had hoped to marry is enough to flatten anyone's mood. But clearly something good happened earlier in the day. So tell me about that?'

It was tempting to claim Rose was mistaken, but the truth was that Beth wanted to unburden herself.

'I swear you have witchy powers,' she said, trying to make light of it. 'Yes, something did happen. Harry was discharged today. He said he was going to miss me, but he also kissed me.'

Rose pursed her lips. 'A real kiss?'

'Well, not a smooching one, but on the lips,' she said, blushing furiously. 'Now I feel guilty.'

'Well don't, dear, I'm rather glad that someone or something has made you perk up. From what you've told me about the sergeant, he sounds a good man.

Now you must concentrate on this service for Jack, meeting his parents, thinking about what you are going to wear, and making that sad journey to Cornwall. But once that is over, you can start living again. You are far too young to stay alone, grieving, for ever.'

'Rose, you are just amazing sometimes, so unjudgemental. I was afraid you'd tell me off.'

'I'm human just like you,' she said. 'You hardly knew Jack, but you've been faithful and devoted to him for a very long and difficult time. It's enough.'

Mr Ramsey was right, it was a long journey to Falmouth, and it had turned much colder. Rose had lent her a black moleskin coat that, although like velvet, was surprisingly warm and fitted her perfectly, and a black felt hat.

'Duncan bought me that coat just a couple of years before he died. He said it was a pity moles only came in black, but I could be stylish in it for his funeral. Of course he died in the summer, so I didn't wear it, but it is rather stylish, Beth, and black suits you.'

Beth sniggered at Duncan saying it would be good for his funeral. Everything Rose said about him pointed to a funny and caring man. 'I feel like a film star in it,' she said. 'I'm glad you didn't wear it for his funeral as I'd take extra sadness with me.'

Rose had made a big Dundee cake for her to give to the Ramseys. She'd used the last of the dried fruit she had stored, another example of her generosity. 'Just don't leave it on the train,' she warned.

Beth had bought some lovely hand cream for Mrs Ramsey, some cigarettes for both Mr Ramsey and Jack's brother, Andy, and a lipstick for his sister, Dawn. They weren't imaginative presents, but there wasn't much in the shops to choose from. The lipstick had been the last one in the chemist's.

She had planned to read on the train, but once on it she found a previous passenger had made the viewing hole in the window bigger, and looking out and seeing Somerset, Devon and Cornwall was far better than reading. Everyone had told her all three counties were picturesque, and she'd have a job to decide which she liked best. They were quite right; the scenery was lovely, one sweet little cottage after another, fields of sheep and cows, fast-flowing rivers, and ancient churches. It was a far cry from London's East End, and Bristol too, with so much bomb damage to the city centre, but the beauty of these new counties brought on a wave of sadness that Jack wasn't showing them to her.

It was dusk when she arrived in Falmouth, and the man who came striding towards her could be none other than Mr Ramsey. He was just an older version of Jack, his features the same, but with a little less hair.

'Welcome to Falmouth, Beth,' he said without even checking who she was. 'You look every bit as beautiful as Jack said.' He took her case in one hand, and put the other on her elbow and led her out of the station. 'We only live ten minutes away, but the hill is a bit steep, I'm afraid.'

After they crossed the road, Mr Ramsey said, 'That bag in your hand looks heavy. Let me have it.'

'It's a Dundee cake,' she explained. 'Mrs Cullen, who I work for, made it. It should be lovely – she's great at making cakes.'

'How kind of her,' he said. 'We haven't had any fruit cake since the start of the war. It seems to be much harder to get foodstuffs daily.'

'It's the same in Bristol. But Mrs Cullen had tucked things away in the larder long before the war began. Mind you, she's given so much of it away now, she's very kind. But tell me, before we get to your house, how are you and your wife coping?'

'Taking it one day at a time. Struggling a bit. It was as we thought, an infection Jack had been harbouring almost since he was injured,' he said, his voice cracking with emotion. 'Just awful. I think Jack would've preferred to be blown up entirely rather than this terrible, prolonged and painful ordeal.'

'Yes, I think he would,' Beth agreed. 'But I kept hoping for a miracle.'

'Me too, but don't let's talk about this back at the house. My wife finds it terribly upsetting. I think that every day since we got the bad news, she's broken down in tears. Though none of us are our normal selves. If you'd come a couple of years ago you would have thought what a noisy, busy family we were. We are all quiet now, but maybe after this service we can start to come out of that.'

'Grief has its own timetable,' Beth said, something that Rose had told her. 'We just have to wait until it passes.'

Mrs Ramsey was small and rotund, in her fifties, but grief had put lines on her face that were probably not there before, and the way she'd twisted her greying hair into an untidy bun and the somewhat grubby floral overall over her dress suggested she didn't care about her appearance anymore. But she hugged Beth tightly, murmuring that she had imagined meeting her for the first time to celebrate their engagement. She got all choked up then and had to go upstairs to recover.

Dawn and Andy were very welcoming, making her tea and offering her a sandwich. But they were subdued, as if they didn't dare speak of anything that might inadvertently trigger a memory of Jack.

Their house was much as Beth had expected, small rooms, all in need of redecorating like most people's homes now. Many photographs, not just of Jack, but Dawn and Andy too. Dawn was a peroxide blonde, petite and pretty, with her mother's dark eyes. Andy also had the dark eyes and a square jaw, and Beth was glad he wasn't like Jack. He was shy; he'd only been in the navy for a year, but didn't seem to want to speak about that. Dawn was chattier. She was working as a receptionist at the doctor's surgery and was no longer seeing the fisherman. She smiled when she said that his smell had put her off a year ago. 'I want to go and work in London when the war is over,' she went on. 'Will you tell me the best shops to apply to?'

Beth was glad when it was time to go to bed. She would be sharing a room with Dawn, and she was so tired she just hoped the younger girl wouldn't keep chatting.

Fortunately, Dawn didn't chat, and Beth must have fallen asleep the moment her head touched the pillow, as suddenly light was coming in round the curtain and she could hear seagulls. It was after eight.

They would be having the wake in the Red Lion, a public house close to the station and the church, and as Beth's train home was leaving at three p.m., Mr Ramsey suggested he drop her case off at the pub this morning.

'We wish you could stay for another night,' Mrs Ramsey said as she dished out boiled eggs for breakfast. 'But will you come again one day, perhaps next summer?'

'I'd love that,' Beth said. She felt so sorry for Mrs Ramsey, who looked drawn and exhausted by her grief. Dawn said last night that she had lost a great deal of weight since they heard Jack was missing. 'It was so cruel that the army and the Red Cross took so long to find him. Poor Mum was imagining all kinds of terrible things. Then she finally gets to hear that one of those things has happened.'

She told Beth too that Jack had said in a letter that he hoped Beth and she would become good friends. 'I told him that if he loved you, then I would too,' Dawn said, and her eyes filled with tears. 'You haven't disappointed, Beth, you are every bit as lovely as he said.'

The memorial service was harrowing, an outpouring of grief from everyone present. So many people there, young and old, plus at least a dozen of Jack's old school friends, now in uniform, and some men who served with Jack and were home on leave. The vicar, however, red-faced, middle-aged and balding, seemed rather more interested in the sound of his own voice than portraying the life of a brave young man who had come to this church since a baby.

The organ was very wheezy and the hymns were played too slowly. But Mr Cox, headmaster at the senior school Jack attended, spoke affectionately of the boy he called 'a bright spark with great promise'. There was also a letter from Jack's captain in the army, read aloud by Mr Cox. He said he felt great regret at hearing Jack had died as a POW, and that Mr and Mrs Ramsey, his brother and sister and other family members should be very proud of him, an exemplary soldier, courageous, tough, and well-liked by both his fellow soldiers and officers. His death was a great loss to the British Army.

Beth found it impossible to eat anything at the wake. She had just a small glass of sherry and watched the clock to leave. Most of the people there were in groups chatting quietly, but if they noticed Beth they didn't come over to speak. She didn't blame them – why should they care about a stranger? And she guessed none of the Ramseys were in the mood to introduce her to people. Aside from feeling isolated, she had been biting back tears all day and felt unable to deal with anyone's memories of Jack on top of her own. She had imagined before she got here that sharing stories would be uplifting, but now she felt she'd been plunged into that dark pit of misery again.

It was after midnight when Beth got back to Bristol. She was cold, forlorn and barely able to put one foot in front of the other, dreading the walk home. Fortunately there was a taxi waiting, when she had expected they would all have gone, and within ten minutes she was opening the front door at Lamb Lane.

'You poor love,' Rose said as she came in. She was ready for bed in her pink dressing gown. 'You look exhausted. I've put a hot water bottle in your bed, and now I'll make you some hot milk and a sandwich.'

'The milk will be lovely but don't worry about a sandwich,' Beth said. 'I think food would just stick in my throat.'

'That bad, eh?' Rose raised an eyebrow.

'Yes, unbearably sad. Jack's mother looked like she was about to collapse. But they were good people, I'm glad I went, even if it was a very long way. They were very touched by you making the Dundee cake.'

'Did you have any of it?'

'No, they didn't take it to the wake. I expect they didn't want to share it with so many people.'

'I didn't tell you before, but I made a little one for us too. Would you like a slice now?'

Rose opened up a tin, and wafted it past Beth so she could smell it.

'Umm, maybe I could manage a small slice, then,' Beth said.

The cake was delicious and comforting. 'I couldn't wait to get back here,' Beth admitted. 'I think that means this is where I belong.'

'I think you belong here too,' Rose said, and got up and leaned over Beth to hug her. 'But one day soon you'll meet the man you are destined to spend the rest of your life with. And no one will be happier than me when that happens.'

23

The black clouds of grief slowly lifted for Beth as the weeks to Christmas passed.

A letter came from Mr Boyle in Ireland asking if she would be willing to let the cottage for at least six months. He had a client, Mr Halstead, who had engineering businesses in both Cork and Dublin. He, his wife and two children had been living in Dublin but wanted to settle near Cork. A six-month tenancy would give them time to find the right property to buy, and they hoped by then the Emergency would be over.

Beth was delighted to accept. She still intended to find some permanent solution for the cottage, but this would ensure the place was looked after until then. She had very few personal possessions left there, having brought most things back on her last visit. But Kathleen would pack any remaining stuff away. She hoped these tenants would keep Kathleen on, and wondered if she could make that a condition of the tenancy.

She wrote back immediately, agreeing and raising the question of Kathleen. That done, she found she was more enthusiastic about plans for Christmas.

'Do you think some of the Jewish children you helped find foster homes and clothes for might like to go to the pantomime?' Beth asked. 'It's *Cinderella* – I saw them putting up posters the other day. I'll gladly buy the tickets, but we need to find out just how many will be needed, and the best day to see the show. I thought Boxing Day would be good.'

'What a brilliant idea,' Rose agreed, beaming from ear to ear. 'I know the right person to ask about how many children. I can get onto that right away. What fun! I haven't been to a pantomime since Myles was about ten or eleven. We used to go every year until then.'

'I've never been to one,' Beth admitted. 'Are they fun?'

'Hilarious,' Rose laughed. 'Terrible jokes, lots of audience participation, the Prince is a girl and the Ugly Sisters men in ridiculous costumes.'

'I used to look at the posters at the theatre in Whitechapel,' Beth remembered. 'I wanted to be dressed like the Fairy Godmother.'

Beth almost never mentioned incidents from her childhood, but that little anecdote made Rose realize why she so much wanted the Jewish children to go.

'We will organize it,' Rose said firmly. 'Leave collecting names and numbers to me. We will need some adults too for supervision. I expect if there's quite a big number we can get a reduced ticket price.'

*

A week later, Beth was in Clifton Village begging sweets from shopkeepers. Her idea was to give a little cone of sweets to every child as they went into the theatre. The cost wasn't a problem, she was happy to pay, it was just the rationing coupons needed. But already Beth had found most shopkeepers were generous, claiming they would ask some of their customers to donate coupons.

Rose had found there were twenty-eight Jewish children to buy tickets for, and so far they had ten adults, including herself and Beth, to supervise. That seemed a fair ratio. These children had been through so much having to leave their parents back in Germany, and mostly they were better behaved than their privileged English counterparts.

As Beth came out of a shop in The Mall at four in the afternoon with a bulging bag of sweets in her hand, she caught sight of someone who almost made her drop the bag.

It was Harry, walking towards her without a crutch or walking stick.

'Beth!' he called out gleefully. 'You aren't going to believe this, but I was just wishing I knew your address so I could find you. I've missed you.'

'I've missed you too,' she said, and was aware her wide smile proved how delighted she was to see him again. 'I thought you'd be fit enough by now to be sent off to some new hellhole.'

'Let's get a cup of tea,' he suggested. 'I'd rather have a pint but they aren't open yet.'

'First I'd better put these in a shopping bag before I drop them,' she said, groping in her pocket for the string bag she kept there.

'That's one helluva lot of sweets!'

'Not for us to tuck into,' she laughed, and quickly explained.

They went into a teashop on Regent Street. At first Beth could hardly get words out. Not only was she excited to see him again, but he looked so handsome. He was clean-shaven, his hair well cut, and his tweed jacket and grey flannel trousers, with a red scarf flung over one shoulder, made him look quite the gentleman.

'Did you go to Cornwall?' he asked.

She nodded. 'It was as sad as I'd expected. But it had to be done. His family needed my support.'

The waitress came over then, and they ordered a pot of tea and some crumpets.

'And since the memorial service?' Harry continued once the waitress had gone.

She smiled. 'Every day is easier. Planning this trip to the panto has helped. And being up at the convalescent home is good too. I'm putting all my energy into thinking about stuff to do for Christmas. But what about you?'

'Well, I've passed the army medical as completely

fit, and any day now I could get ordered to join my mob. They're in Germany now, and with the RAF bombing the guts out of the place I'm not even sure where we'll fit in. No doubt I'll find out the moment I get there. My folks are hoping I won't have to go till after Christmas, but I doubt I could be that lucky.'

'Can't you malinger a bit, say your leg hurts?'

'I would if I thought it would work, but when the army say jump, you must. Once a doc has cleared you, that's it. But you could make me a lot happier if you'd come out to dinner with me tonight?'

She blushed furiously and hung her head.

'Am I that scary?' he said, lifting her chin with one finger. 'After all the quite personal stuff you've done for me?'

'Perhaps it's that,' she managed to smile. 'We aren't supposed to see patients as dinner dates.'

'But I'm no longer a patient, and we are both out Christmas shopping.'

'I *would* like to come to dinner with you,' she said. 'By the way, I don't see you carrying any presents. I hope you've bought something for your mother at least.'

'That's already been done. I got her and my father books they wanted. Luckily they aren't rationed or in short supply. I came out today to try and find some oranges. A tall order, it seems.'

'I don't think you'll be lucky enough to find them,'

Beth said. 'I haven't seen one since the outbreak of war. Or a banana!'

'We had the occasional orange in France, but they were pretty ropey, and sometimes peaches too, which were good. I missed crunchy English apples back then, but now that's all we've got here, I'm sick of them.'

'Are you going to stay in the army after the war?' she asked.

'Yes, well at least for a few years. The whole of Europe will be a mess afterwards, Poles killing Germans, Hungarians getting a lot of stick for siding with the Germans, Italians undecided whose side they're on. As for the Russians, they'll be wanting to fight everyone. We and the Yanks will have to police things.'

'That sounds awful. I only imagined buildings and roads to be rebuilt.'

'If only it were that simple,' he sighed. 'Railways, bridges and hospitals blown up, shortages of food and everything else. No doubt you've heard the stories flying around about concentration camps, the death camps and massacres. Even if it isn't all true it will be a real mess with all the displaced people. It's awful here in the cities, so many people lost their homes, but we weren't invaded by the Germans, so we got off lightly.'

'I liked to imagine all the servicemen coming home as conquering heroes,' she said. 'I didn't think for a moment about the aftermath.'

'Many enlisted men will come home soon after the end, but regulars like me, no chance. But we haven't quite won yet. There's still some serious fighting to be done, and there's the Japanese to crack too, plus lots more stuff in the Far East. But things are looking more positive. And you, Beth, are you going to stay looking after Mrs Cullen? Or go back to Ireland?'

'I don't think I'll ever want to leave Rose. I've just got a tenant going into the Irish cottage for six months. Maybe I'll sell it once the war is over. I just don't know. But after this tea, why don't you walk home with me and meet Rose. She'll be delighted, and it's not far.'

On the short journey home, Harry carried the string bag with the sweets and tucked her hand through his arm. 'That's cosier,' he said. 'When did you last go out to dinner with a man?'

'Over three years ago with Jack,' she said. 'Sad to say, since then I've only been out after dark a couple of times, to the cinema with Rose and to a concert at the church. And last New Year, Rose and I went out. That's it, my frantically busy social life in a nutshell.'

He grinned. 'I shall rectify that. That is if I don't get my orders to go to Germany until the New Year. We'll go dancing, to the cinema, and maybe I'll even come to the pantomime with you and the kids.'

'You wouldn't want to do that, surely?' she asked in astonishment.

Harry shrugged. 'Why not, I like pantos and kids.'

Rose's face lit up when Beth came in with Harry. 'Let me guess! Harry with the broken leg.'

Harry laughed and shook her hand. 'The very same. Sergeant Harry Irwin. I ran into Beth in Clifton Village. We had tea and crumpets and she suggested I come here to meet you.'

'I'm so glad to meet you,' Rose beamed. 'And no crutch or stick. How is the leg?'

'Fine now. I've been walking a great deal and doing the exercises I was given. I even rode my old bike out to Weston-super-Mare the other day. I have to get fit for when I get my marching orders.'

'Well, I hope that isn't before Christmas,' she said, and delved into the big bag of sweets. 'These look good, Beth. How did you manage without coupons?'

'Some were happy to just let me buy without, some said they'd ask for some of their other customers' coupons. Then there were the really nice people who just gave us a couple of free scoops.'

The three of them sat down at the dining table and had more tea, plus the last small slices of the Dundee cake. Harry admired the furniture and was impressed to hear Rose's husband had made most of it. 'I like carpentry too, but I'm certainly not at this standard,' he said, running his hand over the silky surface of the sideboard. That inspired Rose to show him the workshop, which he enthused about.

There were no awkward silences. Rose told him

about her son and daughter-in-law in Canada and their glamorous lifestyle. Harry in turn spoke of his aunt and uncle who had a farm on the outskirts of Bristol, and how he used to help out there, and ride too. 'I wanted to go into the Horse Guards,' he admitted, 'but I suppose they only want the upper-crust types, so I went into the Engineers.'

'More useful than posing on a horse,' Rose said with a giggle. 'The busbies must give the men a headache?'

'But the uniform is gorgeous,' Beth chimed in. 'The red jackets, all that gold braid. Wonderful.'

The time flew by; suddenly it was five-thirty. Rose suggested Harry stay and take Beth out for a meal from there. It was agreed that was a very sensible idea, and Beth went upstairs to change.

'Tell me, Mrs Cullen,' Harry said when Beth was out of earshot, 'Beth doesn't say much about her past, and I've got a feeling some of it, until she came to work for you, was pretty awful. Tell me to mind my own business if you like. But I really like her, and I want to understand.'

Rose looked hard at his handsome, rugged face and saw a real man, kind, strong, dependable and honest. 'Well, it wouldn't be right for me to tell you things told me in confidence, but I can admit she had a pitiful childhood. Yet full credit to her, she made her own rise in life by reading, observation, and having a very good heart to start with. I love her as if she were my daughter. I'm proud of her achievements, and though she was knocked sideways by Jack's death, she's now planning the Christmas panto for the refugee children. So look after her, Harry, she's a diamond.'

Harry took Beth to a restaurant in a hotel in Berkeley Square which he said he'd heard some very good reports of. The reports were not exaggerated; the pigeon pie was excellent, with pastry that melted in the mouth. And the dessert was crème brûlée, which neither of them had eaten before and they loved. It was said the chef was French, and maybe that was why the food was so good. The dining room was comfortable and softly lit. Beth thought it was the nicest place she'd ever eaten in – not that she had much experience of restaurants – but perhaps it was just the company.

Harry was so easy to talk to and so very interesting, making her laugh about when, back in 1939, he was ordered to train newly enlisted men. 'Britain had only a relatively small standing army then,' he explained. 'Most regulars were sent straight away to France. Others like me had to stay and train all the wet-behind-the-ears recruits. Mostly they didn't have a clue. You've never seen so many softies, hardly more than boys, office clerks, teachers and the like. I thought they'd run the first time they heard a machine gun. At least the farm-workers had some muscle and stamina.' He grimaced with presumably an unpleasant memory. 'Then when we got to France, we had a very long march ahead of us. Some of the men hadn't done what they were told to do to treat their new boots and their feet got in a terrible state. Blisters as big as a half crown.

'It was something of a baptism of fire for most of the men, as we saw so many refugees fleeing the Germans with carts and prams laden with their belongings. Their obvious terror gave my men a taste of what was to come up ahead. And of course German planes flew low over us, firing willy-nilly, regardless of women, children and old people. It was hellish!

'I was sent back home soon after to train more enlisted men. But they all surprised me, they got stuck into the training, even when they were almost crying with pain. I had some of these same recruits with me in the retreat to Dunkirk, and I can tell you, Beth, the ones I thought were the softest turned out to be the bravest. I was proud to have trained them.'

Beth saw his eyes glisten with unshed tears and guessed he lost a great many of them during the retreat.

He changed the subject then to ask about when she first went to Ireland. Rather than tell him any lies which later on she might regret, she chose to make him laugh with a vivid description of the Bible-thumping Mrs Griffiths in her awful guest house in Fishguard, the nosiness of her new neighbours, and of getting knocked into the ditch by a passing tinker in a cart. 'The next time I went to England I made sure I could get a train arriving and the ferry departing close together. I think I'd have sooner sat on a train platform overnight than stay with Mrs Griffiths again.'

'So did you make friends with any of the women?' he asked.

'A few to pass the time of day with,' she said. 'But I was aware I was a curiosity, a non-Catholic, no husband and possibly a threat. Kathleen who came to clean and housekeep was the nearest thing to a friend. I wanted to work at something but there was nothing. That's why I came back to England.'

They left the hotel restaurant at about eight-thirty, and on an impulse Beth suggested they walk up Brandon Hill, the park just beyond Berkeley Square. 'I'm sure you already know that by day it's the best view over the city. But there's a full moon tonight so we might be able to see the River Avon, possibly right to the Bristol Channel.'

'It used to be one of my favourite places in summer when I was a boy,' Harry said. 'I used to feed the squirrels, and do roly-polies down the hill. But to see it in moonlight with you, well there are no words for that!'

Beth giggled. It was good to imagine him as a scruffy little boy in short trousers careering down the hill.

It was very dark under the trees leading up to Cabot Tower at the top, and she clung on tightly to Harry's arm for fear of tripping on tree roots. But as they reached the top it was almost like daylight, the moon was so bright.

'Gosh!' Beth exclaimed. 'You can see better than I imagined. The Avon looks like a silver ribbon and the Suspension Bridge like a glorious silver filigree necklace strung across it. I just hope the Germans don't seize the opportunity to bomb here.'

'I think the only real fight left in them now is with their U-boats, trying to sink the convoys of ships crossing the Atlantic bringing us foodstuffs, their attempt to starve us into submission.'

'How are we doing in sinking them?' Beth asked.

'Let's say our navy is doing its best,' he said. 'We won't get told numbers until it's all over. But don't you worry your head about it. We've got Winston Churchill to do that.'

They sat on a bench and just looked out, able to pick out a few landmarks, but in the main it was a patchwork of what they knew were houses, darker spots that could be parks and open spaces, and here and there a church spire or a faint glow of light, possibly from a fire or police station.

'Won't it be lovely when the lights come on again?' Beth said softly, leaning into his shoulder. 'And all our soldiers, airmen and sailors come home. We never knew what we had, did we? Not until everything went bad.'

Harry put his arm around her and cuddled her still tighter. 'That's something most servicemen talk about,' he said. 'I've heard so many of my men claiming they'll be better husbands and fathers if they are spared. The younger ones idealizing the girls they've left behind.'

'What about you?' she asked.

'Well, I'm not a husband or father and I haven't left a girl behind, not yet anyway. But I did promise to myself to be kinder to my dad and mum. I have carried a rosy little dream of a little house of my own, a wife and a couple of kids, with me throughout the war. Just lately that dream has become bigger.'

Her heart quickened at the mention of not leaving a girl behind as yet, and then the wife and a couple of kids. 'More than a couple of children?' she teased. 'Or is it a bigger house?'

He put his free hand on her cheek and drew her closer. 'The dream is you,' he whispered and kissed her.

His lips were so soft and warm, his tongue flickering into her mouth making her insides contract with wanting. She raised her free arm and put it round his neck, stroking the bare skin with her fingers. The kiss went on and on, his hand went inside her coat, cupping her breast, and she lost complete touch with where they were, how cold it was, the time, and everything but wishing to stay in this bliss for ever.

It was Harry who broke away first. 'I knew as soon as I met you that you were the one,' he said softly into her ear. 'When I left Hambleden House I was angry at myself for not asking where you lived, but that was because of Jack. I mooned about, wondering if I should just go back there and wait outside in the hopes of seeing you. But I knew the doctors and senior nurses wouldn't approve of an ex-patient hanging around, so we'd both be in trouble. Then the miracle happened, and I ran into you today in Clifton.'

Somehow, she knew this wasn't the moment to be coy. 'I thought about you so often too,' she admitted. 'The day you left Hambleden House and kissed me, I walked home as if on air. But I felt so guilty, betraying Jack. I cast you out of my mind. I had to, didn't I.'

'I'm very glad I stayed lurking there in the depths, then,' he said with little smile. 'You greeted me joyously today – well, so it seemed to me.'

'I *was* joyous, even more now,' she said. 'But maybe we should go back. It's getting very cold.'

He got up and pulled her into his arms for another kiss. 'I'd gladly die of cold as long as you were kissing me,' he said.

Beth laughed. 'I can't imagine anything worse than you dying of cold in my arms. But there's a tea dance at the Berkeley Centre tomorrow. Could we possibly go to that?'

He tucked her hand into his arm and clicked his heels together. 'Your wish is my command, my lady.'

24

As Christmas approached, Beth was almost holding her breath, praying that Harry wouldn't be given orders to leave immediately.

He had been coming to Lamb Lane every day. He brought the tree in from the garden, and they decorated it together. The three of them made paper chains too and hung them up. He said he could get them a nice fat chicken from his aunt and uncle's farm, and of course Rose invited him to come for Christmas dinner.

'Should I ask your parents too?' she said with her usual generosity.

'Bless you, that's so kind,' Harry replied. 'But the last few years while I've been away, they've been spending the day with their neighbours and their small family, turn and turn about. It's my folks' turn this year and they've got everything organized already. But they'd really have liked to meet Beth and you, Rose.'

'Maybe we can do something at New Year, if you're still here, Harry?' Rose suggested.

They went to the Berkeley for the tea dance, and Beth wore her glamorous coral dress. Harry said she was the most beautiful girl there, and for the first time in her life she believed that.

She felt she was walking on air and basking in warm sunshine because she was sure Harry loved her. Nothing had ever felt so right or good, but she needed a quiet moment with him to tell him about her past.

After the tea dance they took Rose with them to the pictures to see *Dear Octopus* with Margaret Lockwood and Michael Wilding. It was a heart-warming film, and everyone in the packed cinema was beaming as they came out.

While they'd been inside, it had become much colder with a thick frost. As the pavements were slippery, Harry took both Rose and Beth's hands. 'If I go down, we'll all go down together,' he joked. 'I expect we'll have really deep snow in Germany,' he said a bit dolefully. 'Good job my mother knitted me some thick socks.'

'I wish you wouldn't keep mentioning Germany,' Beth reproved him. 'I'll be miserable once you're gone.'

'No you won't,' Rose piped up. 'I won't allow it.'

At that Beth smiled because she knew Rose had fallen for Harry's charm too and wanted to keep him around. But then he was very easy to be with. Beth found it hard to imagine him on the parade ground bellowing out instructions to his men. Even harder to imagine was him armed with a gun and shooting the enemy. She wondered again how men like him could adjust to coming back to civilian life.

In the last couple of days before Christmas, Beth found herself jumping each time the telephone rang, fully expecting it to be Harry telling her he'd got his orders and he'd be leaving that day.

But Christmas Day came the same as the previous days, with him arriving on his old bicycle, a bulging bag strapped to the carrier as usual. One day it had been vegetables from a farm near his parents' home, yesterday he'd brought the promised chicken. But on Christmas morning he had not only presents but a change of clothes, as he'd be staying the night.

Two sets of neighbours popped in during the morning for a sherry and a mince pie, only staying for a short while, but their presence created a festive atmosphere.

The chicken had been in the oven for some time, with Harry in charge of basting it. Rose prepared the vegetables, while Beth laid the table with a starched white cloth, the best glasses and two floral arrangements she'd made with red candles, holly, and silver baubles.

Rose was overjoyed when her son Myles called from Canada mid-morning. She had tears of joy running down her cheeks as she spoke to him.

'It's all so perfect,' Beth whispered to Harry. 'He couldn't phone last Christmas, and although she laughed and said that was the drawback of having a surgeon son, I knew she felt sad.'

'There's many a Christmas I would've liked to speak to my folks,' Harry said. 'When the war is over, I'm going to get a telephone put in for them.'

Rose took Beth to one side just before the lunch was ready and Harry was out in the garden sharpening the carving knife.

'I'm going upstairs for a rest after lunch,' she whispered. 'You must use that time to tell Harry about you.'

'Not today!' Beth exclaimed.

'What better day? Tomorrow we'll be at the pantomime, and the day after he'll surely have to rejoin his regiment. I'm not going to go over why you must tell him, and soon. You know why. You will feel much better for it, I promise you.'

'But what if he's appalled and doesn't want me anymore?' Beth asked, her eyes filling with tears.

'He's not that kind of man, any more than Jack was. So just do it, or risk him worrying so much about what you are hiding that it spoils everything for you.'

The crackers pulled and a bottle of wine consumed, the three of them were glowing from the heat of the fire. The chicken was flavoursome and moist, the vegetables perfectly cooked and the gravy in a class of its own. No one had room for Christmas pudding, and they decided they'd eat it the next day.

'If you don't mind, I think I'll have a little lie down,' Rose said, after gathering up the plates and putting them in the sink. 'I'll do those later.'

'I get the feeling she's leaving us alone on purpose,' Harry said as Rose's footsteps retreated upstairs.

'She is,' Beth sighed. 'She made me promise I would tell you about my past this afternoon, before you have to go back to your regiment.'

Harry got up, took her hand and led her to a sofa. 'It's scary for you to talk about it, isn't it?' he said.

'Yes,' she replied, hanging her head. 'I've been an imposter for so long, I'm terrified of telling the story. Rose is the only one who knows.'

'Well, as Rose is the most principled lady I've ever met, if what you've done hasn't disturbed or frightened her, I don't think I'll be too shocked,' he said with an encouraging smile. 'So just come out with it, sweetheart.'

It was so hard for her to know where to start, even harder to find the right words. But she began with the September day when she met Elizabeth in the Lyons Corner House by Trafalgar Square.

Beth had relived that day a hundred or more times. It was so vivid she could visualize Elizabeth's face, her smart clothes, her poise and confidence. As she told the story, it was like watching a film or a play. She hardly dared look at Harry, fearing he might be judging her and finding her wanting. On and on she went, the air-raid warning, everyone scampering for the shelter, and Elizabeth leading her into Trafalgar Square Tube. She described the crowded scene on the platform, and then the huge blast, and soil and debris raining down on them.

'I must've blacked out at that point,' she said, only then daring to lift her eyes to look at Harry. His dark eyes were wide, not with shock as she had expected, but concern for her.

She went on then to say how she woke up in a hospital bed and the nurse called her Elizabeth Manning, not her real name, Mary Price.

'I should've spoken out then, but I didn't,' she said, wiping angry tears from her cheeks. 'The kind nurse told me Mary Price was dead, but that she had saved me by putting a big handbag over my face. All I got was a nasty cut on my head that needed stitches.'

On she went with the story, stumbling over words here and there, but now she'd got going she really wanted Harry to know how dishonest she'd been. But he still didn't say a word, just listened, even when she related about the money, the fine clothes in the suitcase, and that she intended to go to Ireland and claim the other woman's inheritance.

Finally she got to the end of the story, Clancy's Cottage by the sea, a new life of ease and comfort. She stopped then, waiting for his response.

'Now tell me about your life before all that,' he said firmly. 'The whole thing, what happened to the little girl that made her so pleased to not be Mary Price any longer.'

That was far harder to tell. She was fine telling him about her job in Hampstead, and she had mentioned Auntie Ruth too.

'Your mum?' he said. 'Why aren't you telling me about her? I sense there is a man at the bottom of this, a stepfather, or your mother's fancy man?'

'Fancy man' was an expression Beth had heard countless times in Whitechapel. As a child she hadn't understood the meaning, but she'd learned since then that the expression usually meant a good-for-nothing man or a spiv who used vulnerable women.

She nodded. 'Ronnie. I don't think they were married. Mum met him after my dad died in the Great War. She was very poor, struggling I suppose.'

'And Ronnie said he'd look after you both?'

Again she nodded.

'And how long before he hit you and your mum, and worse?'

'About two years in he was hitting us.'

'And the rest?'

Beth looked up at him, her eyes brimming with tears. She felt he knew the whole story, a sixth sense had told him, but he wanted her to say it. She didn't know why she was finding it so hard to say the right words, when his face held nothing but loving compassion.

'He made Mum go on the streets, and I was ten the first time he raped me.'

She watched his face, and saw his lips quiver and tears spring to his eyes.

'I hoped I was wrong,' he said in a small voice. 'I sensed something when I first met you, but I told myself it was just the sadness about Jack. Rose knows all this, I take it. That's why she excused herself so you could tell me.'

'Yes, and I'm so sorry if it's ruined Christmas for you, but she felt I must tell you.'

'She was right to insist, Beth, something like this cannot be left untold and festering. But I want you to finish the story now.'

It was so hard and shameful to continue to tell him of her mother's descent into drug addiction, just so she could face prostitution, and of course Ronnie's continuing regular abuse, knowing her mother couldn't or wouldn't even attempt to put a stop to it.

'I thought people could see it or smell it on me,' she said. 'The other children at school ignored me, the neighbours – except for Ruth – were the same. I felt I was tainted, and even after I left there and went to Hampstead to work, I still felt the same way.'

Harry moved then and scooped her into his arms. 'None of it was your fault, Beth, both Ronnie and your mother should be strung up. Don't even think she couldn't help what happened. By doing nothing she was as guilty as him.'

His cheek resting against hers was wet with tears.

'Tell me, Beth,' he said after a few moments of silence. 'When you put on Elizabeth Manning's clothes, did you feel you'd stepped out of Mary Price's skin into Elizabeth's?'

Beth had never thought of it like that, but it was true. 'Yes, I suppose I did. I'd lost everything that was Mary's in the bomb blast. Staying at the smart guest house near Baker Street, with money in my purse, elegant clothes to wear, I was a new person. Like a caterpillar becoming a butterfly. I suppose that's awful?'

'No, completely understandable. Even if you'd gone to the police and told them your story, what good would it do for anyone? If Elizabeth had a family it could all be returned to them, but she hadn't, so what were they going to do with it?'

Beth pulled a troubled face. 'Yes, but I pretended to be her. I claimed her inheritance in Ireland. I've lived as her ever since.'

Harry shrugged. 'I dare say plenty of other people have taken another's identity, especially during both wars and other major upheavals. Elizabeth couldn't use it anymore; she had asked you to go to Ireland with her. I see it as recompense for the horrible things you'd been through in your childhood. You've given Kathleen over in Ireland an income, you've been the very best companion to Rose, and you've worked for nothing at Hambleden House. You're hardly a villain,

Beth, you're a good person. If it makes you happier to give the Irish cottage to a worthy cause, then do it.'

'You aren't horrified then?' she asked in a small voice.

Harry laughed. 'Horrified by what that bastard did to you as a little girl, yes. I'd like to cut out his liver and make him eat it. Such trauma would colour most women's whole lives. But I'm certainly not horrified about you taking Elizabeth's identity. I can only admire your resilience, courage and determination. Going off to Ireland alone must have been terrifying. Now, let's put it aside and give me a kiss.'

Harry didn't tell them until the evening of Boxing Day that he'd got his orders to present himself back at Warminster the following day.

The pantomime had been a sparkling success, from leaving Clifton in a crocodile of children aged five to eleven, with the adult minders interspersed between them, to their return with the children singing the songs from the show with rosy, happy faces. Beth had been up front with the tickets, Harry with the cones of sweets, and Rose carrying a bag of damp face flannels to wipe sticky fingers. Harry was in much demand, all the girls anxious to hold his hand, the boys keen to ask him questions about guns and tanks.

Beth loved the pantomime, the terrible jokes, the outrageous costumes of the Ugly Sisters, and even the

Handsome Prince who was a girl. Like the children, she gasped at Cinderella being transformed from a servant into an almost princess with a fabulous ballgown by a wave of the Fairy Godmother's wand. She saw Harry nod and wink at her from a few seats further along the row, clearly thinking Cinderella's story was like her own. She smiled back. He had the youngest girl on his lap and she felt he was her prince.

All the children had learned English in the years they'd been in England, but it occurred to Beth that even if they didn't understand some of the jokes, the plot of the story had universal appeal.

Her mind wandered from time to time, reliving Harry's kisses, and knowing that once they got the opportunity to be alone together it would be almost impossible to put the brakes on and not go further. Telling him about her past had lightened the burden of guilt she'd been carrying. Last night, knowing he was sleeping in the next room, it was so tempting to creep in there. But she hadn't because she had to hear him say he loved her first, and, knowing he was going to leave soon to rejoin the war, it was not the time to take risks.

'Please stay safe,' Beth said now, biting her lip so she wouldn't cry as he returned to the sitting room with his small bag in his hands. 'And write to me?'

She thought he had never looked more handsome tonight – six foot two, his back ram-rod straight, his face still flushed from the cold outside, dark eyes as shiny and black as tar, and his fair hair still unsuitably long for a soldier. He'd said earlier the captain would order it to be cut immediately. Beth liked it that way, little wisps trying to curl around his ears, and she loved his wide mouth and how his lips turned up in a constant smile. She knew from helping him in the convalescent home that his shoulders, chest and arms rippled with strong muscle. And she hoped that before long she could feel his naked chest against her own.

Rose got up to embrace him. 'You'll be in my prayers, Harry,' she said, her voice cracking with emotion. 'I couldn't be prouder of you than if you were my own boy.' She turned away, wiping a tear from her cheek. 'Go and see him out, Beth,' she said.

In the hallway, with the door to the sitting room closed, Harry took Beth in his arms. 'Just one more thing to say,' he said before kissing her until her legs turned to rubber.

'What is that last thing?' she whispered, running her fingers down his sharp cheekbones.

'I love you, Beth,' he said, his forehead against hers. 'I've been wanting to say it all the time over Christmas. Will you marry me? When I get my next leave we could get a special licence for it. That is, if you'll have me?'

'I love you too, and nothing would make me happier,' she replied. She didn't want him to go, but the longer she held him here the worse it would be for both of them. 'But please go now as you've got to leave so early tomorrow, and be careful in the dark.'

'You get back in the warm,' he said. 'We'll soon have a lifetime together with no more goodbyes.'

He moved quickly, shutting the door firmly behind him. But not fast enough for Beth to miss the tears on his cheeks.

25

As church bells rang out for 1945, Beth and Rose raised a glass for the year ahead, and the hope that soon the war would end. Out on the streets people were banging trays and saucepans, blowing whistles, and singing Auld Lang Syne again and again.

Rose was feeling off colour and had a bad cold, so Beth had decided for her they would stay in the warm this year.

There was an atmosphere of real optimism around the city that the war would end soon. People might be getting lean with the shortages of food, fed up with being cold as fuel for fires was scarce, and missing their men terribly, wondering if their lives would ever return to how they once had been, but they were soldiering on under an invisible banner of Hope.

Beth had received a brief letter from Harry that he'd written in a truck taking him and some other soldiers to Dover. He was of course cheerful, making jokes about the intense cold, the awful food, and the stench coming from one of his men's feet. But he reminded Beth that they would marry on his next leave and that he loved her more than he'd ever thought was possible.

Beth didn't expect to get any further letters for a while. She assumed he would be working his way across France, Belgium and Holland, rooting out any straggling German troops en route. She doubted he'd have time to write, or that the mail would even get through. She prayed nightly that he wouldn't be killed. She wasn't sure there really was a God, but if there was, surely he wouldn't take another man she loved from her?

January was cold and grey, and towards the end of the month they heard the shocking news of the German death camps. Whispers about these atrocities had been flying around for some time, but most people felt they were was exaggerated or propaganda. But now there were pictures of the starving prisoners in Auschwitz camp in Poland, and soon after the Allied army went into Buchenwald in Germany, and everyone realized that the whispers had been an appalling truth. They found mountains of dead, emaciated bodies, and barely cool incinerators, still full of human bones. Inside the fetid huts were old people and children too weak to stand. It seemed the rest of the prisoners had been forced into a death march through blizzard conditions.

Beth and Rose could only stare at each other in disbelief that such terrible things could happen. They couldn't bear to talk about it. They listened to the news on the wireless in tears.

Rose, who was still unwell, took to her bed. 'I don't want to live any longer in a world where people do such wicked things,' she told Beth, and it was clear she meant it.

Beth shielded her from any further shocks, warning any visitors not to bring up grim subjects. But Rose didn't want to see anyone, refusing to come downstairs and having all her meals on a tray. Her bedroom was lovely, with two big windows overlooking the garden, although just now it was only bare sticks of bushes and wizened stems of old flowers. Some of the walnut bedroom furniture had been made by Duncan, the natural whorls and squirls in the grain picked out when the sun shone. The heavy linen curtains had a glorious autumn leaves design in reds, golds and orange.

Beth lit the fire in the bedroom each morning, mainly to try to encourage Rose to sit in the green armchair beside it. Although she'd sit there while Beth made her bed and plumped up the pillows, she soon went back to bed. At first she was having a bath most mornings, but after a while Beth realized she was just washing herself at the basin.

'It's too hard for me to get in and out,' Rose snapped indignantly when she reproved her. 'Don't tell me you can't keep clean without a bath. My generation hardly ever had one.'

Beth offered to help her, but she completely

understood when Rose refused. She was afraid of losing her dignity. So she said no more about it, and gave up trying to bully her into coming downstairs.

In the afternoons when Beth wasn't expected at Hambleden House, and in the evenings, she read to her. Sometimes it was an Agatha Christie book, though Rose claimed Agatha wrote the same story in each book and the characters were wooden. But they both loved *The Heart Is a Lonely Hunter* by Carson McCullers, and *The Long Winter* by Laura Ingalls Wilder. Ironically the latter was about a family's hardships living through a desperately bad winter in a little house out on the prairies of America.

'At least we haven't got bears or wolves outside the door,' Rose joked.

Listening to a story removed Rose from reality for a few hours, but Beth was growing more and more alarmed that her dear friend was sinking fast. She was barely eating a quarter of the food on her plate. Her face had grown thin and drawn, eyes that had once sparkled looked dead, even the skin on her arms and legs felt thin and rough.

Beth telephoned Myles in Canada to seek his advice. 'The doctor here just says keep her warm and she will get better,' she told him. 'But I'm really worried. She just wants to stay in bed, and she said the other day she'd seen enough in her life to not want to see anything more.'

'She isn't the first elderly person to say such a thing,' Myles reassured Beth. 'When we get news the war in Europe is over I'm sure she'll bounce back. As long as she's eating and drinking, she should be fine. She's only seventy-four, that isn't so old, and she has no alarming symptoms of something else, I take it?'

'No, her doctor checked her,' Beth said. 'He actually said he was so worn out he wished *he* could take to his bed! I felt that was a bit tactless.'

'Yes, considering he's known my mother all his life,' Myles said with some indignation. 'I wish I could promise to come, Beth. I will try to pull a few strings to see if I can get on a military plane, but it's doubtful I'll be lucky. A ship is also difficult; as you probably know, the U-boats are still patrolling the Atlantic. But I'll do my best. In the meantime, just humour her, feed her and love her, as you've always done. I'm so glad she's got you with her.'

There were times during the bitter winter when Beth felt despair. It was so hard to get provisions, and even harder to turn the few ingredients she did manage to get into something tempting enough to make Rose eat. Finally she managed to track down a black marketeer, and feeling extremely guilty she bought some butter, bacon, flour and a couple of tins of Spam and corned beef at an extremely inflated price.

It was good to make bread again with unadulterated flour, even if she did have to use the hoarded dried yeast which wasn't a patch on the fresh stuff, now impossible to get. As the smell of the baking bread rose up the stairs, Rose looked expectant for the first time in weeks. With a couple of slices, a scraping of butter, and some of the homemade raspberry jam, Rose ate with relish.

'Promise me you'll eat dinner later with as much enthusiasm,' Beth begged her.

'When did you turn into such a dragon?' Rose said but smiled anyway.

'When you began being a bad girl,' she retorted. 'You can stay in bed for now, it's the best place when it's so cold, but at the first sign of spring I shall drag you out, whatever you say.'

Letters from Harry came intermittently, sometimes three together and then none for ages. He had stopped trying to make her laugh with funny stories but instead spoke of imagining the home they'd create together, how he saw the garden, and that he hoped there would be babies too. 'I've got this little daydream of us sitting in the garden on a hot day and a fat little porker of a baby boy playing in water in an old tin bath as Mum told me I used to do. Sometimes I imagine a little girl with your dark hair, pretending to be a ballerina. In this imaginary garden we have a dog, too, and a tortoise. There is an apple and a pear tree, and the rest of the garden is full of flowers you've planted.'

In each new letter there was another imaginary

scene, sometimes a day at the seaside, or one of the children's birthdays with a cake and candles. A visit to a circus, or him teaching the children to swim. All the scenes took place in warm weather, and Beth surmised by that he must be very cold most of the time.

For Beth such imaginings were doubly poignant, as she had no memories like these of her own childhood. But she knew in her heart Harry was giving her these glimpses into the future for that very reason.

She tried to think of interesting or funny things to tell him in her letters. There were a few hilarious moments at Hambleden House, but most of the patients there were so poorly they didn't speak much. The story of the death camps dominated the news and she didn't want to even dwell on that, let alone write about it. But she did write about the imaginary house she'd like to live in with him. It was a real one, a mid-terrace Georgian house she'd walked past one evening before they'd drawn the curtains, and it looked so elegant inside, with wall-to-wall bookcases and a moss-green Chesterfield sofa. She mentally redecorated it in pastel colours and had an imaginary kitchen at the back with French windows overlooking a gorgeous garden, and a view of the River Avon beyond.

In March they heard on the news that the Allied army had crossed the Rhine at Remagen, severely damaging German morale with both the loss of their soldiers and the knowledge they could no longer win. Later in April it was reported that President Roosevelt had died, and been succeeded by Truman.

Spring came late, but a touch of warm sunshine and daffodils bursting into flower lifted Beth's spirits so much that she finally persuaded Rose to let her dress her and bring her downstairs for lunch.

It was only when Beth fished out the pink wool dress Rose had worn their first Christmas together that she saw how thin Rose had become. It hung on her, material flapping around her hips, bust and even shoulders. Almost everyone in England was thinner than they were before the war, but Beth knew she and Rose had eaten better than most people. It was clear there was something more sinister behind this dramatic weight loss.

Beth said nothing, just found a skirt that only needed a safety pin on the waistband until she could move the button, and a jumper that had always been a snug fit. Yet when she helped put Rose's stockings on, she saw her legs were like sticks.

Seeing them like that, it was hardly surprising that she tottered rather than walked. 'You'll have to practise walking again, your muscles have grown weak from lack of use,' Beth said in what she hoped was a jovial manner. 'For today we'll just get you downstairs, and maybe a walk around the garden, then we can gradually extend walking a bit further.'

Lunch was some corned-beef pasties Beth had made with mashed potato and carrots, and jam roly-poly and custard to follow. For once Rose made a real effort to eat, but by mid-afternoon she wanted to go back up to bed.

She turned at the bottom of the stairs, putting her hand on Beth's cheek. 'You have become the daughter I always wanted, Beth, you are so kind, thoughtful and caring. I really hoped I'd be here to see you marry Harry, and have a couple of children. But I don't think I will be now. I want to go and join Duncan, and I want you to promise me that you won't grieve for long.'

'How can I promise that?' Beth asked, holding Rose's bony hand against her cheek. 'My time with you has been the happiest part of my life. I love you.'

Beth put her arms around Rose's waist and almost carried her up the stairs. For once Rose allowed Beth to undress her, and put her nightdress on.

Once in bed Rose caught hold of Beth's hand. 'It's likely I will get weaker soon, but please don't let them take me away? I want to be here with you.'

'Then here you will stay, I promise,' Beth said, hardly able to hold back her tears.

The following morning Beth telephoned Dr Waverly and told him she was very worried about Rose, and asked if he could come as soon as possible. He said he'd come after morning surgery.

Beth was on tenterhooks that morning, afraid of what the doctor would say. She wasn't a trained nurse, after all, and if he insisted Rose went to hospital, she had no right to refuse on Rose's behalf.

The doctor arrived just after twelve, and after briefly listening to Beth explain how Rose was, he went upstairs and Beth followed, even though she expected to be told to stay outside the room. But he didn't ask her to leave, and he was very gentle with Rose, sounding her chest, feeling her stomach, taking some blood, and other basic tests.

'I want to admit you to hospital,' he said to Rose. 'Home is not the place for you now.'

'Yes it is,' Rose snapped at him. 'I might be sick but I'm not feeble-minded. I want to stay here with Beth.'

'Yes, and I want to look after her,' Beth piped up. 'If you think we need a qualified nurse to do things I can't do, we are happy to pay for one.'

He turned to look at Beth. 'I think you've done a fine job nursing Mrs Cullen so far, but what has to come might be too hard for you.'

'There is nothing I wouldn't do for her,' Beth insisted. 'Please don't speak further about hospital, it will only upset Rose.'

'Very well then,' he said. 'Just keep me posted and call if you need me. I'll pop in next week, same day and time.'

Beth went downstairs to let the doctor out. 'What

is the matter with her?' she asked quietly before she opened the door.

'I am certain it is her pancreas,' he said. 'Problems there don't usually show themselves until it's too late. But even if we detect it early on, there is little we can do. She said she hadn't any stomach pain, and neither is she drinking excessively. Is that true?'

'She does sometimes complain of stomach pain, but it goes when she leans forward,' Beth said. 'And yes, she is drinking far more than she used to. I usually fill up the water jug by her bed twice a day.'

The doctor nodded. 'If she develops bad pain I can prescribe something for it. Just ring the surgery. I can see you are already doing a very good job. However, if it gets too much for you let me know.'

After the doctor had gone, Beth took a tray of tea and cake up for herself and Rose. As she walked up the stairs, she thought how joyful everything was with Rose, even sitting with her for tea and cake. She wondered what on earth could possibly happen to make her feel she couldn't cope.

As she put the tray down by the window, she observed that the garden was alight with daffodils, there were green buds on most of the bushes, and it looked lovely in the sunshine. 'If I could borrow a wheelchair for you, would you let me take you for a walk?' Beth asked as she poured the tea.

'No, Beth, I have no desire to go anywhere anymore,'

Rose replied, hiking herself up a little on her pillows. 'I like being here in my bedroom. It holds so many good memories.'

'I hope you aren't going to divulge something racy!' Beth sniggered.

'As if! No – of Myles getting into bed with us on Christmas morning. I can still see him bouncing on the bed. I used to tell him he wasn't to do it, but he did it anyway. Even when Duncan got sick and I nursed him up here, it was a good time. We talked a great deal then, more than we ever had when he was working. The day before he died, he said something I found very odd at the time. But it makes sense now. "I'll be waiting for you, Rose, so you don't need to be frightened when the time comes."'

'You think he knew he was going to die?'

'Yes I do. But that day it never occurred to me. I just brushed it off as a soft remark. That's the trouble with a long marriage, you forget stuff about your partner. Like he was a bit of a wizard, knowing stuff others didn't. I think that was why he was such a good doctor, but it was only after he was gone, I really saw that side of him.'

The telephone rang two days later at eight in the morning. Beth rushed down the stairs hoping it was Harry, but instead it was Myles.

'Good morning, Beth, how is Mother?'

'Much the same,' she said. 'This is a very good line for a change.'

Usually there were strange noises, and the sound would come and go.

'That's because I'm here in Bristol, a place called Hengrove. I managed to get a lift with the military.'

'That's wonderful, Rose will be thrilled!'

Myles chuckled. 'Well, don't tell her, I'll surprise her. I'm waiting for a guy who said he'd give me a lift to Clifton. All being well I'll be there within the hour.'

Beth was already washed and dressed, but now she had to persuade Rose she had to get washed.

Her sheets could do with changing so she used that as an excuse to get Rose out of bed, and also gave her a newly laundered nightdress to put on.

'You are such a fusspot sometimes,' Rose complained. 'I don't feel like washing and you only changed the sheets a few days ago.'

'That isn't so, it was ten days ago. As for washing, you will feel better when you get into a clean bed, washed, and in a clean nightie.'

Rose did as she was told, and once back in her bed, Beth brushed her hair for her and dabbed a little of her Chantilly perfume on her neck and wrists.

'What's that for?' Rose asked. 'I'm not going anywhere.'

'It might give you nice dreams of your past,' Beth said. 'Now, will you eat some porridge for your breakfast?'

'Just a couple of spoonfuls,' she said.

Beth was just going downstairs with Rose's breakfast tray when she heard the knock on the door.

It was Myles of course, looking very dapper in a navy blue suit, a cream raincoat and a trilby, which he swept off as soon as he saw Beth.

He was taller than she expected, perhaps five foot eleven and slender, with neatly cut light-brown hair and blue eyes. The handsome, smooth face of a matinée idol.

Beth put a finger to her lips. 'She's just had her breakfast,' she whispered. 'You can take her up another cup of tea. But if she hears me talking to someone, she'll want to know who.'

He smiled, the same smile as his father in the photograph on the mantelpiece.

'No, I don't need my windows cleaned, they were only done a fortnight ago,' she said in a loud voice. 'But thank you for offering.' She shut the door firmly so Rose would hear it.

Myles tiptoed into the kitchen and put a small suitcase and a linen shopping bag down on the floor. Beth put the gas on under the kettle. Once they'd shut the kitchen door they both laughed.

'Two minutes to make the tea,' she said. 'You must be desperate to see your mother.' She quickly told him what the doctor had said, and a brief rundown on how she was.

'That doesn't sound too good,' he said. 'But it's good to finally meet you, Beth, I know from Mother you've enriched her life. I hadn't realized you were so young though. I had imagined a matron of over fifty.'

'Sorry,' Beth said. 'I expected you knew everything about me.'

'She's never been one to write much about day-to-day life,' he said. 'More local news, questions about us in Canada. We knew you must be important to her as soon as you two met because you got a whole paragraph – that proved you were special.'

Beth made the tea. 'Would you like something to eat?' she asked. 'I made some porridge earlier.'

'I'm fine for now,' he said. 'I'll take the tea up.'

'Just call out if you want anything,' she said. 'I'll be listening at the bottom of the stairs to her reaction on seeing you.'

Beth was not disappointed. She heard Rose gasp in amazement at seeing her son. 'My darling boy,' she exclaimed, and then it sounded as if she was crying.

Beth went back into the kitchen, happy they were reunited.

26

April 1945

Myles was with his mother for over two hours, during which time Beth did some cleaning.

When he came back down, she turned to him from dusting the sideboard. 'What do you think is wrong with her? Was our doctor right?'

Myles looked thoughtful. 'Possibly, but the pancreas is tucked away so problems there are difficult to diagnose. Once they've got going there is little that can be done. I could get her into a hospital for some tests, but when I suggested that she insisted she didn't want anyone probing around her. She wants to stay here with you. I can't blame her for that, Beth, you have clearly been better than a trained nurse. I can't thank you enough.'

'She's not difficult to love,' Beth said. 'My time here has been very happy, even after she became poorly. Now, let me get you something to eat. She usually snoozes till lunchtime – not that she eats much! It's a job to tempt her, there's so little stuff in the shops.'

'Well, I've brought a few things which might do

the trick,' he said, opening up the bag he'd left on the floor. He brought out two sizeable tins of ham, a couple of jars of bottled peaches, some butter, and four packets of cake mix. 'The cake mixes are all the rage in Canada; I doubt they've made their way here yet. The devil's food one is gorgeous. Rich, moist chocolate. Everything you need, apart from an egg.'

'How wonderful!' Beth's smile was from ear to ear. Just looking at the tinned ham made her mouth water. 'We must have some of that for lunch today. And I'll make the devil's food. I've actually got two eggs, which is a miracle. She eats cake more readily than anything else.'

'In that case I'll get out of your hair for a while. It will be good to walk around Clifton again and see how things are.'

'We've been quite lucky here with bombing. Park Street took a hammering, but mostly everywhere else is intact, I think you'll find. After lunch I usually stay upstairs with your mother to chat. I knit or sew, sometimes I read to her, but I'm sure she'd love you to take my place.'

'I can't knit or sew,' he joked. 'And I think she'd like it if you were there with me, conversation always flows better with three.'

Myles poured himself a second cup of tea and scraped some butter on his toast. He'd been here for four days, and sadly he knew his mother was fading fast. Now he was here with her, her mind would've told her body she could let go and die. He remembered as a medical student being told by a very senior doctor that he'd observed this reaction in old people being reunited with a close relative many times. It wasn't a myth, it was true.

Yet despite the inevitable that was to come, these four days had been a happy time. In many ways it was like reliving his boyhood, a far cry from the stress of a large Canadian hospital. But instead of his mother fussing over him, it was Beth doing the fussing. They had talked with Rose, played cards, looked at old photographs, and laughed a great deal.

He owed Beth for Rose's well-being. She managed to make tasty things for her to eat, rubbed cream into her arms and legs to make her feel more comfortable, and was always alert to the possibility of bed sores. She had devised a way of washing Rose's hair in the bathroom basin once a week, then she dried it carefully, teasing out her natural curls so it looked pretty. He thought she was born to be a nurse.

She had only worked one afternoon at Hambleden House since he'd been here, as she really didn't like to leave Rose. He thought the convalescent home were lucky to have a volunteer like her. And he was fortunate to have such a wonder caring for his mother. He just hoped Harry turned out to be as good a man as

Beth and Rose believed him to be, and that they'd be as happily married as his parents were.

After lunch Beth wanted to finish reading *The Long Winter* to Rose, and so Myles said he would go to visit an old school friend and be back at four-thirty.

As Beth always did, she got onto Rose's bed beside her to read, putting a cushion behind her own head. She had been reading for almost an hour when she realized Rose had dropped off to sleep. She was feeling a bit sleepy herself, and as it was pouring with rain she couldn't do some weeding in the garden as planned. So she stayed where she was and closed her eyes.

Myles arrived home at four-thirty as promised, buoyed up with excitement as he'd just heard on the wireless that Hitler and Eva Braun had committed suicide in Berlin. He put his umbrella in the hall stand, hung up his raincoat, and took off his wet shoes.

He glanced into the living room, but Beth wasn't there so he went up the stairs quietly so as not to wake his mother.

Her bedroom door was open just a crack, and he smiled when he saw both women fast asleep, Beth snuggled up to Rose with her arm round her.

He stood there for a moment or two, touched because Rose looked so peaceful, and that Beth was so loving towards her, just as his mother had said in her letters to him. But all at once he had a premonition, and creeping into the room he took his mother's wrist.

No pulse. To be sure he felt for a pulse on her neck and listened to hear if she was breathing. But she had passed – very recently, as her skin was still warm.

Clearly the way she was lying, encircled by Beth's arm, she had slipped away without pain. That was a real comfort, but he had banked on a little more time with her and he felt his eyes well up and a lump come to his throat.

'Beth,' he said softly. 'Wake up, Beth!'

Her eyes flew open. 'Oh Myles, what must you think. I dropped off.'

'It's OK. But Mother has slipped away.'

She leapt off the bed, leaning over Rose as she almost didn't believe him. As the truth hit, her face crumpled and she began to cry.

Myles went to comfort her. 'It was a good death, you there beside her, nice and warm in her own bed. Few people go in such a perfect way. She clearly had no pain or she would've called out. But I must call her doctor now to register her death. Come downstairs with me and I'll make you some tea.'

'It's me who should be comforting you,' Beth said, her lips quivering as she tried to control herself.

'The way she died was the one I would've chosen for her,' Myles said. 'I didn't need to give her morphine, she didn't suffer the indignity of incontinence, or the embarrassment of knowing she was losing her reason. Let's be happy for her, Beth. She'd had a good, happy life, and you can be proud that you were a wonderful, caring companion for her right to the end.'

'But I'll miss her so much,' Beth sobbed.

'And me,' Myles said, and he began to cry too.

It was much later that evening, the doctor been and gone, the undertaker having taken Rose's body to his chapel of rest, and the immediate neighbours notified, before Myles got around to informing Beth of Hitler's death.

'We won't cry for him or even offer a prayer for his soul,' Beth said bitterly. 'But it is wonderful that this means the war is as good as over. It is, isn't it?'

'It certainly is. And your Harry will be able to come home and marry you.'

Rose's funeral was held on 7 May at Christ Church in Clifton, the day Germany surrendered unconditionally. England was virtually holding its breath for the announcement later that day that the war in Europe was officially over. The joy and excitement on the streets were palpable, Union Jacks and banners going up everywhere, and paper streamers and balloons. Public houses rolled out new barrels of beer in readiness for the all-day party that was to come tomorrow.

'It's difficult to mourn anyone seriously on such a happy day,' Myles said to Beth as they followed the hearse driving at walking pace to Christ Church. Many neighbours and friends had joined them. Their sombre clothes looked out of place when every other woman in the neighbourhood had dug out her brightest dress to wear in the even brighter sunshine.

'But Mother wouldn't have wanted sadness all around her,' Myles added. 'Tonight, she'll be tucked in with my father, together for all eternity.'

Beth agreed in principle with Myles, but she still couldn't help wishing Rose could have hung on to see her married. Harry would be very sad she wouldn't be there.

The words that Reverend Humphrey spoke about Rose's life comforted Beth and Myles. He said how countless people had been helped by her as a doctor's wife, and after her husband's death. Until recently she was still fundraising for the poor, sick and troubled people in the parish. 'She made light of it, but all those who knew her were in no doubt she was often working half the night on a new project. She had the rare gift of listening properly to people. She didn't judge, or gossip, she just cared and strove to get the right help they needed.

'I want everyone here today to follow her example. If you succeed, we can make this world a better place.'

Myles took Beth's hand and squeezed it hard during

the service. She could see it was hard for him to control his feelings. He wasn't the much-admired surgeon now, just a man grieving for his mother, and perhaps that was the best tribute anyone could give Rose.

The following day, church bells rang out all over Bristol for the end of the war. Rose and Myles decided they couldn't possibly join the throngs of people celebrating in the centre of town, so they took a blanket, packed a little picnic, and walked over the Suspension Bridge into Leigh Woods.

They found a lovely spot with bluebells all around them, and first discussed the funeral, both agreeing that the final interment was the saddest part.

'I shall have to return to Canada in a few days,' Myles said. 'My wife feels bad enough not being able to come with me, without me lingering longer.'

'When do you want me to move out?' Beth asked.

'Move out?' He looked puzzled at the question. 'The house is yours; Mother left it to you.'

Beth looked at him askance. 'No, you're mistaken, Myles. How can you even think that?'

'It's true, Beth. She wrote ages ago to tell me she'd changed her will, and I assumed she'd told you this. I must confess that in an uncharitable moment before I met you, I even imagined that was why you stayed with her.'

'I think almost anyone would think that,' Beth said,

frowning at the thought of it. 'But how can I accept such a huge gift? The house is full of memories of you as a baby and young boy, of your lovely father too. And there's all the beautiful furniture he made.'

Myles reached out and took her hand. 'I know now that you were never a gold-digger. My mother was very astute, and she'd have realized that very quickly. She loved the house, but she loved you too, and she knew you'd be the keeper of her good memories, Father's furniture included. Don't worry about me, or my feelings – I get everything else, a considerable sum. But the house is yours.'

Beth was in shock. 'I can't possibly accept it, it isn't right.' Her voice was shaky. This was too much for her to take in.

'Of course you can accept it. I know now how much she thought of you, and how you enriched her life. Besides, we have a house in Canada three times the size of Lamb Lane, and we would never come back here to live.'

'I can't believe it.' Beth's voice had dropped to a whisper and she felt faint.

Myles opened the bag of ham sandwiches. 'Eat one,' he ordered her. 'Your blood sugar is running low, and we don't want that. Aren't you glad you haven't got to move?'

'Well, yes I am, very glad, but I never expected this for one moment. I feel guilty.'

Myles put a sandwich in her hand and grinned like a schoolboy. 'The rest of England is whooping it up because the war is over. My mother has handed you an extra dose of joy. So don't look for reasons to be troubled by her generosity.'

It was a very strange kind of day. Peaceful as it was in the woods, they could hear a low rumble of noise coming from the city – singing, bands playing, and people shouting. It wasn't loud enough to disturb, just a reminder that this was a day they were never going to forget.

'Things will be much the same for a while,' Myles said thoughtfully as they walked on further into the woods. 'The blackout will go immediately, of course, but you will have rationing here for some time yet. Slowly the damaged properties will be mended, but there's going to be shortages of paint, timber and just about everything else until they get the factories up and running again.'

'Harry said it would be terrible over in Europe, the Poles fighting the Germans, Hungarians fighting the Russians, and just about every other nationality joining in the revenge fray. There will be rapes, looting, and people starving, much worse than here. And all the displaced people trying to get home.'

'I'm afraid Harry is right, people will want revenge, and there will be savagery. But who can blame them. Imagine the heartbreak for those who had loved ones snatched and taken to work in concentration camps, and who they will never see again.'

'This is all a bit serious for a day which is intended to celebrate victory,' Beth said.

'Yes, we must stop it now, and you, Beth, must understand that you completely deserve the inheritance from my mother. Tomorrow I will contact her solicitor and instruct them to draw up the necessary documents.'

'Are there any things in the house that you want?' she asked. 'I can get them sent to you.'

'Photographs are all I want,' he said, smiling warmly at her. 'That's another job for tomorrow. Now, shall we make our way home?'

A jubilant letter came from Harry the following day. He'd written and posted it before Rose died and the war had officially ended, yet he sounded like he knew Germany was about to surrender. 'There will be a great deal of clearing up and sorting to do here,' he wrote. 'I may get a brief leave soon, but I'll have to come back straight after. But hopefully long enough for us to get married. That is, if you still want to.'

She guessed that by now he would have the letter in which she told him about Myles arriving and Rose dying. But she sat down and wrote another brief and loving letter saying of course she still wanted to get married. The news of the house could wait till he got here.

'I'm really sorry I didn't get to meet Harry,' Myles said as he was at the door, ready to leave, a taxi outside to take him to catch his plane home. He cupped Beth's face in both his hands and kissed her cheeks. 'I will think of you as the younger sister I always wanted. Be happy with Harry and keep in touch. I'd love you both to come to Canada so we can show you what an amazing country it is. Promise me?'

Beth smiled. She liked Myles so much, and wished he didn't have to leave England. 'Yes, I promise. I had started to think of you as my brother in those afternoons when we played cards with Rose. Now go or the taxi might leave. Safe journey home.'

Beth felt very emotional as she waved Myles goodbye. She had enjoyed his company so much and he was her last link with Rose. She wandered aimlessly into the living room and found it too quiet, too empty, and the knowledge that it now belonged to her was scary. Lovely, but scary.

She could sense Rose everywhere, her taste in pictures, the table mats, each a close-up of a different rose, and the cushions, no two the same.

'You will have to learn to put your mark on it,' she said aloud, and her voice seemed to boom round the empty room. 'And you'd better start thinking what to do about Clancy's Cottage.'

She knew she wasn't going back there. It had been lovely but her home was here in England. And while thinking about it, she picked up the telephone and rang Mr Boyle.

'Well, hullo,' he boomed. 'How are you now the Inconvenience is over.' He was jokingly using the wrong word of course, and she laughed.

'Relieved, but Mrs Cullen died just before VE Day. Her son has been here and he's just left, but it got me thinking about Clancy's Cottage and what I should do about it.'

'No tenants in there now, but no doubt enquiries will soon come rolling in,' he said cheerfully.

'I have decided it should go to a charity, preferably for sick children to recover, or city children who need a holiday by the sea. But not a Catholic charity, if that's possible.'

He paused before answering, clearly shocked by what she'd said.

'That sounds like a good and kind plan,' he said. 'As it happens I know the very organization to approach.'

'Great. I thought the dining room, which never gets used, could be made into an extra bedroom.'

'My goodness, Miss Manning, you've been giving this a lot of thought.'

'Yes I have. Not so much lately while Mrs Cullen was sick, but on and off for several months. But my business head tells me now not to give the cottage away. They can have it for a peppercorn rent. Plus pay all the outgoings, including Kathleen's wages.'

'I was going to suggest something similar,' he said carefully. 'I was concerned when you first raised the idea of giving it away, that once you were married or had children you might regret your decision. As your solicitor, and a good friend of your godmother, I felt duty-bound to protect your interests. But it seems you have reached the right decision on your own. So when you are ready I will draw up the appropriate documents. Is there a possibility in the near future of husband and children?' he asked.

Beth laughed. 'Well, I am getting married when Harry comes home, and God willing we'll have children in due course.'

'I sincerely hope so,' he said. 'And congratulations, and please accept my good wishes for a long and happy marriage. May I still send mail to Lamb Lane, or are you moving elsewhere? I always see you in my mind's eye as the Girl with the Suitcase.'

'Yes, I'll be staying here. Thank you too for all the work you've done for me and may do now and in the future. I am going to write to Kathleen and put her in the picture.'

As Beth put the receiver back in its place, she suddenly felt lighter at having made the decision about the cottage. Offering it on a peppercorn rent was down to something Myles had said. Until then she'd never heard of such a thing.

Now she had Rose's room to spring clean. Rose had

said a few months ago, before she even got ill, that when she'd departed, she wanted all her clothes to go to the charity in Jacob's Wells Road to be either sold at a jumble sale or donated to people in need. She had been giving things away for the past year, so it wasn't going to be an onerous job.

At seven in the morning just a few days later, Harry telephoned from the airfield at Hengrove, the same one Myles had arrived at. 'I've begged a lift from a man delivering some engine parts here. He said he'll take me as far as Canon's Marsh. Must go now, he's all packed and waiting.'

Beth felt her heart fluttering with excitement and then put the phone down and ran upstairs to strip off her nightdress and jump into the bath. It would take him less than fifteen minutes to get from Canon's Marsh to her. She barely had time to dry herself and put on a pink summer dress that she'd always received compliments on. Some rouge on her cheeks, lipstick, a dab of Rose's Chantilly perfume and a brush of her hair, and she was back downstairs.

Looking in the larder to see what she had to make a meal of later was slightly worrying. Since Rose died and Myles left, she'd lost interest in cooking and even eating much, so the larder was bare. But there was still a tin of the ham Myles brought, and there were some potatoes, so she could make chips to go with it.

The doorbell rang and she raced to open it, squealing with joy to see Harry even more handsome in his uniform than in the picture in her head. She jumped into his arms, legs winding round him, and he dropped his kit bag and carried her in while kissing her.

'Well, that was a lovely welcome,' he said as he finally put her down. 'You did know it was me? You didn't think you were greeting the postman?'

Beth giggled. 'No mistake. He's old and fat.'

They couldn't stop kissing; it went on and on, getting more and more heated. It was Harry who broke away first. 'A cup of tea is called for, unless you want me to die of thirst?'

'Now that's a romantic thought!'

'I have got a much more romantic one up my sleeve,' he said, tweaking her cheek. 'But first things first. I am so sorry about Rose. She was an extraordinary lady and I liked her so much. I know how fond you were of her, I just wish I could've been here to support you.'

'It's OK, Harry, I've come to terms with it now, and at least Myles was here for her final days. But don't let's talk about sad things today. What's the romantic thing you've got up your sleeve?'

'Getting our special marriage licence. If we go there today, we could get married tomorrow.'

'Really?'

'Yes, really. I have to go back the day after, so it's now or whenever I get leave again.'

Beth felt dizzy at just the size of get married tomorrow. What was she going to wear? Where would the wedding be? Who would they invite?

'What papers do we need?' was the first question.

'Birth certificate. Your identity card. Maybe proof of address.'

At that her face clouded over.

'What's wrong?' Harry asked.

'The birth certificate. Is this going to catch me out?'

'How can it? You've got everything in that name, ration book, letters. You are officially Elizabeth Manning, full stop! Now, let's go, the sooner we get the licence the sooner we can plan tomorrow. Like asking my parents, and whoever else you'd like to be there.'

It was four in the afternoon when they got home, both alight with excitement. They had the precious licence, plus they'd bought a wedding ring at a jeweller's in town. They'd also contacted Reverend Humphrey at Christ Church to ask if he would marry them the next day. He said he would be glad to, at midday.

Harry sent his parents a telegram: MARRYING BETH TOMORROW. CHRIST CHURCH, CLIFTON. 12 PM. PLEASE COME. HARRY.

'That's a bit terse,' Beth giggled.

'Telegrams always are. But Mum knows that. There's a bus which will take them right there, and besides if I was to go over there to ask them, Mum would insist

I spend the night at home, as the groom isn't supposed to see the bride until the wedding.'

Beth put her hands on her hips and made an expression of outrage. 'You aren't thinking of staying with me?'

'I am. I thought we needed to practise before our wedding night.'

Beth dissolved into giggles. 'In that case I'd better make up Rose's bed if it's to be the start of our honeymoon.'

As Beth put clean sheets on the bed she had the oddest feeling Rose was watching her and smiling. It was a good feeling.

As she cooked the chips, Harry went off to buy some wine, and all at once she suddenly felt real delight that this was now her house, and tomorrow she would be Beth Irwin. At the age of thirty-one she wasn't an imposter anymore.

Harry picked her up in his arms to take her up to bed soon after eight. They'd drunk a bottle of wine and Beth was happily tiddly.

He dropped her on the bed, and in one swift movement pulled her dress over her head, leaving her in a silky white petticoat. Then he lay down beside her to kiss her.

'If at any time you want me to stop, just say the word,' he whispered, nuzzling into her neck. 'We don't have to do anything tonight. I just want to hold you and love you.'

'And I want to feel your skin against mine,' she murmured as she unbuttoned his shirt.

It seemed as if their clothes drifted off like magic, and all at once blissful sensations washed over her as Harry stroked and explored her. He was so gentle, but at the same time sensuous, and she felt herself pressing herself ever closer to him. He kissed her from her shoulders, breasts and abdomen, right down to her sex, and she could hardly believe that he was dipping his tongue into her, and taking her to a place she had never imagined, never thought would exist.

The end of it was like the finale of a firework display, strange but wonderful sensations that made her cry out. She pulled his head up to hers, kissing his mouth that tasted of her, and taking hold of his penis, she guided it into her.

'That was incredible,' she whispered later, as they lay soaked in sweat and both their faces wet with tears. 'I had no idea!'

'I love you, Beth,' he said, pushing her hair back from her face and kissing her eyes and nose. 'I'm so happy we can spend the rest of our lives together. I thought this kind of happiness was for other people, but not for me.'

'Me too,' she admitted.

'Has Rose's son said when you've got to leave here?' he asked. 'Because once we're married I can apply for an army house.'

'I don't have to leave,' she said. 'Rose has left the house to me.'

'Really? But—'

Beth put her finger on his lips. 'I'll tell you more tomorrow, about this and Ireland. But this house is ours now, so let's go to sleep so we are bright-eyed and bushy-tailed in the morning, and ready to start our new life together.'

Acknowledgements

A big thank you to Barry Keating for lending me and my friend Jo his apartment in Youghal, near Cork, so I could do some local research. It was kind and generous of you.

Also, a huge thank you to the French baker in Youghal who rescued me from freezing to death when I had sleepwalked out of the apartment in the early hours, in bare feet and nothing but a thin raincoat.

And with no key to get back in. I could have fallen into the sea, as I was on the wharf or even died of hypothermia it was that cold, but thankfully I woke in time to see a van approaching and was rescued. When I tell people I was found by a French baker, they laugh, imagining I have made this up. Of all the people in all the world, a kindly Frenchman in Ireland was my saviour, taking me back to his bakery, giving me tea and a blanket until he saw a light in my apartment block and could get me back in.

I couldn't get warm after that and another thank you is to the landlady of Hearne's, the pub and restaurant in the main street, who lent me her fur coat for the rest of my stay. More kindness and generosity.

Finally, thank you to all the lovely nameless people we met on our travels, especially the nice man in Dunmore East who gave me lots of local information.

Discover the books written
by Lesley Pearse...

WHICH BOOK WILL YOU READ NEXT?

The Long and Winding Road

Telling the extraordinary story of her life, Lesley Pearse's memoir is as heartbreaking as it is heartwarming.

Deception

After the funeral of her mother, Alice Kent is approached by a man claiming to be her father. Faced with this staggering deception, Alice knows she must uncover the whole truth about her mother. Whatever the cost.

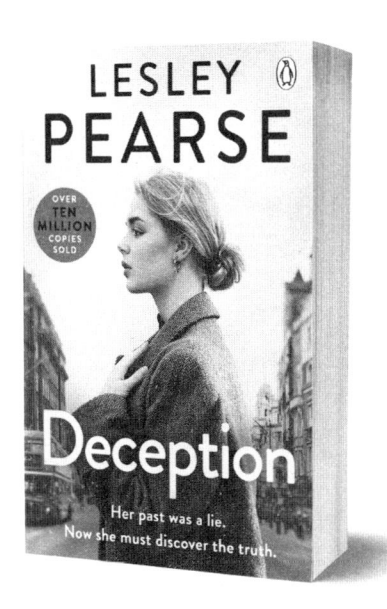

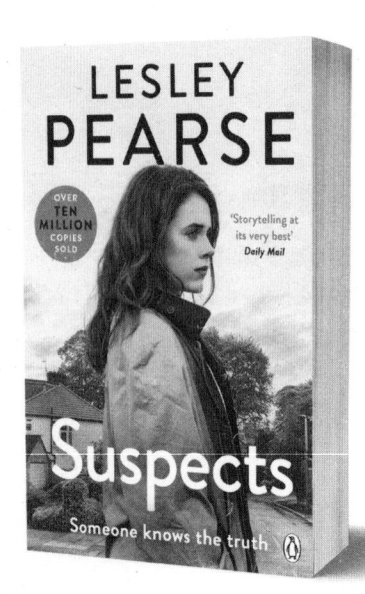

Suspects

When a young couple move into their first home together, a young girl is found murdered nearby. Soon a spotlight is cast on all the neighbours, each hiding their own dark and twisted secrets...

Betrayal

Ten years ago she killed her husband. But the past can't stay hidden forever...

Liar

When Amelia White uncovers a shocking scoop, she begins a desperate search for answers. But to uncover the truth, she must work out who is lying . . .

You'll Never See Me Again

When Betty escapes her marriage, she goes on the run, armed with a new identity. But she never imagined starting again would end in murder . . .

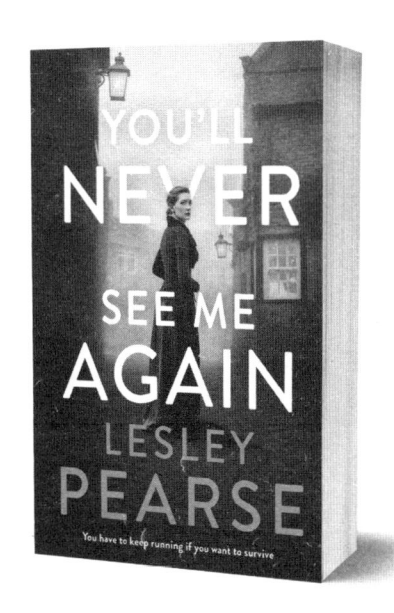

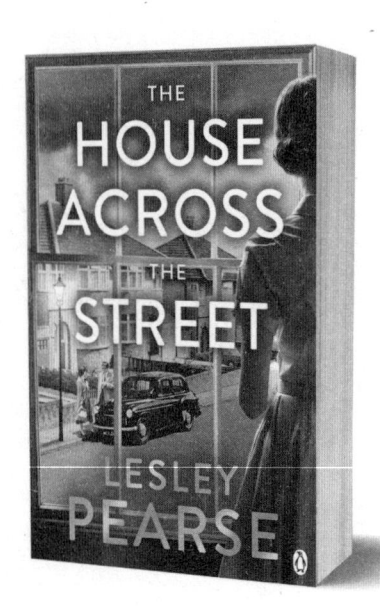

The House Across the Street

Katy must set out to uncover the truth about the mysterious house across the street. Even if that means risking her own life . . .

The Woman in the Wood

Fifteen-year-old twins Maisy and Duncan Mitcham have always had each other. Until one fateful day in the wood . . .

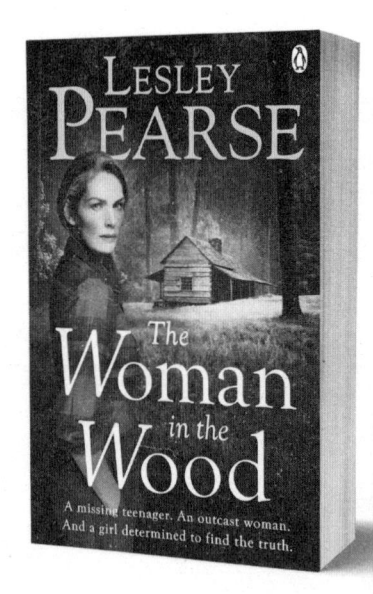

Dead to Me

Ruby and Verity become firm friends, despite coming from different worlds. However, fortunes are not set in stone and soon the girls find their situations reversed.

Without a Trace

On Coronation Day, 1953, Molly discovers that her friend is dead and her six-year-old daughter Petal has vanished. Molly is prepared to give up everything in finding Petal. But is she also risking her life?

Forgive Me

Eva's mother never told her the truth about her childhood. Now it is too late and she must retrace her mother's footsteps to look for answers. Will she ever discover the story of her birth?

Belle

Belle book 1

London, 1910, and the beautiful and innocent Belle Reilly is cruelly snatched from her home and sold to a brothel in New Orleans where she begins her life as a courtesan. Can Belle ever find her way home?

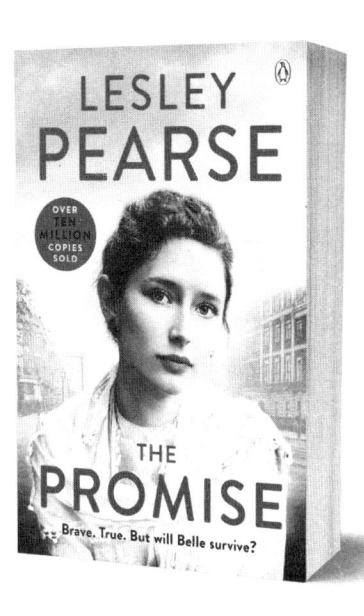

The Promise

Belle book 2

When Belle's husband heads for the trenches of northern France, she volunteers as a Red Cross ambulance driver. There she is brought face to face with a man from her past who she'd never quite forgotten.

Survivor

Belle book 3

Eighteen-year-old Mari is defiant, selfish and has given up everything in favour of glamorous parties in the West End. But, without warning, the Blitz blows her new life apart. Can Mari learn from her mistakes before it's too late?

Stolen

A beautiful young woman is discovered half-drowned on a Sussex beach. Where has she come from? Why can't she remember who she is — or what happened?

Gypsy

Liverpool, 1893, and after tragedy strikes the Bolton family, Beth and her brother Sam embark on a dangerous journey to find their fortune in America.

Faith

Scotland, 1995, and Laura Brannigan is in prison for a murder she claims she didn't commit.

Hope

Somerset, 1836, and baby Hope is cast out from a world of privilege as proof of her mother's adultery.

A Lesser Evil

Bristol, the 1960s, and young Fifi Brown defies her parents to marry a man they think is beneath her.

Secrets

Adele Talbot escapes a children's home to find her grandmother – but soon her unhappy mother is on her trail...

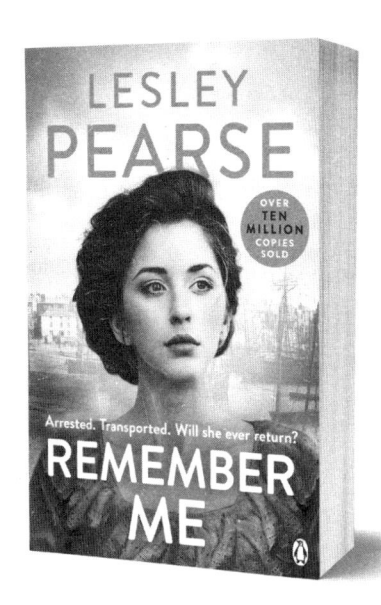

Remember Me

Mary Broad is transported to Australia as a convict and encounters both cruelty and passion. Can she make a life for herself so far from home?

Till We Meet Again

Susan and Beth were childhood friends. Now Susan is accused of murder, and Beth finds she must defend her.

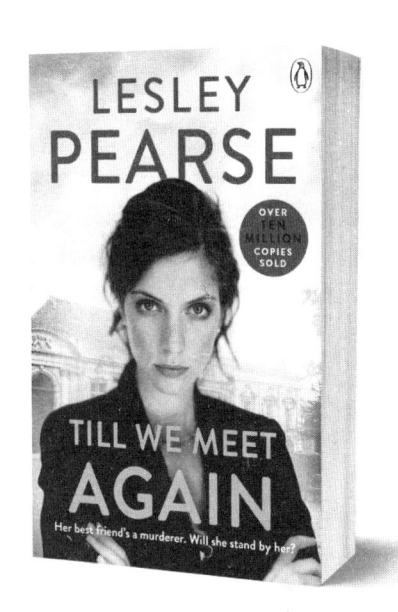

Father Unknown

Daisy Buchan is left a scrapbook with details about her real mother. But should she go and find her?

Trust Me

Dulcie Taylor and her sister are sent to an orphanage and then to Australia. Is their love strong enough to keep them together?

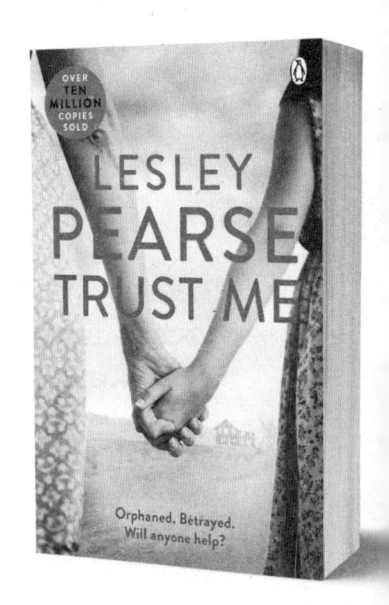

Never Look Back

An act of charity sends flower girl Matilda on a trip to the New World and a new life . . .

Charlie

Charlie helplessly watches her mother being senselessly attacked. What secrets have her parents kept from her?

Rosie

Rosie is a girl without a mother, with a past full of trouble. But could the man who ruined her family also save Rosie?

Camellia

Orphaned Camellia discovers that the past she has always been so sure of has been built on lies. Can she bear to uncover the truth about herself?

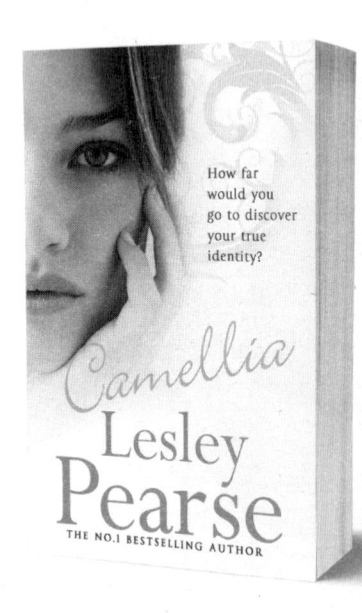

Ellie

Eastender Ellie and spoilt Bonny set off to make a living on the stage. Can their friendship survive sacrifice and ambition?

Charity

Charity Stratton's bleak life is changed for ever when her parents die in a fire. Alone and pregnant, she runs away to London ...

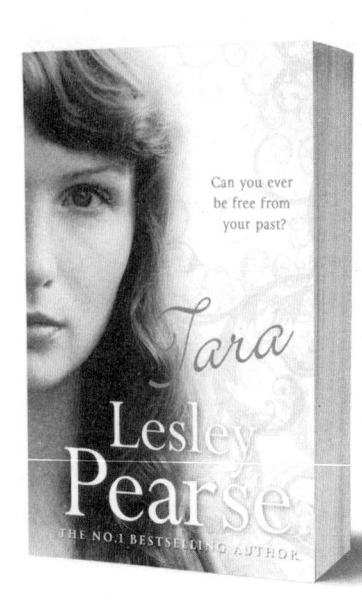

Tara

Anne changes her name to Tara to forget her shocking past – but can she really become someone else?

Georgia

Raped by her foster-father, fifteen-year-old Georgia runs away from home to the seedy back streets of Soho ...

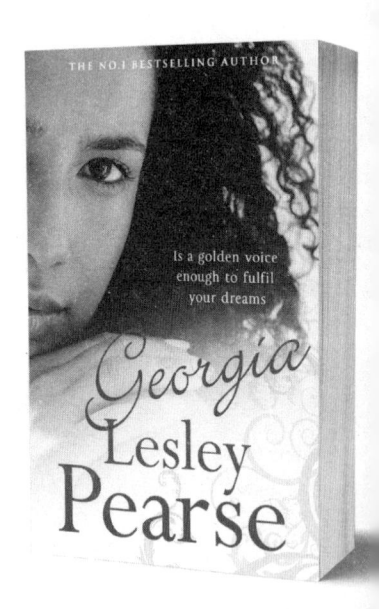